PRAISE FOR *RESCUE ME, MAYBE*

"A story of loss, love and self-discovery, *Rescue Me, Maybe* is brilliant in its subtle humor, intelligent prose and seamless writing. Jackie Bouchard is an excellent storyteller who captures her characters' innermost thoughts and feelings and draws her readers in from the first line." —Samantha Stroh Bailey, author of *Finding Lucas*

"A must-read for dog lovers, fans of women's fiction, and anyone who likes a funny, well-written story about overcoming life's obstacles . . . Warning: Once you pick up *Rescue Me, Maybe*, you won't want to put it down!" —Tracie Banister, author of *Blame It on the Fame* and *In Need of Therapy*

"Bouchard grabbed me by the heart and did not let go until the last page . . . I loved this novel, recommend it for adults and YA readers, and feel that dog lovers will really connect with the plot." —*Readers' Favorite*

PRAISE FOR *WHAT THE DOG ATE*

Named one of the best dog books of 2012 by NBC Petside.com.

Bouchard "writes in a natural, accessible style and Maggie is a profoundly appealing character that the reader roots for. Yes, it's about a broken heart, but it's also quite funny." —Dorri Olds, NBC Petside.com

"Dog lovers take note! *What the Dog Ate* is a cheer-me-up read, the story of a smart woman putting her life back together. Maggie is the character women have been waiting for—she's clever, funny, and REAL. You'll root for her with your whole heart." —Elsa Watson, author of *Dog Days*

"Belongs on reading lists everywhere. It is good reading at its best!" —*Readers' Favorite*

HOUSE
TRAINED

ALSO BY JACKIE BOUCHARD

What the Dog Ate

Rescue Me, Maybe

HOUSE TRAINED

JACKIE BOUCHARD

LAKE UNION
PUBLISHING

Published by Lake Union Publishing, Seattle

www.apub.com

Amazon, the Amazon logo, and Lake Union Publishing are trademarks of Amazon.com, Inc., or its affiliates.

ISBN-13: 9781503947122
ISBN-10: 1503947122

Cover design by Laura Klynstra

Printed in the United States of America

To the hubs: my best friend and, as I like to call him,
my patron of the arts.

You are my lobster.

(And, yes, we know lobsters don't really mate for life like
Phoebe led us to believe on that one episode of Friends.
But "you are my prairie vole" just doesn't sound as good.)

CHAPTER 1

This morning I overheard my husband talking to his penis. He was getting in the shower and thought I'd already left; that's how I unintentionally snuck up on him. Or rather, *them*.

His words stopped me in my kitten-heeled tracks there in our bedroom. A cartoon traffic pileup of emotions plowed into me one after the other: guilt (I'm not in the habit of eavesdropping on Barry, or anyone else for that matter); confusion (I was unaware he had discussions with this particular member of our family unit); embarrassment—for him (it was an awkward moment); and a little anger (does this often happen when I'm not around?).

I raised my arm to push open the bathroom door and say, "Hey, what are you two talking about?" but caught sight of my watch. I only had twenty minutes to get to Montecito, and I try my damnedest to never be late for a meeting, especially with a new client.

Zooming south on the 101, I still felt confused, as if I hadn't had enough coffee or something. Had Barry done anything else out of the ordinary? I replayed the morning in my head. The day had started with our typical Saturday routine: the dog and I slept in while Barry went for his usual long run. I ate, took Marie for a walk, and showered. I'd finished my makeup and was stepping into my linen skirt, still warm from the iron, when I heard Barry come home. Marie's tags jangled as she ran to greet her daddy, and I heard him ask how his "pretty girl" was doing.

I walked out to the kitchen to say hi, and we had our standard "How was the run?" "Fine, how'd you sleep?" exchange.

"Does this skirt look okay?" I turned and gave him the back view, wiggling my hips.

"'S'cute." He pulled up his Coolmax T-shirt up to wipe the sweat from his face. I rolled my eyes at his favorite running shorts, the ones I'd tried to throw away because of the bleach stain. At least he'd left his dirty Nikes in the garage. He padded in his running-sock-covered feet to the fridge, leaving ghost feet markings behind on the hardwood. "Glad I didn't bring Marie. Hot."

Marie perked up at her name and joined her daddy gazing into the fridge. She nose-poked the cheese drawer, then slumped on the mat, dejected when he merely grabbed the orange juice. Barry leaned on the granite counter and guzzled juice from the carton, though we both knew that I would give him grief about it.

"I wish you wouldn't do that. It's gross."

"Not if I finish it."

He stripped off his running hat and pushed a handful of dark, wet hair off his forehead. Having spent fifteen minutes straightening my own flyaway wavy hair, I envied Barry and his run-your-fingers-through-and-you're-good-to-go hairdo. Barry has thick, shiny shampoo-ad hair. He got it from his mom, a gorgeous, petite woman whose parents came to California from South Korea when she was a baby. Next to her, I always felt like an Amazon. One of those B-movie-poster buxom blondes: *Attack of the Fifty-Foot Interior Designer*. Happily, Barry got his height from his Nordic-warrior-looking dad.

"I bought that carton yesterday. You're not going to finish it," I said, reaching for my clutch. "I'm not giving up on you, Bear. I know I haven't had total success training you these past fifteen years"—I paused to check my lipstick in the mirror on the inside flap of my purse—"but one of these days, I'll have you fully dialed in to my specs." I made kissy lips at him.

"Yeah, we'll see how that works out for you." Barry air-kissed my cheek, because he knows not to mess up my makeup when I'm dressed for work.

I jingled my keys, and Marie pranced over, hearing the signal for a good-bye treat. Marie's a big dog—long legged and close to sixty pounds—but she's as graceful as a dancer. She dropped her ivory-colored, curly-haired behind onto the floor. Her dark eyes followed my every move, and her shiny black nose twitched as I got a biscuit out of the cupboard.

I said good-bye, gave Marie her treat, and then headed out with my portfolio. Within seconds of pulling out of the garage, I realized I'd forgotten my sunglasses. (I'm so damn forgetful lately. Barry teases me that it comes with being the Big Four-O—and I tease him right back that he should know, since he's been in his forties longer than I have—but I prefer to chalk it up to stress.) Wearing sunglasses is key if you live in sunny central California and are trying to avoid the Clint Eastwood squinty-eyed look, so I had no choice but to go back into the house for them.

Marie greeted me with her long, silky ears perked up and a "You're back!" expression on her fuzzy face. Marie is an intelligent dog, like most labradoodles—her sweet nature is from her Labrador side, and her brainpower is from her poodle side—but judging time lapses isn't her strong suit. She was poised on her long legs, ready to grab her ball if I gave the word, but I simply said, "Sorry, missy," and ruffled her floppy bangs on my way to the cubby in the kitchen where we stash our mail and keys. No sunglasses. But then I remembered I'd left them on our dresser.

I dashed down the hall. As I neared our master suite, I heard the patter of our rain-style showerhead on the glass tiles and figured Barry was in the shower. I reached the half-open bathroom door and heard his voice. At first I thought he was on the phone, but in the shower? It seemed odd, so I peeked in. There he stood, in all his wiry, nude, marathon-runner glory, his little white butt turned my direction. He had one leg up on the step of the shower, waiting for the water to get warm. His head hung low as he spoke to his crotch.

"This is basically all because of you, Skippy." He reached in to test the temperature. "Or, wait . . . Do you think she planned it that way?" He shook his head and stepped into the shower.

What did I plan *what* way? I stood there balancing on the balls of my feet. Momentum urged me forward, but I had to get going to my appointment. Talking about this would have to wait. Sunglasses in hand, I ran back out to my BMW, leaving Marie looking miffed at the absence of a second good-bye treat.

Which brings me to here and now. While I drive, dodging the Santa Barbara city traffic and the weekend beachgoers, I turn down the radio so I can think. Other than the overheard shower conversation, the morning all seemed normal enough. Barry was maybe a little more taciturn than usual, but he's always like that after a run. Especially a twelve-mile run in the summer heat.

Of course, he didn't seem quite as uncommunicative with his penis. What was it he'd said? "This is all because of you . . . Or do you think she planned it that way?" What did that mean? And what the hell was up with "Skippy"? I didn't know it had a name. My two college boyfriends and the man I dated before I got together with Barry all had names for their penises ("The King," "Patton," and "Benjamin"—after the Dustin Hoffman character in *The Graduate*), but they were all so young. Barry was a very mature thirty-one-year-old when we started dating, and he had never mentioned a name in the years since, so it stunned me. I assumed naming one's penis was something only a younger, less mature guy would do. Not my Bear.

And the name itself. *Skippy?* I mean, it's okay for a Jack Russell or a ferret, but for a penis? It's so . . . preppy. And Barry is the antithesis of preppy. I would have thought he'd go for something more, I don't know, classic, maybe. Wesley or Heathcliff. Or one of his favorite scientists' names, like he did with Marie. Maybe Sir Isaac or Copernicus. Yeah, Copernicus would be an excellent name for a penis. But Skippy?

With a bit of speeding, I manage to make it to my appointment at the Van Dierdons' house, where two bleach-bottle-white smiles welcome me inside. Their home is probably over seven thousand square feet and backs up to an immaculate golf course. My heart beats with covetous lust. The place looks like the grand-prize dream house for an HGTV contest: Spanish-style architecture, beamed ceiling, great room with massive stone fireplace, distressed hardwood floors, and huge oak-trimmed windows overlooking verdant landscaping.

"You have a beautiful home," I say, hoping I'm not drooling, and wondering why they've asked me here. The place oozes perfection.

"Thank you, Alexandra. And thanks for coming on a Saturday," says Mrs. Van Dierdon with her burgundy designer loungewear and perfect tan.

"It's not a problem, and, please, call me Alex."

"Well, Alex, we moved in recently; we're newlyweds." She blinds me with a flash of her anvil-size diamond, and I wish I still had my sunglasses on. "We desperately need your help in the bedroom."

Silver-haired Mr. Van Dierdon lets out a TV-anchorman chuckle. "It doesn't sound very good when you put it that way, little lioness." Her nickname suits her; her gaunt cheeks and slinky saunter give her an on-the-prowl look.

She bats him on the arm. "Tiger, of course that's not what I meant."

I give them my best aren't-you-two-adorable smile. "Why don't you show me the room, and we can get started?"

We hike back to the master suite, and Mrs. Van Dierdon says, "First of all, these doors have to go." She stops in front of partially open French doors leading to their room. They're lovely—dark mahogany frames with frosted-glass panels down the center. "The previous owners installed these, and they're quite annoying when we have guests." She points out other rooms down the hall with the same type of door. "If guests stay up reading, their light shines through these ridiculous doors and keeps us up."

"My bride doesn't need beauty sleep, but *I* do," Mr. Van Dierdon says with a wink.

"I'm sure we can find something more to your liking. I'd never select something for a design simply because it was beautiful. Everything has to work together and work for your lifestyle," I reassure them. "I'm not a form-over-function designer; you can count on that." Designing simply for aesthetics is a huge pet peeve of mine. Sure, it will look great in a glossy portfolio photo, but how are people supposed to live in those sterile, ultrasleek living rooms? Yes, the faucet mounted on the counter-to-ceiling mirror behind the vessel sink gives modern flair to the guest bath, but how's a person supposed to wash their hands without splashing water everywhere?

"I'm pleased to hear that," Mrs. Van Dierdon says. "Now, on to the room." She pushes the doors open, holding her skeletal arms out as I take in the expansive room, large enough to hold all three of the bedrooms in my house. It's pretty, but impersonal. We could be in any top hotel chain. "We're picturing something serene, spa-like."

"Perfect. I can draw up something simple, but elegant. We should start with the color. There are a lot of options for a serene feeling: sea greens, pewter, pale bl—"

"No, no, no." Hubby shakes his head. "Red. We definitely want red walls."

Wifey picks up a page torn from a magazine. "Something like this."

The picture shows what looks like a luxurious resort in the tropics. It's austere, with a color palette in wheat, eggshell, and a lovely shade of celadon. I nod. "I can give you something very similar to this."

They nod back. "Great. But in red."

I spend the next thirty minutes covering their coffee table with photos from my portfolio and design magazines. I show them a formal dining room my employee, Rachel, and I did with garnet-colored walls. "See how this room is so vibrant? You're not going to get the relaxing effect you're after if we go with red." I remind them they got my name from Mrs. Van Dierdon's hairdresser, and isn't Salon Bellissima oh so serene in those luscious creamy tones? (Rachel and I redid the day spa for free early last year before the market dropped; it's been great publicity, which, as a fairly new business in a crappy economy, we need.) Then I pull out the big guns: some research Barry looked up for me on the science of color and how it affects our moods.

"But red's our favorite color." She offers to show me photos of their red-themed wedding.

I draw the last arrow from my quiver. "Have you ever noticed how fast-food restaurants always use red in their logos and their decor?"

"Oh, Alex, we don't do fast food."

"But you've seen the logos, right?" They nod their perfectly coiffed heads in unison, and I continue. "They're red because it's stimulating; they want to stimulate the appetite."

"Stimulating the appetite sounds good, doesn't it, my lioness?"

Lioness growls at Tiger. Time for me to exit, so I stand. "What I'll do is draw up a design for a red room as well as one using beach tones, and you can select the one you prefer."

They show me out, and on the drive home, with the glare of the ocean on my left and the air conditioner and my music cranked high, I think about my job, which I generally love. I thrive on taking an empty space—or better yet, an ugly space—and converting it into a thing of beauty. Someplace my clients can relax. A place where they can walk in the door after a hard day and exhale, feel their shoulders drop away from their ears, and say "I'm home."

But trying to please demanding (and/or confused) clients goes hand in hand with the fun, creative side of the job. If money and the opinions of society (and my mother) were no object, I'd probably turn into one of those reclusive artistic hermit types. I'd get a cabin in the middle of nowhere, hole up there with my dog and husband, and just *create*. Not sure what, since you can only redo your cabin so many times, but I'd make something. Maybe I'd learn to sculpt or throw pots.

However, the reality is that money and the opinions of society (and my mother) matter. Mostly the money. Especially now, since I've, uh, "borrowed" a major chunk of the money Barry was saving for a new car to try to keep my business afloat. And Barry doesn't exactly know. God, I feel sick every time I think about it.

I grip the steering wheel, wanting to beat my head against it. I've got to make these people happy. Sometimes it's hard, though, balancing what you know is right with what the client thinks they want. I wonder aloud, "How can I give them a room that's serene *and* red?" We've got to nail this job so they'll tell their fabulously wealthy friends. My money problems will be over, and Barry will never even know they'd existed in the first place.

I've got to get this contract. I wonder if the Van Dierdons will go for bisque with red accents.

I try to de-stress by mentally drifting back to our serene dream cabin. I need something for Barry to do so he's not underfoot while I'm sculpting. Gardening! He loves that. I picture him tending our veggie patch. Then I hear him say to a summer squash, "Do you think she planned it that way?"

I shake my head to get the image out of my mind. But what did he mean by that?

Could he think I purposely set up my meeting with the Van Dierdons on a Saturday to get out of our usual nap? We've been having some issues in terms of our . . . marital relations lately. We've always kind of been ships that pass in the bed. I'm a night owl, staying up late to work or devour a murder mystery. Barry's a morning person, and I'm still comatose when he springs up to go out on a run. We've always solved this problem with weekend "naps." But since striking out on my own, I've had to do everything I can to get new customers, and sometimes that means weekend meetings. And Rachel can't take the meetings, since I'm the one with the design degree, and it's my company. (I don't want to say Rache is "just" an upholsterer, because she's not—she's more like a fabric whisperer. She does things with a sewing machine and a staple gun that would make a person consider upholstering the fireplace. Or Grandpa. Her work is *that* gorgeous.) Anyway, whenever I've got a weekend meeting, it's adios to the siesta.

I bet that's what he meant. But it's only one o'clock. Plenty of time for a nap. I can get going on some sketches later. A lazy afternoon would be nice, and it'll make Barry happy.

My cozy image of us tucked in our sleigh bed vanishes when I turn into our cul-de-sac and the latest monstrosity on our neighbor's lawn looms large. My molars rub together. The Jansens roll out hideous inflato-decor for Every. Single. Holiday. On Arbor Day, they put out a huge plastic palm tree hiding the real tree in their yard. And, I swear to God, on Mother's Day she puts out a blow-up uterus. Now an immense, angry bald eagle, visible from space, signals the impending Fourth of July holiday.

I shout, unheard from within the sealed sanctuary of my car. "You're bringing down the whole neighborhood aesthetic! Can't you just hang out a flag, like normal people?" Good grief, their trash bin is still out too. Friday morning is pickup day. "And trash cans are supposed to be removed within twelve hours of pickup!"

Leaving their lawn in my rearview mirror, I think: *This is why I love Santa Barbara so much. The city's as crazy about these types of regulations as I'd be if I ran things.*

I whip into our driveway and hit the garage door opener. As the door rises, it reveals Barry's truck isn't there. And then it hits me: maybe *I'm* not the "she" Barry was talking about.

CHAPTER 2

I go inside, collect my usual twenty or so kisses from Marie (makeup be damned now that my meeting is over), then slide open the back door to let her out. All the while I'm wondering if Barry could have been talking about another woman.

An affair? Barry?

I almost laugh, it's so hard to imagine. Maybe that sounds naïve, but I pretty much know where Barry is at all times. He's usually working, running, or gardening. He's an uncomplicated guy and a terrible liar. He can't even manage little white lies. Like when I come home from the hairdresser and he doesn't like my new style, he won't even try to fake it. He'll say, "Your hair. It's different." And then scurry away before I can grill him.

Still, could he be talking to Skippy about another woman even if he's not actually cheating? I replay that snippet of conversation in my head for the eighty-fifth time.

He must have some secret he's hiding. Of course, I've got a big one of my own. But hopefully that will work itself out if everything goes well with this new client. Yes, everything's got to work out, and then there'll be nothing to tell. So focus on Barry for now.

Hmm. Maybe he sent an unintended signal to some woman at work. And now she's after him.

That could be it. He's pretty much awash in a sea of women at work. There just aren't many male librarians at the university. He's tall and thin (some might say scrawny), tan (some might say leathery), quiet and thoughtful (some might say boring). With his dark eyes and hair and reluctant smile, I find him extremely handsome. And I'm sure other ladies do too.

While I'm pondering this, I search for a note. He always lets me know where he is. I remember then that I turned off my phone during my meeting. Yep, there's a message.

"Hey. By the time you get this, I'll be on the road to LA." He lets out a disgruntled snort. "Madeline called. She sprained her ankle, so she asked me to deliver her speech for the ARL dinner tonight." I search my brain cells, knowing he's explained the acronym before. Probably several times. American Research Libraries? Association of Research Libraries? One of those. "She sent me her PowerPoint, but I've got tons to do. Hope your meeting went well. I'll call you later."

Poor Bear. I can hear the stress in his voice. He hates public speaking. Still, I'm pleased. Not because Madeline, the library director, hurt herself, but because maybe finally Barry will get some recognition. Madeline was on track to retire next year, but when the stock market went south last fall, so did her plans. And as long as she's there, Barry's got nowhere to go. He says he doesn't care; he says moving up means more politics and less contact with the students. But I think it'd be good for him. Besides, "library director" sounds way better than "science librarian." And it means more money.

The phone rings. I answer and hear the drone of the freeway in the background.

"You got my message?"

"Yes. Where are you? *How* are you? Nervous about the speech?" I ask, even though I don't need to. I can tell by his tight tone of voice.

"Yeah. There'll be about two hundred people."

"You'll do great. I want to hear all about it tonight when you get home."

"Didn't I tell you? It's a two-day thing. I'll be home tomorrow night."

"You're missing Fuzzy's party?" My sister, Cyn, is throwing a second birthday party for my youngest nephew, Frankie (dubbed Fuzzy by his oldest brother, since he's always vaguely sticky and covered in blankie fluff or cat hair). "If you're not there, I can't hang out with the men. I'll be stuck with the women, and all they ever talk about is babies and pregnancy and their kids' latest, greatest achievements." Barry knows I've come home from these events more than once and had a long rant (or a good cry) because those ladies make me feel like such an outcast.

"I'm sorry." Barry infuses some genuine-sounding remorse into his voice, but I know he's filled with glee. He's also been dreading the party. There will be seven children under the age of eight, plus Cyn's mama posse. But there's no way out. Last year when their middle boy, Bobby, turned four, we called with a sketchy last-minute excuse about why we couldn't make it after all, and she totally saw through us. We can't try that again. "Take Marie along. She'll help you face the LPs." (Barry's code acronym for kids: Little Pains-in-the-ass.)

"Yeah. Maybe." I picture the party, seeing kids hopped up on too much sugar racing around, yelling, and beating a piñata until its battered body yields more of the high-fructose corn syrup they've made their god. If I make it out of there without a migraine, it'll be a minor miracle. "Damn it, Bear. This is a total drag."

"I know. But I couldn't say no to Madeline."

"Oh hell. I still have to get Fuzzy's present. I better go. Good luck. Call me tonight."

And tonight when he calls, I'll ask him about what I overheard this morning. I didn't want to get into that while he was driving. Maybe I should text him and ask him to call me when he gets there? Or maybe that's a conversation best held in person. I chew my lower lip.

Marie appears at the sliding glass door, taking my mind off things. I let her back in.

"Hey, baby, wanna go to a party with me?" She wags her tail, which I take as a yes.

"You can be Mama's ally." I crouch down to hug her, and we both take a moment to sigh and enjoy it. I break it off, knowing I need to get to the mall.

I have no clue what a two-year-old boy wants for his birthday. Last year, I ordered a bunch of kids' books online and had them delivered. Cynthia e-mailed me that it was "lame." I told her that books are *not* lame.

Or did she mean it was lame that we didn't show up to the party?

Anyway, no matter what I get Fuzzy, shopping for it will be a chore. It'd be more fun with backup. I dial Rachel, because she's a mom. Granted, she has an eight-year-old girl, but she still ought to be able to help. Besides, I need to tell her about the new clients.

"I've been hoping to hear from you. How was the meeting with the Van Dierdons?"

"It was . . . interesting. Their house is to die for. Want to meet up at La Cumbre Plaza and I'll tell you about it? I need to get a present for my nephew."

"Sounds good. My mom can watch Kaitlin. Meet you at the fountain in an hour."

A little over an hour later, we bask in the fluorescent lights of KB Toys, in the boy aisle. They don't exactly label it, but it's obviously intended that way, as primary colors abound and the toys are all construction- or sports-themed—in comparison to the aisle we just passed, swathed in pink and lavender, everything beribboned and bejeweled. Maybe I could've handled this on my own.

"Does he like cars?" Rachel asks, pushing a handful of straight brown hair back behind her ear. She grabs a mustard-colored stuffed dump truck, then tugs at the felt eyes and smile sewn onto the truck's front. "You've got to make sure these bits won't come off though."

"That's not exactly what I had in mind." Cyn will pay for calling my gift of reading lame. "He's pretty rambunctious. I thought maybe something he could burn off some energy with." I wander down the aisle while Rachel continues scanning the shelves.

"How about this?" She sounds excited, so I spin around, hoping she's found the perfect toy so that we can leave and go get iced mochas. "A bowling set!"

"Ooh." I reach for the box to inspect it. "Nope. The pins are fabric. Too quiet."

"You want to get him something noisy? Isn't that kind of cruel? I mean, for the parents."

"They have three boys aged seven and under. They're used to a decibel level on par with living under a flight path." I stroll down a few more aisles, past the stuffed animals and board games. I come to an aisle labeled "Music" and see it: My First Band! "Rache, over here."

She comes and I show her the box, which is the size of a large overnight bag. "Oh no." She shakes her head. "Drums? A tambourine? Cymbals! That's mean. Get the bowling set."

"It's not mean. It's creative. They'll put on *Barney's Greatest Hits* and have a jam session. With the bowling set, they'd have to take turns. They're not great about that. With this, they can each take an instrument and all play at once. It's perfect." I head toward checkout.

"I never realized before that you don't like your sister." Rachel smiles as she says this, so I know she's at least half teasing.

"I like my sister. But she bugs me sometimes with her 'I'm a mother; what have *you* done for the world lately?' act. You know how some mothers can be."

"What do you mean?" She narrows her eyes at me as the line moves forward.

"Well, you know how some women can act—now, I'm not talking about you here—but all some women want to talk about is their kids, and they act like they've done this great service by bringing their children into the world. But not you! You're a great mom, and Kaitlin's super cute, but you don't go around advertising it all the time. Ya know? You still hold adult conversations. But my sis . . . she acts like she's the Mother Teresa of mothers sometimes." I'm rambling. Rachel gets quiet, and I'm afraid I pissed her off.

After we leave the toy store, I buy each of us an iced coffee. She picks up the conversation where I left off.

"I think having a career helps me have an identity beyond being Kaitlin's mom. I mean, I'd love to stay home with her, but it's not an option. And I know what you mean about the moms with the giant *M*'s on their chests—I find it's usually the ones who don't work. There's this whole . . . rivalry between the working moms and the stay-at-homers at Kaitlin's school."

"Seriously?" We find a table in the shade and sit with our drinks.

"It's not overt or anything, but they have this subtle way of making you feel like Joan Crawford if you bring store-bought cupcakes to a school party."

"I'd be in trouble. I'm a terrible baker." I take a sip of my sweet, icy coffee. "Oh, hey, before I forget, remember I said I was going to stop by the women's shelter on my way home the other day?"

"Yeah. Could they use that leftover paint and fabric?"

"They said they could absolutely use the paint, but the fabric . . ." I shrug. "They don't have a sewing machine there."

"Since I don't have any client work at the moment, I could see if they need some curtains whipped up or something."

I smile and tap the end of my nose. "I was hoping you'd say that. I was thinking you could work on that while I work on the drawings for the Van Dierdons." I pull a Post-it out of my purse. "I've got the measurements. It's just two small windows." I hand her the note, and she reads my scratchy writing. "Too bad we can't also donate some money. Wouldn't it be amazing if we were making enough to be a corporate sponsor or something?"

"Someday," she says. We both cross our fingers, then I crook mine against hers, and we tug. It's our own version of a pinky-swear promise combined with a please-let-it-happen wish.

"I hope so," I say as we reach for our drinks again. "Anyway, until then, I figure we can at least donate leftover materials and some time."

Rache waves the Post-it note, fanning her face. "I can crank these out easy this week. Before we get busy with the Van Dierdon job. We're in for that, right? How was the meeting?"

"I sure hope we're in. They didn't say they're considering another firm, but they have to love the design or they'll go looking for someone else." I describe their palatial master suite and how they want it turned into a serene spa. She blows a puff of air in an "easy-peasy; been there, done that" way, until I add, "But they're fixated on having red walls."

She has the same "what the hell?" reaction I did. I sketch on a napkin while we toss ideas around.

Rachel, who has removed her glasses to look at my sketch, taps the plastic frames on the table. "We need this job. We've got nothing else coming in right now."

"Don't remind me." Rache doesn't know the half of it.

She puts her glasses back on and rubs her forehead. "And Mason is behind on child support. Again. If we don't get this job, I might have to do something drastic."

"Like what?" I fold the napkin sketch and stick it in my purse. I try to imagine what drastic measures I could resort to if we don't get this job. I've got to start replenishing our savings account and paying off my credit cards. Before Barry finds out.

"Look, don't freak out." She holds up her hands. "But Beverly called. The upholsterer she hired when we left isn't working out. She wants me to come back."

"You can't be serious." I was about to take a sip of my coffee, but now I set it back down so hard that it sloshes over the edge of the cup. I pluck a wad of napkins out of the dispenser. "Do you remember how many times she made you cry? The upholsterer 'isn't working out.' Ha! That's Beverly speak for 'I haven't been able to crush her spirit.' I can't believe how many years I put up with her. We both hated working there; you can't go back." I crumple the napkins and throw them on the table. My hand feels sticky.

"I know she can be a bit . . . difficult."

"Difficult? Calculus is difficult. Final Jeopardy is difficult. Beverly is a demanding, unreasonable dictator. She's Idi Amin in a sweater set."

"I know she's that way with her staff, but her clients like her—and she says they're busy. Even in this economy! I need steady income. I don't have a Barry like you do to fall back on." She pushes her hair behind her ear again. "We've given it a good go. But the housing market sucks right now; people aren't redecorating. It's not our fault. There's no shame in going under."

"We're not going under." My pulse pounds in my temples. Yes, it's true, I've got Barry to fall back on financially if my company fails, but I need this to work or I'll have . . . what? In this society, in order to count, a woman has to have children or a career, or the complete package of both. I know my mom is disappointed I haven't provided her with additional grandchildren, so it would be nice to have a successful "baby" of a business to show off. And I want Barry to be proud of me too. Plus, I can't even imagine how angry he'll be if he finds out I spent most of his car fund. And I don't want to let Rache down either. I'm the one who talked her into leaving Beverly's, and I can't let her go back there. She'd be miserable. I have to make this work.

"We're fine. But we have to ride this out. You can't leave me. Nobody knows fabrics like you." This can't be happening. I can't lose Rachel. And I can't bear the idea of Beverly winning. Beverly's sneering face appears before me, and again I hear her last words when we quit: *"Good luck; you're going to need it."* "I can loan you some money," I blurt out. "I mean, the business can." She doesn't need to know the money will come from Barry's and my personal savings. There's still some money in there. And she'll pay me back as soon as we finish this new job. "It'll be an advance. Tell me you're not quitting."

"I wouldn't have to borrow money if I went back to work for her."

"But you'd be giving up your dream. And your dignity. She'll make you crawl if you go back. And it's just an advance. We'll get this job with the Van Dierdons, and they'll love our design, and they'll tell all their rich friends, and everything'll be great. You'll see." I squeeze her hand in a vise grip and hope she's getting the "I'm not letting you go" message.

She finally squeezes my hand back. "Okay. Let's see what happens with the Van Dierdons. But this has to be an official loan, with interest and everything. It's not charity."

"Of course. Yeah. We'll do it all official. Everything's going to work out," I say, trying to convince myself as well.

Crap. Everything's riding on this red room.

*

That night, I'm on the sofa, surrounded by abandoned sketches. It's been a long day, and all my drawings look like crap. I've given up and am having a glass of wine and massaging paw balm into the bottoms of Marie's feet (got to protect my girl from those hot summer sidewalks) when Barry calls.

"Hey, it's late. I thought it was an after-dinner speech." It's a relief to hear his voice. I've been anxious, waiting all evening for him to call and checking my phone to see if I'd forgotten to turn the ringer back up.

"It was, but there was a reception after. And you know how wild and crazy we librarians get around free chardonnay." It's nice to hear that the tight-lipped Barry from this morning is gone, and my husband sounds like his usual self—or at least a slightly tipsy version of his usual self.

"Don't tell me—there was a wet cardigan contest."

"Hey, now." He laughs. "I'm allowed to poke fun, but you're not." He tells me the speech went well, and I tell him I had no doubts. But I grill him about what he wore.

"Your suit's still in the closet. Please tell me you didn't wear those ratty old cords. I wish I'd been here while you were packing." I rub Marie's ear, and she leans into my hand. She turns her soft brown eyes up to me, and they're filled with love. Or a desire for the ear rubs to never stop.

"I like my ratty old cords. Besides, trust me, the fashion police haven't been here, and if they do show up, they'll be too busy to bust me." He yawns loudly. "Sorry. I'm beat. And I want to try to get in a run before the breakfast session, so I better get some sleep."

"Wait, I—" I hadn't planned to do this over the phone, and I'm not even sure it's the right time to bring it up, but I decide to strike while his lips are loose with chardonnay. "Is . . . is everything okay?" I stop rubbing the dog's ear.

"Uh." He hesitates. I realize I'd been hoping he'd answer with a resounding, *Everything's great!* I can feel the miles between us. "Why, why do you ask?"

"I . . . You didn't seem like yourself this morning." Marie puts her paw on my knee, and I reach for it.

"Boy, nothing gets by you."

Marie pulls her paw away; I must have squeezed it too tightly. "So there is something?" My heart starts to pound.

"Something happened at work on Friday. I need to talk to you about it, but we've both been coming and going. I was sort of in denial at first, and then when you got home last night, I was asleep. Then today was crazy. I don't want to get into it on the phone."

Oh, dear. This doesn't sound good. He was in denial about it?

"Okay." I'm not sure what to say. I wish he'd just spit it out. "But . . . is it bad news?"

"No. *No.* It's . . . it's complicated. I'll explain when I'm home."

"Is it something to do with work? If you don't tell me, I'm just going to worry."

"It's nothing to worry about. It's—it's best if I explain it in person. It's nothing. I mean, it's *something*, but it's nothing bad. I'll see you tomorrow night."

We hang up and I spend the rest of the evening trying to watch TV or read, but I can't concentrate. I give up and turn off the lights. "Come on, Marie, let's go to bed." She runs ahead and jumps on the bed. I join her, and we end up sprawled out, her with her head by my knee, me reaching out to stroke her soft flank while I think. What could his news be? He's getting laid off? Oh hell. He did say the governor announced big cuts in the state's school funding. Getting laid off would be bad, *very* bad. Although Barry wouldn't understand exactly how bad. Please, don't let it be that. We *cannot* afford that.

When I get lost in my worries and stop petting her, Marie twists to rest her head on my thigh. "Come here, baby," I say, patting the bed just beside me. She gets up and rearranges herself, curling into a ball next to me.

I practice breathing in tandem with her, hoping it will help me relax and fall asleep. But it's no good. My mind drifts back to Barry. What the hell else could his news be? There's simply no scenario that could have happened at work, involve his penis, and not be bad. Penises and libraries do not mix.

I contemplate getting up and having another glass of wine.

Nah. I roll on my side and spoon Marie. She stretches her long legs, then pushes her back against me, snuggling in even closer. All I need is this sweet girl.

As I've done so many times before, I stop obsessing over my troubles by telling her the story of how we found her at the shelter: about her first day home, when she stole Barry's running socks off the bathroom floor and chewed holes in them (thereby training him to put them in the hamper), and about how she's found her "forever" home. I tell her how we rescued her, and how she rescued us from our grief over the loss of our previous dog, Louis. And then we finally both fall asleep.

CHAPTER 3

These houses all look the same, I think as I pull into my sister's neighborhood in Thousand Oaks. Cynthia and her husband, Jamie, used to live near us, but after their first son, A.J., came along, they moved away from pricey Santa Barbara so that they could afford a bigger house. Now they have their bigger house, but they're in a neighborhood where they could pass toilet paper to the neighbors through the bathroom window. At least the Sunday morning traffic was light, so I made it to their house in under an hour, with Marie whining excitedly in the backseat and pawing the window for the last five minutes, since she could tell where we were heading as soon as we got off the freeway. I'm early because I know Cyn will need party-prep help, and because I plan to get in early, get out early.

On the plus side, at least my anxiety about getting through this party is taking my mind off my anxiety about what Barry needs to tell me.

The sun beats the top of my tired head (not unlike how Fuzzy will soon be beating the drum in his My First Band! box) as Marie and I approach the door, gift bag in one hand and a cooler shielding my fruit salad in the other. Marie races ahead to the porch, excited to see her little buddies. I reach for the doorknob and hear wailing, probably from Bobby, their four-year-old with a low frustration threshold. My head already hurts from lack of sleep. It's going to be a long afternoon.

Inside, it turns out the noise is from Fuzzy, not Bobby. He's planted in the foyer, naked, arms akimbo, his face a vivid red—probably the shade the Van Dierdons want. Of course. Fuzzy turns two today, so here he is, being terrible.

Marie approaches him with trepidation. She nose-pokes his bare backside, bringing a louder scream from Fuzzy. Marie slinks off in search of the other boys, whom we can hear playing—sounds like some sort of shoot-out—in the family room.

My sis comes down the stairs holding a cute red, white, and blue outfit on a munchkin-size hanger. She waves hello and stops in front of Fuzzy.

"I'm sorry, Frankie, but you can't wear your PJs to the party." Cyn points at me. "Look, here's Aunt Alex. Don't you want to get dressed and give her a hug?" I know this is the wrong tack, as I'm not Fuzzy's fave person. He glares at me. I get the feeling that even in his narcissistic two-year-old mind, he knows he's not my favorite either. (I have to confess I prefer A.J., who, at age seven, can be reasoned with.)

"No!" He shakes his head like a terrier with a rat, turns, and stomps down the hall.

Cyn shrugs. "He'll snap out of it. Or we can bribe him into this getup with cupcakes."

"I don't remember Mom ever bribing us. The way I remember it, it was pretty much her way or the highway." I've seen the boys run roughshod over Cyn many a time, but she rarely raises her voice with them. "In fact, I got spanked a time or two. And I turned out okay."

"She never spanked me."

"I rest my case," I mutter. Of course Mom never spanked her. Cyn was born six years after me. With two miscarriages in between, the doctor told Mom it was unlikely she'd have a second child, so when Cyn finally came along, she headlined as the Miracle Baby. I remember

Dad would point at Mom's stomach, tight as a watermelon, and say, "There's a baby in there." I remember having a very "yeah, so?" attitude. No one mentioned the baby was coming *out*. They sprung her on me. One day I was still the only child, sole princess of all I surveyed. Next thing I know, Mom and Dad are bringing Cynthia home, and Mom is beaming like this screaming ball of baby is the best thing that's ever happened to her. That ever *will* happen to her. I don't actually remember this part, but Aunt Iris says the first time they introduced me to Cyn, I may have squeezed her a little too tightly. I'm sure I was merely trying to give her a warm welcome-home hug, but apparently they thought I was trying to suffocate her. I *do* remember feeling brushed aside while everyone fawned over the baby. That may or may not have been the day I stopped playing with my dolls and began to play solely with their dream houses instead.

It was definitely the day Heidi, our terrier mix, and I became besties. Oh, I'd loved Heidi before, but after Cyn was born, we really bonded. While Mom and Dad fussed over the new baby, Heidi and I consoled one another. Heidi became my constant companion by day and my security blanket each night. At the time, I didn't know the phrase "unconditional love," but that's how I felt. She became the forerunner of all the pooches I've had in my life.

My mind now runs through a slide show of all the dogs I've loved, stopping at Marie. Thank God I brought her along. I'm probably going to need a security blanket to get through this party. I can see Marie through the opening to the family room, she's playing dead for A.J., who's wearing a cowboy hat and hog-tying her feet. "Oh, A.J., just pretend, okay? Don't really tie her feet up."

"Okay, Aunt Alex," he says in a grudging voice, but at least he complies, and then he and Bobby run over to say hi and give me hugs. Marie follows along and nose-pokes my hand. I'm not sure if she's just checking in with me or thanking me for saving her from being hog-tied.

Cyn tells the boys to go get dressed for the party, then heads for the kitchen. Marie stays with me, as I follow along after Cyn, surveying the scene. Legos flood the family room floor. The dining room table hides under canary-yellow plastic place mats, half-empty cereal bowls, and spilled milk. It smells like a mix of ant spray and cupcakes. A grape-jelly stamp of a hand stands out on a cream-colored wall. The area rugs are shoved against the baseboards, signaling that the boys have once again turned the hardwood floors into their hockey rink. In the kitchen, cereal boxes, dirty dishes, unfrosted cupcakes, and two six-packs of beer jockey for space on the counters. I'm glad to see the beer.

Marie trots over and sniffs at the jelly handprint, situated perfectly at her nose height. After a quick glance back at me, presumably to see if I might try to stop her, she starts licking the wall. I *would* stop her, but at least she's helping to make a dent in the mess.

"Ready for the party?" I ask. Cyn pushes through the saloon doors into the kitchen, and I brace my shoulder for impact as the doors swing back. "Give me a screwdriver, spackle, and some paint, and in like thirty minutes, these doors will be history." This is, conservatively, the tenth time I've made this offer.

"A.J.'s still in his cowboy phase. He loves them."

I point at the cupcakes. "Are these Mom's recipe?" Maybe I can sneak one before lunch without the boys seeing.

"Of course. Did you think I'd use a boxed mix?" She holds a bowl of Sponge Bob–yellow frosting out to me. "Can you frost them while I get dressed?"

"Maybe you should frost them while I straighten up." I demonstrate being better suited to this task of cleaning by grabbing two cereal boxes and putting them in the pantry.

"I've got to get the boys dressed. Unless you want to help them?"

"That's okay. I'll frost." I take the bowl. "But what about cleaning up?" Scanning the room, I hope the look on my face adds "this mess" to the end of my question.

"That'll take five minutes."

I want to say, *No, it will take two days, a power washer, and a hazmat crew.* I don't really care if her house is messy. She's always been messy. It's just the thought that people will be here soon for the party . . . it makes me cringe. I'm mortified for her, but obviously she doesn't care, so I guess I should try not to care as well. I shrug and attempt a smile. "Okay. It's your party."

Thirty minutes later, cupcakes line the now-clean counters like frosted soldiers, and the dishwasher hums its way through the breakfast dishes. My three nephews, now clothed, sit at the bar and beg for cupcakes. Marie's black nose peeks over the edge of the high counter as she balances on her back legs, trying to see what the boys are so interested in. A.J. tells her to get down and sit; Bobby and Fuzzy parrot their older brother. The boys love to boss Marie around—it's a welcome change of pace for them. Marie makes their day by obeying. With their success at "sit," they begin firing all the other commands she knows at her. She looks so cute, running through all of them at top speed: she shakes with A.J., high-fives Bobby and Fuzzy, then plays dead, then sits again. I laugh and tell them to go easy on the poor girl. "I think she's earned a treat," I say. I snitch three slices of strawberry out of my fruit salad and hand each of the boys a piece to feed her.

After the treats are dispensed, the boys turn back to me and rest their elbows on the bar. Although dressed, they are not what I'd call *ready.* Their toffee-colored hair sticks out in various directions: up for A.J., out for Bobby, and in strange swirls on Fuzzy. Fuzzy's face, predictably, sports a shiny veneer of some type of juice. A long white hair from Fernando, their Persian cat, adorns his right cheek. I assume Fernando's gone into hiding, since he's not as big of a fan of Marie as the boys are.

"Tell you what: I'll let you guys share the bowl if you go pick up your toys." I hold up the stainless-steel bowl streaked with the remaining frosting to display the bounty that awaits.

"Mom always just gives us the bowl," A.J. says.

I assess them for a moment. They can't be trusted with the tidying job anyway. "Fine. Have at it." I push the bowl across the counter, and they clamber onto their knees and fall upon it. "Don't get any on your clothes," I say over my shoulder. "And don't give Marie any," I add, as Bobby extends a frosting-laden finger in the dog's direction. The finger changes course and pops into his own mouth as he looks at me with wide-eyed innocence.

I know I said I wasn't going to care, but I can't resist doing at least a tiny bit of straightening up while Cyn's getting dressed. Marie, realizing she's not going to get any frosting, follows me into the family room. I've trained her to put her toys away, so I hand her a ball and point at an oversize chest. "Toys! Away," I say. She helps as I shove, toss, and cram everything in the box. If Marie can be trained in this art, why can't the boys be as well? Oh, wait, they *can* be; it's just that Cyn does everything for them.

I go to the powder room to wash up. The hand towel feels damp, in an I'm-the-439th-person-at-the-truck-stop-to-use-it way. I grimace, pull it off the rack, and find a fresh replacement under the sink.

When I come back out, Cyn appears, ready for the party. Lime-green, form-fitting Bermuda shorts show off her tan legs, and a matching plaid sleeveless top with the shirttails tied in a knot reveals her brown stomach. I have to hand it to Cyn—she looks great, thanks to her regimen of running while Fuzzy rides in the jogging stroller and Bobby and A.J. pedal their bikes alongside. She strikes a cocked-hip pose, and I know she's waiting for me to say how cute she looks.

I ask if she got a new outfit for the party and leave it at that.

She looks around and asks, "Have you been cleaning again?" This is not said with a "thank-you" tone, but with a "did you take my favorite earrings?" accusatory tone, which I've heard before. (And I didn't *take* her earrings. I borrowed them. Big-sister prerogative.)

"Just a little." I untie my apron and head for the kitchen, ignoring her harrumph.

Jamie comes through the door lugging the gas tank for the barbecue.

"That took forever," Cyn says. "I thought you were going to help get ready for the party."

"You know how crazy Home Depot is on weekends."

"Yeah, that's why I've been telling you to do it every night this week."

"Some of us work. Some of us like to relax when we get home after a long day. I don't see why you couldn't have done it this week."

"Don't start with the 'I'm the only one that works around here' thing."

I know Jamie has been repeatedly asking Cynthia when she's going back to work. She had a good job as a dental hygienist in Santa Barbara before they moved, but the boys have given her an out. She's forever dreaming up work-from-home ideas, and the various projects she's started (custom-embroidered booties, hand-painted T-shirts, baby-shower favors) clutter their fourth-bedroom-turned-office/craft room/storage space. I'm not sure what her latest venture is.

The doorbell rings, averting a full-blown argument, and the boys and Marie stampede to answer it.

*

Over the next fifteen minutes, the doorbell rings as each new group of guests arrives. Each time, the boys and Marie rush to the door. I tag along to make sure Marie behaves.

Last to arrive are Cyn's best friend, Bess, with her husband and three kids. In the ruckus, while everyone kisses and hugs hello, their middle daughter, Olivia, heads straight for Marie.

"Oh, a puppy!" she says.

Although I've met Cyn's friends several times, this is the first time I've brought Marie along. Olivia charges Marie, arms extended for a hug. The girl's face is only slightly higher than Marie's.

I know Marie will be fine—she's been rushed at and hugged a million times by the boys and by Rachel's daughter, Kaitlin—but I wince to see a child run so trustingly at a strange dog.

"Hang on!" I jump between the two of them, crouching down to Olivia's level and catching hold of her hand. "Hi. Remember me? I'm Alex." She looks taken aback, but nods, so I continue. "That's my dog, Marie. She's very friendly, but you should *always* ask a doggy's owner if it's okay to say hello. And a lot of doggies don't like hugs, so ask about that too. Okay?"

She nods again but doesn't say anything.

"So did you want to meet Marie and give her a hug?"

Enthusiastic nodding.

I let go of her hand. "Okay, just be gentle. All right?"

Olivia carefully circles her arms around the dog's neck. Marie wags her tail and kisses the girl's ear. Olivia giggles, then looks up and beams at me.

I smile back and tell her what a great job she's done.

*

While the guests are loading up their plates with lunch, I go to use the powder room. It's occupied, so I head upstairs to the boys' bathroom, hoping it won't be too gross. If it is, I'll just give it a quick cleaning in case any other guests use it.

At the landing, I hear voices in the master bedroom. I'd seen Maya carrying her baby upstairs with a diaper bag, but didn't realize anyone else was up here.

"Who brings a *dog* to a kid's party?" I recognize Bess's voice.

"I know, right?" Maya replies. "I wonder if she even asked Cynthia if it was okay." I did, as a matter of fact. And Cyn said it was a great idea since the boys love Marie so much.

"Did you see her lecturing Olivia?" My face burns. "What a lot of nerve." *I wasn't lecturing her,* I want to burst in and say. *I was just trying to teach her not to charge at strange dogs so that she doesn't end up getting bit in the face someday!*

But there's no point trying to defend myself. It will just make them dislike me all the more. I get that we don't have a lot in common, but what did I do to make them actively shut me out? They've never once tried to pull me into the group conversation or asked about my life.

I'm transported back to my first day of Girl Scouts, when Amy Sue Simpson whispered, loud enough for me to hear, "Look at the freak" when I walked in. My legs were covered in dozens of itchy red welts, plainly visible under my uniform. Back in the days of flimsy flea collars, Heidi had brought a flea infestation into my bed. I shudder, remembering. I was terribly allergic to the bites and scratched myself raw. Mom had to buy one of those horrifying flea bombs and kept us all out of the house for a day.

"Stay away from her," Amy Sue had said. "She's probably contagious."

I want to tell these ladies I'm *not* contagious. *My lack of interest in child rearing isn't catching!* We're all women who love our families and want the best for them. Surely there's some common ground there?

I creep back down the stairs, feeling like a scabby-legged outsider once again.

And Cyn wonders why Barry and I try to get out of these parties. It's going to be a long afternoon.

CHAPTER 4

"Have you picked out a name?" Bess asks Maya, who is not perceptibly pregnant.

Also at the table besides Bess, Maya, Cyn, and me, is the fourth momsketeer, Veronica. Actually, Veronica is still a wannabe mom. (Earlier she announced she's ready to stop having her life be "all about *me*," at which the rest of them nodded, and, I expect, struggled to keep from glancing in my self-absorbed direction.) Luckily, I've been to enough of these events that we've moved past the usual intrusive line of questioning about my breeding prospects. At the first few get-togethers, it was all "You're sure you don't want kids?" "Who'll take care of you when you're old?" "You're just going to let your ovaries wither on the vine?" Okay, no one ever asked that last one aloud, but they said it with their slit-eyed looks.

At this point, I'm not sure whether they've (a) accepted that I'm a freak, (b) decided I'm too old to pester about it anymore, or (c) taken to secretly pitying me for hiding my true feelings and deep regrets about never having children. I'm afraid it's the last, but whatever. Maybe I'll have the last laugh someday when Barry and I have enough money left to entice the boys away with a promised inheritance so that they'll take care of *us* in our old age instead of their parents.

We sit around the patio table, spread with the remains of our barbecued burger lunch. Cyn and her friends encircle one end, and I'm at the other end, surrounded by the empty chairs that recently held their husbands. The men snuck off to the garage to ooh and aah over the 1973 Camaro Jamie's been refurbishing. An oscillating fan in the corner of the patio drowns out some of the noise of the kids and Marie running through the sprinklers and playing on the Slip'N Slide in the big backyard. The boys holler, the girls squeal, and Marie barks with joy. And Veronica watches as if there's a risk of drowning death.

I nurse my now-tepid beer and try not to look too bored. I'm not sure whether the mothers can see through the Stepford-wife smile plastered on my face. I'd lay good odds they can't because they've gotten used to ignoring me. What I really need right now is a nap. I didn't sleep much last night, and between the hot weather and the huge burger with half a beer, I'm ready for a snooze. Or maybe I should go run through the sprinklers with Marie and the kids. It'd wake me up, and be a helluva lot more fun than sitting here.

"I got one of those baby-name books," Maya says, "but it's such a daunting task. Julio wants something unique—maybe a character from one of his favorite books or something."

I want to open with a joke, "I hope his favorite book's not *The Lord of the Rings*; Frodo would make it tough to survive high school." But these ladies don't joke about these things. Still, I actually have something to say for once. This feels like common ground, so I say, "Actually, we've done that with our dogs. We named them after Barry's favorite scientists. Marie's named after Marie Curie. Our last dog was Louis. As in Pasteur."

They look at me, probably shocked that I can speak. After all, I had nothing to offer on getting into preschool, Maya's annoying babysitter who keeps trying to plunk the baby in front of a *Baby Einstein* video, and, oh hell, I don't remember the other riveting topic. Probably because I was amusing myself imagining a line of alternate *Baby Einstein* DVDs: *For the sports-minded parent, there's* Baby Jordan. *Or if you're hoping for a financially savvy baby, try* Baby Trump. I'd almost laughed out loud at the thought of *Baby Trump* in a diaper and outrageous comb-over. Anyway, the fact I've been sitting here, mute, until this point causes all heads to swivel my way. Cyn gives me an actual encouraging smile, but the rest of them simper as if to say, "That's nice, crazy dog lady," and then turn back to one another. I don't know why I bother.

"Do you know the sex yet?" Cyn asks Maya.

"No, but I'm hoping for a girl. One of each would be perfect."

"God, I'd love to have one of each," says Veronica. She stares longingly at Maya's still-flat belly, and I do honestly feel for her. Cyn told me they've been trying for ages.

"I'd love to have a girl. I'd dress her up in pink, and we'd go shopping together." Cyn's eyes soften. She looks out into the yard at her three rowdy boys. A.J., crouched behind an overturned bucket hollers, "Incoming!" and tosses a water balloon at Olivia. Marie dives in front and takes the hit, earning the dog another big hug from the girl. Cyn turns back to the table. "I told Jamie I want us to try for a girl."

The other women chime as one: "That's great!" "How exciting!"

"Are you crazy?" Again, every head turns in my direction, only a lot faster this time and without the previous perfunctory smiles. I know Jamie can't have reacted positively to this. Their original plan was to have two children, and then Cyn would go back to work, at least part-time, when Bobby got into preschool. But then—surprise!—Fuzzy came along. "Can you guys afford another kid?"

"Thanks for your support." Cyn glares at me, and Bess pats her hand. The stupidity of bringing this up while she's got her mama posse behind her hits me, but I press on.

"I'm just saying, doesn't Jamie think you're going back to work soon?"

Bess looks at me, opens her mouth, and then clamps her lips together. She turns back to Cyn. "What did Jamie say?"

Cyn chokes back tears. "He said I was crazy!" The ladies openly glare at me. Maya gets up to comfort Cyn and offers her a clean Sponge Bob napkin.

I get up too, but to take a stack of dirty plates inside. I can hide in the kitchen for a good while if I unload the clean dishes from the dishwasher and reload it with the lunch mess.

Several minutes later, Cynthia comes in. Marie troops behind her, leaving a trail of wet paw prints. I grab a rag out of the pantry. "Shoot." I wipe Marie's feet. "She's making a mess."

"It's okay. I'll have to mop later anyway." Cyn sniffles. Her pert nose glows pink. She's managed to have a good cry without smudging her eye makeup, a talent I've always envied.

"I'm sorry, Cyn." I give her a hug. "It'd be nice if you could have a girl. Jamie sort of acts like the boys are solely *his*." Cyn let Jamie pick out their names (although she retained veto power), which came from his NASCAR and Indy racing addiction. He loves to watch racing with the boys, all piled together on the sofa; they wrestle during commercials. He plans to get them into baseball as soon as they're old enough; A.J. and Bobby already play T-ball. Tuesdays he takes them to Hooters for two-dollar chicken wings. Well, I'm guessing on the last one.

"You're right though." She hangs her head. "Jamie says we can't afford another baby."

It can't be easy living steeped in so much testosterone. It *would* be nice, no matter how unrealistic, for Cyn to have her little girl. "How about a Chihuahua? There are a gazillion that need rescuing. And you can dress them in pink and take them shopping!"

She laughs and looks slightly cheered; I don't have the heart to tell her I was serious. Instead, I say Marie and I need to get going.

"You're not staying for the singing and the presents?"

"No, we've got to get home." I fib about what time Barry will be back. Besides, I'm not sure I want to be here when Jamie and Cyn see the band set, which I'm starting to regret. Rache was right: I should've bought the fabric bowling set. I ask Cyn to say my good-byes for me, then hug her once more. Cyn gives Marie a hug good-bye too. I grab a cupcake, and Marie and I dash outside.

In the car I lean back in my seat for a moment, happy to have survived another of my sister's parties. Barely. Maybe I should start lining up excuses for Bobby's fifth birthday, which is coming up in a few months.

*

I'm surprised when I get home and find Barry's truck in the garage. I guess I didn't fib to Cyn.

As I let Marie out of the backseat, I can't help but worry about Barry's supposedly-not-bad news. If it's not bad, why did he come home early? I pause for just a moment before opening the door into the house.

"You're home." I find him making spaghetti sauce in the Crock-Pot. It's too hot for spaghetti, but he cooks when he's anxious. Marie rushes to greet him, but then her nose shoots straight up as she realizes there's ground beef in the vicinity. She acknowledges Daddy with a few hand licks, but then it's back to sniffing at the stove top and counter. She looks at me, at the stove, at Barry, then back at me again, hoping for a handout.

"I missed you girls," he says. We peck hello. "It's no fun to come home to an empty house. How was the party?"

"Ugh. Same as always. We weren't expecting you back yet." I put my hand on my hip. My trepidation about his news is momentarily overridden by annoyance. "Hey, how long have you been home? You could have stopped by the party, you know, and helped me face those people."

"I'm sorry you had to go alone, but I just got home about fifteen minutes ago. I couldn't concentrate on any of the presentations, so I left early."

"Uh-oh." Barry is usually über-focused on three things in life: work, running, and our garden. His not being able to concentrate on one of them is not a good sign. "So are you going to tell me what's going on?" I look down at the neon-yellow cupcake in my hand. I didn't want to get crumbs in my car, and figured I'd enjoy it at home. But now Barry's here and about to tell me his news that's so big he couldn't concentrate on whatever it is librarians normally enjoy concentrating on, and the thought of eating the cupcake makes my stomach churn. I toss it in the sink, where it lands with a thud. "Should I have a seat or something?"

He puts down his wooden spoon and wipes his hands on a kitchen towel. "This might be a bit of a shock." He rests his hands on my shoulders.

Is this about me? Oh God, maybe this is it—time for me to dive in and confess everything about the credit cards and how I've raided our savings account. "Before you say anything, I'm sorry I've been kind of crabby. The business hasn't, well, it hasn't been   "

"Why are you bringing this up now?" He takes his hands away, and I miss the warmth and weight of them. "I'm trying to tell you something. I need you to listen."

I anchor my lower lip between my teeth and give him a go-on-then nod. If things don't work out with the Van Dierdons, I'll have to suck it up and tell him the truth—all of it—but now is not the time.

"This girl came into the Science Library on Friday. I noticed her because she didn't look like the usual science or engineering student. Too, I don't know, punk or something. She looked like a skunk—her hair was half-black, half-white. She had raccoon-eye makeup and these red-and-black-striped tights." He only gets wordy like this when he's nervous or upset. I want to say, *Get to the point, Bear.* My brain races double time, trying to beat him to the denouement of his tale.

"She's pretending to look at the oversize books by the reference desk, in front of where I was working. She's fingering the spine of the *Encyclopedia of Industrial Chemistry*, and she keeps glancing over." Some young girl's got a crush on him? Big whoop. "She finally approaches, so I ask if I can help her. She asks if I'm Barry Halstad, and I say yes." He takes a deep breath, then blows it out while pushing his hair back off his forehead. "And then she says . . . 'You're my dad.'"

"She what?" My mind, which has been racing, racing, racing, now suddenly skids out on the curve he's thrown up before it. I stand up straight and search his face, trying to see if by some small chance this might be a very bad joke.

He points at me. "I'm pretty sure my face had that same expression."

"I need to sit down." I turn one of the dining room chairs toward the kitchen and fall into it. "Go on." This has to be a misunderstanding. He'll get to the punch line soon.

Barry leans against the kitchen counter. "So I'm standing there, thinking there's no way in hell, when she pulls this yellowed Polaroid out of her purse and says, 'You and my mom kinda had a thing in the late '80s.' It's a picture of Jade and me on this camping trip we took in the Redwoods."

I bristle at Jade's name. Barry doesn't notice; he's too busy twisting his wedding band around and around on his finger.

"And then I look at her," he continues, "and she is a bit like a Goth version of Jade. Her eyes are the same lavender-blue." Does he have to add *lavender*? Isn't plain blue sufficient? "She's got the same pointed chin. And I'm thinking, 'Wow, this is Jade's daughter.' And then she says 'I mean, I guess that *thing* you guys had, it turned out to be me,' and gives me this awkward half smile, and she's got the Halstad fangs." He raises his upper lip to show me the pointy-tipped canines that run in his family. Like I don't remember them.

"You're assuming she's your kid based on a snapshot and some pointy teeth? Come on. You know I love your little fangs, but a lot of people have them." This is not Barry's kid. Barry and Jade do not have a kid.

"It's not just that. She looks like me. Like me and Jade."

"Holy shit, Barry." I have no idea what else to say. The churning in my stomach relocates to my brain. In all the dozens of possible scenarios I'd been imagining, this one never came up. The thousand monkeys at the thousand typewriters in my overactive brain *never* would have come up with this. A daughter. From his first love. Holy shit.

CHAPTER 5

I stand up. "Whiskey. I need whiskey."

I go to the pantry and take my time reaching for the bottle. Barry's had a few days to get used to this news, but it's just slapped me in the face. Closing my eyes, I imagine the photograph the girl showed Barry, of him and Jade, young and in love. I open my eyes and turn to find him standing there with a cocktail glass. I'd been so lost in thought, I didn't hear him get the glass from the hutch. He takes the bottle and pours me three fingers' worth.

Pausing to inhale its mellow vanilla and charcoal scent, I take a swig and finally say, "Why now? Where's she been the past . . . how many years has it been? How old is she?"

"She's got to be eighteen. Remember our blind date?"

"Of course I remember." The date had been so bad that when I saw him again three years later, at the wedding of our mutual friend Paula—the one who'd tried to set us up—I refused to talk to him at first. Apparently, he'd remembered our date differently, since he wouldn't give up until I danced with him. We've been together ever since. "I know you don't remember it that way, but it was the worst date ever."

We'd met for lunch at my favorite Mexican place, where Barry proceeded to burn Jade's name into my brain by saying it about four hundred times. Of course, I didn't know then that he only turns wordy when he's upset. He went on and on about her in terms that were sometimes reverential, sometimes angry, and sometimes amused, but all tinged with anguish. He'd even pulled out a picture (he brought a picture of his old girlfriend on our first date!); with her dark hair and fair complexion, she looked like a blue-eyed version of Snow White. Or rather, a lavender-eyed version.

He had been so raw, an open wound sitting across from me on the crowded patio of La Super-Rica Taqueria. I remember thinking that if someone took the time to pull him from the emotional wreckage and nurse him back to date-ability, he'd be a find. But you'd have needed the Jaws of Life to pull him from that mess, and at the time, I was young and looking for fun, unarmed with the proper heavy equipment. I remember wondering why Paula had set us up if Barry was barely out of a devastating breakup. As he talked, I realized they'd broken up months earlier. But the night before our date, he'd run into Jade at their favorite dive bar, and it had set all those old feelings of love, loss, and rejection running in their hamster wheel.

It dawns on me what he's saying. "You mean, that night—you're saying it happened the night before our first date?"

"It had to have been."

"I didn't realize you had sex that night." I don't know why this makes me angry. I feel like he cheated on me, which is ridiculous, since he hadn't even met me yet. "Swell."

"Of course I wouldn't tell you *that*. When I saw her at the bar, I thought I could convince her to come back to me. I . . . never mind. Anyway, you and I started seeing each other in '93. And our blind date was almost three years to the day before Paula's wedding. So, the girl, she's got to be eighteen."

"The *girl*," I repeat. "What's her name?" Is he hesitant to use her name because it means acknowledging her existence?

He runs his hand through his hair. He goes to the Crock-Pot and stirs the sauce, fast. Marie gets up thinking he's finally going to give her the pan he used to brown the meat. I've blocked out everything but Barry and the whiskey glass I'm clutching, but now I realize she's been waiting to lick the pan all this time. If she whined or harrumphed in her usual way, I didn't hear.

Barry also notices Marie. He sets the cooled pan down on the kitchen mat. Keeping his back to me, he returns to stirring his sauce. "This might sound strange—but her name's Marie."

"What?" The dog and I both look at him. Marie, seeing he has nothing else to offer, goes back to her pan, while I walk over and take the spoon out of his hand. "Your *daughter* has the same name as our *dog*? Why is that?" My voice gets louder with each word.

"Why are you mad at me? I didn't know she existed until three days ago."

"What would you have done if you did know?"

"I'm not sure. I . . . This still hasn't sunk in. I can't believe I've had a child out there all this time."

"Okay, let's start slow. Why does she have the same name as our dog?"

"I don't know. I didn't name her." He glances at me and sees my "you must have *some* idea" look. "It might be because . . . one time Jade and I got into this discussion about our favorite names. I told her I'd always liked the name Marie, because Marie Curie was such an amazing woman. I don't know, maybe it's a coincidence."

"Women don't casually talk about favorite names, Barry." I roll my eyes. "Jade wanted to know what names you had in mind for a baby."

Barry gets a distant look in his eyes. "That would explain the big fight we had that day."

I know that Barry and Jade only fought when the subject of babies came up. He filled me in on our blind date: how much they'd loved each other, and how Jade only broke up with him because she desperately wanted children, but he didn't. When Barry and I started dating, I took every opportunity to reassure him that I'd never wanted kids either, that it would never be an issue for us.

I know Barry loves me. But I've always felt like he loved Jade more. I bet if she'd told him she was pregnant, he would've married her. He'd have forgiven her for tricking him. I know she could've managed that, because she seemed to have some kind of spell over him. I'd seen how much he loved her, how devastated he was to lose her, on that first disastrous date. Yes, he was over her a few years later when we met up again, but still . . . I always felt like Barry's consolation prize.

So why didn't Jade tell him?

"Back to my original question. Why now? Why didn't your daughter ever try to find you before?"

"I don't know. We didn't talk for long. She dumped the news on me, then said she'd give me some time to digest it. She gave me her cell number and another number for the place where she's staying." He reaches into his pocket and pulls out a folded piece of notebook paper, the edges frayed where they once clung to the spiral binding. He drops it on the counter. "She wants to have dinner. With us. I told her I'm married. She asked if we had any kids, and I told her just the dog."

"I hope you didn't tell her the dog is named Marie too."

"No, of course not. I said I'd talk to you, and we'd figure out a night to have her over. She said she wants to get to know me."

"Okay." I take a swig of whiskey. "Dinner. We can handle that." I'm trying to process everything. Barry's a dad. But if she's eighteen, he's missed the hard stuff, right? The news is a shock—but eighteen. We missed all the annoying LP action and most of the rebellious teen years. Now he just needs to take some time to get to know her, see her once in a while. They'll start slow. Become friends. They'll e-mail and talk on the phone or text occasionally. Maybe years from now, he'll give her away at her wedding. Will we have to help pay for it? Okay. Sip some whiskey. I'm getting ahead of myself, as usual.

"We can do dinner. She's visiting, right? Do they still live in San Francisco?" When Barry and Jade broke up, she moved back there, where she'd grown up. She got a job as a research scientist with a biotech firm and, as far as Barry knew, never returned to Santa Barbara following their last . . . encounter after the dive bar.

"Like I said, we didn't talk much. She said she'd explain everything over dinner. But she's not just visiting. She's, um, starting at the university in the fall."

"Oh. She's going to UCSB? She's moving here?" That's a new twist. I'd been thinking she came to town to find Barry. They'd review their life stories and then she'd leave. But moving here is a very different thing. Will Jade visit? Does this mean she'll be back in Barry's life? What if he sees her and all those old feelings resurface? Okay, focus. "I thought you said you're supposed to call her at the place where she's *staying*, not *living*."

"It sounded like it's a temporary arrangement." He shrugs. "We'll find out when she comes over. Let's have her over soon, okay? I want to . . . does 'get it over with' sound wrong?"

"No. I feel the same. This is a lot to absorb, but I want to meet her. Find out where she's been. And why she's coming around now."

"You sound so suspicious. I hope you're not going to grill her."

"No. I just wonder if she wants something. If she does, you're going to have to insist on a DNA test. Do you think she might ask for money? For school or something?" Or what about past child support? Is that a thing? Could Jade come after us? Good God, we don't have that kind of money. We don't have *any* money. But Barry doesn't even know that. Yet. I begin to regret the whiskey, and push the glass away.

He shrugs again, and it seems his shoulders might never drop. "I don't know." He sounds frustrated. "Maybe she just wants to get to know me. We have to give her a chance."

"Okay." I occupy my hands by getting a pot for the noodles. "We'll give her a chance. And a DNA test."

"Let's have her over tomorrow, okay? It's hot for spaghetti, but everybody likes it, right? I made a ton, so there'll be plenty left over. The sauce is better the second day anyway."

"That doesn't give me much time to get ready." I set the pot on the stove.

"This isn't one of your fancy dinner parties. You don't have to 'get ready.' Besides, Anna comes tomorrow, so the house'll be clean. And I'll cook. You don't have to do anything."

"But we've got those gorgeous new plates, and I haven't had time to shop for matching napkins yet." Though suspicious and worried about the whole thing, I can't help the fact that my mind goes to creating a perfect party. It may be awkward; I may be freaking out about the specter of her mom; we may not have anything to say to one another, but the table will be lovely.

"Please don't get all crazy. She's not going to care about the napkins. She's coming so we can all get to know each other."

I say okay, but I picture my work schedule for tomorrow and know there's time for a quick run to Bed Bath & Beyond. And I've got a coupon. We can afford new napkins.

"I'm anxious for you to meet her. To see if you think she looks like me. I think she does. I think she's . . . *mine*, so I want to get to know her. God, I've been dying to tell you about this, but there hasn't been a good time to talk."

"If I'd known you needed to talk, I could have stayed home Friday night." I'd taken Rachel out for drinks for her birthday.

"You told me how much Rachel was looking forward to it; I didn't want you to disappoint her. I thought we'd talk when you got home, but then I fell asleep. Oh, Lex, I've been going crazy keeping this in." I can almost see the stress falling away from his shoulders and his brow now that his secret is out. He goes to get his own glass for some whiskey, but I stop him.

"I've been going crazy too." I hand him my glass to finish. I'm happy to see he's more like my usual even-keeled Bear now. "I could tell something was up. But you're right. It's not bad news. Just shocking. And I understand why you waited until the time was right to tell me."

Barry's words to Skippy come back to me: *Do you think she planned it that way?* He must have meant Jade, and how she "accidentally" ran into him that night long ago at his favorite bar.

"Can I ask you something?" I check the water to see if it's boiling, then put the lid back on and turn to face him. "Skippy, huh?"

His eyebrows raise, signaling he's wondering how I know.

"I overhead you, uh, chatting with our mutual friend the other day."

He stares at the ceiling for a moment, clearly embarrassed. "You know Jade's family is wealthy, right?" Of course, brainy, beautiful, *and* rich. As if I'd forget. Her dad had started a sourdough bread bakery with something like the last twelve cents in his pocket and turned it into a national grocery store staple, plus a chain of upscale sandwich shops. "They had a boat they kept at Morro Bay. We used to go there sometimes on the weekends. She was always 'Captain,' I was 'Skipper,' and well . . ." He shrugs, then retreats behind his whiskey glass.

I should have known this would also be related to Jade.

I turn to the stove again. "From now on, I'm going to call him Copernicus."

*

Early Monday evening, after searching for fabric samples with Rachel for the Van Dierdon project, I come home with a shopping bag filled with robin's-egg-blue napkins and a little present for Barry—an apron that says "Cooking = Math + Science." (Everything was over half off; a mere blip on the credit card radar.) I find Barry and our dog in the kitchen. He's tearing up lettuce leaves like they're the pages of a diary he doesn't want anyone to read, and Marie strains to watch, the tip of her shiny black nose at the edge of the counter, clearly hoping he'll toss a crouton her way.

He phoned earlier to let me know he'd had a brief conversation with Marie—the girl, obviously, not the dog (and no, I'm not ready to refer to her as "his daughter" yet)—and that she's coming at six thirty. I asked him if she'd said more about, well, anything, and he said it was just a brief, awkward invite. He gave her our address, and that was it. We also decided to call the dog by one of her many nicknames, Baby, for the night. The evening's going to be awkward enough without letting the girl know she shares her name with our dog.

I rub Marie's—I mean Baby's—neck while she wriggles and tries to lick my wrists. I move on from the dog's neck to Barry's and massage his tense muscles. He pauses to enjoy it.

He nods at the shopping bag, looks at his watch, and shakes his head. "You have thirty minutes for your final stress-prep madness. You'd better start spit-shining the baseboards."

"I'm just going to set the table. I'm not going to get all crazy." Good grief. *One* time I get down on my hands and knees at the last minute to elbow-grease a scuff off the baseboard, and I'm forever branded as the crazy baseboard lady. (I do *love* our baseboards though—five inches high, painted with semigloss Picket Fence White: they look stunning against the Cinnamon Latte walls.)

"Everything looks good anyway, right?" I scrutinize the kitchen. A thumbprint stands out on the stainless-steel fridge. I pluck the towel off Barry's shoulder and buff the spot until it shines. A few tomato seeds have snuck off Barry's cutting board. I grab a sponge from under the sink and wipe the counter around him. I know he thinks I'm anal with my over-the-top sprucing (and, okay, he's probably right), but hey, he's got little quirks that drive me batty too. So we're even. And at least my quirks leave us with a sparkly clean house. "Oh, hey, I brought you a little something."

I get the apron and slip it over his head. He smiles and gives me a smooch.

"Very handsome," I say. "There's chilled wine, right?"

"She's not drinking age."

"Not for her. For us. We should have a quick glass before she gets here." I pull a bottle of pinot grigio from the fridge and pour two glasses. "Here. You need to loosen up."

Barry stops tossing the salad and takes a healthy sip. "Is it rude to drink in front of a guest who can't? I didn't get any soft drinks. All we have besides alcohol is water and blue Gatorade."

"Crap. I can't believe I didn't think of that. I'm not used to having nondrinkers in the house. I could run to the store. Get some juice and soda. Maybe some flavored water?"

"No! There's no time. I need you here. You're good at filling awkward silences."

"Bear, she's coming to get to know you. It'll be fine. Be your usual lovable self." I hope I've reassured him, although I'm worried about the evening myself. "Drink your wine and try to relax. I'm going to change. And I'll bring you something to put on over that T-shirt."

He looks down at his chest and rubs the lettering peeking out over the top of the apron, which reads "Beam me up, Scotty." "But this is my favorite. It's soft. Maybe she's a *Star Trek* fan."

"Maybe she is. But I think it sends the wrong message. I'm going to bring you that nice Tommy Bahama shirt I bought you last year."

"I'm not crazy about that green color."

"It's not green; it's sage." I pick up my cool glass of wine and head down the hall.

Standing in my closet, I paw through my clothes, wondering what one wears to meet one's husband's love child. Ugh. I consider not changing, but my business outfit sends a "let's get to it—what do you want with us?" message. I need something that says, "We're warm. We're friendly. We'd like to get to know you. But don't try to put any crap over on us." I decide on my polished cotton black walking shorts, white J.Crew T-shirt, and black sandals with silver trim.

After changing, I check the mirror, smoothing my hair and fluffing the ends. I stare hopelessly at the creases in my forehead, dabbing at them with powder, then head back to the kitchen with the Tommy Bahama shirt and find Barry staring into the pasta pot full of water on the stove. His wine looks untouched beyond the initial slug he took.

"The water's never going to boil that way," I say.

"Huh?" he snaps out of his thoughts and stands straight. "Oh, right. Watched pot and all."

"No, I mean you have to turn the fire on." I reach past him and light the burner. "Put this on." He takes off the apron and slips the shirt on over his T-shirt while I sprinkle salt in the water. When he's buttoned up, I hand him his wine. "Drink this."

He sets the glass back on the counter. "I'm not ready for this, Lex. What do I know about being a dad?"

"She's almost nineteen. The hardest part's in the past. She just wants to get to know you." I can see his stress level ratcheting up again. "Talk to her like you'd talk to one of your students."

"She probably doesn't want to talk about how to do citation searches in PubMed."

Marie, I mean Baby, barks, and we catch the sound of a car out front.

Barry eyes get wide. "She's here."

We grab our wine and gulp. We wait for what seems like an interminable stretch of time for the doorbell to ring. I take another big slug of wine and motion for Barry to do likewise.

"Why hasn't she come to the door?" he asks. "What's she doing out there?"

"I don't know. She's probably as nervous as you are. Maybe she's getting up her courage." I hope she's not swilling alcoholic fortification, though, like we are.

We stand there, staring at each other, straining to hear every sound. Marie/Baby senses our tension and strains forward as well. Her ears go up and back. She runs to the front door and lets out several sharp barks before the bell rings.

"Mar—Baby, shush!" I scold as I push Barry toward the door. "You open it," I whisper to the back of his shoulder. "I'm right behind you."

Barry pulls the door open a little too forcefully.

Her hair captures my attention first. It's just as Barry described: half-black, half-bleached white, only I'd pictured one side black, the other blond. Instead, jet-black roots give way to bright-white ends, like they've been dipped in paint. It's spiky in the back; she's turned away from us—checking out our front lawn or taking in the neighborhood. There's a split second of confusion before she turns to greet us, because a tiny leg juts out from her hip. Mere confusion amplifies into full-blown, mouth-agape speechlessness as I find I'm staring at a female, teenage version of Barry—with a baby in her arms.

CHAPTER 6

A baby.

Barry's kid, or alleged kid, has a kid. Which means new papa Barry just became new *grandpa* Barry.

I hear a small sound come out of Barry's mouth. It might have been the beginnings of "welcome" or maybe "what the . . . ?" My money is on the latter, because it's all my own throat keeps trying to push past my lips.

The baby looks like a blue-eyed Nancy Reagan—she's all big round head on a long skinny body. Her head totters on her twiggy neck just like the former first lady's.

It seems like hours pass, and all I can come up with to say is some variation of *holy shit*. Even in my state of near-catatonic shock, however, I know Emily Post would not advise welcoming guests into one's home with the greeting "Holy shit." Of course, these are no ordinary guests—they are, holy shit, *family*.

Barry turns into the Madame Tussauds' version of himself. There's no way he'll recover before me, even if I smack the back of his head (as I am tempted to do) to jar some words loose.

I'm about to say hello when the dog, always excited to have company, noses past us to sniff the baby's bare foot. Startled, the girl takes a step back and pulls the baby higher against her chest. The baby, however, is undeterred and reaches down for the dog.

"It's okay," I say, breaking the silence. "She loves kids."

"You're sure?" Marie repositions the baby on her other hip and tentatively holds her free hand out. The dog sniffs it and wags her tail.

"She's used to my nephews. Honest. She'll be gentle."

"What's her name?" Marie asks, accepting a few licks on her hand.

"Her name's Marie," Barry says. He's apparently found the power of speech, but our plan not to bring up the dog's name flew right out of his addled head. The girl's forehead wrinkles.

"But we usually call her . . . Baby," I say. How stupid that sounds now. "Or Bunny. She has a lot of, uh, nicknames . . ." It's going to be a long and awkward night. I make the usual kiss-kiss sound at the dog and pat my thigh so that she'll stand by my side. "Come Ma—I mean, Bunny. Give them some breathing room." I hold out my hand to the girl. "I'm Alex. You must be Marie." I almost add a "too" on the end.

She shakes my hand with a surprisingly firm grip for such a slight girl. "This is Ruthie." She turns to look at the baby and tickles her neck. In profile, the girl is even more like Barry. Her nose has the same slope, and her cheekbones stand out like his, her thick bangs hanging low over her left eye. Ruthie coos and Marie smiles at her. And there they are—the pointy little teeth known to run in the Halstad family.

Our gray matter has barely absorbed the fact that Barry has a teenage daughter, and now here she is, holding a baby. I want to shut the door so that Barry and I can let this sink in before attempting semi-intelligent conversation, but there's no opportunity to even share a meaningful, if dumbfounded, look. Instead, I nudge him with my elbow so that he'll get out of the entryway. He steps back to let them in.

"Welcome," I say. "Let me take your purse." She sloughs her huge army-green bag off her shoulder and I catch it, although it's so heavy it almost hits the floor before I recover. The dog stays beside me as I set the bag down next to the couch, but she leans away from me to sneak in a few sniffs at the closed fabric flap. "Would you like to sit? Dinner's almost ready." I wait for Barry to dive in, shooting him a quick look.

"Would you like some blue Gatorade?" he asks. He brushes his own thick bangs off his forehead, and he looks like an unsure teenager himself, instead of the forty-six-year-old father—no *grand*father, shit!—that he actually is.

"Or some water?" I add. "I'm afraid we don't have any soda in the house."

"That's cool; I don't drink soda. Water's fine. It's not bottled, is it? I try not to drink bottled water. Like, tap's cool."

"It's not bottled. It's filtered. From the fridge dispenser."

"Okay. Cool."

"I'll get it." Barry flees, leaving me with his progeny. I hear the clatter of a wineglass against the counter and hope he's not only finishing off his drink but also bringing refills.

"Please, have a seat," I say. She swings the baby off her hip and sits. I take the loveseat across from her and give the dog the hand signal to sit beside me, which she does, leaning her weight against my leg. Holding Ruthie on her lap, Marie looks around the room. She speaks, but I can't hear what she says over Ruthie's sudden air-horn shriek. Meanwhile, the poor dog sits up straight and whips her head around to show me the whites of her eyes. She's not a fan of loud, high-pitched noises. I tell her it's okay and nod my head so that she knows she's allowed to go. She races off, probably to seek refuge with Barry. "Sorry. What was that?" I ask.

"I said 'nice place.'" Ruthie squirms, and although she no longer shrieks, she now emits relentless "uh, uh, uh" noises. "Is it okay if I let her down?" Marie glances around. "I'll keep an eye on her."

You and me both. "Sure, go ahead. So how old is she?"

She lets the baby slide off her lap, but keeps Ruthie protectively between her feet. Ruthie collapses onto her diapered bottom, protruding like a puffy white cloud beneath the hem of her black summer dress. "She's fifteen months."

Right here is where a mom would know to ask, *Oh, so is she walking/talking/doing tai chi/learning Mandarin now?* I'm sure fifteen months means something to most ladies, but I know nothing of developmental stages. I go with: "What a cute dress." I *want* to say, *Why are you here? Why now? And why do you have a baby?* But I ignore the voice in my head.

"It's an unusual color choice for a baby girl's dress."

Marie tilts her head and smiles a scrunched half smile at me. I remember Barry describing her awkward smile. Maybe she's not quite as self-confident as her handshake made her seem. "I made it myself. I'm not, like, into girly colors." That's fairly obvious, considering her charcoal-colored top and short, flowy black skirt, paired with the striped leggings Barry had mentioned.

"You sew, then?" While I make conversation, Ruthie surveys the room. I'm worried about what might attract her attention—our electronics equipment in the media console? The glossy books and pretty candles on the coffee table?—but luckily, Marie is prepared. She pulls a bright-purple plastic key ring out of her bag and clatters it over Ruthie's head while she tells me her grandmother taught her to sew. "Ruthie's named after her," she adds. Ruthie reaches for the keys and seems fascinated for what I hope will be a long while.

Barry comes in carrying a water glass and, bless him, a refilled wineglass for me.

"The spaghetti's done. We can eat," he says to me.

"I hope you like spaghetti," I say to Marie.

"Yeah—if it's vegetarian."

I shoot a look at Barry that hopefully transmits: "You are supposed to ask people if they are vegetarian or have allergies when you invite them over."

Marie can obviously tell from the exchange of looks between Barry and me that we're not having vegetarian spaghetti. "I should've mentioned it. Some plain noodles with cheese'd be fine." She makes that funny little smile again. At least she's trying to be accommodating. She scores points for that.

"I already put the meat sauce on the noodles," Barry says, earning him another look from me. "Sorry. I saw you had the big pasta-serving bowl out."

"We can cook some more noodles," I say to Marie.

"No, it's cool. If there's, like, bread and salad or whatever, I'll be fine." She's so thin, I believe she probably subsists on bread and salad, so although the crazed über-hostess within me wants to make her some nice cheesy pasta, I let it go. Besides, there's still an uncomfortable "we don't really know what to say to each other" vibe (mostly exuding from Barry). I figure it's best to get us all to the dinner table where we can preoccupy ourselves with eating.

"What about the baby?" I ask. "Is she a vegetarian too?" I've never heard of such a thing, and it feels stupid to ask, but I'm assuming like mother, like daughter. I don't know. Do babies need meat? Are they like dogs?

"No. She's not. Not yet anyway. She's not a huge eater, so I feed her whatever she'll eat. I mean, within reason." She carries Ruthie, following Barry and me to the dining room. I can see she's looking around for the furry Marie, and she freezes when the dog comes out of the kitchen. I call the dog over to Barry's chair at the far end of the table and give her the *down* and *stay* hand signals. She lies down with her chin on her paws, eyes upturned to watch the activity in the room. "Good girl," I coo at her. "Barry, why don't you get her a treat since she's being so good? Maybe one of her chew bones to keep her busy during dinner."

While Barry retrieves a bone from the pantry, I turn to the table, set for three. How will this work? "We don't have a high chair, so . . ."

"She can sit in my lap. And you can just put some spaghetti in, like, a plastic bowl."

Swell. I foresee my white tablecloth covered in little red-sauce handprints. Marie must be thinking the same thing, since she looks at the table, then down at the cream-and-sage-colored area rug under it and adds, "Do you have a plastic tablecloth? Or two?"

After some rearranging, and one more "Staaaaay" from me to keep the dog from "helping," we have two plastic outdoor tablecloths spread on the dining room table and on the floor underneath Marie and the baby's chair. I feel better about this arrangement—although the orange and yellow daisy-print oilcloth, which looks so cute on our patio table with our bright-yellow picnic set, clashes horribly with my robin's-egg-blue, silver, and white tablescape. Also, I'm wondering how good of a pitching arm this kid has. Are two tablecloths enough? Is there time to drape the room in plastic sheeting?

We engage in some innocuous patter about the weather while we eat. The baby seems content to chase noodles around her bowl and occasionally attempt to stuff one in her mouth. Every other one ends up on the floor. Although we've taught our dog not to beg during meals (she always lies next to Barry's chair while we eat), she quickly learns that the "uh-oh" the baby emits, sounding almost like the ding-dong of a doorbell, means food on the floor. A tired old chew bone cannot compete with food. Each time there's another "uh-oh," the dog lifts her head and the gnawing on her bone ceases. Marie looks over at the dog, who's being such an angel, and says, "She wants the noodles, huh?"

I smile and nod. "She's the first round of cleanup crew around here."

"Um, okay," Marie says.

Barry releases the dog with a chipper, "Okay." We all listen to the sound of her tongue on the plastic, while Ruthie squirms in her seat to watch the activity under the table. Chortling, the baby drops another noodle, obviously on purpose this time, then squeals and claps her hands when the dog stretches forward to slurp it up. Her mom may not be eating much, but at least we're providing dinner and a show for the baby.

"Okay, that's enough, Roo," Marie says before Ruthie can get her little fingers wrapped around another noodle.

With the show over, and the dog settled by Barry again, we return to our exciting topic of the weather. It's not normally this hot here; it's so much cooler in San Francisco. Barry joins in with some research he read on weather patterns. Then we fall silent.

To fill the conversational gap, I ask, "So, Marie, what made you decide to apply to UCSB?"

"I figured if it was good enough for my dad, it was good enough for me."

Barry and I exchange looks while Marie crunches into a crouton. So she knew about him before she started applying to schools. But before I can ask how long she's known about Barry, she continues.

"My friend Sarah and I came to check it out last year, and we loved the campus and stuff. My *mom* wanted me to go to Berkeley," her tone changes when she mentions Jade, becomes flatter, "so I could live at home and Ruthie could keep going to the same day care and stuff. My mom's been pushing Berkeley on me for years. I was like, 'Enough already.'" She rolls her eyes and stabs her fork into a hunk of lettuce. "I was ready to get out on my own. Well, *our* own." She squeezes Ruthie tighter within the circle of her left arm. "Anyway, now I know why she didn't want me to go to UCSB." She glances at Barry.

He notices we're both staring at him. He swallows. "Didn't she want you to meet me?"

"She told me you were dead."

I freeze midchew. Barry puts down his fork. "Dead?" we ask in unison. Barry glances over at me, and we exchange a surreptitious "what the *hell*" look with each other.

"Yeah. That's messed up, right? Like, I knew you were my dad all along. She gave me some pictures and told me about you and stuff. But she told me you died before I was born."

"That seems kind of . . ." I want to say *cruel*, but finish with "extreme."

"Totally. Not to mention completely harsh. I grew up thinking I was, like, half orphan, you know? And then when it was time to start picking a college, and I said UCSB, she started laying the Berkeley stuff on thick. But I applied anyway and got accepted. And she was acting all bizarre. So then, the other day, I'm surfing the school site, and I find this page listing new classes. It catches my attention 'cause it's got this Cultural Roots of the Japanese Horror Film class listed, and I'm thinking, that sounds cool, and I go to click the link, and I see your name."

She's been addressing most of this to me, but turns to Barry before continuing.

"It's some class you're doing for science freshmen on how to use the library or whatever." She pauses, and Barry nods. "And I swear, like, your name looked huge." She extends the fingers of her right hand several times. "This giant, throbbing neon sign: 'Barry Halstad.' And I totally froze. I probably would've stared at the screen for days, but Ruthie started crying. I didn't even hear her, or like I heard her, but her crying sounded underwater. My mom came in to see why I was ignoring Ruthie, and I pointed at the screen."

She flicks her bangs out of her eyes and takes a big drink of water.

"So you only recently found out I was alive?" Barry asks.

"Yeah. Like just a few days ago. My mom and I had this massive fight, and I started making plans to move here early. I wasn't supposed to move until September first."

"What did your mom say? Did she explain?" I ask. Luckily, we've all eaten a good portion of our dinners during the banal weather talk and ensuing silence because now our meals sit forgotten. Although I continue working on my wine. And quietly top up my glass.

Marie shrugs. "She tried." She eyes Barry once more from under her bangs, then turns her attention to a wayward lock of Ruthie's hair. Ruthie tries to squirm away, but Marie keeps fussing with her hair. "She said you didn't like kids. And that she was trying to protect me from a big letdown. She said she didn't want to tell you because she didn't want you to feel a sense of obligation to us." She leaves Ruthie's hair alone. "But I think we should've, like, given you a chance, y'know? It wasn't for her to decide. I told her it was just another way for her to control my life, and I started making plans to move."

Okay. This explains a lot. Although I still don't understand Jade's motives.

Barry clears his throat. I'm sure he has no idea what to say to this poor girl. I try to guess what he might say, and can't. I hope something comforting will come out of his mouth. "We shouldn't judge your mom. I'm sure she thought she was doing what's best."

Of course. The "defend Jade" route. Saint Jade could never do any wrong in Barry's eyes.

"I know." Marie's voice is still monotone. "She's always got my best interest at heart." She emphasizes "best interest" with a snarky lilt, signaling she's heard this a time or thirty.

Marie pushes the remaining bits of salad around her plate. Maybe Barry was right to take Jade's side. After all, it's not as though you can bash a kid's mom in front of her. The corners of her mouth flash upward when Ruthie grabs a Parmesan cheese shaving off Marie's plate and stuffs it in her mouth. But then the brief smile is gone.

She sighs. "My high school had this annual picnic—a father-student thing. It was always on a Friday, and after lunch they'd let us go home early. I used to beg Mom to let me skip school that day. But my mom's a total fanatic about school. She'd never let me skip unless I was, like, dying." She considers the baby on her lap and adds, "Or giving birth or whatever." She displays another uncertain half smile. "Anyway, she used to always say stuff like, 'If your dad were here, I'm sure he'd love to go.' And after I found out she lied, I kept remembering her saying stuff like that. It wasn't just one lie, you know? It was like this constant *stream* of lies." She looks down at her plate and mutters, "Totally eight-forty-three'd."

"Excuse me?" I say.

"Oh, I try not to swear around Ruthie. My friend Sarah, she works at a restaurant where they get fired for swearing, so they came up with code numbers for different cuss words. Eight-forty-three means totally," she lowers her voice to a whisper, "eff'd up."

"Ah," I say.

"Hey, are your parents dead?" Marie shoots a look at Barry. "My mom told me I didn't have any family on your side."

Barry nods. "They both died a few years ago."

"A few years ago? Man, another huge lie. What a total nine-seventeen my mom can be." I don't ask what that translates to, but I can guess. "She told me——"

She breaks off as Ruthie fusses in her arms. Now that her bowl is empty and she's snitched the last bit of cheese, she has no further entertainment. She clearly wants down.

"Sit still, Roo." Marie forms her napkin into a makeshift puppet.

"Noooo." Ruthie holds her spaghetti-sauce-covered fists to her eyes and rubs them, adding vermillion eye shadow to complete the look she's already got going on her lips and cheeks. She whips her head back and forth. The message is clear: she finds no charm in her mother's feeble napkin puppet. Ruthie points at the dog, still settled by Barry's chair. "Og. Og."

"She wants to pet the dog," Marie says, her eyebrows crinkled with concern.

"It's okay. The dog'll love it. Let me grab a damp cloth first." I don't want saucy handprints all over our lovely ivory-colored pooch. I dash to the kitchen and back.

I hand her the cloth and settle on the floor next to the dog's hind end so that I can keep an eye on the baby and make sure she's gentle with the dog.

I watch Marie clean Ruthie's hands, and hope she'll do as thorough a job as I would. At least the hubbub with the baby has ended the uncomfortable feeling in the room caused by the giant unanswered question swinging like an ape from our chandelier: What would Barry have done if he'd known of Marie's existence?

Marie sits cross-legged on the floor with Ruthie, warning her to "be nice to the puppy." Our patient pup, used to my rambunctious nephews, knows she's about to be literally rubbed the wrong way and stretches out on her side. Ruthie giggles with delight as the dog laps at her fingers. *That's my girl! Get any spaghetti sauce her mama missed!*

While everyone watches the dog and baby, I think about how this isn't the evening I'd imagined. Barry and I had prepared ourselves for the fact that Marie might be angry and have a "where the hell have you been all my life?" chip on her shoulder. But now I understand why she's suddenly appeared, and why she's so happy to see Barry. Her chance to get to know her father, which she thought she'd never have, is suddenly here; something she must have longed for often as a child is now a reality. I still have my hand resting on the dog's hip, but now, instead of watching Ruthie, I watch Marie. Her big blue eyes study Barry, bent over in his chair and rubbing the dog's ears. When Barry looks up to find Marie staring at him, she looks away.

"Would anyone like dessert?" I ask.

"Not for me, thanks," Marie says. "I don't eat sugar. That's one thing I try to not let Ruthie have either. She can be hell on wheels if she eats sugar."

"Barry doesn't eat it either."

Marie smiles at him. "Cool," she mutters.

He's obviously scored points in her book. I've got to try to get Barry talking, get off the heavy "I thought you were dead; my mom's a lying nine-seventeen" path this conversation has taken and into some lighter stuff. Find out what these two have in common. It's way too much to absorb everything at once, but some basic getting-to-know-you stuff is where we have to start, right? If we were in a musical, I'd break into song, and we'd all be hugging by the end of it and breathing heavily from dancing around the dining room. But we're not in a musical, so instead I'll start with dessert.

"It's sugar-free vanilla frozen soy milk," I say. It's not as bad as it sounds, and it's all Barry will eat, so if I don't want to eat dessert alone, I have to cater to his tastes. "And I've got raspberries to put on top."

"Okay, sounds good," Marie says. "I'll give Ruthie bites of mine."

We get up from the floor. As I head to the kitchen, I say to Barry, "Tell Marie about how you tried to go vegetarian that one time."

Barry shakes his head. "She doesn't want to hear about me and my weak will."

"Yeah, I do." Marie settles back into her seat with Ruthie.

"It was in college." Barry tells the story of how his mischievous roommate set out to thwart Barry's fledgling vegetarianism by making the most savory carnivorous meals he could think of: meatloaf, grilled steaks, BLTs.

Marie is laughing as I set dessert on the table.

"All my good intentions undone by a slice of bacon." He shrugs. "Weak-willed."

"I bet you could give up meat if you tried again," Marie says.

Barry shakes his head. "Nah. I've tried. I get cravings for a burger after a week. But we do buy organic grass-fed beef, free-range chicken . . ." He pokes at his dessert. I guess he's worried about being a disappointment to his daughter. Seeming uncool. It's sweet.

"Barry runs marathons," I say. Most folks are impressed by that.

"Hey, I run too." A happy, Halstad-fang-filled smile spreads across her face. "I used to run track. Uh, until—" She jiggles the baby, who licks her lips in a frustrated effort to reach every bit of the frozen soy milk. "I was on the cross-country team. I wanna do a marathon someday."

They talk about distances and speeds, and that segues into nutrition and favorite running shoes and past injuries. Barry talks about some research he read on recovery drinks, and I sit back and eat my raspberries, feeling pleased with myself for discovering a shared interest.

Eventually, they exhaust the topic. Silence. Spoons scrape bowls. The dog sits up, her curls peeking over the edge of the table. Like Pavlov's dogs, she knows that the sound of silverware hitting ceramic means a lickable dish is in her immediate future. Barry sets his dish down, and Ruthie contorts to watch. We listen to the dog's tongue polish the bowl clean. Barry knows I cringe when he does that in front of guests, but at least it's holding the baby's interest.

Now what do we talk about? I shoot Barry an intense glare while inclining my head toward the girl, hoping he'll leap in with a new topic. He gives me a deer-in-the-headlights look that lets me know I'm alone in the role of conversation instigator.

"So Marie." Think of something. Anything. "Where are you staying?"

"We're at this motel with my friend Sarah. She's starting at UCSB in the fall too. The apartment we're renting together isn't available until September first. She came down with me now 'cause I needed some help getting settled with Ruthie."

"That was nice of her."

"Yeah. I left Ruthie with her that day I came to see you at the library," she says to Barry. "But she's going back to San Francisco for the rest of the summer to work and save money for school. She's, um, leaving on the holiday." Wednesday is the Fourth of July.

"What'll you do until September?" I ask. As soon as the words leave my mouth, I get a bad feeling that I shouldn't have asked this particular question.

"I'm not totally sure. That's, uh, part of why I wanted to come over." She fusses with Ruthie's hair again. "I know I just met you guys and all, but you seem cool. And I don't want to go home, 'cause I'm still massively pissed at my mom. But I can't afford to stay in the motel." Her pointed chin juts out. "My mom said she'd pay my way during school, but she won't fund my 'running away' for the summer." She says "running away" in the long-suffering voice most teenagers have perfected. "So I was kinda hoping Ruthie and I could, y'know, crash here?"

She pauses a second before rushing on. "We wouldn't be any trouble, and it's only until September first. And I was thinking that way, um, my dad," she glances at Barry, "and I could get to know each other. Make up for lost time and stuff. And I'll totally help. I'm not a great cook, but I can make breakfast. And I swear I'll help clean, and . . . and I know you guys probably want to talk about it and that's cool." She gets up, swinging Ruthie onto her hip. "We should go. Ruthie gets wired if she doesn't go to bed on time. So maybe you guys can think about it and let me know? Because if I can't stay here, then I have to go back with Sarah on Wednesday. But I'd really like to stay."

Barry and I stand as well. Marie heads to the living room for her bag. Furry Marie trots along behind her. I widen my eyes at Barry. He mouths "What do I say?"

"Nothing," I mouth back. *I'll handle this.*

We follow her into the living room. She swings her bag over her slender right shoulder, and it seems to balance the weight of Ruthie, riding her left hip. The dog stretches her neck, sniffing at the bag again. There's got to be some food in there. Marie notices the dog and side-steps away. I pat my thigh, and although the dog heaves a sigh, she stations herself next to me.

"So Marie," I say, "you know we don't have any baby furniture. No crib, or high chair, or things like that."

"I didn't expect you to. I brought all that stuff in my SUV. Well, not a crib, 'cause Ruthie and I can share a bed, but everything else. We needed it at the motel anyway, and I figured that way we'd be ready when school starts."

"And the house isn't exactly baby-proof." I wave my hand at the living room to signal that this is obviously not a home intended for grubby, grabby hands.

Marie looks around. "I could totally help with that. We wouldn't have to do much. Move a few things, put some baby locks on cupboards." *And cover all our area rugs and furniture with drop cloths,* I want to add. "Ruthie's a good baby. I promise we won't be much trouble."

Oh, wait. The dog. Isn't she afraid of the dog? How would that work? "And of course, the dog's used to having the run of the house." I reach down and gently tug at furry Marie's ear. "We don't crate her while we're at work."

Marie studies the dog, who wags her tail, wondering what fun thing will happen next.

She might be our out.

Marie holds out her free hand and the dog trots forward to lick it. Ruthie flails to reach the dog, and Marie bends down so that Ruthie can pat the dog's soft head.

"She seems like a really gentle dog," Marie says. "And I wouldn't want Ruthie to grow up with any of my fears. I know I can be a little overprotective sometimes. My mom has *totally* ruined me for bugs," she confides. "I don't want to do that to Roo. She's never really been around a dog before. I think it would be good for her."

I open my mouth, but she presses on while heading for the door. "Anyway, you don't have to answer now. Like, sleep on it, and maybe—" she looks at Barry, "call me tomorrow?"

Barry opens the door for them. Her SUV doesn't just sit in our driveway, it dominates it. Good gravy, the amount of crap she could have crammed in there behind those tinted windows. I picture boxes and baby accoutrements being trooped into my lovely, uncluttered home, but my vision is cut short as Marie thanks us for dinner and says good-bye.

"It was really great to meet you." She looks at Barry, then away. Barry shifts from foot to foot. He was probably going to do the rote "Nice to meet you too," but realized what an odd thing that is to say to one's child. He runs his hand through his hair, then pats her shoulder.

"Barry'll call you." I jump in for him. She smiles and leaves, and the three of us follow them out, stopping on the porch; at the car, Marie takes the baby's arm and makes her wave. I give the dog the hand signal for *sit*, then tell her, "High five." She holds up her right paw for a moment, returning the baby's "wave." Marie points, telling Ruthie, "Look, the doggy's saying bye-bye." She attempts to coax a return bye-bye out of Ruthie, but all Ruthie says is, "Og." Clearly, dog-Marie has made an impact on the baby, even if we didn't.

Barry shoves his hands in his pockets, and I wave again as they pull away.

When they're out of sight, I shut the door and lean against it, the dog nuzzling my hand. "Wow. That was unexpected. I mean, she seems like a good kid. But a baby? I was *not* ready for that."

"Yeah, that was . . . different." Barry—always the master of understatement—squats down in front of the dog. "Who was the best puppy tonight?" he says in a soft voice, rubbing Marie's ears. She flicks her tongue at the end of his nose, and he smiles and stands up before she can get more licks in. He heads toward the kitchen, unbuttoning his shirt as he walks away.

"There's no way we're letting them move in, right?" I call out after him. He keeps walking. I sit on the floor next to the dog, taking over ear-rubbing duty. "You're the only 'baby' we need in this house, aren't you?" I say softly. She lets out a little half groan, half harrumph and leans her head into my hand. I'm pretty sure she's with me on this, so even if Barry's not, it'll be two-to-one in favor of the girls not moving in.

CHAPTER 7

I sit on the floor for a few more minutes with the dog, scratching her tummy while I think about what a crazy night this has been. Hearing Barry scraping plates in the kitchen, I give Marie one last pat and join him in the kitchen.

"So, seriously, Barry . . . we're not letting the girls move in here, right? It'd be one thing if it was only her, but a baby too?"

"She seems like a good kid, huh?" Barry stands at the sink, rinsing dishes and loading them into the dishwasher. I grab the wine bottle off the table and split the remainder of the pinot grigio between our glasses. "Funny that she's a runner too." His eyes still look half-dazed, but what might be a proud smile starts to form at the corners of his lips. "Maybe she and I could go for a run together."

"And, what, I get to babysit while you do that?" I don't want to rain on his father-daughter bonding ideas, but come on. He knows I'm afraid of babies. They're so easily damaged. This one's old enough that that weird soft-spot-on-the-head thing is probably toughened up, but still. It's not the same as dog sitting. I nudge his shoulder and hand him his glass. "That is *not* happening."

"Of course I would never expect you to babysit. Maybe Marie's got a baby jogger in that monster car. If not, maybe we could get her one? A little, I don't know, make-up-for-lost-time present?" He leans against the sink and looks into his wineglass.

"That's a super sweet idea, Bear." He's seeming less freaked out by the minute. Meanwhile, I'm completely freaking out. How is he so calm about this? He's obviously blocking out what my sister's house is like: nothing but noise and toys. If I could give birth to a rational, fully formed five-year-old, I *might* sign up for motherhood, but little kids scream. A lot. And have no volume control. And sometimes they cry, no, *wail* for no apparent reason. A surround-sound memory blares in my head of Bobby's conniption fit the time A.J. picked out all the orange M&Ms from a bag they were sharing. I remember wanting to yell, *They all taste the same!* Barry has always agreed with me on this stuff. I need to remind him of that if he's got it in his crazy head that we should let them move in.

"So what are you thinking? About them moving in?" I ask *again*. I drum my fingers on the countertop. I knew she wanted something. I knew there'd be more to this dinner than simply a touching "Getting to Know You" sing-along.

"I realize I haven't had a lot of time to process this, but I feel like I owe it to her." He turns back to the sink. Possibly because he doesn't want to see my facial expression.

So if I say they can't move in, then I'll be the lone bad guy. How do I talk some sense into this man? I know my "the house isn't set up for it" argument won't fly. He couldn't care less what the house looks like, so I work the noise angle. "Remember when my sis and the boys spent the night last New Year's Eve?" Barry loves his quiet time after work. "Remember how loud they were? And how Bobby had that screaming fit?"

"You can't compare three boys with one baby," Barry says. "And Ruthie seemed calm. Did you see how gentle she was with Marie?"

Marie, crashed on the mat in front of the stove, thumps her tail softly at the sound of her name.

"You're saying you're okay with this idea? Need I remind you that you're the man who coined the term 'LPs'? Until little pains-in-the-ass are old enough to be reasonable, they're tyrants. Little Kim Jong Ils. Demanding. Petulant. Given to extreme crankiness. You know how much we cherish the calm and quiet of our sanctuary here." And the cleanliness. We cherish the cleanliness.

"I know, but I feel like it's the right thing to do." After loading the dishwasher, Barry walks over and rests his elbows on the counter next to me. He slowly swirls the wine in his glass. "I can't help but wonder what I'd have done if Jade had told me about this way back when. I'm afraid I would've been a jerk. Told her she'd tricked me and I didn't want anything to do with them. I'd like to think I would have done the right thing, but . . ."

"You're a good guy, Bear. You always have been. That's why I grabbed on to you and wouldn't let go." I reach over and squeeze his arm. "You'd have done the right thing. I'm sure you'd have been there for her." I can't help but wonder what Barry means by "the right thing"—does he mean he'd have married Jade? I'm hoping he means he'd have provided financial and emotional support. I don't want his mind traipsing down a path that involves an imagined wedded life with his ex. Where the hell would that've left me? Will he be plagued by what-ifs now? "Things work out the way they do for a reason."

He blows air through his lips, then straightens. "I keep thinking about how I'd told Jade a hundred times I didn't want to be a dad. Now I am one." He runs his hand through his hair. "I feel like letting them stay here is a way to . . . make up for me not being around."

"You don't have to 'make up' for anything. You didn't know. Besides, *we* have always agreed on the not-having-kids thing, and now you have one, plus a grandkid. And that's just how things are now, and it's . . . I mean, we'll get to know them, and it'll all be great, but letting them move in? It's all happening too fast."

"It's only for two months. And I know it's all happening fast, but these are the facts." His voice starts to get louder. "Unbeknownst to *me*, turns out, I do have a kid." The door of the dishwasher isn't quite closed all the way, and he kicks it shut with his foot. Okay, maybe he's not as calm about all this as I thought. Maybe he *is* pissed off at Jade after all. He grabs onto the edge of the sink, his back to me, and exhales loudly. "I don't know. This is . . . it's overwhelming."

I go over and rub his back. It's hard to see him so stressed out. "It *is* overwhelming. So maybe we need to put the brakes on, just for a bit. Maybe it's best if she goes home and reconciles with her mom." Jade's reasoning seems sound to me: Marie should go to Berkeley, live at home, keep her routine with the baby. It's the same UC system. It must be possible to transfer. Maybe if Marie and Jade made up, Marie would also realize what's best. And Barry's obligations would be reduced to occasional e-mails and once-in-a-while visits. Barry may think he's ready for them to move in, but neither of us is equipped to go overnight from dog parents to grandparents with a live-in baby. It's a hell of a change after a decade and a half of the status quo.

"You can still get to know her if she's back home, over the phone and e-mail. And then she'll move here in the fall, and by then you two will have a good foundation to start really building a relationship." To *me*, that sounds like an excellent plan.

"I just . . . I don't know, Alex. This may be guilt talking, but I feel like we can't say no. And we've both got Wednesday off for the holiday and no plans, so it's a good day to help them move in. I know it's asking a lot, and I know it's going to be crazy around here if we do this, so . . . what do you think? You get to make the call."

Typical. He generally lets me have the final say on everything—household decisions, investments, vacations. He's easygoing, and he knows what a control freak I am, so he rolls with it. So if I say no,

I'm the . . . what was the number Marie used? Oh yeah, I'm the nine-seventeen. I'm certain he hasn't thought through what a major shift this'll be in our lives. *Major*. Like tectonic plates ramming into one another. I'm about to say something along those lines when he looks at me imploringly with his beautiful deep-brown eyes.

"It won't be that bad," he says in a rush before I can speak. He must have guessed from the look on my face that I was about to object. "It's not like she's dumping the baby on us and leaving. And it will give me a chance to get to know Marie." He puts his hands on my shoulders and raises his eyebrows at me. "Come on, whaddya say?"

I want to say *no*! But . . . he doesn't ask for much, and I can see this means a lot to him. And it *is* only two months. Besides, how hard can it be? He's right—it's not like we'll have to take care of Ruthie on our own; her mom'll be here. Hoping I won't regret it, I reluctantly let a quiet "Okay" slip out. "Call her tomorrow and tell her."

He squeezes me in a tight hug. "You're the best. I love you, Alex." He kisses my cheek with a loud smooch. "I'm going to call her right now." He rushes off in search of her number, leaving me alone with the dog.

Marie sleeps peacefully, not knowing her world is about to get nutty. She'll be my ally in this. I know she'd prefer the quiet of our peaceful sanctuary. I poke at her haunch with my toe. She lifts her back leg, exposing her tummy for rubbing. I crouch down and oblige while whispering, "Hold on to your tail. We're about to have a baby on board."

*

Two days later, when Sarah heads home to San Francisco, Marie and Ruthie are on our doorstep again. As Barry said, it's a good thing we have the day off, because it takes most of the day to unload her car and get them settled in the guest bedroom. Furry Marie trots along, back and forth, with each trip. A box of tissues falls from a stack of boxes in Barry's arms, and the dog grabs it and brings it to me, more or less still in good shape.

Afterward, Marie says, "Maybe we should do a walk-through and talk about Ruthie-proofing the house." Marie phrases it as a statement, but her quirky smile pulls her face into a questioning look, as if she's waiting for some sign of approval. I wonder whether she's always like this or it's the new surroundings. After all, she's just moved to a new town with her baby in tow. It's a lot for a young girl on her own. I smile back.

"Sure." I lead the way to the living room while Barry goes to start dinner. The dog is usually Mama's girl, following me everywhere, but if there's activity in the kitchen, I can't compete with that. She prances after Barry, the Lab side of her brain always preoccupied with food. From the way she holds her tail high, swishing it back and forth, I know she's thinking she can wheedle a treat out of Barry.

I turn back to human-Marie. I know she's right that we need to baby-proof the house, but I've worked hard to achieve the perfect look, and I'm not eager to make significant changes. The house needs to look like a living advertisement for my services. After all, you never know when a neighborhood mom stopping by with her cookie-selling Girl Scout needs a new master bath. *Be marketing all the time!* Maybe we'll only need to make a few minor tweaks.

"For starters, the coffee table probably oughta go," Marie says.

"Go?"

"Yeah. Those sharp corners. Ruthie could hurt herself."

I designed our gleaming dark-walnut coffee table myself, and had a carpenter build it. "It's the centerpiece of the room," I say. "It anchors the area rug and the other furniture."

Marie looks around, and I think she's finally appreciating the room. "I see what you mean," she says, and I smile. "I guess we can duct-tape Styrofoam on the corners or something."

Oh yeah, that's gonna look great . . .

"But," Marie continues, "she might use it like a big drum." *Please tell me you two didn't move in here with a My First Band! set.* "We should cover it up. Do you have any more of those plastic tablecloths?"

On cue for her drum solo, Ruthie weaves toward the table. She raises her hand, holding her purple plastic key ring. I'm about to dive for her when Marie takes hold of Ruthie's key-wielding hand and helps her toddle on to the next potential hazard.

Is the table a threat to Ruthie, or the other way around? "Maybe you're right. It's dangerous. I'll get Barry to put it in the garage."

Marie moves on, inspecting the artful display of treasures from our travels I've created on our built-in shelves: a small Murano glass bowl from Italy, a framed photo from our honeymoon in Napa, a bowl of sea glass collected on beach walks. My favorite shelf displays various bottles I have treasure-hunted at Antique Alley downtown over the years, each holding a small scoop of sand from various beaches we've visited: a slender bottle with white sand from Bora Bora, a Depression-era cruet with Bermuda's famous pink sand, a sea-glass-green apothecary bottle with black sand from a lovely drive on Maui's Hana Highway, and a cobalt-blue inkwell with a reminder of one Christmas spent on Cape Cod. The final bottle, a pear-shaped flask, holds chocolate-brown sand from Rockaway Beach, where we stopped on the way home from our honeymoon.

The collection always transports me back to those lazy, romantic vacations with Barry. God, we could use one this year. We haven't been on a real vacation since I quit working for Beverly and started on my own. We needed to start saving some money. Unfortunately, I've never been great at that. (Except when Barry insisted I save up for my BMW. Thank heaven he did, or I'd have a car payment to worry about now too.) For the little bit extra I ended up socking away, we might as well have gone on another beach vacation. We could have at least afforded a road trip to San Diego.

"These knickknacks should probably go," Marie says.

"Those aren't knickknacks." I point at the Murano bowl. "*That* is an expensive objet d'art." I admire the bottle collection and think, *These are my cherished memories, my* life *with Barry!*

"Yeah. 'S' pretty. But we should probably move it all up on a higher shelf. Or maybe hide it out of sight. Shiny stuff attracts her attention."

What is she, a raccoon? A magpie?

Marie reaches out and tugs one of the shelves, testing its sturdiness. "Are these built-in?"

"Yeah. They won't budge."

"Good. She might try to climb them."

"Can't we just say, 'No, don't touch'?" *Shouldn't she learn certain things are off-limits?*

"I try to reserve no for the big stuff. Like, stuff that could hurt her—a hot stove, or something totally gross on the ground. Other than that, I try to use positive language with her. Do you think you guys could do the same?" There's that funny, questioning smile again. "I don't want her to be raised in an environment that, like, squelches her natural curiosity, y'know?"

It's the same technique we use with the dog. Save "no!" for dead stuff in the street, that sort of thing. Otherwise, accentuate the positive. Maybe this'll be easier than I thought. I can think of Ruthie as a puppy with prehensile abilities.

"Okay," I say. "I'll put this stuff away." The top shelf has doors on it; I can hide things out of sight up there. Ruthie, still holding Marie's hand, shakes her plastic keys, then throws them to the floor, where they land with a clatter.

"Oh." Ruthie's lips form a circle. She looks startled for a moment, then grins. Marie picks up the keys and hands them to Ruthie, who shouts "No!" and throws them down again. This plays out twice more, and I'm left wondering why Ruthie gets to say no, but we don't.

Marie dangles the keys, coaxing the baby forward. "Come on, Ruthie. Let's go check out the kitchen."

"No!" Ruthie says. She plops down on the dining room rug, seemingly content to stay there and play with her keys and leave the kitchen inspection to us.

Following along after Marie, I hope the sigh that slipped through my lips wasn't as audible as I fear it was. I station myself at the counter between the two rooms so that I can keep an eye on Ruthie while Marie goes into the kitchen.

Barry stands at the stove, caramelizing onions to top the veggie burgers he'll grill for our holiday dinner. (The dog, predictably, sits beside him begging, but since onions are toxic to dogs, she's out of luck this time.) Barry came home from the store last night with bags overflowing with bright colors and leafy greens. He's making a meatless meal tonight to welcome Marie, but I hope she doesn't think we're going vegetarian while she's here. It's one thing to accommodate a guest, but come on. We're talking two months.

"Is it okay if we poke around in here while you're cooking?" Marie asks Barry.

"Sure, no problem," Barry says, smiling at the girl.

"That smells yummy," Marie says as she reaches to open the cupboard under the sink. The door handle slips from her grasp when the plastic clip we've installed engages. "You've already got a baby lock?" The dog, intrigued by what's going on and probably also by the smells from the trash, comes over to inspect.

I point at the dog sniffing at the slight opening in the cupboard door. "It's because of her. She kept getting in the trash." Something little humans and dogs have in common—they both like to get into things they shouldn't and put questionable items in their mouths. At least this is one place where we're a step ahead of the game. (I glance over at Ruthie, and, sure enough, she's sucking on her plastic keys.)

"Cool. One less thing to do." She holds her hand out and lets the dog sniff at it. The dog noses her hand, trying to work some snout and ear rubs out of the girl. Marie smiles and obliges. I'm so glad to see that human-Marie is not afraid of dog-Marie anymore. Human-Marie seems glad too, judging by the pleased "Gosh, she likes me!" look on her face. Still rubbing the dog's floppy ears, she says, "It's funny about her name being Marie too, huh?"

Barry bends his head over the stove, leaving me to deal with this. "Yep," I say.

"My mom named me after Marie Curie; she's my mom's idol. What a coincidence."

"It sure is." I hope my face forms a convincing "how about that?" look. "It might get confusing, so we'll call her Bunny. She's got a million nicknames. She'll adjust fine."

"Or you guys could use my nickname: Wren. My middle name's Renee, so Ren for short. My friends spell it with a *W*. You know, like the bird? Sarah teases me about my bird legs." She kicks out a skinny limb. The striped leggings are gone, replaced by fishnets with a hole in the knee under baggy black shorts and a vest over a white tank. She's not exactly what I'd call Goth, since she's not sporting a ton of dark makeup, but she's definitely got a punk-rock vibe going. She's not June Cleaver's image of motherhood, and it's not a look I'd go for, but I have to admit, the girl's got style.

"Okay, Wren," I say. "What else do we need to do in the kitchen?" Ruthie flings her keys, and they skitter across the dining room floor. I retrieve them for her.

"As long as there's nothing glass in any of the other cupboards, they'll be fine—like, if it's just pots and pans and stuff. But if there're things you wouldn't want her pulling out, you need to move that stuff or install more baby latches."

I go into the kitchen and pull a notepad out of a drawer. "I'll make a list, okay, Bear?" I pat him on the back. I don't want all our pots and pans dragged out, even if she can't hurt them. "He can install them in the guest bathroom too."

"Add electrical socket plugs to the list," Wren says. "We don't want fried baby." She says it so deadpan, you'd think we were talking about a menu item.

"Gosh, no," Barry says. "I'll buy one of those medicine cabinet locks too."

"She can't get up on the bathroom sink, can she?" I ask. *What is she, a little monkey?* I peek over the kitchen counter and am relieved to see Ruthie still sitting on the rug and not scaling the dining table. My mind races through the alarming number of ways Barry and I might manage to kill this tiny human. Two months. That's eight weeks. Almost sixty days stretch before us like a gauntlet to be run, with my only goal a living baby at the other end.

"No, I don't think she can climb up there, but I thought I'd use that long counter for a changing table, since there's no dresser in our room." The thought of my lovely granite countertops being used for such a purpose . . . I want to cry.

"You're not going to, like, leave her alone with us ever, are you?" Barry asks, pushing his hair off his forehead. Apparently, he's also been mentally enumerating the ways we might accidentally fry, maim, blemish, harm, mar, hurt, impair, impale, or otherwise damage the baby.

"Relax," Wren says, laughing at our worried expressions. "You guys are funny. This isn't going to be any big deal. You'll see."

*

Even if Barry, furry Marie, and I aren't ready for this baby, the house is. It looks not unlike someone's beach getaway, closed for the off-season. My beautiful sofas, which Rache custom upholstered, are draped in spare sheets to thwart sticky hands and thrown sippy cups. All my perfectly placed collectibles, painstakingly stacked books, and the photos of Barry, me, and the dogs that once graced the bookshelves and end tables now hide in locked cupboards. Everything that was once on the bottom shelves of our bookcase now fights for space on the top two shelves. (Wren has assured me that Ruthie can't climb that high.) My beloved coffee table is in the garage, wrapped in old blankets. My dupioni silk curtains, usually such a grand frame for our picture window, now look ridiculous draped over the finials to keep them away from Ruthie, who apparently thinks floor-length curtains are in place solely for games of peekaboo. (Apparently, this is a favorite game at Grandma Jade's, where the design is all about utility for curtain-climbing grand-babies. Grandma Jade. That makes her sound so old. Of course, she *is* eight years older than me, since she's two years older than Barry.) The merino wool area rug has been rolled up and relegated to the garage, replaced by a cheap but plush substitute I picked up at Target. I chose a pale-honey rug for its Cheerios-esque coloring, since I'm sure Ruthie's little fingers and tiny shoes will soon be flinging and crushing the cereal—or at least their sugar-free equivalent—into the ground.

The dining room is more of the same: hems lifted on drapes, a plastic tablecloth over our highly polished dark-wood dining table, the area rug rolled up and stashed in the hall closet.

I imagine Wren and Ruthie's moving in will coincide with a new routine of daily vacuuming, which will make furry Marie unhappy. We chose to rescue a labradoodle on purpose, knowing they don't shed much, which means less vacuuming. But now, with a baby in the house, our Dyson will get a workout. If only I had the money to fit in twice-weekly visits from Anna for the rest of the summer.

As I take the last vase from the dining room buffet table to pack away in my closet, I think, *Good-bye beautiful house,* then start humming the chorus to "See You in September."

CHAPTER 8

Their first morning in our house, I wake to Ruthie's shrieks. It sounds like a full-blown tantrum. Reason number one why dogs are better than kids: no tantrums. Sure, maybe there's some wild barking at the mail carrier, but no shrieking. Never any shrieking. Barry's already gone, lucky bastard. Two mornings a week, he leaves early and goes for a run on campus while it's still nice and quiet there, then showers at the gym. You'd think he could have picked a different day, since this is the first morning with our guests, but no. He's missing the meltdown, which seems completely unfair, if you ask me. I grab his pillow and put it over my head, trying to drown out the noise. Marie, usually asleep on our bed or on the rug at the foot of it, is nowhere to be seen, so I assume she's hiding somewhere quiet. If there is such a place.

After a few more minutes, I give up and toss Barry's pillow aside. I groan and pull on my robe.

At least I smell coffee as I stumble down the hall. Please don't let Wren speak to me until I've had some. Barry must have set it up with the autotimer for me. Bless him. Probably a peace offering since he knew I'd be annoyed with him for ducking out so early.

Wren doesn't hear me come down the hall over Ruthie's screaming, so I catch a glimpse of her face before she realizes I'm there. She holds a spoon in one hand, and her chin rests in the palm of the other. The corners of her mouth and eyes droop.

Poor kid. It can't be easy trying to make her way on her own. Especially with a baby. God, I was still a baby myself at eighteen. And I was always such a daddy's girl. I can't imagine missing out on all that. I think back to how my dad always brought Cyn and me a treat from the candy display by the checkout whenever he went to the hardware store; I'd always share mine with him. We used to give Heidi baths together in a big metal tub out in the backyard, and it always turned into a water fight. He noticed my preference for dollhouses over dolls, and built me a three-story mansion. The floors and ceilings were grooved and the walls left loose so that I could change the room sizes by moving the wood slats from one groove to another. I was constantly redecorating that thing.

Wren notices me and sits up straight. She flashes half of a smile at me. The kid puts up a good front. Points for bravery.

"Morning," she shouts to be heard over the baby. They're seated at the dining room table, wrestling over a container of pale-blue yogurt. Another reason dogs are better than kids—you never have to fight to get them to eat a meal; dump food in bowl, drop bowl on floor, done.

From the violet sheen on the lower half of Ruthie's face, I'd say she's winning their wrestling match and hasn't ingested much. She flails her arms and shakes her head. Aha, there's furry Marie! She's seated at attention next to Ruthie's high chair, happy to help out if the only goal is to reach the bottom of the yogurt container. At least Wren has accepted Marie. Thank God, because I can't imagine how this would've worked otherwise. And thank God this is Marie and not Louis. Oh, how we loved that dog, but he wasn't as accepting of strangers in the house as Marie is. I still never go twenty-four hours without thinking of him, but right now, I'm so grateful for Marie's easygoing nature.

Wren makes buzzing sounds and zooms a spoonful of yogurt in for a landing, but the airport is closed. "No," the baby says, shaking her head. Wren tries coaxing her in a chirpy voice that's incongruous with the torn white T-shirt she's wearing, which features Sid Vicious's face screaming into a microphone. (I only know it's Sid because "Sex Pistols" is scrawled across the top in bloodred.)

"Morning." My reply comes out gravely, the way my voice always is first thing.

"Do you have a cold?"

"No." I always sound this way precaffeine. "I'm fine. Just need coffee."

"It's just, I wouldn't want Ruthie to catch anything. I'll try to keep her away from you if you're sick."

I clear my throat. "You know, I do have a little scratchiness. I might be coming down with something." Maybe I can buy myself a buffer of space if I play this up. Maybe they'll retreat to the guest room and I can enjoy my coffee in peace. I'm so not a morning person, and I was really hoping she wouldn't be either.

"Sorry about all the noise." She doesn't appear to be preparing to retreat. "We kept Ruthie up too late last night watching fireworks. She's a super crab-head this morning." *Yes, I heard.* "Do you always get up this late?" She twists and looks at the clock in the kitchen over her shoulder. "Is my dad still sleeping?" *As if that were possible.* "Do you have any tea? I didn't want to poke around the cupboards."

"Coffee" is all I manage to say as I fill my favorite white ceramic mug with the cursive silver *A*. This is too much conversation before caffeine. I turn my back on them and get my 1 percent milk out of the fridge. At least Ruthie has quieted down.

"I'm not into coffee. I normally drink yerba maté. I brought some with me, but we finished it at the motel. I'll get some more. You should totally try it. It's, like, way better for you than coffee. Ruthie, come on, one more bite."

I take a long sip from my mug. "We have tea. Feel free to poke around the cupboards." I take another sip. "Sorry, I need to have some coffee first thing. Barry's gone already. He's a morning person."

"That's something else we have in common." Her half smile stretches into the full version. I want to add, *yes—but he never talks this much in the morning.*

I top off my mug and pull the filter, heavy with wet grounds, out of the coffeemaker. As I dump it in the trash, Wren lets out a distressed "Oh!"

"What's wrong?" I raise my eyebrows at her.

"It's . . . I didn't know you were gonna throw that away. Don't you guys compost?"

"Uh, no."

She looks out the sliding glass door. "I noticed your herb garden out there, so I thought maybe . . ."

"Yep. That's Barry's doing. I'm not much for yard work."

"Cool. Maybe I'll talk to him about starting a composting pile." *So now we have to start dumping our trash out in our backyard? Swell.* "Hey, do you think it's okay if I call him Dad?"

One more big swig of coffee. "Uh, sure."

"And is it okay if Roo calls him Grandpa?"

I smile. It's kind of cute to think of Barry as Grandpa. "Sure." Of course, then it occurs to me that I don't want to be step-granny Alex. "And maybe she could think of me as Aunt Alex. I'm used to that anyway, with my nephews."

Wren points at me and says to Ruthie, "Say good morning to your auntie Alex."

Ruthie grimaces in my direction as if pondering such a wordy greeting. She settles for waving both arms at me and shouts, "Tee Lexsch!"

It's pretty adorable, and I can't help but laugh. T-Lex. That's me—like T-Rex in the morning. On that note, I take another gulp of coffee, then dig around in our tea stash. I hope Wren doesn't expect me to make it for her, because I need to shower and get to the office to meet Rache and do some more work on the design for the Van Dierdons. I set two boxes of tea samplers on the counter—one a mix of herbal delights, the other filled with caffeinated options.

"Oh," is all Wren says when she sees the boxes. Clearly, this is not the organic, fair trade, locally grown loose-leaf breakfast beverage she had hoped for. "That's cool. I'll get something when I go out."

I'm glad to hear they're going out. The thought of leaving a veritable stranger (with a baby, no less) alone in the house was weird to me. I still think we didn't give this arrangement enough thought. We didn't ask what they'd be doing all summer while we're both at work. (Seriously, what will they be doing?) We didn't talk about meals or house rules or restrictions. At least she's new in town, so she probably doesn't have any friends to invite over. Does she?

"All done!" She raises Ruthie's hands, and they both yell "Yay!" Ruthie, tantrum forgotten, smiles wide and blows a thick, yogurt-y bubble.

Wren hops up from her seat, then tilts her head toward me, reminding me of the bird she's nicknamed for. "Hey, I know I said I'd be in charge of breakfast, so what can I make for you? Toast? Cereal? I make killer pancakes. I don't suppose you have any almond flour?"

"Sometimes I skip breakfast on weekdays." I glance up at the clock, although I know only three minutes have passed since we both looked at it. "I've got to get going."

Her arms fall to her sides. "But it's the most important meal of the day." She actually wanted to make breakfast for me. That's sort of sweet. "Besides," she lowers her voice and inclines her head back toward Ruthie, "it doesn't set a good example if you skip it. Especially when I have such a hard time getting her to eat as it is."

The baby smears fallen blobs of yogurt around the tray of her high chair, then lets Marie lick and slurp at her fingers. Happy babbling noises from the baby ensue. So Marie's already gone over to the baby's side. From the relaxed, swishy wag of her plumelike tail across the floor, she apparently finds the baby a great addition to the house. *Traitor.* Personally, I think a walk-in closet with an attached dressing area would be a better addition. Anyway, as for the baby . . . well, it's day one, so I'm willing to be open-minded for Barry's sake. But I'm not going to sit down and eat breakfast just because Ruthie, who's already eaten, needs a role model. That's what her mother's for. I'm the step-grandma. Isn't that the deal? Grandparents get to do whatever they want with the kids, right? Isn't that why everyone's so gung ho about the gig?

"I promise you can make a huge breakfast on Saturday, but right now I've got to get going. You have the spare key Barry gave you, right? You two . . ." I almost don't say it, but the über-hostess in me won't let it go unsaid, "make yourselves at home."

*

I return from the office that afternoon and am immediately greeted *not* by the dog, as usual, but by a crunching sound as my pumps grind sand into the hardwood floor. Removing my shoes, I feel enough sand under my toes that it's like I'm at the beach. I carefully wipe off my feet, but in the hallway outside the guest bath, I find more. Enough for the Santa Barbara Sandcastle Festival. I hear music playing behind the guest bedroom door and assume Wren and Ruthie are tucked inside. Along with my dog. I take a peek at the guest bath. It's as I feared—another beachfront on the tile floors and in the tub. Wet, sandy beach towels lay in a discarded heap.

And what's with all the stuff plugged in on the counter? Wren's taken the liberty of adding an outlet extender, turning our usual two outlets into six, and every one of them has something plugged in: a hair dryer, two chargers—looks like one for a phone, one for a tablet—a night-light, a flatiron, and a baby-wipes warmer. It's a good thing we have a long counter in there since it's also piled with hair products and baby-butt ointments (all labeled "natural" or "organic") and a leaning tower of diapers. Nothing "green" about those.

If we have anyone over while they're here, I'm going to have to get her to cram all this crap under the sink.

I sigh and turn my attention back to the mounds of sand. Should I start cleaning or have a discussion about rules with our new guest? Remembering my own lackluster cleaning efforts as a teen, I go change into shorts and a T-shirt, then return to tackle the mess myself.

While wiping sand out of the tub, I consider that this is yet another way dogs are easier than kids. You simply hose them down in the front yard when you get home from the beach. I wonder if she'd consider that with Ruthie.

If Ruthie's napping, running the vacuum might wake her, but I remember that Cyn's boys could sleep through heavy construction at that age. Besides, it's *my* house, and a broom alone is not going to cut it. Sand is murder on hardwood flooring. We just had it put in a few years ago, for Pete's sake, and the distressed look is *not* what I am going for.

At the roar of the vacuum, Wren pokes her head out of the guest bedroom door, allowing Marie to escape and dash for our bedroom to hide from the scary machine.

"I was totally going to do that after Ruthie's nap," she yells over the loud hum. She takes a step forward and closes the door behind her. "I can do it now, if you want."

"It's okay," I yell back. "It'll just take a few minutes."

Fifteen sweaty minutes later, I'm done vacuuming. I hope this heat wave breaks soon. It's usually hot here in the summer, but not *this* hot. The windows and back sliding glass door all gape wide open. Marie slinks back out of our bedroom now that it's safe and finally comes to say hello. I kneel down and sit back on my heels so that we can have a proper greeting. "It's about time," I whisper into her ear as she wiggles in my arms. "You're a little traitor." I kiss the spot between her eyes, and she gives me several on my chin. When she's done kissing me, she goes and flops in front of the back screen door, panting.

I get up off the floor. "You know, it's okay to turn the air-conditioning on during the day."

Wren and Ruthie are now on the living room rug, working on a stacking puzzle. "It seems like a waste for just the two of us."

"The dog likes the AC too. So that's three of you." No response. I'm sure she's pondering the massive carbon footprint I leave as I stomp through life. Me, Sasquatch. Her, Kermit. Well, excuse me, but leaving your chargers plugged in all day is *not* green. Not to mention the monster SUV she drives. "I'm going to run it for a bit." I close the windows and sliding door and lower the temperature on the thermostat.

"You want something cold to drink?" I ask as I head to the kitchen. Maybe I should point out that the fridge is energy efficient.

"I'm fine. I've got some water."

"So besides hitting the beach," I ask as I return with a glass of wine in hand, mentally adding, *and bringing a good portion of it home with you,* "what did you two do today?" I sink into the sofa, pull my feet up under me, and take a sip of my wine. I usually enjoy some quiet time when I get home from work, but now the agenda includes cleaning and socializing. Will it be like this every day for the next two months? Since my business isn't exactly overrun with jobs right now, I've gotten used to getting home before Barry gets in. I usually turn on some music and relax on the sofa with a glass of wine and one of my design magazines. In fact, the latest issue of *Coastal Living* tried to flag me down from the kitchen counter, and I'm itching to flip through it while I sip my pinot grigio. But instead, I'm overheated from vacuuming and stuck making small talk with this stranger who's now family. *Thanks, Barry.* I hold up my glass in a silent, annoyed toast to him and take a big swig of my wine.

Plus, Thursdays are "date night." We don't usually go out to eat on the weekends because our favorite spots get so crowded, so Thursdays are our night to have a cocktail and then head to a restaurant. Obviously, that won't be happening tonight. Barry texted me this afternoon that he could make his "famous" Thai chicken salad for dinner, skipping the chicken for Wren's portion. Thank heaven Barry's generally in charge of the cooking. I avoid it enough when it's just the two of us, but I'd be completely stressed about trying to figure out a vegetarian and a baby-friendly option every night. Oh, shoot. Barry told me to get some chicken out of the freezer. "Hang on a sec," I say. No chicken inside, but the freezer in the garage holds two packages. I put the chicken in the microwave to defrost (Wren would probably frown on that) and contemplate leaving the "cage-free" sticker from the wrapping on the counter so that we can earn some points with the girl. *Don't be silly*, I tell myself, and throw it away. If I left it there, she'd just lecture me on the antibacterial wipe I'd have to use on the counter afterward.

Back on the sofa, I pick up our conversation. "Anyway, what else did you do?"

"Before the beach, we stopped at the park rec center. Ruthie loves your park."

"So does Marie. But there's a rec center?"

"Yeah. You've never been?"

"You mean the building? I thought it was for the gardeners and park employees."

"They have classes and stuff there. I Googled ideas for me and Ruthie for this summer, and they have a Mommy and Me class, so I signed up."

"Sounds like fun," I lie. I have no idea what goes on at a Mommy and Me class, but whatever it is, no thank you. Give me an obedience class full of rambunctious puppies any day.

"Um, yeah. We'll see." She takes the puzzle apart so that Ruthie can put it back together again.

"You don't sound super excited about it."

"It's just . . . you know, it's probably not teenage moms. I'm sure I'll be the youngest one." She brushes her hair off her forehead in a move so like Barry's that I stare a moment too long. "But it'll be nice for Ruthie to play with some other kids."

Poor thing's only a kid herself. It can't have been easy, what she's been through these past couple of years. And it's not an easy road she's got ahead. I should probably stop whining about missing my precious alone time and our date night and my pretty house and try to be more supportive. I try to think of any of our friends or Barry's coworkers with teenagers we could introduce her to. No one comes to mind. Our procreating friends all have young kids, and they'd only be interested in Wren as a potential babysitter.

Hanging out with just her baby and us is going to make for a long, boring summer for Wren. Poor thing. I visualize my last summer before college. Except for a part-time job to save up some money, it had all been tanning and boys and diving into the cold surf and driving around with my best friend, blasting the radio and wondering where we could get some beer. At least she can do the tanning part. Although from the look of her pale complexion, she's not into that.

I need to think of some fun things for her to do.

Barry comes home then, interrupting my thoughts, and there's a hubbub as both Marie and Ruthie try to greet him at the same time. It occurs to me that maybe Ruthie hasn't had many men in her life. Maybe Barry is a novelty to her. Barry squats to greet them simultaneously, pulling Ruthie into a hug with his left arm while Marie kisses his right cheek. Within moments, Barry is ignored as Marie moves on to the baby, and it's another lovefest of squeals and frantic kisses. We all have to smile at that.

Later, at dinner, even though it's not the same as date night at our favorite sushi spot, Barry's Thai salad is a hit. Even Ruthie seems happy with her "deconstructed Thai salad," as Barry calls it—chunks of chicken, some mandarin oranges, carrots, and a few other veggies presented on her compartmentalized plastic plate that reminds me of old TV dinners. I work the cage-free-ness of the chicken into the conversation. Wren bursts my balloon by saying, "You know it just means they open the doors for them."

"I don't know," I say, smacking my lips. "This chicken really tastes like it ran around outside in the fresh air." Luckily, we're almost done eating, since the conversation smacks right into its closed cage door after that.

After dinner, Barry introduces Wren to *Star Trek: The Next Generation*. Sadly for him, it turns out she's not a *Star Trek* fan, but she says she is willing to give *Next Generation* a try, so they start streaming season one.

They sit together on the sofa. Barry seems comfortable hanging out with her, and she seems happy to simply be with her dad. It's sweet, listening to him tell her how watching the original *Star Trek* as a boy influenced his love of science. "You could be a science nerd *and* an adventurer," he says in a hushed voice.

That night in bed, he asks how I think it's going.

"Okay so far, I guess. But I'm annoyed with you for sneaking out of here this morning." I jab him in the arm with my index finger, then waggle it at him. "You so owe me."

"I'm sorry." He grabs my finger and squeezes it. "Have I told you lately how amazing you are? Really, I know this is all really awkward." He kisses the end of my finger, then lets go of it. "Awkward and overwhelming. I woke up at four and started stressing out. It's just so weird to me to think back to all those years that I had no idea Wren existed." He chews his lip. "I couldn't fall back to sleep, so eventually I just got up and went for my usual run. I'm really sorry."

"I'll let it slide. This time. It *is* overwhelming." I pat his arm. "Anyway, I'm also a little annoyed about all the sand they tracked in today. But I have an idea for that." My mind wanders to other ways they might ruin my house. "Oh, man, how sturdy do you think diapers are?"

"I should know the answer to this how?"

"You're a science guy. You must know something about plastics. Isn't that what they're made of?"

"I never thought about it before. I assume from the sound they make that they're made from some sort of polyethylene. Why?"

"I just don't want them ruining those sheets. Those are the most expensive sheets in the house. Eighteen hundred thread count. Egyptian cotton."

"Why does the guest bed have the best sheets? What're we sleeping on?"

"Oprah says you can tell a lot about a person by their sheets."

"So what does it say about us that the best sheets aren't even on our bed? We don't even have guests that often." He lifts the edge of the sheet I toss over our bedspread every night to keep it clean in case Marie sleeps with us. "And what about the dog? What's the thread count for her sheet?"

"Maybe I could switch them out the next time I do laundry. Maybe they won't notice."

"You're crazy, Lex. I'm going to sleep."

He rearranges his pillow and folds his hands on his chest. Marie leaps onto the bed and spreads out between us while I think about how soon I can offer to do laundry and switch out those sheets. With so many sets covering the sofas, do I even have a spare?

Inventorying our linen cupboards in my head starts to make me sleepy. As I begin to drift off, I think how weird it is having these people in our lives.

But then it hits me, and I'm jolted back awake. Despite the chaos they've brought to our house, they're a buffer. If they weren't here, I'd have to break down and tell Barry about the money troubles I've gotten into. God, I should have told him ages ago, when I first started running up the balances on my credit cards, but things just got away from me so quickly. But now, having the kids here gives me a reprieve. Of course I can't bring up my big financial mess in front of guests. Which gives me time to get my act together and set things straight. If we can get this job with the Van Dierdons, and a few more after that, everything'll be fine. Hopefully, he'll never need to know.

I lie awake for another hour or two, stressing over details for the Van Dierdon job.

CHAPTER 9

I leave the office a little early—it's Friday and things are quiet—and stop by KB Toys again. I remembered seeing some cheap kiddie pools there while shopping for Fuzzy's present.

Hoping to convince Wren it's less hassle to cool Ruthie off in the backyard rather than at the beach, I cart home a jungle-green pool shaped like a turtle. We might still have to deal with wet feet tromping through the house, but at least wet feet are easier to clean up after than sandy feet. I've got my superabsorbent mat on the patio at the back door for Marie, so hopefully a major portion of the water will be gone before tiny feet scamper indoors. And Barry's pretty well trained in the art of wiping Marie's feet before she comes in, so how hard can it be to train Wren in the same technique?

"I bought something for Ruthie!" I announce as I enter the house. No sand greets me today, but a nose-curling smell has replaced it. And it's ridiculously hot in here again.

"Oh," Wren ducks out of their room; Marie squirms out from behind her and runs to greet me. While accepting her kisses as I rub her sides, I consider the depths of her traitordom. I cup her chin and look into her eyes. Where is my peace-and-quiet-loving Mama's girl?

I thought she'd miss the usual serenity around here, but I guess she's decided it's a huge step up from being home alone all day. Still, it's annoying how even once I'm home, she chooses to hang out at Ruthie's side over mine. I sigh, kiss her between the eyes, and stand straight. Still looking down at her, I try to fathom what's going on in that furry head. It's got to be the dropped faux-Cheerios.

"Ruthie's napping," Wren says. She points at the pool. "Cool. She'll love that. It was a total pain finding parking at the beach yesterday. Plus, by the time I carried her and our umbrella and all our stuff down there, I was a ball of sweat. It's been so fricking hot." Her usually spiky hair droops, giving away the "fricking" heat as clearly as her tank top, baggy shorts, and bare feet.

I move on through the house with the pool, heading toward the yard, and Wren follows. I feel myself wilting. No wonder Ruthie's napping. It's a sleep-inducing sauna in here, and my silk top hangs close on my skin. The funky smell intensifies near the kitchen. Stopping by the counter that separates the kitchen and dining room, I rest the pool atop my foot and look for signs of some experiment gone wrong. Has she been making meth in here? The clean kitchen yields no clues. "So what's that smell?"

"Man, I'm really sorry. Totally raunchy, huh?" Her face contorts into her funny twist of a smile. "I made kale chips. Ruthie loves them. So does Marie! You should try them. I made some yesterday, and Marie was all over them."

"Really?"

"Yeah! But don't worry. Apparently, kale's great for dogs too, I Googled it. Well, unless they have kidney problems. She, uh, doesn't have any kidney problems, does she?"

"Nope."

"Oh, phew. Anyway, I got distracted and totally eight-forty-three'd them. Kale smells *really* bad when you burn it." She didn't have to add that last part. The house smells like rotting broccoli. And no wonder it's been so damn hot in here when I come home: there's been no AC running *and* she's been using the oven. Crazy kid. "The smoke set off the alarm, and Marie was all freaked, so I took the battery out." She points at the detector on the wall.

"Oh yeah. Marie hates that thing." I look at the dog with a sympathetic smile.

"She hid under our bed."

"Poor baby." I pat Marie, who is poised to dash outside with us. At least Wren cleaned up, but please, God, don't let her make that again. Please don't let her insist that I try kale chips this weekend.

Unfortunately, the open windows do nothing to dissipate the smell. The air sits, heavy; no breeze stirs. I heft the pool up again and open the screen door. Marie runs out ahead of us.

I set the pool down on the patio. "Let's get this situated, then I've got to change. I'm dying." I fan myself with my hand, hoping to relieve the sweaty sheen on my forehead.

"I wasn't sure," Wren says. "About the AC? I know you said it was okay, but it seems like such a waste. But now we'll have the pool, and we can cool off in the backyard." She flicks a stray pebble with a chartreuse-painted toe.

"Seriously. You can run it. It's a small house, so it doesn't take much to cool it down."

"Okay. I guess I got the cheap gene from Grandma."

"Didn't your grandparents make a lot of money from the bakery?" I drag the pool out to the grass, and Wren picks up the other side. "Let's put it over there." I point at the far end of the yard, where Barry has staggered slate tiles and filled in the area with pea gravel. We walk sideways with the pool. "Anyway, your grandparents. I thought they were wealthy."

"Yeah, but not when they met. They were, like, dirt poor at first, and Grandma never got over it. She hated spending money on clothes or electricity or whatever. I loved her a lot, but she could be kinda nutty. She was always following me around switching off lights. If I said I was cold, she'd say, 'Put on another sweata.' And San Francisco's cold, like, practically all the time. 'Put on another sweata.' She must have said that to me ten thousand times." We shimmy the pool back and forth, making sure it's level.

"We can move those chairs to the side." Wren helps me shift the Adirondack chairs, and I note they could use a fresh coat of paint. "Did your grandparents live with you guys?"

"No, but they lived around the corner. I used to go to their house while my mom was at work. I'd spend the night if she worked late. Which was, like, all the time."

"You said your grandma taught you to sew?"

"Yeah. She had this ancient machine. I'd go buy cheap stuff at the Salvation Army, then tear it apart and make it into something else."

"Resourceful." I sit in one of the chairs and check if it's level. It rocks, so I get up to adjust it a bit. "Didn't your mom take you clothes shopping though?" Some of my favorite memories of my mom are of shopping with her and Cyn at the annual back-to-school sales. We'd come home exhausted, but after a snack—usually some of Mom's homemade cookies—we'd be revived and hold a fashion show for Daddy. If I had a daughter, I think that shopping sprees, mani-pedi outings, and trips to the hair salon would be some of the best parts. I'd try going for a manicure with Marie, but she gets her nails done at the vet's office.

"No. She's always busy with work." She shoves her hands in her pockets. "And beyond her power suits, she's not into clothes." She says "power suits" with a dismissive voice.

"Did your mom ever get married?" That question might seem out of the blue, but since she's telling me about her childhood, I figure I'll slip it in. I admit it: I Googled Jade after Wren turned up. She works at Acadia Pharmaceuticals, a top biotech company. She not only works there, but naturally, she's a *star*, recently promoted to chief operating officer and the first woman to hit C-level at the company. But all I found was career info: her work bio on the Acadia site; a LinkedIn profile; and a few business articles and interviews, including a profile in *San Francisco Business Times* online, where coworkers raved about how wonderful she is to work with. *Natch*. But nothing about her personal life. It's as if she doesn't have one. She doesn't even have a Facebook page. But I suppose Jade is too busy with her important work to waste time on social networking.

"No, she never dated much. I thought it was because she was part of this tragic romance. You know, young love sundered by death," she says in a dramatic voice. "Ha. Another lie."

Hmm. So Jade never married or even got serious about anyone. I itch to pry some more, but don't want to press it.

"So you said you knew about Barry your whole life, right?"

"Yeah, from as far back as I can remember."

"Didn't you ever Google him?"

"No," she looks at me and smiles her crooked, questioning smile. "Obviously I should have, huh? But my mom said he died before I was born, and that was before the Internet was even a thing, so I just didn't expect there to be anything about him online. And she gave me a box of pictures and cards he'd given her, stuff like that. I just thought that was all I'd ever have from him." She scoffs. "I asked her one time when I was, like, eight if we could write to his parents or go visit them. I said I wanted some pictures from when he was little, like me. That's when she told me they were dead too. She made it sound like he didn't have any other family. End of story."

Poor kid. I give her an understanding smile. "Remind me tonight, and after dinner we'll look through Barry's baby pictures. He was a cutie."

We go back inside, and I beeline for the fridge. I need something cold to drink before I do anything else. If I were alone, I'd opt for the wine—after all, it's five thirty somewhere—and sip it while pondering

Jade's lack of a love life. But since I have an underage guest, I opt for something nonalcoholic. For now anyway.

Before Wren turned up, our fridge was practically biblical—pretty much just water and wine. But with the girls living with us, we've stocked up on various organic juice options. I was never one to drink grape juice—except for the fermented variety—but I have to admit, it's thirst quenching.

"Juice?" Wren nods, and I grab two glasses. As the ice cubes clunk out of the dispenser, I let an extra one fall into my hand. I toss it to Marie, who crunches it happily. I note Wren's shorts again while handing her her juice. It's true, they're baggy, as I'd first assessed, but they also have an interesting level of detail. They're cuffed, and then bunched up on the outer side seams with nicely contrasting white twill ribbon run through a silver D-ring, and what looks like it was probably once a man's striped tie acts as a belt to keep them on her skinny frame. She looks adorable in them.

"Did you make those?" I point at her shorts after she takes the glass from my hand.

She runs through her usual half smile/shrug combo. "Yeah. Used to be pants and a tie."

While we chat, I sweep the battery off the countertop and into the junk drawer. I make a mental note to put it back in the smoke detector later. "They're super cute. You're good."

"Yeah?" She looks down at the pants as if I've pointed out a spot on them.

"Yeah. And they look comfy." I set down my glass. "Speaking of shorts, I better go change." I say over my shoulder, "Why don't you fill up the pool? Ruthie can try it when she wakes up."

On cue, fussy sputtering sounds crackle over the baby monitor that's standing in the kitchen cubby.

I go change while Wren grabs Ruthie, who has woken up a hot, sticky, crabby mess. One good thing dogs have in common with little ones is a propensity for a lot of napping, so you have a chance to get some stuff done, but dogs even beat babies on that front, because they don't wake up sweaty and wrapped in damp diapers.

Wren carries a face-rubbing Ruthie in an olive-green two-piece out of their bedroom and announces they're going to try the pool, if I'd like to come watch.

Marie runs to greet the baby, whose face blooms from scrunched with annoyance to openly joyful. I have to agree with Ruthie; there's nothing like one of Marie's greetings to cheer you up. The way she wiggles and wags her tail and kisses you, it's like you've been gone for months and she's overjoyed that you're back.

Ruthie blinks her sleepy eyes at me, points at her top and says, "Kini."

I shoot a questioning look at Wren. "She means bikini," she explains.

"Oh!" I laugh. "That's a cute kini you've got there, Ruthie." She holds her hands to her chin, tilts her head, and gives me a coy smile that's sign-this-kid-up-for-modeling adorable. "Well, let's get Esther Williams here into the pool," I say, and now it's Wren's turn to look confused. "She was a movie star who dove into a lot of pools," I say. "Way before your time."

Luckily, the Adirondack chairs are in the shade, so I settle there with my "juice" (now a chilled glass of chardonnay; I decided to move on to the adult grape drink). Wren steps barefoot into the pool, then lowers Ruthie in. I reach out and dip in a toe. The pool sits in the sun, so the water's not fresh-from-the-hose cold. Ruthie flumps down on her diapered bottom and begins to splash her hands, mimicking her mom's efforts to get her to play in the water.

Marie, who'd been hanging back munching another ice cube, trots over and plops her front paws into the pool as well. She stares at me with a look that seems to say, "Really? For the baby?" Then she lowers her head and laps thirstily at the water, although a full bowl of fresh water sits in the shade by the back door. Ruthie points at Marie, shouts "Og!" and splashes some more.

Wren pulls a couple of Ruthie's bath toys—a plastic tugboat with a walrus captain and a panda bear wash mitt—out of her pockets and drops them in the water. She sits beside me, extending her pale skinny legs into the pool, using her narrow white feet as a backrest for Ruthie.

"Thanks for buying this for her," she says. "She loves it. Probably going to want to be in here every day."

"Beats hunting for parking at the beach, right?"

"And beats trying to get the sand off every flipping inch of her."

"Hmm, yes, there's that too," I say as if that hadn't occurred to me.

We sit in silence for a while, laughing as Marie runs to get her tennis ball, then plunks it in the water. I toss it onto the grass for Marie, entertaining both baby and dog, since Ruthie squeals each time Marie brings it back and drops it in the pool.

When Marie tires and lays down in the shade to work on tearing the fuzzy yellow covering off the ball, I close my eyes and rest my head against the back of my chair. "Let's order pizza when Barry gets home," I say. "It's too hot to cook."

"Cool," Wren says. "Ruthie loves to gnaw on the bones. I mean, you know, the crust."

Another thing dogs and babies have in common. "We call it that too. Marie also loves the bones." I smile.

Wren looks at Ruthie. While gently tapping her toes on the baby's back, she says, "I wanted to tell you again, thanks for, like, letting us move in and stuff. You guys have been really cool about . . . about everything."

She's looking in Ruthie's direction, but her eyes are unfocused, and she chews her bottom lip, apparently lost in thought. As much as I'd prefer to be spending this summer with just me, Barry, and Marie in our tiny house, I can't help but feel sorry for Wren. I have to wonder if some people in her life have not been "really cool about everything." It can't have been easy to deal with getting pregnant at her age. Especially when she has a superwoman overachiever for a mom.

I wonder where Ruthie's dad is in all this. Wren has offered up zero info on how all this went down. Barry and I have whispered in bed, wondering. We'd also discussed how this was yet another way dogs are better than kids. You can spay or neuter your dog, but try it with your hormone-crazed teenage boy, and people will call Child Protective Services on you. You can give them the safe sex lectures and lead them to the well of contraceptives, but you can't make them drink. Just like dogs, teenagers sometimes act without anticipating the consequences. Anyway, we didn't want to pry. We figured if or when she was ready to tell us, she would. Maybe this latest thank-you is her way of saying she wouldn't mind talking a bit. But I hesitate, waiting to see if she'll volunteer more. I sip my wine, simply say "You're welcome," and nod while offering what I hope is a look of smiling encouragement to go on.

Ruthie, meanwhile, has become fascinated with the ears on the panda wash mitt and tugs at them. We watch the baby, accompanied by the sounds of a tennis ball being scalped.

"It feels like vacation here," Wren finally says. "It's way more relaxing than our house."

"Sometimes a change of scenery is good for everybody." I decide to dig a little. "It can't have been an easy past couple of years. I remember what it was like when I was picking colleges and getting ready to move away from home for the first time. And you were doing all that with a baby as well."

Wren starts chewing her lip again. No half smile this time.

"That must have been hard, huh?" I prompt.

"Yeah. The last two years haven't been the greatest. My mom's always on me about school and stuff. And . . ." She scrunches her wet toes up on Ruthie's back, making the baby squirm, though her focus doesn't shift from her panda.

"And what?"

"It's just, you're right. All this picking a school, and trying to get in and stuff, and making up for the time I was out . . . It's been really stressful, and the stupid part is . . . I don't even wanna go to college." She looks at me for a moment and then back at Ruthie, with a face like she's said too much.

Hmm. I may be out of my depth here. I wasn't prepared for this to turn into a life counseling session. "But what would you do if you didn't go to school?"

She rolls her eyes and flops back in her chair. "Gawd, you sound like my mom. 'You can't throw your life away,'" she says in a high-pitched nasal whine. "Like it's a felony or something not to go to school."

"Oh, I didn't mean it that way. I meant, what would you *like* to do?"

"I want to, y'know, get a job or . . . I dunno. I'll figure something out. I don't think school's the place for me. But my mom wouldn't hear anything different."

"Sure, college isn't for everybody. There are other things you could do—vocational school maybe, or . . ." Oh hell, I don't know what to say. I know that both Wren's parents were big brainiacs in school, and that both have master's degrees, so I doubt Barry or Jade would want me counseling their daughter on taking an alternate route. While I'm trying to think of what else to say, she sits up and looks at me.

"Can I tell you something I never told anyone else?"

Oh God, what's she going to say? "Of course." I fortify myself with a swig of wine.

"When I found out I was pregnant, my boyfriend, well my *then* boyfriend—who turned out to be a *total* douche—oops! I mean, a total ten-twenty-one—anyway, he wanted me to, you know . . . fix things." She glances at Ruthie while whispering "fix things."

"Obviously you made other choices."

"Yeah. Because, like, not because I thought it was the right thing to do, necessarily, but . . ." She looks down and scratches at the peeling nail polish on her left thumb. She continues in barely more than a mumble, "But because I thought if I had a baby, it'd be a good excuse not to go to college. I thought my mom would have to get off my back."

Ruthie starts to fuss, so Wren grabs the fluffy beach towel I'd brought out. Wrapping the dripping baby in the towel, she sets Ruthie on one of the slate tiles and rubs her dry while she keeps talking in a quiet tone.

"I hope that doesn't sound super terrible. And like the dumbest idea *ever*. I mean, I love her, and I can't imagine *not* having had her, but, well, at the time—"

"It's okay. I understand." I admit, I once considered lying to my own mom and telling her Barry couldn't have kids. Evidence to the contrary now sitting before me, it's a good thing I rejected that idea. Of course, I also never told her the truth—that I never felt a maternal urge. I guess I wanted her to think, for as long as possible, that maybe someday Barry and I might have kids. I wanted to delay crushing her, to avoid being a disappointment. I know how Wren feels. It's not easy to tell your parents you're not going to be who they want you to be, that you're not going to live the life they'd imagined for you.

Maybe Wren needs to suck it up and just tell her mom the truth. Do as I say, not as I do, right? Isn't that how most parents roll? "Have you tried explaining your feelings to your mom?" I ask.

"Yeah, but she won't listen. She says the only way she'll support me is if I'm in school. If I drop out, I get cut off. She doesn't care about what *I* want."

"I wish I had some words of wisdom. But you should at least give school a try. Who knows, maybe you'll love it." I lean forward in my chair and rest my elbows on my knees. "Personally, my college years were some of the best times I ever had. You'll meet a lot of new people, make friends, take interesting classes, maybe discover new interests. College can be a blast. It's very different from high school."

"Yeah, it's cool it's not like high school. But still, it's probably more fun if you're not a single mom." She hoists Ruthie onto her hip. "I better get her out of this wet diaper. Thanks again for the pool." She bops Ruthie on the end of the nose with a corner of the towel, and says, "Tell Auntie Alex thanks for the pool." Wren points at me, reminding Ruthie who the heck Auntie Alex is. "Go on, say thanks."

"Tee Lexsch!" I want to roar like a dinosaur every time she says that. "Fanks," Ruthie chirps. "Fanks!" she continues to call out as Wren heads across the yard and into the house. Marie comes to stand next to my chair, then shakes her whole body from nose to tail, sending a spray of water all over me. I hold up my hands as a shield and squeal, but it's so hot out, it actually feels good. I can't help but laugh.

Hmm. This is one way babies are better than dogs—easier to dry off when they're sopping wet. But with a dog, "guidance counseling" only involves a leash.

*

Later that night, after watching both Marie and Ruthie gnaw on the pizza "bones" at dinner, and after Wren loaded the dishwasher and I quietly reloaded it (I know it's insane, but I like it just so), Barry, Wren, and I pore over his baby photo album. Wren has a good laugh about how skinny he was in some of his prepubescent photos. He was an adorable, scrawny little thing.

Afterward, Barry and I go to our room while Wren stays up watching TV. We lie in bed whispering, Marie stretched out on her back between our legs with her feet flopped open, hoping one of us will rub her belly. I can't resist her, so I oblige.

"How do you think this is going?" I ask, my eyes adjusting to the dim light.

"Pretty good." He rolls onto his side to face me. "You?" He reaches down for a few rubs of Marie's belly as well.

"Yeah. Not bad. Not as bad as I thought it might be. Didn't really appreciate the lecture on paper napkins during dinner, but she seems like a good kid."

"It wasn't a lecture. She's right. Cloth napkins are better for the environment."

I stop rubbing the dog, who rolls over onto her side, and fold my arms across my chest. "In case you hadn't noticed, we mostly do use cloth around here, but it was greasy pizza. She's a walking contradiction—all gung ho green, but she drives that huge boat of an SUV around. And have you seen all the stuff she's got plugged in in the bathroom? A baby wipes warmer? Leaving her chargers plugged in all the time? Come on. That's not green."

"I'm sure Jade bought her the SUV to be sure they were safe."

"Yes, tanks are safe. And heaven forbid Ruthie should experience the horror of a chilly baby wipe on her butt."

"Don't you like her?"

"I do. I like her. But I can't help it; I get annoyed when she lectures me about coffee grounds and paper napkins."

"She's right about the grounds too. I've been meaning to start a compost heap."

I poke him in the arm. "There. Right there. It's that word, *heap*. That concerns me. Is there going to be a heap of trash in our yard? Do we have to be *that* green?"

"It's not technically a heap. Well, it is, but it's in a bin. And it'll be on the side of the house. You'll never see it." He adjusts his pillow and rolls onto his back again.

"You don't have to do this to impress her. We're already super green; I mean, what's greener than *not* having babies? Think of the millions of diapers we've kept out of landfills."

Barry laughs.

"I'm not joking."

"Okay, you're right. But please don't say that the next time she suggests another way we can reduce, reuse, or recycle. Hey, speaking of diapers, shouldn't she be using the cloth kind? Wouldn't that be greener?"

"Please don't suggest that. She'll be running up our water and electricity bill with the constant laundry. And how is *that* green? Anyway, I'm sorry. I really do like her, but I just needed to vent a little. She's a sweet kid."

"Jade's done a good job with her."

I bug my eyes out to keep them from rolling, even though I know he's staring at the ceiling. Oh God, is he thinking, *What if Jade and I had raised her together?* "From what she told me, it sounds like her grandmother raised her more than Jade. She's mentioned a few times how Jade's completely wrapped up in her work."

"Jade always was a go-getter. Super determined."

I want to say, *She sure was a go-getter where your sperm were concerned,* but decide against it. "Sounds like Wren might not be quite as determined as her mom. At least, not about school."

"What're you talking about?" Barry rolls over to face me. I suppose he assumed any offspring of his and Jade's would come out of the womb hugging an e-reader (*Nine months! I got a ton of reading done!*) and possess the same love of learning they both have. I mean, I loved college myself, but I enjoyed the whole experience—the classes, the freedom, the social side. I know from talking to Barry about our university years that he was much more immersed in his classwork. I'm sure he was always in the chemistry or computer labs. I know he spent most Friday nights at the library rather than out partying, and I assume, from things he's said in the past, that Jade was the same.

I relay the afternoon's conversation, and he makes concerned, and rather fatherly, "huhs" during my retelling.

"She's got to go to school," he says when I finish. "What's she going to do with her life without a degree?"

"Shh. She'll hear you. And I don't know. I'm just repeating what she said."

"You told her she needs to start in September, didn't you?" He lowers his voice again.

"*Yes.* I said she should keep an open mind, and see how this first quarter goes, and maybe she'll find she loves it."

"You should have said she needs a degree," he props himself up on one elbow. He looks like he might hop out of bed, march down the hall, and tell her himself. Marie harrumphs at all the movement on the bed and jumps down. As she settles on the throw rug, she emits a loud sigh.

"Sorry, Marie." I continue, "Maybe it won't be her thing though. Not everybody needs, or wants, to go to college."

"Sure, but—"

"Lots of very intelligent, successful people are college dropouts. Bill Gates, Steve Jobs, and um . . . the Facebook guy . . ." I try to come up with a few more to make my case, but my mind goes blank. "Besides, we barely know her. We don't know if she's a good student." I hold up a finger. "Oh, Lady Gaga! I read an article about her the other day. She's a college dropout too."

"Swell." Barry falls back onto his pillow. "I wonder if Wren can sing."

"That's just it; we don't know what her skills are. I mean, besides sewing. I don't think we're in a position to push her any one direction."

"You're right, I guess. She needs to go to school, but if we push, she might rebel more. We've got to be subtle. You did the right thing." He leans over and kisses me good night, then pulls the sheet up and shuts his eyes. "You're right, again. Like always."

Normally I'd play along with this banter, reminding him that yes, I *am* always right, and asking him what he'd do without me. But guilt weighs heavily tonight, like a wool blanket.

Maybe I'm not always right. Maybe I don't *always* do the right thing. Here's hoping everything will work out and he'll never need to know.

I seriously consider curling up with Marie on the floor and telling her adoption story again (at least in my head), but instead I lie in bed and fret until long after midnight.

CHAPTER 10

Saturday morning brings a cheerful scene. Ruthie slept through the night, and there's no sign of her "super crab-head" alter ego. Since I don't have to make breakfast, Marie and I get in a lovely walk before it gets too hot. Barry cuts his usual long Saturday run short (unheard of!) in order to be home in time for our big happy-family breakfast. And Wren makes fabulous almond flour and pumpkin pancakes and has fun tossing bites to Marie. Possibly best of all, Wren stops trying to foist her sweaty-feet-smelling yerba maté breakfast drink on me and seems resigned to the fact I'm sticking with coffee.

Three days down, fifty-four to go. But who's counting?

I offer to clean the kitchen since Wren cooked (and since I don't trust her to clean it to my standards), and Marie follows me. Her Labrador side showing again, she's no doubt hoping one more pancake will be found. Luckily, there's an extra one, so I tear it into four chunks and have her run through her best repertoire of tricks for me: *shake*, *high five*, *roll over*, and *play dead*.

The three generations of Halstads stay and chat in the dining room (well, two chat, the third babbles). Barry gasps, and I turn in time to see Ruthie's sippy cup sail through the air. Fortunately, it's empty, so although the lid pops off, only a few drops of juice trickle out. Wren jumps up, but I'm there with my sponge before she's fully out of her seat. Mr. Clean's got nothin' on me.

Wren's apology is interrupted by the ring of her phone. She pulls it out of the depths of her baggy army pants and glances at the screen. "My mom." She frowns and shoves the phone back in her pocket.

"You should take it," I say. "She might be worried about you guys." Things have gone okay for a day or two, but I'd still welcome the chance to have our peaceful life back. Maybe it's not too late for Wren to make up with her mom and spend the rest of the summer in San Francisco. Then we can all continue bonding in the fall, when Wren's got her own apartment. I finish wiping the floor and head back to the kitchen.

"I'll text her later. There's nothing for her to worry about." Her phone chirps, signaling a message. "*Gawd.* She's relentless." She doesn't look at the phone.

"Does she still work at Acadia Pharma?" Barry asks. I'm not surprised he knows employment info about his ex. It's standard procedure to Google one's former lovers, isn't it? But that's another place where I don't fit the norm. I couldn't give a fig about my exes and have never looked up a single one. But, of course, I've Googled Barry's ex. Obviously, Barry hasn't done so recently, or he wouldn't have to ask.

"Yeah. She loves that place so much, she might as well be married to it." Her phone chirps again. "Give it a rest already." She slumps in her chair, sighs, and pulls the phone out again. Head bent over the screen, she sits up straighter. "My grandpa died."

"Oh no," Barry and I say together. "I'm so sorry," I add, joining them in the dining room.

Another chirp. "She wants me to come home. For the funeral at least."

"Was he sick?" Barry asks, while I add, "Were you close?"

"No. And not at all. I was close to my grandma, but she died three years ago. Grandpa said it was a good thing, so she didn't have to see what a disappointment I turned out to be." She nods at Ruthie while her jaw clenches. "He was kind of old-fashioned. And kind of a dickhead. Sorry. I shouldn't say that." She inclines her head toward Ruthie. "And I know you're not supposed to speak ill of the dead and all that stuff. But he was." She adds, muttering, "I forget the number for dickhead."

"Did he live near you?" Barry asks.

"Yeah. My mom used to take food over for him after Grandma died." She shakes her head. "It was just takeout, but she'd wrap it up on our plates and pretend she made it. It wasn't like he was too feeble to cook—or get his own takeout—he just expected to be waited on. Total old-school chauvinist." She squints. "He's not going to know if I don't go to his funeral. Even if he did, he wouldn't care. He didn't give me or Ruthie the time of day."

Another chirp from her phone. She looks, then sets it facedown on the table.

"But your mom will care if you miss the funeral," I say. "You should go."

Barry puts his hand on Wren's shoulder. Ruthie squeals and winds up to toss her munchkin-size spoon, but Wren's quick and stays the baby's pitching arm. Linked arm to arm to arm, the three of them look so much alike. I can see this time is important for Barry. For *them*. Maybe I shouldn't be trying to get rid of her. After all, this situation isn't Wren's fault. It's Jade's.

"For a couple days, anyway," I add. "You could fly back right after the funeral."

She waggles the cell phone. "Yeah, that's what my mom said. She wants us to come home tomorrow and stay a few days."

"Your room'll be here when you get back." I pat her other shoulder, and she looks up and smiles at me, without a hint of her usual uncertainty.

*

In the wee hours of Sunday, we wake, once again, to shrieking. So much for the last couple nights of Ruthie sleeping like a worn-out puppy. They don't have to catch their flight until midmorning, so I shove earplugs in, roll over, and go back to sleep.

With the earplugs in, I manage two more hours of sleep, waking when Barry grabs a decorative pillow from the floor—where he always tosses them, rather than in the pullout storage under the bed like he's supposed to—to shove behind his head. Even through the earplugs, I hear Ruthie crying. Marie gets up, goes to the door, whines to go out and check on things, then comes back to my side of the bed and nose-pokes my arm.

"Why doesn't she nose-poke you? She can see you're awake." I pull out my earplugs in time to hear a loud wail from Ruthie. I twist to look at Barry, knowing he'll be reading on his iPad—probably news of some sort: world events or sports updates or the latest tech talk.

"Maybe she's appealing to your mothering instincts. She wants to see what's distressing the baby; maybe she thinks you do too."

"What about your fathering instincts? You go see what's wrong."

"I'm of no use in a wailing baby crisis."

"Well, just because I have ovaries doesn't mean I know what to do. It's not like ovaries come with a Babies 101 manual. Let's face it, Marie's the best one to send. Open the door for her."

Barry throws off the sheet and lets Marie out. A moment later we hear Ruthie's gurgling giggle. Then there's a coughing fit that sounds like it came from an old man.

"I give up." Barry gets up, and I pray he's going to make coffee.

I try the earplugs again, but it's no good. I pull on my robe and scuff down the hall to find Wren cuddling Ruthie while the baby rubs her knuckles into her ears. Marie paces around their chair, trying to get at the baby. Her ears shift at every little sound from Ruthie, and her eyes are soft with concern. It's pathetic that my dog has more of a maternal instinct than I do, but I can't help how I'm wired.

"She's got another one of her earaches. This happened the last time we went in the ocean too."

Yeah. If they left that much sand in the house, how much was left in Ruthie's ears?

"Uh-oh." I have no idea what one does in this situation. "Do you have any medication?" I recall Marie pawing her ears and shaking her head when she had an ear infection brought on by too many romps at the beach last summer. With a dog, you head to the vet and get drops.

"She woke up in the middle of the night. She had a fever, and I figured it was her ears. She gets earaches a lot. I Googled a twenty-four-hour urgent care place and took her." She holds up a white paper bag. "I got a prescription." Ah, so sort of the same as with a dog. "The doctor said it looks like only a mild infection, but she still said Ruthie shouldn't fly until she's better."

"So you guys won't be able to fly out today? How long does it usually take the drugs to kick in? Maybe you could go tomorrow instead."

"The funeral's Tuesday and my mom wants me to help her before. I'm still pissed at her, but if you guys would . . . I could maybe . . ." The baby starts to cry again, and Marie stops her pacing and nudges Ruthie's foot gently with her nose. "It's okay, Roo," Wren soothes. She strokes Marie's head and thanks her for being so concerned about the baby. Then, looking from Barry to me, she says, "I don't know when she'll feel better, so I should probably get on that flight. I promise she won't be this fussy once the medicine kicks in."

She wants to leave us alone with the baby? The *sick* baby? I want to scream, "No! You can't leave us with this tiny creature!" Is this appropriate mother behavior? Shouldn't she be opposed to leaving Ruthie with people she just met? Granted, Barry's the grandfather, but she barely knows us. I would never leave Marie with strangers, for Pete's sake. I know Wren's only eighteen, so maybe she's not thinking this completely through like an older, more worry-prone mother would, but still, this is crazy.

I look at Barry and blink several times, Morse-coding him my panic. "Let's talk about it while we eat," he says, fleeing to the pantry. "I know Alex needs her caffeine injection, and I could do with some myself." *Way to dodge the issue, Bear.*

"Can I have some too?" Wren asks. I tilt my head at her in surprise, and she adds, "I hardly slept last night." Her normally bright-blue eyes are heavily lidded. I realize what I thought were smudges of makeup leftover from last night are, in fact, dark circles. Poor kid looks exhausted.

"Was she fussy all night?" I tentatively reach out and rub Ruthie's back.

"No, she didn't wake up until four. It's just—I'm kind of nervous about seeing my mom."

I immediately know what will happen. Wren will get on the plane; she needs to see her mom. As long as Barry and I can work out baby-sitting between our work schedules, and call in reinforcement from Rache and Anna, our housekeeper, Wren will leave Ruthie with us. We'll have to fend for ourselves with an earache-afflicted child for a few days. On the one hand, I'm terrified of all the things that can go wrong. But on the other, Wren should try to patch things up with her mom.

Selfish thoughts prod me again: my best hope of getting them out of the house is Wren reconciling with Jade. *This could be your chance,* the devilish side of me rejoices.

So, selflessly, for the sake of Wren's relationship with her mother, and also completely selfishly, for my own hope of regaining our calm, quiet, way-less-messy life, I say, "We can watch her." Knowing somehow that between Barry, Anna, Rache, and me, we'll figure it out, I muster as much certainty into my voice as I can. "We'll be fine. You go ahead and get on that flight."

Oh dear. I hope this isn't a crazy idea.

CHAPTER 11

"This is a crazy idea, right?" Barry whispers to me after breakfast as Wren goes to finish packing. "I mean, is it wise of her to leave her baby with us? *Inept* us?"

"I know," I whisper back. We huddle over the sink, pretending it takes both of us to rinse and load the dishwasher. "It's like how you're always complaining about the freshmen's brains at school."

"You mean how they're not fully functioning? Studies have definitely showed the nerve cells that connect teenagers' frontal lobes with the rest of their brains are sluggish. The messages are being sent, but it takes them a while to get there."

"And the frontal lobe is the part of the brain that might say, 'Hmm, I wonder if it's a bad idea to leave my baby with these morons.' Right?"

"Exactly. But *our* frontal lobes work properly, so maybe we should renege on our offer."

"No." I finish loading the dishwasher and reach for a towel to dry my hands. "Her mom needs her. And it's going to be okay. We can get Rache and Anna to help us." I hand him the towel. "Oh! And Cynthia! I'll call her. We can use all the help we can get."

It's only seven thirty in the morning, but I know it's not too early to call as the boys get up with the sun. Cyn answers on the second ring, and I hear the usual commotion in the background—the boys screaming, the television blaring, and one new sound: cymbals clashing. Uh-oh. She's going to kill me. And now I'm calling to ask a favor. I better word this carefully.

"You're up early," Cyn says, stifling a yawn. She knows I like to sleep as late as possible on the weekends. Pretty sure she's jealous about it, since she never misses a chance to goad me about my "beauty sleep." I tried to tell her once that she and Jamie should take turns sleeping in on the weekends, but I suppose that's impossible with the noise level over there.

"It's kind of a long story." I haven't talked to Cyn since I left Fuzzy's party. Where do I start? "Um, what would you say if I told you our family has a new baby girl?" She wanted a baby girl, and now the family has one. Yay! She won't be able to resist, right?

"Did you guys get a puppy? What does Marie think?"

"No, not a puppy." I'd better start from the beginning, with the conversation Barry and I had last Sunday. If I cut to the chase, she'll ask a million questions, so I might as well give the full report. As I do, she occasionally interjects an "ohmygod" or a "what?" but mostly listens quietly while I tell her about Wren and Ruthie.

"They moved *in?*" I'm sure she's thinking of how I follow the boys around the house with a bottle of spray cleaner and a damp rag every time they're here. "How are you feeling about all this? Hang on." She covers the phone, but I can still hear her muffled shrieking at the boys: "A.J., put your brother down! And Bobby, get off the coffee table!" I hear what sounds like another adult and assume Jamie must be helping to corral the children. He couldn't possibly be sleeping through that madness.

"It's all happened so fast, my head's still spinning. But Wren's a good kid. And it's nice to watch her and Barry interact. They're weirdly similar. It kind of blows my mind, actually." Okay, here's where I've got to be careful. If I let on I need her help, she'll suddenly be too busy. Or she'll make me squirm and beg. "So I thought maybe you'd want to meet the latest addition to the family. Ruthie's super cute! She's past that new-baby-smell thing"—*that's a thing, right? Like new-car smell?*— "but she's still at that cuddly stage I know you enjoy. I'm sure you'll fall in love when you meet her." *And then maybe you could watch her all afternoon for me while I finish my drawings for the Van Dierdons?*

Normally, I know my sister would not hesitate at the chance to get her hands—and nostrils—on a baby, but as she pauses, I hear another adult voice again. And then a donkey-bray laugh I'd know anywhere.

"Was that Daddy?" I don't wait for an answer. "They just got home from their cruise yesterday," I add, stating the obvious. Our parents are retired and living in Temecula, a fast-growing city about two hours southeast of Cynthia's. To be at my sister's house this morning, they'd have to have either gotten up at five, or driven there last night after flying home from their European Riviera cruise. I haven't even talked to them yet, because I figured they'd be too tired and would call me once they felt up to it.

"Mom said they woke up really early because of the jet lag. And they felt so bad about missing Frankie's birthday, they decided to drive here." She makes it sound all very matter-of-fact, but I also note her slight gloating tone.

She knows she's Mom's favorite. She knows *I* know. No one ever has to voice this. It's understood among the three of us. Oh, of course, Mom trots out the "I don't have a favorite; I love my girls equally" bromide every once in a while on my account, but we all know where my name falls on the best-daughter roster. We've known (or Mom and I have anyway) since the day Cyn came home from the hospital. And it's gotten more pronounced as the years have passed.

When Mom, who'd never written anything beyond the annual family Christmas letter before, wrote a bestseller, *What to Expect When*

Your Daughter's Expecting, it further cemented their bond. After all, the book's certainly not about me. It's not very original, being a rip-off of the *What to Expect When You're Expecting* megahit, but it's exceedingly popular with baby-boomer grandmas. I bought a few copies to be supportive. Not that it mattered. My measly copies (in one of which Mom wrote "Thanks for being a good sport!" when I played fangirl and asked her to sign it) were a drop in the bucket of the bazillions she sold. Mom and Dad were able to retire early and go on fabulous European cruises. All because my sis is a breeder. And no thanks to me.

"She says hi," Cyn adds.

I say nothing.

"She wants to talk to you." I'm sure Cyn is now waving my mother to the phone.

"Hi, honey!"

"Hi, Mom," I say, my voice a monotone. I try to hide how hurt I am that I haven't heard from them yet. Didn't even get a postcard, for Pete's sake. Or maybe I shouldn't bother to hide it. "I assumed you'd made it home okay yesterday."

"I was going to call you later and tell you all about the trip. It was wonderful, but we were so exhausted when we got home yesterday. Being a tourist for three weeks is tiring! You know I love to go-go-go, and we went-went-went on this trip."

"But you recovered by this morning and felt like a long car ride? After all that flying yesterday?"

"We woke up so darn early. It's going to take a while to get back on this time zone. And we brought the boys so many fun things. You should see the matador and bull marionette set your dad picked out for Frankie when we were in Spain."

"A matador and a bull? But bullfighting is so cruel."

"It's not like the puppet's got an open wound or anything. It's part of Spanish culture. It's—oh, never mind. Anyway, when your dad suggested we hop in the car and come up here for the day, I couldn't resist.

We felt so bad about missing Frankie's party. Anyway, how are you? It sounded like you had some big news for your sister. What was that all about?"

I don't want to recite the whole saga again. "Cyn can tell you." And I'm sure she'll relish telling how my picture-perfect house, which she comments on every time she comes over (in a voice that's supposed to sound complimentary, but is just plain snotty), is maybe not so perfect anymore. "Can you put her back on?"

"Okay, hon. I'll call you one day this week and tell you all about the trip. Oh no, you'll be working during the day. And I'll probably be going to bed early every night. Next weekend, okay? I'll talk to you then!"

I hear Cyn take the phone back. "Never mind," I say. "I thought you might want to come up and meet the baby, but clearly you're busy with visitors."

"What about meeting Wren? Didn't you think I'd want to meet her too? I could come for a little while. Jamie's out golfing, and I'm sure Mom and Dad would love some alone time with the boys."

"Wren'll be gone by the time you get here. She has to fly home for a couple of days for her grandpa's funeral. So you'd only be meeting the baby."

"She's leaving her baby alone with you guys? For a few days?" She titters in an annoying, high-pitched way. "Do you have reinforcements lined up or something? Oh, wait a minute." Her amused tone fades. "That's why you want me to come. You need a crash course in baby care, right? This isn't about me getting a chance to cuddle the latest addition to the family."

"Okay, yeah. I could use some help. Maybe a few pointers. Killing Wren's kid while she's gone would probably put a damper on Wren and Barry's fledgling relationship. So can you come for a bit and help me out?" My mother and sister share a deep addiction to babies, so I realize what might happen once Cynthia tells Mom the story. "Do you think

Mom would want to come meet her too? That's a lot of driving for her in one day. Are they staying over tonight?"

"No, she said they have tons to do at home—mountains of laundry and mail. They want to get on the road by about three. I'll ask, but I'm not sure if she'll want to come up. I could be there by ten. Whether she comes along or not, I'll have to leave your house around one thirty."

A few hours of How Not to Kill a Baby is better than none. And hopefully I can get some work done while Cynthia gets her baby-girl fix. "Thanks, that's perfect. I'll see you soon."

When I get off the phone, I call and schedule a cab for Wren. The original plan was for Barry to drive her, but I don't want to be alone with Ruthie right away. Or at all, if I can help it.

The next call is to Anna. She has two teenagers; she'll know what to do. Monday is her usual cleaning day anyway, but I'm hoping she can stay all day, plus part of Tuesday as well. I'm definitely going to need someone to babysit on Tuesday when I have my appointment to deliver the design plans to the Van Dierdons. Thank heaven, Anna says she'd love to meet the baby and will rearrange her schedule and help out. I don't care what those extra hours are going to do to our budget. I'll figure it out. I can skip getting my hair colored at the salon again. This is a necessity, after all.

I find Barry looking through his e-mails and checking his calendar on his phone. "Anna says she can help part of the time this week, but can you come home early on Tuesday and Wednesday?"

"Since it's summer, things are quieter than usual, so the timing's perfect," he says. "I've got meetings both mornings, but can watch her in the afternoons. Do you think I'll have to change a diaper? I've never done that before."

"It's not rocket science."

"Yeah, well, rockets don't poop."

"You can handle it."

"Can we handle it, though? What've we gotten ourselves into?" His eyes dart back and forth, and he reaches up to run his hand through his hair. "We better let her sleep in our room." I imagine he's remembering how Wren said that she and Ruthie would be fine sharing the guest bed, but she wanted Ruthie's side against the wall so that she couldn't fall out. He's right; we can't let her sleep in there alone. Thank God we have a king; we can fit her between us. Marie's going to love that. Me? Not so much.

"Good idea."

His eyes go wide. "Wait a minute. Don't babies sometimes . . . die in their sleep? Seriously, what have we done?"

Trying not to feed his panic, and to calm myself down too, I reassure him that sudden infant death syndrome is only a problem with tiny babies. I have no idea if this is true, but I make a mental note to research it later. "We'll get through this with help. We've got Anna, and Cyn's coming this afternoon. It'll be fine. But I can't think about it too much or I'll start to freak out. I have to do some straightening up."

Barry knows nothing mellows me out more than a good cleaning session (except maybe a glass of whiskey), so he lets me go. I know he's probably itching to get out for a run—we each have our coping mechanisms, and it's too early for whiskey—but I hope he'll at least wait until Cyn gets here.

"Marie, toys! Away," I say. She helps me collect her and Ruthie's toys from the living room floor, and we drop them in the basket I keep hidden behind the sofa.

Once the floor's picked up, I run the vacuum, which Marie flees from, as usual. Then I tackle the kitchen. It's only Cyn coming, but still, I like everything to look nice. Or as nice as possible, what with the design modifications we've had to make.

While I'm polishing the sink, my cell rings. The call is from Cyn's house. Crap. She should be on the road by now. *Please don't let her say she can't come after all!*

"Hey, haven't you left yet?" I answer without saying hello.

"Oh, were you expecting me to come along?" my mother replies.

"No, I thought you were Cyn. Is she on her way?"

"Yes, she left a bit ago. She gave me the short version of what's been going on there. A baby! I can't believe it."

Didn't she say she wasn't going to call me again until this weekend? But, of course, now there's a baby involved. "Yes, a fifteen-month-old girl. Her name's Ruthie."

"I was so tempted to come along! Tell me everything."

"I don't have time right now. Maybe we can talk this weekend, like we'd planned."

"But a baby girl! I'm so tickled." She sounds positively gleeful. "It's so ironic though."

"What do you mean?" I pause in the midst of wiping down the countertops.

"Your sister's been praying for a baby girl, and now you have one. I can't wait to meet her. Maybe I could drive up and visit? Maybe Wednesday?"

Hmm. At the moment, I do have a babysitting gap that morning. Still, it chaps my hide—and my pride—that when it was only Barry and me, she was content to wait until next weekend for a mere phone call catch-up. But now that there's a baby involved, she's suddenly willing to drive up and see us ASAP. I can't remember the last time my parents drove up just for a visit and not for some major holiday or birthday celebration. Usually if we want to see them, we either have to meet up at Cyn's or go to their place. Annoying. But . . . I need the help. "Let's play it by ear. I've got to go. I'll call you later, and we'll figure something out."

"And then you'll tell me the whole story? Cyn said that you told her that Wren and Ruthie both look a bit like Barry. I can't wait to meet them! I bet Ruthie's adorable."

"She is. She's long and lean like Barry, and she totally has his nose, but she's got blue eyes and curly hair. Anyway, I've really got to go now, Mom. Tell Daddy I said hi, and I'll talk to you—Wait!" I almost scream, afraid she'll have hung up already. "What's the deal with SIDS?"

"Oh, silly! That's only young babies. Ruthie will be fine. But I could come stay overnight on Tuesday if you'd like." My mother never stays over at our house. If we have an evening event at our house, my parents go home with Cynthia and Jamie and spend the night at their place before heading home.

"It's okay. We can handle it. I'll talk to you later." I toss my phone aside. *Can we?* Maybe I should've taken her up on that sleepover offer.

I attack some stains on the coffeemaker, polish the front of the fridge, and spray and wipe down the counters. When I'm done, the room offers up no other obvious areas to pounce on, so I pop the sponge in the dishwasher and give up on cleaning any more before Cyn arrives.

I check on Wren, who is packed and ready to go. She's propped against a pile of pillows on her bed, holding a sleepy-looking Ruthie and reading her a story. Marie is curled up on the bed with them. Shoot. I never thought to put a spare sheet on the top of the guest bed too. I'm running out of sheets.

"I made some notes for you and my dad," Wren says, holding up a few sheets of lined paper torn from a school notebook. "Like, Ruthie's favorite foods, tips on getting her to sleep. Stuff like that. I'll have my phone with me all the time. Other than the flight, I'll just be a text away."

"Please keep it charged up and with you at all times." This is an unnecessary thing to say to a teenager, but I say it anyway. I'm assuming she'll keep it on during the funeral. She can set it to vibrate, and I'm sure she's practiced in the art of surreptitious texting. "Anna, our housekeeper—she's a mom—will help babysit while you're away." She smiles, probably pleased to know that someone with actual baby experience will be around as backup. Still, if I was her, I'd be worried. But then, she doesn't know me and my clueless-about-little-ones ways that well yet. "I called a cab. It should be here soon." I leave her to spend a few minutes alone with Ruthie.

When the cab arrives, I hand Wren cash to pay for it. She asks me to give Ruthie a million kisses for her while she's gone. I'm unwilling to commit to anything above double digits, but I know Marie will happily make up the difference, so I nod and smile. Barry's keeping Ruthie occupied in the backyard while Wren drives off. We all agreed it's better if she doesn't witness her mother's departure. As the cab pulls away, I wave and hope I don't look too worried, but I can feel the furrows between my eyebrows deepening.

And now I'm closing the door and wishing a whole boatload of wishes: please let Jade and Wren make up (they *are* going to make up, right? I mean, what better place than a family funeral to put things into perspective); please let Wren's flight bring her back safely and right on time Wednesday night; and, most fervently, please don't let grievous bodily harm come to the baby while she's under our care. Sure, we'll probably inflict a wee bit of emotional damage on her—we're bound to suck at this because we don't know what we're doing—but it'll be short-term, right? She'll forget about the horrors of missing her mommy and being trapped with Grandpa and the scary T-Rex lady as soon as Mommy's back, right?

Right?

"Oh, Marie," I say, bending down for a quick hug. "I hope this goes well."

As I stand straight, I hear Ruthie calling for Mama from the backyard.

It's going to be a long four days. Luckily, we have the one thing that always makes the baby smile.

"Go get her, Marie," I say, and follow the dog out back.

CHAPTER 12

"Oh my God, she's adorable!" Cynthia squeals when I answer the door with Ruthie attached to my hand. "Hi, sweetie!" Cyn squats down so that she's eye level with Ruthie. Marie leaps in, taking the opportunity for lots of kisses, which makes Ruthie giggle as Cyn lets out a "Bah!" and pushes Marie away.

"Marie, give your aunt some breathing room." I drop Ruthie's hand—she sways, but stays upright—and grab Marie's collar instead.

"Come here," Cynthia crooks a finger at Ruthie, who eagerly hobbles forward. She puts her fingers into her mouth and sucks them, smiling at Cynthia, who's making goofy wide-eyed faces. "Who's the cutest little thing ever?" Cyn asks. I answer in my head: *Marie! I mean, look at that face! Those long, wavy-haired ears!*

Ruthie toddles into Cyn's outstretched arms and collapses against her.

"Oh my God, these curls!" She runs her fingers over the dark corkscrew curls on Ruthie's head, pulls one out, and lets it bounce back into place. "What's with the black dress though? Is she in some kind of mourning for her great-grandpa? Is that a cultural thing or something for her family?"

"Only if Goth counts as a culture."

"Huh." Cynthia holds Ruthie away from her, assessing her black pinafore and white T-shirt underneath. "I'm your great-aunt Cynthia," she says to the baby. "And you are the cutest little Goth baby ever!" I'll give her that—with her long, skinny limbs and big, round blue eyes, she *is* the cutest little Goth baby ever. Cyn extends Ruthie's hands, and the baby shows off some of her best dance moves, grooving to an unheard beat. Cyn looks up at me. "So does this mean Wren's Goth?" She stands, and we move to the sofa, Ruthie clutching Cyn's index finger while she walks.

"Not really. She doesn't exclusively wear black. She mixes it up with a little gray, white, some red every now and then. And as far as I've seen, she doesn't have any tats, and only double-pierced ears. She's got a pretty unique style. And she runs too. Or she used to. Can't picture those Goth types running."

"No way. Imagine their eyeliner after only a mile." Ruthie's eyes droop as she collapses against Cynthia's knees. Marie, settled beside me, lifts her head and tenses like she's ready to dive into position and cushion the baby if she falls. Cynthia wraps Ruthie in her arms and hoists the baby into her lap with a practiced ease, and Marie relaxes again. "Somebody needs a nap," she coos at Ruthie. "So Wren seems like a good kid?"

I shrug. "Yeah. I mean, we haven't known her that long, but she's sweet with Ruthie. She could've come in here with a major chip on her shoulder, but she just wants to get to know her dad. And she doesn't have that 'I'm smarter than you' entitled attitude that a lot of teenagers seem to have these days. You know?"

"Well, that's good parenting. My boys won't be like that either."

Of course not. "I think she actually spent a lot of time with her grandma. Sounds like her mom and grandpa are—well, *were*, in her grandpa's case—workaholics."

Cyn snorts. "Those have-it-all moms think they have all the bases covered. And then look what happens." She lifts her elbows to indicate the baby encircled in her arms.

I don't want to engage in that discussion with Cynthia, since I don't have a horse in the stay-at-home-moms versus working-moms race. Generally, I'd probably take the opposite point of view just to be contrary with Cyn, but I suppose I do relate better to the working moms. After all, I love my job, so if they *want* to keep working, I say, more power to 'em. (And if they *need* to, well, then we should probably all cut them some slack.) I don't think we can necessarily pin Wren's pregnancy on Jade's possibly lax parenting. Still, I'm not about to jump to her defense. Best to end this line of chat anyway, since I hear Barry padding down the hallway.

"Hey, Barry," Cyn says when he appears. "Or should I say, 'Gramps'?"

He looks at his bare feet. "Yeah. It's, uh, been an interesting week."

"If that's not the understatement of the year," I add.

He waves at a sleepy-eyed Ruthie, who sucks her fingers while resting her head on Cyn's chest. "Looks like you ladies are all set here, so I thought I'd take Marie for a little run, okay?" He heads for the door before I can answer. I know he needs to fit in a run on the weekends or else he gets grumpy, plus, I didn't have time to take Marie for a walk this morning due to all the chaos. Luckily, it's cooler today. I've been petting her as she leans against my legs, and now I nudge her with my knee. "Go with Daddy." She races after Barry, knowing there's a run in her future.

After they're gone, Cyn says, "Somebody's tuckered out," and heads toward the guest room. I'm bummed Ruthie's nodding off. I could have handled a napping baby by myself. I'd hoped she'd stay up while Cyn's here, then sleep later. Like, the rest of the day. So as I follow Cyn into the guest room, I tug on Ruthie's fingers, slung over Cyn's shoulder.

"Look who's up again!" I say in a loud, cheerful voice. Ruthie rubs her left eye with her fist. She lets out a pitiful sputter, but then spots the bookshelf. "Ook," she gurgles in a throaty voice while pointing.

"She loves her books," I say. "Bet she'd love it if you read to her."

Cyn settles down with Ruthie between her legs on the area rug. (My beautiful celadon-colored rug that I hope will still be beautiful by the time they move out; I didn't bother to replace this one with a Target cheapie because I imposed a "no food or drinks other than water" rule for the guest room.) Cyn pulls a few of Ruthie's books off the shelf and asks Ruthie, in a high-pitched voice not unlike the one Barry and I use with Marie, if she'd like to read about the fuzzy bunny.

Ruthie indicates she would indeed enjoy such an activity by yanking the book away from Cyn and slapping at the pages. She's fully awake now. Hopefully, the reading won't immediately knock her out again.

"So . . ." I edge toward the bedroom door. "You think you could entertain her for a bit while I get some work done? Maybe like an hour, and then I'll take a break, and we can eat lunch." I pull the folded sheets of scrawled notes from my back pocket and wave them. "Wren left instructions about what and how much I should feed her, so I'm good to go on that front."

"You asked me here to babysit? I thought you wanted me to meet the new family member. I thought we were going to hang out for a while."

"We will. We'll hang out, as soon as I get some work done." I hold up an index finger. "Just one hour. I wouldn't ask if this weren't such a massively important project. Okay?" She looks annoyed, but I back out of the room before she can object.

An hour later, I find Ruthie sound asleep (*darn it!*) slumped over a stuffed pig she stole from Marie's toy basket. (Maybe I need to alter the toy laundry cycle from every other week to once a week while they're here; hope she didn't suck on that thing.) Cyn is still in the guest room with her, cranking out rapid-fire sit-ups on the floor.

"Eighty-eight, eighty-nine," she says under her breath before noticing I've come in. "Hold on." She continues her crunches. "Ten more." She collapses back on the rug as she hits one hundred. Her abs, even after three children, are tighter than mine ever were or will be. "She fell asleep a few minutes ago, so I thought I'd get in some sit-ups."

"Are you and your perfect abs ready for lunch?" Cyn always amazes me with how quickly she gets back in shape after looking like a bowling pin while carrying each of the boys. It's impressive. Yet another thing you don't have to worry about when you choose dogs over babies—having a dog doesn't involve stretch marks.

"Don't give me grief about my sit-up routine."

"I'm not giving you grief. That was a compliment. Your abs are, in fact, perfect."

"It's the way you say it. Like it's shallow or something." I hold out a hand and pull her up. "You have your perfect house and your perfect career and your perfect marriage and your perfect . . . haircut. My abs are the only thing I have control over in my life."

I laugh, although she's probably not joking. "I don't have a perfect career, or a perfect marriage, or a . . ." I fluff my chin-length hair. "Do you really like it this way? It's shorter than she usually cuts it." If only I could have afforded to have it colored and highlighted too.

"Yes. It's perfect. I assume we're now going to have our lunch on perfect place settings."

"You're the one with the perfect all-American family, with your two-point-two kids. Remember me, the freak who never wanted children?"

"You're not a freak." This is the closest Cyn and I have ever come to discussing my childless-by-choice life. It's good to know she doesn't think I'm a freak, but maybe she's just saying that.

"You don't think?"

"No, you know what you want, and who cares if other people don't understand?"

I'm about to say *Yeah, but what if one of those people is your own mother* when she says, "I'm starving. Let's eat. What're we having?" At least I know now that she doesn't share her friends' view of me as a weirdo. It's a good feeling.

I smile at her. "I'm starving too. We're having egg salad sandwiches. But, um," I point at Ruthie still asleep on the floor with her pig pillow. "Do we leave her there? Do we wake her up to eat?"

"We'll let her sleep for a bit, and then we can feed her when we're done. Did Wren pump some breast milk for her before she left?"

"Huh?"

"Well, Ruthie's still pretty little. Wren should still be breast-feeding her. Isn't she? Even at night?"

"I have no idea. I mean, I don't think so. She never said anything."

Cyn's mouth takes on the same disapproving line I've seen our mother exhibit many a time. "She really ought to be breast-feeding her until at least age two."

"I don't know what to tell you. That's something you'll have to bring up with Wren, but I'm assuming that ship's sailed." Good grief. There's the stay-at-home moms versus the working moms, and now we've got breast-milk wars too? Of course, I guess it's no different than when we used to take Marie to the dog park when she was an overly energetic puppy. We'd get the raw feeders versus the kibble people, and folks arguing about the best training methods. Why does everyone have to be so judgmental all the time? Why are folks always trying to shove their choices down everyone else's throats? *Live and let live, people.* "Let's just go eat, okay?"

"Okay," she says, with one last flattening of her lips and a dismissive lift of her eyebrow. "Anyway, Ruthie'll be fine. We've got the baby monitor, so we'll hear if she wakes up."

I don't even know if it's okay to leave her on the floor or not. If we put her in the bed, will she fall and break her skinny little neck? How do I possess a uterus but not know the answers to these types of questions? Maybe I am a freak. Again, dogs: easier. They sleep anywhere.

"Okay. I hate to leave her on the floor like that though."

"We're going to put her in the bed," Cyn says like I'm the biggest idiot ever. She squats, flexing her toned legs, and gently lifts the baby. She sets her down and scoots her to the far side, against the wall. "We'll barricade her in with the pig and the sheep." Cyn gathers stuffed animals from the floor. "She won't fall out." Luckily, Ruthie sleeps the sleep of the medicated, oblivious to the rearranging.

We hear Barry and Marie coming back in from the garage as we head to the kitchen.

"How was your run?" I ask. I notice that Marie ducks into the guest room to check on the baby, then trots straight to her water bowl by the back door for a long drink. "So egg salad sandwiches. That sounds good, right?" I ask Cyn.

"Only if you have the light mayo."

I give her a "please, what do you think?" look.

"Good," Barry says, heading for the fridge. "Hot."

After he gulps down half a bottle of orange Gatorade, he asks if I got much work done.

Cyn gives me the same flat-lipped expression I just gave her, which in her case reads: "Even Barry knew you called me here to babysit while you worked. Don't deny it."

I concentrate on the bowl of egg salad and ignore her. "A bit," I say to Barry.

"Did you show Cyn what you're working on?" He reaches around me and, while trying to distract me with a kiss on my temple, steals a hunk of yolk out of my bowl. Marie sits on my foot, also hoping for a handout. Barry obliges.

"No." I wave my wooden spoon at him like a sword. "And get out of my egg salad. Want me to make you a sandwich?"

"Yeah. I'll have it after I shower." He turns to Cyn, seated at the table. "Check out the beachy design she's working on. It's fantastic. Almost makes me want to let her redo our room." He starts to walk out. "Again," he tosses over his shoulder. It's true. I've redesigned our room, oh, a time or six since we've been together. But come on—we bought the house just before we got married, so we've lived here twelve years. He resisted the first time, saying the bedding was still good, the colors were "fine." I told him he was going to have to get used to being married to a designer, and convinced him there was no easier way to change the look of a room than a fresh coat of paint and some new fabrics. I've been lucky he always indulges me and even helps roll on the new paint.

"You wanna see?" I ask Cyn. She's never taken much interest in my work, except when I designed the boys' rooms for her as a housewarming present.

"Sure."

Spreading my sketch pad and project board on the dining room table, I show what I've got so far and explain what else is left to do.

"Barry's right. Your room would look great like this."

"If it were three times bigger."

"The color scheme, I mean. It's perfect for your house."

I won't be redoing our master suite, or any room in this house, until I get my business running smoothly, but Cyn doesn't need to know that. "For the moment, I'm still happy with the look we've got." I turn back to the kitchen, hoping she won't catch my bald-faced lie.

*

Cyn's gone and all three of my other roommates are napping. Usually I'd also be "napping" with Barry on a quiet Sunday afternoon, but with all the craziness around here, I still haven't finished my two designs for the Van Dierdons. I'm supposed to deliver them on Tuesday, so there's still some time. But these have to be perfect, so no rest for this weary designer.

My cell rings, and I snatch it up, paranoid that the slightest sound will wake the baby even though she's a room away.

"Alex, dear." The *dear* is stretched to two syllables, and right away I recognize the voice. "It's Mrs. Van Dierdon."

I'm surprised she's calling on a Sunday, and I scramble to come up with her first name, but then remember she never told me what it is. "Hello, Mrs. Van Dierdon. How are you?"

"I'm fabulous. Now, I know we talked about you submitting your design ideas to us on Tuesday, but I'm hoping you can bring them by tomorrow instead."

"Certainly." So easy to lie over the phone. "In fact, I'm putting the finishing touches on them right now." I'd like to stick to the original appointment, but I need to do everything I can to make this woman happy. Crap. Now I'm going to have to stay up late to get these finished. "Tomorrow would be fine."

"How's first thing? Say ten thirty?"

"Sure. That'd be perfect."

"Wonderful. You see, the other designer we've been talking to dropped her drawings by today." *Other designer?* I thought they were only considering my firm. "She was so enthusiastic! She called and said she knew we weren't expecting her design until Monday, but she was so excited about it that she couldn't wait to show us. And now that we've seen what she's come up with, we're excited to get moving too."

"Of course. I understand. It's no problem." *Crap!* Competition. "I'm very excited about what we've come up with as well. I think you'll love it."

"Excellent. Oh, by the way, the other designer, Beverly Caldwell, said she knows you. Well, I wasn't surprised. Santa Barbara is *such* a small town. Especially when you run in our circles. Don't you agree?" *I wish I ran in your circles, lady. I run rings around the outside of your circles.* But she's right; it is a small town. Ugh. Beverly. "Anyway, she told me you used to work for her." I wonder what the hell else she said. She was so pissed when Rache and I quit. Instantly erected a wall of ice between us. "She said if we like your design better, we really should thank *her*; she says she taught you everything you know." Mrs. Van Dierdon chuckles while I feel my hair begin to spontaneously combust.

Okay. Keep cool. Don't snap at the client.

I force out a chuckle of my own. It's so fake that anyone with half an ounce of empathy would recognize that. Luckily, Mrs. Van Dierdon is not that sort of person. "Oh, that Beverly. She always was a kidder."

"Yes, well. I'm glad that's all arranged. We'll see you tomorrow morning bright and early, at ten thirty."

I say good-bye and hang up while wondering if ten thirty qualifies as bright and early. Maybe for someone who lives Mrs. Van Dierdon's ladies-who-lunch lifestyle.

I look over my designs. As promised, I'm giving them two options to choose from: the red, yet peaceful, room they wanted, and a serene suite done in beautiful turquoise, pale sea foam, and sandy beach tones, with a few spots of coral to make things pop.

Personally, I prefer the beachy design, but I'm almost certain they'll pick the red room. I'm pleased with the solution I came up with, giving them everything they asked for. As they enter, there'll be a red accent wall, behind the massive custom-designed headboard. Every time they walk in, they'll see that burst of bright, bold color. But when they're lying in bed, they'll be facing fawn-colored walls. The headboard and bedding will be shades of ivory and sand, with accent pillows in burnt sienna, deep chocolaty browns, and vibrant reds. Rache found some fabrics with textures so rich that it's all going to look amazing. There'll be a few other red accents—the pillows on the chaise and a gorgeous bowl I found in a catalogue—but mostly, it will be soothing to the eye, with splashes of color here and there.

They have to love it. They have to. I can't even consider the alternative without feeling like my heart has switched places with Rachel's pincushion.

Eyes on the prize.

I visualize getting the job. A vision made so much sweeter when I picture Beverly losing out.

CHAPTER 13

I finish my yogurt and put the bowl on the floor for Marie to lick. I set Ruthie on the kitchen mat and call Marie over. Before she can start licking the bowl, I cup her furry chin in my hand and look into her deep-brown eyes. "Watch the baby for me, okay?" I say, hoping she'll somehow understand. I tousle the soft curls on both their heads, then jog to the guest bathroom to put on my mascara, hoping I can trust Ruthie not to get into anything during those sixty seconds. Or trust Marie to come tattle if she does. I don't trust either of them enough to chance taking the extra ninety seconds to cover the distance to my own bathroom. Fortunately, Barry stayed with the baby this morning while I showered and got mostly ready or I'd still be running around in a robe with dirty hair. (How do mothers get anything done?) But now that he's left for work, I'm anxious for Anna to get here. If only Marie could signal to me if the baby gets into something.

After harrumphing at all the products still plugged in on the counter (at least the chargers went to San Francisco with Wren), I apply my mascara, then take an extra few seconds to once more powder the dark circles under my eyes. Except for the baby, none of us slept much last night. Although Ruthie wasn't fussy, Marie and I kept raising our heads to check on her every time she made the slightest peep or murmur, and Barry, each of the three times he got up to go to the bathroom, would place a hand gently on her back. "Still breathing," he'd announce.

Please let us all sleep better tonight!

On my way back to the kitchen, I hear the sound of a ceramic bowl inching along hardwood—Marie must be licking the bowl pretty vigorously if she's moving it across the floor. I come around the counter to find Ruthie licking the bowl on her hands and knees, and Marie standing by, head cocked with a "Hey, wasn't that supposed to be for me?" expression.

At least Marie is not one to fight over food.

My hands go to my hips. "Ruthie. What are you doing?"

Grinning, she falls back onto her pudgy behind, her lips rimmed with pale pink strawberry yogurt. "Oggie." She chortles, apparently finding her impression of Marie terribly amusing. I have to agree; it is amusing. And darn cute. Hmm. Maybe that's the way to get her to eat her yogurt every morning. "Silly puppy." I smile and give her a good-doggy pat on the head while wondering if the dog licked the bowl first.

While I'm still standing over Ruthie, I feel her cheek and forehead. She seems perfectly normal. No fever, no ear rubbing, no fussiness. Hooray for the medicine, but still . . . if Wren had waited just one day . . .

My cell rings. It's Anna. I hope she's not running late. It's only quarter to eight, so I've still got plenty of time before I have to leave for the meeting, but I asked her to come early so that she could watch Ruthie while I finalized my pitch. I worked on the drawings all last night, but I still haven't perfected exactly what I want to say.

"I'm not going to be able to come to work." She sounds like a puny version of her usual bubbling-with-energy self. "I think I have the flu."

"You can't be sick. You're never sick." I start to feel sick myself.

"I know. I feel terrible, but I can't babysit the little one like this. I'm running a fever."

"I'm begging you, Anna, don't do this to me. Today of all days, I absolutely need you here." A sick day. She's never needed one before. This can't be happening. I beg her to come anyway, but she insists she's too contagious. "The baby can handle a small dose of the flu, right? You could wear a mask, couldn't you?"

"No, the baby can't get the flu. Not on top of her earache."

"Her earache seems completely under control."

"No, really, I cannot come." She promises she'll be well by her usually scheduled Monday next week, moans a last "sorry," adds a distressed "Ireallyhavetogonow," and hangs up before I can offer any more objections.

Crap!

A replacement. I've got to have a replacement. I put Ruthie in her high chair so that I can make phone calls. Cyn? No, Bobby's on half days at prekindergarten, and with the hour drive, there's no way she'd be back home in time to pick him up.

Rache! She doesn't have any work to do for me right now, so she can earn some of her pay by babysitting.

I try her cell, but get voice mail. "I desperately need you to watch Ruthie. Wren left her here with us, and—oh, it's too much to explain." I'd texted Rache last night, so she already knew the meeting had been moved up. She knew the whole long-lost-daughter-and-grandbaby situation too, since I'd poured out the story in telenovela installments at work every day last week. But she doesn't know Wren left us alone with the baby. "I'll tell you the whole thing when I talk to you. Anna was supposed to babysit, but she called in sick with the flu. Who the hell gets the flu in the summer? Call me back immediately. I'm begging you, please! You know how important this meeting is." I hang up and for good measure text: *CALL ME*, with about a dozen exclamation points.

I pray she'll call, and in the meantime try Barry. He doesn't usually answer his cell while he's working, so I call his office phone at the library. Thank heaven he answers. "I need you to come back home, like, now."

"Is it Ruthie? Oh my God, is she okay?"

"She's not going to be okay when I leave her here with Marie as her babysitter."

"What're you talking about?"

I tell him about Anna and how I have less than two hours to figure out a babysitting arrangement. "I can't screw up this meeting. I can't call these people and postpone. That'll make us seem unreliable, and then they'll pick that witch Beverly over me, and . . . They're not going to give me this job if I put them off. I've got to be there at ten thirty, so you've got plenty of time to get back here."

He swears he can't leave. Some "critical" meeting that he "can't possibly miss," but I'm only half listening to his reason for why the stupid thing is so damn important, something about more budget cuts. Whatever. *This* is urgent.

"Barry, she's *your* grandkid. You need to fix this. I need you to either come home right now or come up with a solution."

"I'm sorry, Alex, but I absolutely cannot come home. Can't you get Rache to help out? She works for you, after all."

"I tried Rache. She's not answering."

"Maybe she'll still call you back. And if not, well, you'll have to take Ruthie with you," he suggests.

"Take her with me? Take a baby to a client meeting?" I let out an angry, maniacal laugh.

"Maybe they like babies. Babies and dogs sell."

"So you're suggesting I take Marie as well? Thanks for helping out." I hang up as I hear him saying something else into the phone. *Please, God, let Rache call back in time.*

Ruthie starts to cry from her high chair, but I don't have time to deal. I've got my citron-colored silk tank top on, with my robe over it. I haven't picked out a skirt or shoes yet. I thought I'd have time to do that after Anna arrived. "I'm coming, Ruthie! I swear," I yell, although I run the opposite direction. Marie seems to think that chasing after me looks fun, so she also runs away from the screaming baby. "No, Marie," I stop and point. "Go see Ruthie!" Marie does a "what was I thinking?" double take and runs back to the baby. Thank heaven I hear Ruthie giggle—Marie to the rescue!—as I run to my closet while praying Rachel will call.

*

I always endeavor to be ready for the worst-case scenario. It helps when planning a major decorating project to assume some sort of mess will set you back in terms of both budget and timeline. Like our recent job at the Banisters'. The plan called for built-in bookcases in the master suite. When the existing shelving was torn out, we found mold damage in the wall shared with the en suite bath. Luckily, I'd padded a few extra days into the project plan, and although we were overbudget with the necessary fixes to both rooms, we still came in on time.

So now, planning for the worst—that I'm alone in this—I figure I'll use part of these two hours to take Ruthie to the park. If we go for thirty minutes or so, it'll wear her out. A tired puppy is a good puppy, and I'm hoping the same applies to babies—as long as I don't overtire her, I guess. I need her to be mellow if I do end up dragging her along. Thirty minutes will still give me plenty of time to come home, freshen up, and change into my work clothes.

The bonus is that Ruthie can't damage anything at the park. Well, not anything *I* own anyway. Maybe a plant or two will suffer.

Once there, Marie wants to pull me along at our usual quickstep pace and check for new smells since our last visit, while Ruthie wants to toddle along at her stop-and-smell-the-roses-and-then-put-the-roses-in-your-mouth pace. I pull with my left hand on Marie's leash, trying to slow her down, and drag Ruthie along with my right, trying to speed her up. Frustration levels escalate for all three of us. Not to mention the fact I'm getting a kink in my back from leaning down to hold Ruthie's hand.

I give up and let Marie loose. It's not technically an off-leash park, but she'll come right back to me if I call her. I keep an eye on her so that she won't stray too far into the bushes and out of sight. She trots along, leaving no leaf unsniffed, while Ruthie and I resume our stop-start pace. As a test, I call Marie, and she trots back. I pat her fluffy head and release her again, confident that at least my furry angel won't get into trouble.

After about five minutes of walking like Quasimodo so that I can keep hold of Ruthie's hand, I'm relieved when Ruthie decides she's a big girl and can totter on her own. She flails free of my grasp, and I'm happy to let her go so that I can stretch my back. I saunter toward the swing set, and she follows. I call for Marie, who trots along behind, then stops at the edge of the sandy play area and begins inspecting the perimeter.

While Ruthie explores, I run over my pitch in my head. We spend a few minutes on the swings, then she's off to the metal rocking horses. I help her get her skinny leg up and over the thing, and she rides like Annie Oakley for about three minutes before the thrill wears off. Next she points at the slide. It's a short slide, so I hold her hand the whole way up the stairs, hang on to her at the top, and help her fly down. The first attempt brings peals of laughter. The second time, she smiles. But her third time at the top, she notices some older boys kicking a soccer ball around on the grass.

"Ball, ball." She freezes, squatting at the top of the slide, and points with her whole arm, giving me an imploring look.

"We didn't bring a ball, Ruthie. We've got all these other fun things in the playground." The swath I cut with my free hand takes in the swings, the rocking horses, and a miniature climbing rock, but she's uninterested.

"Ball!" Ruthie shrieks. She emits her usual stressed "eh, eh!" sounds and tries to pull out of my grasp.

A mother swinging her little boy stares. I smile and mouth a sheepish "hi," then turn back to Ruthie, whose wrist I'm clutching with an eagle grip. I picture myself trying to explain to Barry and Wren how Ruthie managed to fall down the slide. Meanwhile, an older girl, maybe six or eleven (who knows?) has skipped to the bottom of the stairs and stands waiting her turn.

"Okay, we'll get you a ball." Hopefully, with her short attention span, she'll forget about the ball if I can distract her for a minute or two. "But you need to sit and come down the slide. Okay?" Ruthie wriggles and squirms. She's trying to stand, while I try to pull her into a sitting position. It's possible I'm hurting her wrist, but there's no way I'm letting her loose six feet off the ground in what looks to be the early stages of a tantrum.

"Can I have a turn?" the waiting girl whines.

"Aren't you kind of big for this? Wouldn't you prefer the jungle gym?" I thrust my chin toward the iron bars at the other end of the playground. "This slide's for tiny kids."

She turns toward a woman bent over her phone on a bench. "Mom! This lady said I can't play on the slide."

The woman looks up, apparently wondering who is daring to cross her darling. She marches toward us.

"Sorry, no, I didn't say that. A misunderstanding." She keeps advancing. Ruthie continues to wiggle and "eh!"

"Ruthie, please. Come on!" She ignores me. I remember what the training books said when we first got Marie. Simple one-word commands. "Sit!" I say with as much "I'm the boss" authority as I can muster. She sits. "Good job!" I help her down the slide, scoop her up, and begin our retreat as the woman reaches her daughter.

"Slide's all yours." I try to sound friendly. I smile broadly.

Ruthie points at the boys playing soccer again. "Ball."

"Oh all right; we'll head over there. And then we should get going." I'm hoping Ruthie will be happy watching the boys play for a few minutes. I look around for Marie. I'd lost track of her while trying to keep Ruthie from falling off the slide. I spot her at the far end of the park, heading toward a couple stretched out on a picnic blanket. They're so busy staring into each other's eyes that they completely ignore the remains of their picnic lunch. Marie, however, follows her nose straight toward what looks like a large chunk of Subway sandwich.

"Marie, no!" I yell, as I scoop Ruthie up in my arms and start to run. But it's too late. At this distance, I can't compete with turkey and cheese, or whatever other delicacies beckon. Marie darts at the sandwich, and in the flash of a few inhalations, it's gone.

The couple rolls over. "What the . . . ?" the man says as we come closer.

I yell apologies, and Ruthie hollers and points as we run toward and then past the ball she thought she was about to get her hands on. Running with her is awkward. I set her down; I'm almost to Marie now anyway.

"I'm so sorry!" Marie snuffles for crumbs at the empty wrapper. The couple laughs.

"It's okay. We were done," the young man says.

"But still, Marie!" I scold her, and she draws her head into her shoulders. "Naughty girl. She's normally good about coming when I call her. But . . . was that turkey? It's her favorite."

"Yep, with provolone. Really, it's okay." The girl pats Marie's hanging head. "We were going to throw the rest away. She's so cute, you can't be mad at her. What kind of dog—" She stops petting Marie and points. "Your baby's tearing off in the other direction."

I spin around and see Ruthie heading into the middle of the soccer game as fast as her uncoordinated legs will carry her. "Oh hell. Sorry, again. Marie, come!" I take off after Ruthie, shouting "Sorry!" to the boys and waving my arms at them. "Mind the baby!"

Fighting for the ball, the boys are oblivious to the tiny tyke about to enter in the midst of their kicking legs. I scream, "No!" at Ruthie, but she either doesn't hear or ignores me. As two of the players clash, the ball shoots off to the left. "Excuse me," I yell. "Baby coming through!"

I swoop in and grab her as the teenagers come to a confused halt. They all stop, turn, and stare.

I gasp out another apology. I've got the baby in my left arm, and catch hold of Marie's collar with my right hand. I hustle them over to a bench to catch my breath and put Marie's leash on her.

"Okay." I sit Ruthie on the bench. "You two are a handful." She ignores me, engrossed in picking the peeling green paint. Marie grins, hot and happy after her romp and ill-gotten sandwich gains. "I don't know about you two, but I'm exhausted. Auntie Alex is now a stinky mess," I say in a happy voice as I waggle my finger in front of Ruthie's nose. "Auntie Alex is going to need to take a birdbath. So you ready to go home?" Ruthie shakes her head. I remember what I'd learned earlier and try it again. "Ruthie, home!" She looks up at me, apparently surprised by my curt tone after the happy-happy voice I'd been using before. I hope I'm on to something, but am fully aware it's probably too good to last.

I stand and help her off the bench. Quasimodo returns as we clomp toward the car, leash in my left hand and hot little mitt in my right. It hits me there's an easier way. I unhook the leash from Marie's collar; attach it instead to the clasp on Ruthie's overalls, and we're off again. At least Marie is tall enough that I can hang on to her collar while standing straight. I hustle them both along, head down. I don't even dare glance toward the playground because I can feel both mothers, still there with their kids, giving me the stink-eye.

*

Egad. A peek in the bathroom mirror shows crazy-lady hair, circles under my eyes, and a shiny face. At least I'm mostly cooled down from blasting the air-conditioning in the car on the way home. I peel off my T-shirt and shorts and take a quick birdbath at the sink, splashing some cold water on myself. Once my makeup is touched up, I grab the blouse I had on earlier, when I thought I was in the clear to get ready for work.

Oh no, not now. A pale violet blotch from this morning's yogurt skirmish mars the front of the blouse. I don't have time for this! Ruthie refused to eat the blueberry flavor, screaming "Ink! Ink!" until I gave in and traded her for the pink strawberry yogurt. God, dogs are so much easier. Marie eats whatever I put in front of her, even though it's the same damn thing, day in and day out. And she loves it! Of course, Ruthie wants to eat the same damn thing day in and day out too: pink yogurt. So maybe that's where we're going wrong.

I yank my blouse off, making my hair crazier. I decide to go with it, fluffing it to the max, then spraying it like crazy. I hope they'll think I'm going for that 1960s bombshell look, although the look calls out for a perfect cat-eye, which I don't have time for because I plan to use the last ten minutes before we leave for a little something else I've got in mind. I grab my aquamarine blouse (and my liquid eyeliner—in case I hit a long red light). The tiny mother-of-pearl buttons fight me as I run down the hall.

"I'm back!" I run past where I left Ruthie in her high chair with a frozen Go-Gurt. (Pink, of course.) I figured she needed to cool down too, and a snack is in order since I don't want a hungry baby screaming during our meeting. I dash to the kitchen, knowing Ruthie's too messy to pick up out of her chair. I am *not* getting yogurt on my favorite top. I wet a kitchen towel and give her a thorough wipe down, then pull out one of the turkey hot dogs we use for Marie's "high-value" training treats and dice a hunk into small pieces.

"Who wants to do something fun?" I address both Ruthie and Marie. The success with the one-word commands at the park gave me an idea, and we've got a few more minutes before we have to leave. Just enough time for a training session.

I carry Ruthie into the living room and have her stand, holding on to the edge of the sheet-covered sofa. Marie follows along, sniffing at the hot dog.

"Okay, doggies, sit!" I say, using the accompanying hand signal. Marie sits, since she knows the drill. Ruthie looks at Marie, then me. I take her hand and repeat, "Sit!" She plops down next to Marie, and I praise them both and dole out hot-dog bites.

"Okay, this is a tough one . . . Ready?" I hold out my palm flat toward them, like a stop sign from a crossing guard. "Stay!" I walk quickly around the corner into the kitchen. I wait a few seconds, then return. They're both in the exact same spots. "Good doggies!" More hot-dog bites all around.

"We've only got enough time to try this one more time. I hope you're a quick study, Ruthie." I help Ruthie to stand and run them through the signals one more time. Ruthie does great, but it's possible she's only mimicking Marie. Oh well, a little practice is better than none.

"Hooray! You're so smart!" I applaud and Ruthie joins in. "We're going on an adventure! Who's going to be the best baby ever?" I talk in my excite-the-dog voice, hoping it works on babies as well. If I have no choice but to bring her along; she'd better be in a good mood. If she melts down into one of her fits, piercing the quiet of the Van Dierdon mausoleum, I won't have Marie there to put an end to it, and they'll shove us right back out the door. For this to work, she has to be sweet, adorable Ruthie. Super crab-head Ruthie must not make an appearance! Dang, I wish I could bring Marie. She definitely wants to come, bouncing along after us (my excite-the-dog voice really works), but no.

I toss her the last of the hot-dog bits, and although she looks disappointed, she retreats to make sure she's found every piece.

Ruthie's in the cutest of her Goth-baby looks—a black jumper trimmed with what looks like burgundy ladybug fabric and only reveals itself to be skulls if you look *very* closely. And I was smart enough to put a big bib over it while she was eating her Go-Gurt. As I hook her into her car seat, I say, still in my happy voice, "I hope you aren't too sticky." Although it's taking every ounce of energy not to use my bitchy, stressed-out voice, I continue using my perkiest tone. "Don't touch Auntie Alex's leather interior! Or she'll turn into T-Rex!"

Ruthie grins and points at me. "Tee Lexsch!"

At least Barry helped me install her car seat last night, when the three of us went out for frozen yogurt. (Sugar-free, of course. It mostly went okay, except for the Sca-Ream-Ing while she waited for her treat. Mortifying. I swear I will never again make judgy eyes at people in stores with tantrumming toddlers.) The car survived unscathed because Barry sat in the back with her, singing for her entertainment and making sure she didn't touch anything. Now I wonder why I didn't line the backseat with plastic tablecloths as I did in the dining room. Must do that later. I give her hair a fluff, spit-wipe a missed spot on her dimpled cheek, and we're off.

On the way, I manage to whip out my liner and pull off a pretty good cat-eye at an extra-long light. I also make up a song, crooning for Ruthie since (next to Marie) singing seems to bring out the best in her. "I hope you like the design I've made, with the headboard covered in silk brocade. It's a serene and peaceful oasis for you both, with your big-toothed faces," I sing, while occasionally making eye contact with Ruthie in the rearview mirror.

We pull into the Van Dierdons' sweeping driveway. One of three garage doors (designed to look like stable doors) is open, revealing what must be Mrs. Van Dierdon's S-Class Mercedes. I know it's hers because the license plate reads "SIZDEUX."

Size two. Shoot me now. I make gagging sounds and roll my eyes, while Ruthie laughs. "Can you believe her?" I ask Ruthie. I wonder if ladies larger than a size six ever fantasize about rear-ending her. As a member of that group, I'd venture to say yes.

I park in the shade of the huge eucalyptus tree branching over their driveway. What if I leave the windows down? Nobody's going to snatch her out of the car. And . . . *No, no, no, no, no! I am not leaving the baby in the car. Not even if I'd only be inside for two minutes. It's July, for Pete's sake. I won't leave Marie in the car at all in the summer, and there's no way I would consider leaving Ruthie either. You are a bad, bad devil.* I almost cast a withering glance at my shoulder, I'm so sure there's a wee pointy-bearded, soul-stealing fiend seated there.

Barry, this is all your fault, I silently curse him. *And it's your fault in more ways than one. If you'd kept it in your pants, we'd be going about our usual happy routine. Or if you'd come home this morning like I begged you to, I wouldn't be sitting here tempted to leave the baby in the car.* I squeeze the steering wheel in frustration.

Ruthie burbles in the backseat, and I blink a few times, then close my eyes for a second to regroup.

My teeth still grind, but I need to shake it off before going in to see Mrs. SIZDEUX. I try to get into my "aren't you two adorable?" mode. At least Ruthie's in a lovely mood. She's babbling along with my grousing and blowing bubbles out her perfect bow-shaped lips. If the Van Dierdons like babies (*oh please, oh please, oh please*), then they won't be able to resist her. And they'll think I'm a good person too, no? For helping out during this family emergency. That'll win points for our team, right? Then again . . . if they don't like babies, I'm screwed. Even if Ruthie is pulling maximum cuteness ratings at the moment.

On their porch, I can't decide if I should hold the baby or hide her behind one of the giant potted junipers on either side of the double doors. I decide to set her down and see if she'll stand behind me for a minute, so they don't notice her first thing.

Her hands are cold and slightly sticky on the back of my leg. I plaster a smile on my face and ring the bell. I'm worried about Ruthie remaining upright and quiet for as long as it will take them to cross their acreage of hardwood floors to get to the door.

Please, God, I pray, although I'm probably not in good standing. *Let this go well!*

CHAPTER 14

After what feels like an eternity, Mrs. Van Dierdon's smooth, smiling, perfect face appears, welcoming me in. "You're right on time, and I can't tell you how excited we are to see what you've got for us!" She glances at my portfolio while extending a skinny arm to signal I should enter.

I hold up my hand. I can't just walk in; I'm either going to have to lead Ruthie in by the hand (a move fraught with the potential for resistance and frustration and tears—possibly on both our parts) or pick her up. It's safest to pick her up, but before I do, I decide it's best to first explain her presence. Mrs. Van Dierdon follows my glance down to Ruthie, who chooses this moment to release my leg and topple backward onto her padded behind.

"Oh!" Ruthie and Mrs. Van Dierdon emit the word in unison.

"Why, Alex, you didn't tell me you have a baby." Mrs. Van Dierdon rushes forward, batting me out of the way, and scoops Ruthie up. Mrs. Van Dierdon is wearing an all-white (*size two, I'm sure!*) ensemble: crisp and polished cotton capris, a tank top with a sheer diaphanous blouse over it, and a chunky necklace. The look shows off her tanned skin and silver hair. The perfect shade of ruby lipstick completes the outfit.

I offer up another prayer: *Please don't let there be any spots of yogurt I missed on the baby! And please don't let her upchuck on what has got to be a ridiculously expensive outfit!*

"Actually, I—"

"She's adorable!" She whisks the baby inside, jouncing Ruthie on her hip and nonsensically babbling to her. "Who's a woodgy woodgy widdle woo?"

"Did I hear the bell?" Mr. Van Dierdon comes into the foyer, also dressed in summer whites. With his trim Bermuda shorts, loose linen shirt, and Top-Siders, the two look like an ad for the Santa Barbara tourism board. Or maybe for Viagra. He stops short at the sight of Ruthie in his wife's scrawny arms, then lets out a gasp and snatches Ruthie away, not even asking who she is. Scurrying toward the living room with her, he picks up where his wife's babbling left off.

Mrs. Van Dierdon trots after him. "I had her first, Bunny!"

"She's mine now, Kitten," he calls over his shoulder. Bunny and Kitten? At least it's an improvement over Tiger and Lioness.

As I shut the massive front door and follow along behind, I can't help but smile. Maybe Ruthie will help us land this job after all!

In the living room, they sit on the sofa, Ruthie on Mr. Van Dierdon's knee, and fire questions at me: "How old is she?" "Does she know a lot of words?" "Does she like *Arthur*?" I don't even understand that last one (*Arthur who?*), so I simply say yes. Ruthie watches us converse and laughs. She flaps her arms, and they both clap with delight. *Go, Ruthie! Flap, little girl, flap!*

Finally, I get around to explaining she's not my baby. Not wanting to sound like we live in a soap opera, I gloss over details, simply saying she's my husband's granddaughter, and that we're babysitting for a while.

"I'm so sorry to bring her along like this; I would never normally bring a baby along to a professional meeting." In fact, I would pretty much never bring a baby anywhere. "But there was a family emergency."

"Nonsense," Mr. Van Dierdon says, and his wife adds, "We're delighted to have a little one here." They're so enamored with Ruthie it makes me wonder if either of them has children from prior marriages. I look for displayed photos of kids, grandchildren, something I might have missed on my previous visit, but no, it's all black-and-white shots of the happy couple. Or the pensive couple. Or the romantic couple. Stylized photos of them walking on the beach—*the* perfect shot for the tourism board—or gazing at one another seated beneath a willow tree. Judging by their home, I wouldn't have picked them as child-loving types, but I'm oh-so-grateful that they are.

Ruthie begins to fuss, and I realize the giant army-green purse Wren left us to use as a diaper bag still sits, forgotten, at home. How could I be so stupid? One thing dogs and babies have in common is their need for poop patrol, and I always have spare plastic bags when I take Marie out. How could I forget something so fundamental for Ruthie? *Poop. Please don't let her poop!*

Mr. Van Dierdon bounces Ruthie a few more times on his knee while his wife tickles Ruthie's chin. No luck; she squirms and tries to pull away. Mr. Van Dierdon hoists her from his knee and moves her to the white buttery-leather sofa. "Maybe you'll be happier here," he says, tucking her up against the gorgeous silver-gray silk throw pillows.

Please, Lord, do not let her be wet. I'm pretty sure that couch is a Poltrona Frau, which means it probably cost more than Barry's truck. Ruthie makes a "you're all beginning to annoy me" sound and smacks herself in the face. Fingers located, she stuffs several of them into her mouth.

I may not have the diaper bag, but I have car keys! I dig in my purse, hoping my keys will make a decent replacement for Ruthie's purple plastic set. I've got to entice her off that sofa.

"Here, Ruthie!" I jingle the keys in front of her, and she clutches them. I grab hold of her and set her on the area rug. Thank heaven, the spot she vacated looks dry.

We talk about Ruthie for a few more minutes. Their perfect silver heads track her every move. My portfolio seems forgotten, although not by me. I've got to get Ruthie out of here while she's still charming. And dry.

"Well." I pick up my portfolio and set it across my lap. "Are you ready to see what we've come up with?"

The couple turns back to me, and Mrs. Van Dierdon claps her hands, her rings clacking together. "Oh yes! Let's see!"

Mr. Van Dierdon suggests we go into the dining room so that I can spread my design boards out, and we stand. I'm not sure about leaving Ruthie behind, and hesitate. "Maybe we should—"

"She'll be fine. She can see us from here," Mrs. Van Dierdon extends her arms, taking in the huge room spread before us and the dining area, with seating for ten, across the way. Yes, if her vision is good, she can see us. "She'll be fine," she repeats.

They seem to know babies, way more than I do anyway, so I trust their judgment and figure it'll be okay to leave Ruthie. She's jangling my keys and occasionally sticking the leather fob with the silver BMW logo into her mouth. *Eeesh.* At least she's quiet and happy. I decide not to take any chances and leave her my cell phone as an additional toy. It's turned off, so there's no way she'll be dialing South Korea or texting weird messages to Barry. "After you," I say, and let them go ahead of me. I hiss, "Stay," then quickly give Ruthie the *stop* hand signal. Hopefully, she'll comply without Marie here to show her the way.

The Van Dierdons sit on the far side of the table, and I take the chair opposite. One more glance at Ruthie reassures me she's holding her stay, so I sit and unzip my portfolio. I can only see the top of her curls over an ottoman, but the jingle of my keys tells me she's still occupied.

"Oh," they say—again, in unison—as I pull my first color sketch out. It's not the same delighted "Oh" Ruthie elicited, however. *Uh-oh.* I keep going and pull out the project board, covered with fabric samples and paint colors. "Huh," Mrs. Van Dierdon says. These are not the most enthusiastic sounds I've heard from them this morning, but they still haven't seen the full plan.

Undaunted, I prop the sketch up with my left hand. "This," I say with a flourish of my right hand, "is your new master suite." I wait. They study the sketch, their eyes scanning the drawing, taking it in. No reaction passes across their placid faces. But maybe with all that Botox, their faces can't show much expression.

I look once more to check that Ruthie's head hasn't moved, then dive in to my presentation. "I think we've managed to capture all the elements we discussed in our previous meeting. Now, I know you mentioned wanting a red room, so this accent wall behind the headboard will give you that dramatic pop of color as you enter. We pick up the red again in the accent pillows on the chaise lounge and in touches here and here on the built-in shelving." As I talk, I encourage them to run their fingertips across the samples. Rachel found some fabulous fabrics, including a subtle floral print for the chaise lounge with the tropical resort feel they requested.

As I continue talking and pointing out details, they slowly nod. They're seeing it come to life! I've worked every last one of the things they wanted into this design. They have to see it's exactly what they asked for. Of course, maybe they're beginning to realize they asked for a bit too much . . .

Luckily, I've got a backup plan. "Now, as I mentioned I would, I put together a second design with a beachscape theme." I pull out the other board. "As you can see," I say while handing them each some fabric samples to fondle, "it's the same layout, but we've replaced the reds with turquoise and this pale-sea-foam-blue shade. This room would be a perfect complement to that amazing ocean view you have from your master bedroom."

The hint of a smile begins to play across Mrs. Van Dierdon's perfect satin-red lips.

Ohmygod, she might actually like it. She might realize I was right in steering them away from the red idea. Hmm, I wonder if Beverly gave them only a red room. Damn, I'd love to see her drawings. A discreet glance around for any possible project boards leaning against a wall or on a credenza turns up nada.

Mrs. Van Dierdon has begun to make happy "oh" sounds as she goes through the fabric selections for the seaside room. She takes a square of turquoise velvet and strokes it against her husband's cheek, playfully bumping him with her shoulder. "What do you think, Bunny?"

"Kitten, you know I'm happy with whatever makes you happy."

Oh, please, let her be happy. Is that purring I hear?

I hold my breath, waiting for her to say something, when a clatter breaks the silence. It is quickly followed by a clunk and the unmistakable hailstorm crash of breaking glass. Ruthie lets out a distressed, ear-shriveling scream and starts to bawl.

We leap from our chairs. For a split second, I can't see Ruthie's head, although I can still hear her crying, so I know she's alive.

I beat the couple to the living room and find Ruthie in a heap on the floor. It looks like she tried to scale the built-in shelves, and judging by the fact that my cell phone now rests in the midst of a mosaic of broken glass, I'm guessing she got frustrated with her efforts and instead chucked my phone at the vase that used to stand alone on the center shelf.

Please don't let it be a priceless vase.

The Van Dierdons are again in unison. "Oh. Oh. Oh" is all they manage; each "Oh" slower and sadder than the previous one, like wind-up toys running out of juice. "Bunny" stands with his mouth hanging open, while "Kitten" collapses into the nearby armchair, with one final "Oh."

"Ruthie!" In the commotion, I forget the "don't say no to the baby" rule. "No!" I yell. I'd like to think I yell because she's scooting toward the broken glass, but I'm frustrated she's wreaking havoc, right when I thought Mrs. Van Dierdon was about to say she liked the design.

Ruthie looks at me as if she's lost every living relative, every stuffed toy, every last bit of comfort she ever had in the world. Clearly, she's not used to being told no. Or yelled at. Her eyes widen and she trembles, recoiling as if I'm the most horrifying thing she's ever seen. She points at me and lets out the longest, loudest wail I've heard from her. "Waaaaaaaa!"

Mr. Van Dierdon turns on me. "Don't scold the baby! This is your fault. You should have been keeping an eye on her."

But . . . Mrs. Van Dierdon was the one who said she'd be fine. I want to scream in frustration. Why did I listen to this woman? I knew I should have brought Ruthie into the dining room with us.

"I wasn't scolding her; I was afraid she'd hurt herself," I try to explain myself as a woman, whom I presume to be their housekeeper, bustles into the room—a plump lady in a periwinkle uniform with gray braids twisted on top of her head. Where was this motherly looking soul when I needed someone to watch the baby while we talked business? *Now* she appears?

She sees the baby crying and the rest of us gaping like useless mannequins and springs to scoop Ruthie away from the broken glass.

"Sweet pea, what happened?" she coos as Ruthie buries her beet-red face in the neck of this total stranger. Ruthie hates me. The Van Dierdons hate me. Fantastic. The woman switches Ruthie to her other arm and scrunches her nose. "Whew. She needs changing. I'll do that, then come back with the vacuum." She looks at me. "Diaper bag?"

"I, uh, I forgot it." They all look at me like I'm an idiot. "It was a bit of a last-minute thing that she ended up coming along."

"I'll think of something." The housekeeper turns on her heel.

Mrs. Van Dierdon looks like a silver-haired Raggedy Ann doll in the armchair; her arms hang limp at her sides, her unblinking eyes stare at the empty shelf where the vase had been.

"Oh, Kitten." Mr. Van Dierdon crouches beside her chair and rests his hand on her shoulder. I'm hoping he'll say something like, "It's no big deal. We can get another one." But he says nothing more.

"I'm so sorry," I start. My first instinct is to say, "Of course, I'll pay to have the vase replaced," but I wonder how much money we're talking about here. I've never dealt with anything like this before. Oh, we've had minor things happen in other homes—a picture frame fell, a wall got scratched—but we've never damaged anything beyond an easy fix. I take a deep breath. Okay, this is what business insurance is for. "Please don't worry about a thing," I manage to say with something like confidence. "I can have it replaced."

"No," Mrs. Van Dierdon says. "You can't."

"Perhaps I could—"

"No, there's nothing you can do." She blinks. "My grandfather made that vase. He was a glassblower in Venice. It was a one-of-a-kind wedding present for my mother. She passed it down to me."

Oh my God. Who displays something with that much sentimental value on an open shelving unit? This is why God made display cabinets with actual doors on them.

Shit.

I don't know what to say. I lick my lips, certain my lipstick has worn off by now, and swallow. The confidence I'd mustered earlier deserts me. "Is there anything I can do, any way at all that I can make it up to you?" My voice sounds small, incongruous with my hulking figure, towering over them while they huddle at the armchair.

Mr. Van Dierdon stands and says, "It's best if you leave."

"Of course. Let me get my portfolio." Maybe there's still some slim hope they'll hire us. If they love the design, they might overlook today's madness. I zip up my portfolio, leaving the samples and project boards on the table.

"You can take those as well." Mrs. Van Dierdon has followed me on her silent kitten feet into the dining area. She waves dismissively at my work.

"Of course." I scoop everything under my arm, desperately wanting to be out of here. So much for the slim hope we might still get the job.

I grab my purse, slink toward the front door, and reach for the knob.

"Aren't you forgetting something?" Mrs. Van Dierdon says in an arch tone. I turn as the housekeeper reappears; Ruthie toddles along, clutching her hand, happily gnawing on a dinner roll. What appears to be a dish-towel-turned-cloth-diaper protrudes from under her black jumper.

"I didn't forget her," I say. Okay, I'm an idiot, but I'm not *that* much of an idiot. I wouldn't have driven off without the baby. "I was going to load my things in the car and come back." I shift my purse to my other arm, already overloaded with my portfolio and the useless crap for this stupid project, march over, and take Ruthie's hand.

Please don't let her scream. "Let's go home, Roo," I say in a feeble imitation of my get-the-dog-excited voice.

Mercifully, we both keep it together.

I load Ruthie in the car, and we drive home in silence. She falls asleep, while I wonder if they're going to want that kitchen towel back. It's probably the Mercedes-Benz of kitchen towels.

CHAPTER 15

We get home, and I shift sleeping Ruthie from the car to the bed. I barricade her in with stuffed toys, then lie down on the floor with Marie. She seems to understand my mood, and she tones down her usual crazy kisses to sweet, tender ones instead. She bats at my arm with her gentle paws, and I snuggle into her and try not to cry. Finally, I get up and turn on my phone.

A half-dozen texts from Rachel sit waiting for me. She's so sorry she couldn't watch Ruthie; she was at the office finishing the curtains for the women's shelter. She didn't realize her phone had fallen out of her purse and was back in the car until it was too late to reach me. She sends good luck. She wants to know how the meeting went. The final message says she assumes the fact she hasn't heard back from me is good news.

Um, no.

God, I never thought to try calling the office phone. She told me she was going to finish the curtains Tuesday while I was meeting with the Van Dierdons. When the meeting got moved to Monday, I was just so stressed about the meeting going well, I didn't stop to think she'd move up her timeline as well.

Now I understand the phrase "no good deed goes unpunished."

I don't know how I'm going to tell her we aren't getting this job. I wonder if she'll accept Beverly's offer. Probably. Whatever I say, I have to stay upbeat so that I can convince her not to leave me. I take a deep breath, let it out, and call her.

"Hey!" She answers on the first ring. "How'd it go?"

"They seemed to like the beachy design." Might as well start with some good news.

"Great. When do you think we'll hear back?" I hadn't told Rache that Beverly was also in the running. I thought it might freak her out, but I did text her that there was another designer in the mix. "Hey, what happened with Ruthie? You must have got somebody to watch her, yeah?"

"No, I didn't. I had to take her along."

"Oh, dear. How'd that go?"

"It started out great, actually, but . . . look, I think they liked our take on their master suite, but I doubt we'll get the job." I leave unsaid that we wouldn't get it if we were the last firm in town. "There was a bit of a mishap with the baby, and they were pretty pissed when I left."

"What the heck happened?"

"I'm too tired to go into it right now. Let's just say I may have to put in a call to our insurance company."

"Holy cow, did she burn the place down?"

"No, she broke a vase. Probably a priceless vase. The whole thing was completely eight-forty-three'd."

"What?"

"Oh, sorry. It's something Wren says so we don't swear in front of the baby. It means totally eff'd up." I'm swept under by a wave of exhaustion. I want to hang up and crawl in bed. "Look, just because we're not getting this job doesn't mean you have to go back to Beverly."

"Ugh. Beverly."

"Have you heard from her again?"

"Yes. She's called me three times. I told her we were about to land a big job."

"You didn't tell her where, did you?"

"No, I wouldn't do that. I mean, I said Montecito, but I didn't name names. Anyway, she's been pretty relentless. But after the last call she said she'd wait. That I'd be calling her."

"That total nine-seventeen."

"I can guess what that means. I don't want to call her. Is there any chance at all we could still get the job?"

I can't paint this as a rosy picture. "There's no way. We'd have a better chance of being asked to redo the Sistine Chapel. But I'll find us something else. Don't give up on me yet. I can afford to pay you until the end of this month, and by then—"

"But will you be able to afford to pay yourself too? I don't want to be on the payroll with no work to do. It's not right, and it's not fair to you. I should bite the bullet and go back to Beverly. She said they're busy right now. I don't know how in this economy, but they are. She said I could work overtime if I want to make some extra money."

I can't compete with that. "I don't want to lose you, Rache."

"I know. And, believe me, I'd rather work with you than Beverly a million times over. But I've got bills piling up, and Mason is totally unreliable with Kaitlin's child support, so I need steady income. If it was only me, I'd eat ramen noodles and cancel my cable and move to a smaller place until we could get things going again, but I can't do that. I've got to put Kaitlin's needs ahead of my own."

"Even if it means crushing your spirit?"

"You're not making this any easier."

"I'm sorry. You're a good mom. And the best upholsterer in town. You're too good for Beverly. I'm going to keep this business going, you'll see. And one of these days, I'm going to walk into Beverly's sweatshop and scoop you out of there. It's going to be very *An Officer and a Gentleman.* The rest of the schmucks who still work for her will cheer while I carry you out."

Rache laughs, but her chuckles slowly give way to tears. "Holy cow, I'm going to miss you. I hate quitting. I feel like a rat abandoning ship."

"The captain and this ship are not going down. I'll keep this thing afloat. Somehow." I *have* to keep it afloat. Shit. "You do what you've got to do, but someday we'll work together again. Deal?" I pray what I'm saying is true. At this point, I'm not sure if I'm trying to convince her or myself.

"Deal. I love you, Alex. I'm so, so sorry I can't stick this out with you. I hope you don't feel like I'm letting you down."

"God, no. I love you too. And I feel like I'm letting *you* down. I'm the one who talked you into leaving Beverly in the first place."

"No, you didn't let me down. It was good to get out of there for a while. To see how it can be to work somewhere fun."

"All right, look, I've got to go. Ruthie's napping, and I should check on her. We'll talk soon."

"Really soon, I hope."

You and me both. Because if I don't turn this around, I'm doomed.

*

Tuesday morning, though I have no reason to go to the office, I'm up early. Barry has to leave for work, so that means I'm on baby duty. Again. Barry swore he'd only be gone for the morning, so I'm on my own for at least the next few hours. He owes me. Big-time. This is his grandbaby, after all.

I'm not up for cleaning yogurt off everything, so instead I opt for the simpler bowl of white-devil-free faux-Cheerios. Dry. Cleanup will be easy-peasy since Marie sits next to her, catching dropped O's, and

Ruthie plows through them once she invents the game of One for Me, One for the Dog.

While pouring more coffee, I think how I can't wait for Barry to get home. I begged him not to leave this morning. After yesterday, I told him I was *not* in the mood to deal with *his* grandbaby. But he said he couldn't miss yet another "crucial" meeting, and he promised to be home in time for lunch. I'm not up for reading every one of Ruthie's books to her again, and I have no idea what to do to entertain her next. (Sadly, a stack of baby DVDs did not come along in that car full of crap Wren and Barry schlepped into the house. Why can't Wren be like other mothers and plug her kid into the TV? How did we end up living with the only teenager in the world who's not hooked on electronic entertainment?)

Feeling rebellious, I find a cartoon channel and plop Ruthie down in front of a show with surfing tigers. I leave her stacking puzzle nearby for added distraction. Marie lies down next to her, and I wish dogs made better babysitters. After yesterday's fiasco and another try-not-to-roll-over-and-crush-the-baby night in bed, I'm even more exhausted and want to go back to sleep, but I can't leave the baby alone. I settle for crashing on the sofa and staring into space while surf tunes play in the background.

Even with the post-traumatic stress from yesterday's meeting—I hear the vase crash to the floor and Ruthie's wailing cry over and over; I see the Van Dierdons turn their shocked and disappointed faces at me again and again—I almost manage to drift off. My cell rings, jolting me back to the present.

It's Mrs. Marx, the client whose living room we recently finished redoing. And who, unfortunately, already made her last payment, which I spent long ago. *Please let her be calling with another job!*

"Hello, Mrs. Marx. How are you? Still enjoying that beautiful living room?"

"Yes, it's lovely, and Douglas is still ecstatic about the fireplace you found." We'd mounted a sleek high-end gas fireplace on the wall. "Even though it's summer, he still likes to turn it on! You know how the temperature drops here at night when you're right by the ocean. He opens the French doors so it's certain to be cool enough for a fire. I think he just likes having another remote to play with."

"I'm pleased to hear that." *Please say you have another job for me.*

"Yes, the room's wonderful." She pauses. *And so you'd love me to do an equally wonderful redesign of your master suite, right?* "It's just . . . the curtains." *Oh, damn.* I had to fight her on that fabric. "The gold is too much for me."

"Not gold, Mrs. Marx. Champagne." I emphasize the word and hope the celebratory vibe that usually accompanies the beverage rings clear in my voice. "Curtains are like a frame on a piece of art. You want to show that art off to its fullest. And those curtains are the perfect frame for that room."

"Every time I walk into the room, I'm startled. I expect to find Liberace sitting at a candelabra-topped grand piano in there."

You'd think the curtains were studded with rhinestones the way she talks. There's the slightest sheen to the fabric when the light hits it just right. It's gorgeous. But oh, how I struggled with her over every fabric, paint, and accessory choice so that she wouldn't end up with a bland and boring beige living room. If that's what she wanted, why didn't they stick with the old room? I must have asked myself that question a dozen times while working with her. "Think of them as beige with pizazz. Beige on steroids." I remember she mentioned loving to cook and hope she's an Emeril fan. "Beige kicked up a notch."

"The room's amazing. And I know I agreed to the curtains, but . . . you must have caught me on a Xanax day." She titters, but I doubt she's joking. "I have a swatch of the perfect replacement picked out. Of course I'll pay for time and materials."

If she's not happy, she's not happy. And I need the money. Maybe it will be enough to cover the Nordstrom bill I got yesterday.

"Of course. I want you to be comfortable. If you'd like to make a change, I can fit you into the schedule right away." Lord knows I've got nothing else going on. "I can stop by this afternoon if that works, and you can show me the swatch you've picked out."

Oh, crap. I've lost my seamstress. But it's only curtains. Basically a bunch of big rectangles. I'll take the old ones down and use them for a pattern. It'll be fine.

*

"I did some research before heading home," Barry says as he comes in the door. Marie rushes to greet him, while I shush them both.

"Ruthie's sleeping! If you wake her up, I'm running away with the mailman."

"Idle threat," he whispers. "He's way too short for you. So how was this morning?"

"She was an angel while you were gone. I didn't even have to put the leash on her." Barry laughs, and I remind him we agreed not to mention the park incident to Wren when she gets back. She's been texting, e-mailing, and calling to check on Ruthie a half-dozen times per day, but we've been keeping our replies short and of the "she's fine; don't worry" variety. Actually, it's been great to have her only a text away, because we've had to ask for advice, especially at bedtimes and bath times. I'm glad we're more than halfway through this babysitting gig. Maybe Ruthie will come out of this alive after all.

"Hungry? I was going to heat up the leftover salmon and put it on top of a salad."

"Sounds good. I'm starved." Barry joins me in the kitchen.

"You should be; it's almost one o'clock." I glare at him, then take some of my irritation out on a stalk of celery, chopping it roughly. At least Ruthie was good while he was gone. If she'd fussed the whole time, I'd let him make his own damn lunch. "I thought you were going to be back by twelve thirty." I don't have to be at Mrs. Marx's until three, but he's on the clock now. If she wakes up, she's his problem.

"I know. I'm sorry I'm late, but I had an idea!" He dashes back for the work satchel he'd dropped on the dining room table and pulls out three DVDs with brightly colored covers. He fans them out: with *Winnie the Pooh* on top, and other cartoon delights behind. "I stopped at the public library. These ought to help us get through the next day and a half."

"We should've thought of that sooner." He rejoins me in the kitchen and puts the salmon in the microwave before helping me with the salad. "Anyway, you said you were doing some research. About what?"

"Babies. In terms of exploring their world, they're a lot like dogs at this age, using their mouths to experience new things."

"I saw that in action at the park. Ruthie tried to eat a ladybug. When I convinced her not to, Marie came over, sniffed it, and ate it." Barry laughs. "Seriously, how is this info going to help us get through these next two days?"

"It's probably not going to help with that, but I find her . . ." he pauses while slicing a cucumber. "Fascinating. At this stage, she'll start exploring the world more visually. I was reading about self-recognition. Remember when Marie was a puppy and tried to play with the puppy in the mirror? Apparently, babies are the same, viewing their reflection as someone else. At around fifteen months, they begin to understand that the little critter in the mirror is them. I don't know that Marie sees *herself* in the mirror, but she certainly learned that her reflection's not another dog. I'm going to try some experiments with Ruthie and see if she recognizes herself."

"That's great, Bear. You're in charge this afternoon, so when she wakes up, you can do all the experimenting you want. I mean, as long as you're not talking about hooking her up to electrodes or anything."

"I'm going to put something new on her—say, a bow on top of her head—and see if she reaches for the reflection, or for her own head."

"You'll have to report the results to me. I need to go see a client this afternoon."

"You're leaving me with her?" He stops chopping, knife poised over the cutting board.

"Yes," I say through gritted teeth. "*I* was alone with her all day yesterday plus this morning. It's *your* turn. Besides, I have work to do." One measly job that will require a trip to the fabric store, cutting straight lines and sewing straight hems, and then, unless something else comes along, I'll probably be headed straight to debtor's prison.

Thank God I'm not living in a Dickens novel.

Barry doesn't know that I don't have any other jobs lined up after this minor curtain-fixing deal. Of course, I told him about the job in Montecito falling through—thanks to his wannabe-jungle-gym-climbing granddaughter—and about Rache quitting. "Told" makes it sound like I related an anecdote. It was more like I ugly/angry-cried when he got home from work Monday while the story gushed out of me in gulping gasps.

He was very sympathetic, and apologized—again—for not being able to leave work because of the last-minute, all-hands-on-deck budget-cut meetings. Still, he didn't understand why I was so upset. Rache quitting, he agreed, was a "drag," but he tried to reassure me that I'd be fine on my own. That was my opening. I should've told him everything. I almost did, but he was so sweet—saying he'd make it up to me for not being there when I needed him, telling me he appreciated how great I'd been with Ruthie, bucking me up over the loss of Rachel—that I lost my nerve. I couldn't tell him the business was on the brink of falling apart. As for Rache, I said Beverly offered her more money. Which is the truth, even if it isn't the *whole* truth. And as for the business, well, I didn't say anything beyond how much I'd wanted to get the job with the Van Dierdons, thinking it would be our gateway to the Montecito crowd.

Barry is opposed to debt. Other than our home loan, and then the equity line of credit I convinced him to get so that we could spruce up the house (a designer *cannot* live in a house with shag carpeting, plastic faucet handles, and linoleum kitchen counters ringed with burn marks), Barry generally pays cash. If it's something expensive, like a new truck to replace his ancient beast, he squirrels money away until he has enough.

And since Barry is the science-minded one, and I've got the business brain, I've always been in charge of our finances. I reconcile our checking account, pay the bills, and organize our taxes each year.

So when I pushed both my work and our personal credit cards close to their limits, well, I started dipping into our savings account. I know I should have told him, but I thought it'd be temporary. Only it kept getting worse. The well was there, and I couldn't stop myself going back to it whenever a new expense popped up. Need to run another ad in *Montecito Magazine*? Dip into savings. Rache needs an advance? A little dip'll do ya. Next thing you know, it's snowballed into this huge flipping secret.

I should get it over with and tell him, but I don't think he'll understand. Especially about the Nordstrom credit card. I *need* to look my best for this job. It's nothing like his job. No one cares what the head of the science library is wearing. In fact, it probably gives him street cred if he looks like his science-nerd students, in his sad cords and faded flannel shirts. But that's not how my job works. Who's going to trust me to give them a gorgeous design if I don't look precisely put together myself? He thinks I can "wear whatever." Ha! So yeah, there were some shopping trips to Nordstrom. And a few to Ann Taylor as well.

Then there was also the equipment and furniture for my work studio: the huge table and sewing machine for Rache in the back, the built-in shelving in the front reception area, the lovely vintage desk I whitewashed, my gorgeous white leather and chrome desk chair, and the barrel chairs Rache reupholstered in rich bisque brocade. After all, sometimes we meet clients there; it's got to exude my sense of style. And we decorated that salon and day spa in Montecito for free. It was great advertising—after all, we knew the wealthy clientele would be in at least every six weeks to get their roots redone, if not monthly for a facial. I'm sure the job would've paid off already, if the economy hadn't nosedived. We finished a few jobs before the market started going south, plus the Van Dierdon job *almost* came from that. But then the market crashed, and those who didn't lose a ton of money held what they had left more tightly to their chests.

Of course Barry sees the financial news. He knows times are tough all over; he's mentioned drastic cuts to their library budget. And I've hinted that things aren't exactly booming. But still . . . he doesn't know that I've got nothing else on my calendar after this measly curtain job.

I've never kept something this big from Barry before. I don't want to lie; I didn't set out to. I knew the business would be hard to get off the ground, and there might be tough times, but I thought we'd eventually start to make money. I believed in myself, in my passion for design, so much so that I didn't consider failure an option. All the money I spent—it was an investment. In my career. In me.

But things look grim. I might have to admit to Barry that I'm a failure.

He looks so desperate at the thought of me leaving him home alone with Ruthie. Even with dread in his eyes and the wrinkles on his brow, he's so handsome. I can't tell him I screwed up. He'd be so disappointed. I want to make him proud.

I can still turn this thing around. I should probably do some more advertising. There's a bit of money left in our account . . . A couple of big jobs is all I need. Especially now that I don't have an employee to pay. I can do this. It's going to be okay.

"I promise I won't be long." I stroke the side of his face. "But I told Mrs. Marx I'd stop by today. Think of this as special bonding time with Ruthie. If you run out of things to do with her, teach her the sign for *roll over* or *come*. Anyway, Marie'll help keep her happy. Plus, you've got me, my mom, Wren, Cynthia, and Anna on speed dial, so no worries." I count off on my fingers. "But if there's a problem, you should definitely try all of them before calling me."

CHAPTER 16

At Mrs. Marx's house, I'm not surprised to find she's selected a sad beige linen blend for the curtains.

"This is much more suited to my taste."

"If this is what you want, this is what you'll have." I confirm she got it at the home fabrics place on Los Olivos. "I'll head over there as soon as I measure these existing drapes. I have a step stool in the back of my car; I'll go get it."

"No need. I've got one in the pantry." She motions for me to follow her. This gives me a chance to comment on her dining room and kitchen. I've seen them before—we toured the house to get a sense of her style before starting work on the living room—so I know they're refined, but bland. Like a cream-colored cashmere sweater, both rooms could use a lot of accessorizing to jazz them up.

As we walk past the huge dining room with its eggshell walls, basic oak table, and a chandelier that looks like something my grandma would've loved, I ask, "Now that you have your lovely new living room, I wonder if you've given any thought to updating the dining area?"

Mrs. Marx stops short. "Oh. No, I hadn't actually." She turns to me, then looks at the room. "I think it's quite elegant."

Must tread carefully. "Yes, of course, it's *très elegant*." These ladies eat it up when you sprinkle some French into your phrasing. "But it's an old-world elegance that, while lovely, is perhaps a bit out of step with your new, more modern living room. It'd be very easy to give the room a minor . . ." I don't want to say face-lift, so I search and find the perfect word. "Rejuvenation."

"Hmm. Rejuvenation. I don't know. Let me think about it. And discuss it with Douglas. He's fussy about these things."

I want to drop to my knees and beg her for the work, any work. I want to shout like those annoying carpeting commercials: *I'll do any three rooms for the price of one!* But I know how these ladies operate. I've got to play it cool. If there's anything the ladies in this zip code don't want to be associated with, it's a ship that's going down. So in my best "it doesn't matter to me" voice, I say, "If you decide to go ahead, let me know. Soon. I'm about to be snowed under." By credit card bills. I lean in conspiratorially, "For a favorite client like you, of course, I'd slip your job into the project schedule first."

Her simpering smile tells me I've hit the ego bull's-eye. "Of course, if we have any more work done on the house, you'd be the one we choose. But for now, let's focus on getting these drapes done." Crap. I've got to do a good job on these or she'll never hire me for anything else. And I've got to do as good a job as Rache did.

But I haven't the first clue how to work that beast of a sewing machine I bought for Rache. It occurs to me that a hack job on these curtains could be the final nail in my business's coffin. Curtains, as it were.

*

I'm not up for a visit from my mom, but I have actual work to do, and with Anna still sick and Barry back at work this morning, I had no choice but to call last night and ask her to come.

It's pretty much the same routine as when Cynthia got here. "She's so cute." "She looks like Barry." "Oh, those curls!" There must be a Cute Baby checklist. Curls, boinged. Check. Tummy, tickled. Check. Cheeks, nibbled. Double check. Meanwhile, I rate nothing more than a glancing hug, and Marie is ignored outright, until she can't stand it anymore and nose-pokes Mom's elbow.

"Yes, yes, Marie. Hello," Mom says to the dog, then goes right back to making kissy lips at Ruthie. Marie, apparently adopting an "if you can't beat 'em, join 'em" attitude, opts for kissing the baby as well.

Mom sits with the baby on the sheet-covered sofa. "Tell me everything about Wren and the baby." While I oblige her, she never takes her eyes off Ruthie, handing Ruthie her car keys, tickling her belly again, and pausing for a round or two of peekaboo.

When my tale is done, and with Ruthie engrossed in the contents of my mother's purse, Mom looks down to where I'm sitting cross-legged on the floor, rubbing Marie's belly. "Do you remember when you were little and you'd say you were either going to have no children or five?"

"What made you think of that?" I'd only say that because Mom was always trying to get me to play with dolls, and Cyn always wanted me to play house. I'd say I wanted either a house full of kids or none, though even at that young age I somehow knew it would be none in the end. But I also knew my mom didn't think that was normal. I remember once when Cyn wanted to play, she handed me her favorite baby doll and said, "You be the mama this time." I said, "No, I don't wanna be the mama. I'm okay being the aunt." Mom overheard us and said, "Oh, honey, someday you'll want to be the mama." There was a glow in her eyes, and I knew from the empty feeling I got inside that she wouldn't want me to tell her she was wrong.

From then on I started saying the line about "none or five." I didn't want to completely lie, but I also didn't want to let on I wasn't like the rest of the family. My mom and my aunt would laugh when I'd say it.

"Sounds kind of drastic. Why not one or two?" I'd explain that one was no good. I knew that having a sibling was special. I told them a kid should have a brother or sister, but if there are only two, they'll fight (like me and Cyn!), so an odd number was better. Three was no good, though, because then someone would be stuck in between the all-important eldest and the much-fawned-over baby. Best to have five, so three of them could share the middle-child burden.

I'd actually forgotten I used to say that. Why is she bringing it up now? I shrug. "I was right, anyway. I always said none or five, and I've got none."

"But now you have this sweet pea here. Lordy, if you'd had five. Ha! I can't imagine." She looks around the room, noticing all the changes made for Ruthie's sake. "You must miss having your beautiful things around."

"That makes me sound kind of shallow." Oh, how I miss my beautiful things.

"I don't think you're shallow. You're a designer, for heaven's sake. Of course you want to be surrounded by beautiful furnishings. It's who you are."

Yes, that's right. I'm the career woman. And Cynthia's the mom. And since I'm not a mom, there's no other role for me, so I better get to the fabric store. I've got to nail these curtains, then convince Mrs. Marx that they need to redo that boring dining room to go with their fabulous Liberace-free living room, and get my career off life support. Because if I'm not the career woman, who the hell am I?

"Anyway, what made you remember that?"

"I was thinking . . . I know you always said none or five, but it's not too late to have *one*. You only just turned forty. Lots of women have babies well into their forties these days. I read the other day that the birthrate for women aged forty to forty-five is at a record high."

Oh, crap. Though I have never said it flat out—"Barry and I will never have children"—I thought she'd accepted it as fact by now. I inspect the inside of Marie's ears and wonder if Mom notices my lips tightening.

"I thought you might feel different now, after seeing what it's like having a little one in your life."

"I've been around Cyn and the boys enough to know what it's like." *Besides, having Ruthie here hasn't exactly been the rosiest ad for reproduction.*

"Having children is such a huge part of life. I worry you'll regret it someday if you don't experience having a child yourself."

I think back to the conversation I had with Wren, both of us worried about disappointing our mothers. I'd advised Wren to tell Jade what she honestly wants out of life, so I probably should do the same now.

"I know that's a huge part of your life. But it's not something I want." I look down at Marie. She paws at my hand, either comforting me or encouraging me to continue rubbing her belly. "I know you don't understand, or maybe don't even believe me, but I didn't get the mothering gene. I don't want to have a baby. I've never once felt that need. Besides, what's worse: to not have a baby and live to regret it, or to *have* one and regret it?"

Ruthie moves from playing with Mom's keys to leafing through her checkbook. Mom strokes Ruthie's hair. "I know you wouldn't regret it."

I want to scream, "You're not listening!" Instead, I yoga-breathe and count to five. "All I know is, I've never once had an iota of an urge to have a baby. I'm pretty sure that's nature's way of telling me I'm not cut out for motherhood."

I'd once told Barry I thought maybe we were slightly more evolved than the average person because we didn't want kids. My theory was that Mother Nature knew the planet was overpopulated, so she'd pegged some of us to go against all those years of precedent and actively avoid procreation. Barry went into a high-level discussion of how evolution is based on various members of the same population having different traits, and how those traits must be "heritable." Since there would be no offspring to pass the "nonparenting gene" on to, there was no way for this to be part of an evolutionary process. In other words, we're freaks of nature with no reason for our disinclination to reproduce. Unlike, oh, every other living creature on the face of the planet.

So what will my mother's reaction be? Her face gives away nothing: she's worn the same blissed-out smile ever since she opened the door and saw Ruthie. If she's disappointed to find out the truth, she covers it well.

"Having a baby changes your perspective," she says. "All you want is what's best for them."

I fight the urge to grab a pillow off the couch and scream into it.

Okay. At least she doesn't think I'm a freak. But she's apparently deaf to what I'm saying. Maybe I'm speaking in a register only dogs—and dog-moms—can hear. I don't know why this is so hard for her to accept.

"Why do I need my perspective changed? What I want right now is what's best for my family—and my family means me, Barry, and Marie."

"And now this doll too, and her mother."

"Yes, you're right. We have extended family now. But we're never going to have a baby of our own. We're one-hundred-percent sure. I mean, Barry's taken steps"—I make a scissoring motion with my fingers—"so it's not going to happen." There. I can't make this anymore clear. There's no other way to spell out that we are *not* going to have a baby. Her face remains the picture of serenity. Honestly, I'd expected a tear or twenty, but either she's *still* not getting it or she's experiencing some kind of baby contact high. "Right now, our focus is on our newly extended family: helping Barry and Wren establish their relationship, and not accidentally killing Ruthie before Wren gets back."

Mom laughs. Ruthie looks up and breaks into a huge grin. "You're not going to kill her." She raises her voice half an octave. "Unless you bake her in a pie and eat her up!" She makes nom-nom-nom noises while mouthing Ruthie's hands, to the baby's delight. Marie runs over, also wanting a nibble or two of Ruthie pie. When they're done play-eating the baby, Mom continues. "Look at the number of morons out there in the world with children. They all do fine. You and Barry are smart, successful, well-educated people. You can handle this."

I wait for yet another baby comment, but she's silent.

When I'm sure she's not going to poke me one last time with the baby cattle prod, I stand. "What I need to handle right now is this project for my client, so I better get going."

I show her Ruthie's room and where her books and the library movies are stashed. We discovered last night that this movie thing is a serious bonus of having a baby rather than a dog—you can prop a kid in front of a movie and she's happy. Mesmerized, even. *God bless you, Walt Disney!* If only the same thing worked on rambunctious puppies. Mom follows, holding Ruthie on her hip. Marie tags along.

"She doesn't eat much, so try to get whatever you can into her." I point to the fridge. "She likes pink yogurt, and there's tons. Don't be surprised if she wants to eat it out of the bowl like a dog."

Mom laughs again. "You used to do the same thing."

"Yeah? Funny." I kiss Mom's cheek. She holds Ruthie out for one, and I oblige. "Thanks for watching her." I kiss Marie twice on the soft spot between her eyes, and toss her a jerky treat.

As I drive away, I wonder if Mom will finally stop making comments about Barry and me having children. With the new information I gave her, she has to, right? Although, considering her past, I won't be surprised if the next time she brings it up, she has statistics at the ready about how successful vasectomy reversals can be. Plus, the name and number of a doctor who can help with that.

Maybe I should have tried the "we're more highly evolved" argument on her.

*

Though my mom seemed unfazed by it—maybe *because* she seemed unfazed by it—our conversation drained me. I'm glad this is a small job. It's all my brain can handle right now. At least I've said my piece, which is a relief. How she reacts to it is her issue, not mine. I can feel the weight lifting off my chest. Or off my ovaries, anyway.

At the office, I measure the old curtains. I'm already in over my head, and I text Rache for help figuring how much yardage to buy. It's only been two days, and she's already back at Beverly's. Damn that Beverly—she's such a nine-seventeen. She didn't waste a minute in snatching my girl back, and I bet she totally gloated about it. A few minutes later, my phone chirps.

Get extra half yard/panel for the bottom hem plus facing at the top.

I dash off a thank-you text and hope it doesn't sound as frazzled as I feel.

Happy to help. Call if more ????

As an added bonus, she sends another text a few minutes later: *Should be able to pay back the advance soon.* Thank God. I wonder if we have the same definition of *soon*.

At the fabric store, they measure off the yards with only inches to spare. The manager says she can order more, but it'll take three weeks. Great. No room for error. Luckily, I find some of the same fabric in another color, so I get a yard to practice on. Rache had also texted: *Practice and make sure the tension's OK on the foot.*

I replied: *WTF's a foot?*

Instruction book in top drawer of sewing table. Easy-peasy.

Yeah, easy for her to text.

At the studio, I adjust the tension on the sewing machine and attempt a seam on some of the test fabric. (At least I figured out what the foot is.) It looks fine on top, but when I flip it over, the stitching hangs loose and loopy. I overcorrect, resulting in too-tight stitches and a massive knotted ball of thread. The fabric sticks and won't budge. I yank it out, which snaps the needle in two. And, of course, there are no spares, so it's back to the fabric store. At the office again, even with the "easy-peasy" instruction book, it takes forever to put in the new needle, and then I'm baffled by how to rethread the stupid machine. Tendrils of tension creep up my neck and into my overtired brain. I can't even adjust the tension in my own life. How am I going to adjust it on this stupid machine? I almost text Rache again, on the verge of frustrated tears, but instead give up and lock up the office.

Of course a damn *sewing* job would be the first thing to come up after losing Rache.

My luck had better turn around soon.

*

"I'm home," I yell when no one greets me. From the car situation, I know Barry's home and Mom's gone.

The house sits silent, but I hear Barry's "surf tunes" playlist blasting out back. I detour to the bedroom to change, and swallow two ibuprofen.

In the kitchen, I watch the backyard scene through the window while getting myself a glass of ice water. Ruthie "helps" Barry with the weeding. She squats beside him, plunging skinny fingers into the rich soil that Barry has carefully cultivated (*without the help of compost, Wren!*) and pulling up cloverleaves. She holds a plucked stem out for Barry's inspection, and he praises her the same way he does with Marie: "Good job!" Marie sticks her nose in to inspect the proceedings and tries to eat the cloverleaf. Barry goes back and digs out the roots Ruthie missed.

Who'd have thought the guy who coined the term "LPs" would be smiling and gardening with his very own LP? They're pretty cute together.

I can't believe Marie hasn't heard me yet, but then Barry's blasting the music pretty loud. Getting his grandkid hooked on the classics early, I guess.

I rap on the kitchen window and three heads turn. Barry waves, Ruthie shrieks, and Marie barks and lopes to the back door. As for Ruthie, I'm not sure if that was a shriek of delight or terror. *T-Rex returns! Our fun here has ended!*

I step onto the patio and crouch down to say hi to Marie. "What're you guys doing?" I ask while Marie wiggles and tries to get me to scratch her behind.

"We're weeding, aren't we, Ruthie?" Barry sits back on his haunches.

"Veed!" Ruthie squeals and plods toward me with a weed held out as if it's the finest flower. Okay, I have to admit it's adorable. She scrunches up her face, and it looks like she's attempting a *Bewitched* imitation. For a second, I hope she'll wiggle her button nose and make all my problems disappear. Hmm. In that scenario, wouldn't she disappear too?

"Thank you." I accept the offering and grab her muddy hand before she can touch my lemon-chiffon-colored shorts. Her jumper holds enough dirt to plant succulents down the front. Why was today the day we dressed her in khaki instead of her usual black? "She's filthy, Bear."

"Yeah, and she's having a great time."

"Don't let her touch anything when you come in, and don't forget to wipe Marie's paws."

"Do I ever?"

"Yes. Yes, you do." I waggle Ruthie's hand up and down. She thinks it's a new game and starts to bob and dance. "It's straight to the tub for you when you come in, missy."

"You'll help me with that, right?"

"Yes, I'll help. I'll go get the bath ready." I drop her hand. "Go finish weeding with Grandpa."

I slip inside the sliding glass door as she slaps both hands on it, leaving muddy prints. I point enthusiastically at Barry. "Gan'pa. Veed!" she yells, then races back to Barry.

Great. Now I've got to wash the windows.

I run a tepid bath, then call Barry to bring in the urchin.

We work together, bathing her. Barry distracts Ruthie, making goofy faces and singing silly songs. (Her favorite is his version of the Bee Gees' "Stayin' Alive," only he changes the words to "takin' a bath"; she joins in on the ah-ah-ah-ah's.) I do the hard work, washing her hair and getting the dirt out from under her tiny nails. Marie provides the yuks for Ruthie (and earns a "yuck!" from me) by attempting to drink the dirty bathwater.

Barry rubs Ruthie dry and keeps singing while I untangle wet curls. Not an easy job, but luckily Barry's on a roll with his hits from the '70s and '80s.

"'G'in," Ruthie says, demanding Barry repeat the tune.

"You've got yourself a fan there," I say. Barry pulls her jammies off the bathroom counter and helps me wrestle her into them.

"Is it too early to put her PJs on? Isn't she going to get her dinner all over them?"

"We'll wrap her in a towel, in addition to her bib," I suggest.

"'G'in!" Ruthie shouts.

"Okay, one more." Barry holds a finger in front of her nose and launches into the English Beat's "Mirror in the Bathroom." I have to laugh at that. For the first time today (or this week?), I feel a bit more relaxed.

While he continues singing, I suggest plugging the child into the TV while we enjoy cocktail hour. Lord knows we've earned a cocktail or three after surviving almost four days with Ruthie with no blood loss. Well, except when she scratched me in bed the other night. I complained to Barry that she'd punched me, but he countered, "Newton's second law of motion defines force as the product of mass times acceleration."

"So?"

"So she doesn't have much mass, and speed's not her forte, so you do the math."

"Seriously, Bear. She punched me." In the morning, when I showed him the marks on my arm, he had to concede that she'd at least clawed me. (If Newton had anything to say about clawing, Barry didn't mention it.)

Barry puts on *Arthur* while I get the wine. (*Oh! That's who Arthur is. He's an aardvark!*) We collapse on the sofa with exhausted sighs. Marie gracefully leaps up next to me and rests her head in my lap. I rub her ears, and she lets out a contented groan.

"We made it." I clink my glass against Barry's. "Only a few more hours until she's back." We learned early on not to say Wren's name (or refer to myself as Mama around Marie) as it agitated Ruthie. She'd look around, bottom lip puckering, and more often than not it would lead to tears and cries of "Mama!" But as long as we kept her otherwise occupied, or had Marie there to distract her, she did pretty well being left with virtual strangers. I think it's good that Wren's raising a kid who's not too clingy.

"She texted me while you were in the kitchen," Barry says. "Flight delay. She'll be back around eleven."

"Eh." What's a few more hours at this point?

"There's more. Uh, Jade's coming along."

"Wait. What? They made up?"

"I don't know. It's just a short text."

"Let me see." I grab his phone. *So you know—my mom's coming too.* What does this mean? Maybe they made up, and she's coming to help Wren pack so that they can all drive home together. Maybe we'll be able to enjoy the rest of the summer in peace. No more waking in the night to crying, no more having to be "on" all the time playing hostess, no more constant reminders of Jade's new role in Barry's life as the mother of his child. *And* I'll be able to buckle down and figure out how to save my business. Not to mention my marriage, if I can get my finances in order before Barry suspects anything. I scan the living room and think, *The cherry on top will be getting our beautiful house back!*

His phone buzzes again while I'm still holding it. *Don't worry—she booked a hotel.*

I read it aloud, then hand back the phone. "Duh. It's not like we'd ask her to stay *here*. How weird would that be?" Crap. I'd been so busy thinking about the possible good-news spin on this development that I hadn't thought about the fact this means Barry will probably see Jade again. For the first time in nineteen years. "This is going to be weird anyway, isn't it?"

"Very." Barry—master of assessing a situation in as few words as possible.

I wonder what he's really thinking. And what's he going to think when he actually sees her?

But . . . he doesn't need to see her. If she's coming to help Wren pack, they can do that while Barry's at work. I should be able to orchestrate that.

There's room for Jade in Wren's car, even when it's filled with all of her and Ruthie's stuff, right? They could always strap Jade to the roof.

CHAPTER 17

The cab pulls into the driveway just after eleven. Barry had texted Wren to say he'd pick her up at the airport, but she insisted she didn't want to be any more trouble. She raps lightly on the front door, although she has a key. We'd normally be asleep, as Ruthie is, but Barry wanted to wait up and welcome her "home," and I decided I better be there too, to get the scoop on what's going on with Jade. Barry gets up to answer the door, and Marie runs to assist.

I mute the TV as she comes in and receives a thorough kissing from Marie, who has really taken to her human sister. Wren's become surprisingly relaxed with the dog—a testament to Marie's beautiful nature. We ask about her trip, the funeral, and the flight.

"It was all good." Wren sets down her bag. "I know Ruthie's probably asleep, but I'm gonna go peek at her." She tiptoes into the guest bedroom.

When she comes back, she flops down on the loveseat while Barry and I share the sofa. "I didn't wake her up, even though it was tempting. She's such an angel when she's asleep, huh? Oh, I missed that peanut! How'd it go? For reals."

"Fine," Barry says.

"Fine?" Wren tilts her head and turns to me. She may have only known us a few days, but I'm sure she's noticed that Barry's not the one to go to for a detailed report.

"For reals," I say. I'm not about to blame Ruthie for losing out on the job at the Van Dierdons', or Rache quitting, or the imminent collapse of my career. But I *do* blame her for pushing over the first domino. And there's plenty of blame to go around: Wren for not waiting one more day to see if Ruthie would be well enough to take along; Barry for refusing to come home and help; the flu bug that felled Anna. And, okay, me too. I should've known to keep an eye on her at the Van Dierdons'. If only I'd brought her into the dining room with us! It's a good thing the coffee table's in the garage or I'd beat my head against it seven or eight times. Instead, I chew the inside of my cheek, then answer, "We had a, uh, a babysitting snafu one day, but other than that, things went well. My mom and my sister helped out."

"Oh, how cool Ruthie got to meet her . . . what would they be? Her step-great-aunt and step-great-grandma, right?"

"Yeah. They both fell in love with her."

"She didn't get to meet my grandma. And she barely hung out with her great-grandpa, since he made it clear how much of a disappointment I was."

"Sorry." Barry offers a sad smile, but doesn't expand on that thought.

Hoping she won't be as reticent as her dad, I ask again, "So the funeral was okay? I'm sure your mom was glad you were there."

"Yeah, Sunday and Monday we ran around organizing stuff. The funeral went okay, I guess. But it was kinda weird." She kicks off her scuffed black boots; her big toe pokes out of a hole in her tights. Of course, there's also a hole in the knee, so I'm sure she doesn't care. She pulls her feet under her. "Everyone said how great he was, and how he'll be missed." She shrugs. "But I realized the people saying that stuff were all bakery employees. He didn't have any real friends there. And it was only me and my mom for family." She wrinkles her nose, exaggerating her usual uncertain half smile and revealing, once again, the pointy little fangs she inherited from her dad. I wonder if Ruthie will have those too. "Sad, huh?"

Barry and I nod.

"How's your mom doing?" I ask. "Did you guys get a chance to talk things through?"

"Not really. I'm still mad at her over the whole making-me-think-I-was-a-half-orphan thing. She tried to talk to me about it some, but then we sorta had another fight."

"About?" I ask. Barry would probably let the comment go. Well, obviously they haven't made up.

"About my grandpa. She could tell I wasn't exactly feeling it at the funeral. She gave me some grief for not 'acting right.' But I wasn't going to pretend to feel something I don't. Anyway, I got pissed 'cause I took the time to go up there and be there for her, and I had to leave Ruthie behind and everything, but I still went, even when I'm mad at her, and then she goes and gives me shit." She covers her mouth. "Sorry. I mean, two-ten."

"It's okay," I say. "Ruthie's not here; we understand." Barry channels Marcel Marceau.

"I said her funeral would be the same, just a bunch of work people because that's all she has time for."

"Oh. Ouch," I say.

"Yeah." She adjusts her feet, pulling her knees into her chest. "I felt kinda bad after. But it must've got to her, because next thing I know, she tells me she's taking the rest of the week off work plus a few days next week—which she totally never does, especially since she already took two days off for the funeral—and she's coming along back to Santa Barbara with me. She said she missed Ruthie—well, me *and* Ruthie, but I'm sure she mostly meant Ruthie. I couldn't change her mind. She said she was coming whether I wanted her to or not."

So she's not coming to help Wren move back home. Why, then? "Do you think she wants to come over here? Check out where you're living?"

There's probably no way to keep Jade and Barry from seeing one another now. What if Barry feels a stab of regret when he sees her? It's only natural he would think about the one that got away, what might have been. After all, she was his first great love. Maybe the greatest love of his life.

And here I am, the consolation prize.

I'm not as pretty as petite Jade. I know she's still the great beauty she was years ago. Sure, that picture of her on the company site could've been airbrushed to within an inch of its life, but I'd bet the rest of our meager savings it wasn't. And I'm not as smart as her either. She's got a master's in biology and is the COO of her company. I have a degree too, but I feel like compared to *biology*, mine is in Playing with Colors and Pretty Fabrics with a minor in Kissing the Client's Ass. And at the moment, I can't keep my company in the black, let alone lead it to the top of the NASDAQ.

She and Barry would've been an amazing team.

Two-ten. How is he not going to see that when she's here, in the flesh?

"I dunno," Wren answers, calling me back to the present. "I mean, she doesn't have to come over here. Ruthie and I could go meet her at her hotel, or a restaurant or whatever. But I think she might want to talk to my dad." She peeks out from under her bangs at him. Her eyes, rimmed with heavy eyeliner, blink once, twice. Then she looks at me. I wonder if Barry sometimes thinks of Jade when he looks at Wren's blue, no *lavender*-blue, eyes.

If he's going to see Jade, I want to be there too. Maybe this will be our chance to get some answers out of her about why she never told Barry about Wren, and how she thought she could get away with acting like Wren and Barry were nothing more than chess pieces. Or maybe

I could get her alone and smack some answers out of her. However it goes, I want as much control over the situation as possible.

"No, let's do it here." I look over at Barry. "See if she wants to come for dinner tomorrow." I can't tell if he's silent with anticipation or trepidation about seeing Jade for the first time after all these years.

*

"Tomorrow" finds me painstakingly cutting out curtain panels. I smooth and resmooth the fabric across Rache's giant cutting table. Correction, *my* cutting table. Mrs. Marx's living room has fourteen-foot ceilings and three separate picture windows with double case-ments, so I've got six huge panels to make. I hear my dad's voice in my head saying "measure twice, cut once," so I measure four times just to be sure. The fabric is boring but pricey, and although Mrs. Marx is paying for time and materials, she's not going to want to pay for extra if I mess this up. Nor is she going to want to go curtainless for another three weeks if we have to wait for more fabric to arrive.

Once they're cut, I iron the hems down each side, turning the raw edges over once, then a second time, to form a clean finish as Rache had always done. It's fiddly work, and the steam from the iron burns the tips of my fingers before I remember that Rache said to turn the steam off so that it won't stretch the fabric out of shape. After hours of hunching over the ironing board, my back aches. I don't have time to start sewing, which is just as well because I'm worried the curtains are going to look like a Home Ec 101 project by the time I'm done.

All this messing with the fabric has ruined my nails, so I stop for a manicure appointment on my way home. Mitzi works on my hands, and I sink back in the chair. "You haven't been here in ages," Mitzi says while I shut my eyes.

"Trying to save some money," I say.

My budget troubles return like noisy crows, chasing away my fleeting moments of calm. *Can't think about money right now. Have to get through tonight with Jade. But seriously, what's my problem? I could've done my nails myself. Then again, when I'm in this deep, what's a few more bucks?* I shut my eyes again, worried another tension headache lurks.

At home, fingers freshly painted blush pink and contrasting nicely with the bouquet of magenta zinnias I bought for the table, I find Barry in the kitchen marinating salmon steaks while Marie supervises. I convinced Barry to get home early from work so that he could cook, since he's way better at it than I am.

I wave to Wren and Ruthie, playing in the pool out back. Marie does love the baby, but fresh meat or fish tops all, so for once she's not at Ruthie's side. And she has no more greeting for me than a quick, desperate glance that pleads, "Can you get him to give me some of that?"

Barry tells me Anna's still here, finishing up our bathroom.

"Hello," I call out as I enter our room. I go to the closet for the summer dress I've picked out. (Oh, how I wanted to go shopping for something new. I've lost five pounds from the stress lately—so at least there's one upside—but I had neither the time nor the credit on my Nordy's card to go shopping. Luckily, I remembered a dress I moved to the back of the closet when it got too tight. Hooray for it fitting again when I tried it on last night. Boo for it being five years out of fashion. But if Wren's right, and her mom's "not into clothes," then Jade won't notice.)

"Sorry I'm still here." Anna emerges from the bathroom with a bucket full of cleaning supplies. "I know you said it's a special occasion tonight, and since I missed being here Monday, I wanted to make sure that everything looks tip-top."

"Thank you so much for fitting us in. You're feeling better?"

"Much," she says. "I'll get out of your hair now."

"Thanks again. I know the house was extra dirty."

"The wee ones make as much mess as ten adults." Anna grins. "But they bring so much joy, who cares, right?" She heads out before I can say I do indeed care. I wish I could afford to have her come every other day while they're here.

As she bustles down the hallway, I can't help but think, *if only she'd been here Monday!*

God, I need a glass of wine.

I change and head back to the kitchen. "Smells good, Bear. What about Wren, though?"

He points over his shoulder at the fridge. "Got a portobello mushroom for her."

He has a glass of wine going, plus one for me. I want to dive in and float. An in-progress salad waits for more attention—cherry tomatoes rest atop the torn romaine filling our biggest wooden salad bowl, while the cutting board holds a cucumber and a handful of radishes.

"So, nervous?" I try to sound casual while I grab a paring knife and begin carving radish roses. I may not be the best cook, but I can garnish like nobody's business.

"*Nervous* isn't exactly the word."

Please don't let *excited* be the word. I dig into another radish.

"Any idea what you're going to say to her?"

He shrugs and shakes his head while adding a dash more salt to the salmon.

I glance out back to make sure that Wren's still busy with Ruthie. "How about, 'are you kidding me? You stole my freaking sperm?' Something like that?"

He lets out an irritated, almost rumbling sigh. "Yes, I'm pissed. But what's done is done. And yes, I've got questions for her, but having it out with her isn't going to change anything."

I almost strain my ocular muscles suppressing an eye roll. Of course he's not going to get into a fight with Do-No-Wrong Jade. I check out back again. Wren carries Ruthie, wrapped in a beach towel, toward the house. I set down the final radish rose. Opening the sliding door, hot air seeps inside. Thank heaven Wren's started using the AC. "How was the pool?"

"Great," Wren says. "I'm going to get Ruthie dressed before my mom gets here. I could go without a lecture on making sure she doesn't sit around in a wet diaper." There's that halfhearted smile again. "And then I can help make the salad or whatever."

"Nah, we've got it under control." Now, how do I keep this evening under my control?

*

I send Wren and Ruthie to answer the door when we hear Jade's rental car pull up. Ruthie's the main one she wants to see, after all. (At least I hope she is.) And this way they can say hi while I hold Marie back and assess Jade.

Yep, as gorgeous as the photo on the company website. But Wren was wrong about Jade's fashion sense. She's wearing slim ivory capris and a cyan-blue tank that brings out her eyes. I'm guessing her car back home has a personalized plate that reads: SIZZERO. Her dark hair is back in a ponytail—but not a lazy, pulled my hair up in a scrunchie-because-it's-hot pony. No, this is a no-nonsense coiffure, every hair slicked perfectly against her head, then gathered at the nape of her neck in a tortoiseshell clip. Despite the heat, she looks elegant, cool, and beautiful. I should've known Wren would be an unreliable witness as to someone else's fashion sense.

Her hair gleams as she turns her head, taking in Ruthie, then Wren, then Ruthie again. With her hair back, I get a good look at her face. She seems practically makeupless, and although I know she's forty-eight, I'd have guessed she was closer to my age. Fine lines fan out around her eyes as she smiles and coos at Ruthie, but her forehead remains smooth. I wonder if she's visited the doctor for a round of injectables, but then she scrunches her face to play-bite Ruthie's arm, and her forehead scrunches too. Damn. She's naturally freaking beautiful. Yep, this is what the grand prize looks like.

I smooth my hair and glance at Barry, who's watching the scene between baby and grandma from under his eyebrows. The expression on his face is inscrutable.

"Gamma," Ruthie says repeatedly. She makes a breathy "hee" sound, the tip of her tongue sticking out between her perfect rosy lips. Wren shifts from one Doc Marten–covered foot to the other.

Jade strokes Wren's cheek. Wren looks like she's fighting the forces trying to drag the corners of her mouth down into a scowl. She waves a hand to welcome her mother inside. "Come in," she says.

Finally, Jade notices the rest of our familial unit—Barry, looking as uncomfortable as Wren, and me, holding back the wriggling Marie.

She heads for me first. "You must be Alex." She extends a hand, so I let go of Marie, but then she says, "Oh, what am I doing? We're practically family." She pulls me into a hug scented with the floral notes of what I'm guessing is insanely expensive perfume.

It's an awkward hug, since I have at least eight inches on her. Bending at the waist, I feel like the lumbering beast that I am. Why do I never feel tall, thin, and glamorous? Shouldn't she be the one feeling inadequate—short and stunted next to lofty supermodel-height me?

"How tall and lovely you are!" I stand straighter, basking in the compliment. (God, I'm pathetic.) "I'm a munchkin next to you. Did you model?" Before I can answer, she continues. "Barry, you did good." She throws a playful elbow out, nudging him. "And *you*." She takes him in, hands on slender hips. "Except for some grays, you look exactly the same."

"You too," Barry mumbles.

She runs her hand over her sleek hair. "Well, minus the grays though, for me." *Oh, that was snotty.* Yes, Barry's gone a bit gray, but he's just as handsome as he ever was. She laughs—no one else joins in—then adds, "Give me a hug, you big goof." I study Barry's face as he steps forward, but it's a blank mask. I'm glad at least to see he doesn't pull her into a tight squeeze; it's a perfunctory encircling of her in his arms.

"Would it be okay if our dog says hello to you?" I ask, interrupting their hug a fraction of a second after it starts. I've been giving Marie the silent *sit* and *stay* hand signals and periodically giving her the eye to make sure she stays. She's barely keeping her fluffy butt on the floor, staring, waiting to be released.

"Of course." I give Marie the okay, and she races to greet Jade, who holds out a hand for a thorough sniffing and then reaches for Marie's favorite itching spot—behind the ear. I'm stunned when Marie takes the smallest of steps backward. And she didn't even try to lick Jade's hand. Maybe she doesn't like Jade's perfume.

"Oh, shy, huh?"

Uh, no. Not usually. But then Marie's always been an excellent judge of character.

Before I can say anything, Jade continues, still smiling at the dog, "So Wren tells me her name's Marie as well." She seems unused to referring to her own daughter as Wren, and it's nice of her to play along in our efforts not to confuse the dog, but a knowing smile plays across her lips as she looks at Barry. What an intimate moment this might be, if only the wife weren't standing here, ready to tap a sandal impatiently on the floor.

Turning back to Wren, she grabs her by the arm, steering her to Barry's side. "Let me look at the two of you together for a second."

They look so similar, both wiry and obviously feeling awkward about being scrutinized. Barry's hand goes to shove his hair off his forehead, but he must see Wren make the same move, so he instead scratches his ear.

"I always knew she looked so much like you. But to see you together . . ."

"You could have seen us together a lot sooner, eh, Jade? I mean, if you'd really wanted to." Barry looks pointedly at Jade, and puts his right hand on his hip.

The loving gaze she'd been giving her daughter stops, and she blinks a few times, her face turning more serious, businesslike. "Hmm. Right. Look, I'm sorry things were sprung on you like this, Barry. I did try to call you at work and warn you Wren was coming, but I kept getting your voice mail, and it didn't seem appropriate to leave the news in a message. And I didn't have your cell number." She might as well be explaining a cost overrun to a business partner. "And as for telling you sooner, well, if I had to do it over again, I'd do it all the same." She smiles, and I can't believe how easily she's dismissing all of this. "Everyone always says, 'things happen for a reason,' and I'm sure there's a reason our situation worked out this way." *Um, yes, the reason is you,* I want to say. *You orchestrated Barry getting you pregnant, then hid it from him. And you probably would have gone on hiding it from him—and from Wren—if she hadn't stumbled upon the truth.*

Wren rolls her eyes in the background, and when I make eye contact with her, she makes an exasperated face. When Jade turns her way, Wren blinks, returns her face to a neutral expression, and busies herself with the buttons on Ruthie's jumper.

"What's done is done." Jade clasps her hands together. A flick of her head makes her ponytail swish across her shoulders. Apparently, she's switching to another topic; perhaps the ponytail swish is a move she uses in meetings at work. Barry looks at me, his jaw clenched. I wrinkle my eyebrows at him in an "I can't believe this woman" look. I flick my chin at him, urging him to say something.

"Jade, maybe I could speak to you for a moment, uh, in the kitchen," Barry says. *Oh no, Barry. I meant you should say something here, where I can listen in. Not in the other room!*

"Oh, why, certainly," she says with a surprised tone. She bats her eyelashes, and I want to yank them out, one by one.

Wren and I are still standing in the entryway. I shrug at her and motion that we should go sit. I hear Barry ask Jade something in a hushed, strained voice, but I can't make out what he says. I'm struggling to listen in, but Wren starts talking.

"So this is kind of awkward so far, huh?" she says with a nervous titter.

Ruthie, on Wren's lap, starts to fuss, and Marie rushes over, nose-poking her bare leg to check on her. Wren starts talking to the dog, thanking her for being so sweet. Ruthie giggles and claps now that Marie's here.

"Ball, ball," Ruthie shouts.

She loves to watch Marie play with her ball. Marie obliges, rushing to her toy basket to fetch her squeaky ball. Marie sits, chomping on the ball. It squeak-squeak-squeaks each time she rearranges it in her mouth.

I can just barely hear Barry's and Jade's hushed voices over the commotion. They might be getting louder, but so are the dog and the baby.

Wren mouths at me, "I wonder what's going on in there?" tilting her head toward the wall separating us from the kitchen.

I'm so tempted to suggest she take the dog and the baby outside to play so that I can eavesdrop and find out, but instead I just shrug. I try to act nonchalant, while straining my ears to hear. Things seem to have gone silent in the kitchen. Is it a standoff? Or are they sharing a reconciliatory hug?

A moment later, Jade reappears. There's a slight flush of color to her cheeks.

"So, Alex, I understand you're a designer," she says as if nothing's happened. She scans the living room, sadly still Romper Room–chic, then looks me straight in the eye and says, "What a beautiful home you have. I'd love a tour."

I'm dying to go check on Barry in the kitchen, and to find out what they talked about. "Wren," I say with a tight smile, "how about if you give your mom the tour? You can show her where you and Ruthie are staying."

"You can show her," Wren says. "I'm going to help my dad." She emphasizes *my dad*. I hear the refrigerator door shut a little too loudly. Marie tags after Wren and the baby, probably hoping something good came out of the fridge that she can partake in.

Damn it. I just want to join everybody else in the kitchen, but instead I adopt my fake-happy work voice that I use with clients who annoy me. "Alrighty, then." I lead Jade down the hallway. "Let's start at the back of the house." I open my hand, signaling for Jade to start down the hallway first, and try to sneak a peek at Barry in the kitchen, but his back is to me.

Although I don't want to be giving this tour, I can't help but feel the designer in me showing off our master suite and the third-bedroom-turned-office with some pride, since these are the only rooms untouched by the Babies "R" Us decorating team.

"This takes my breath away," Jade says upon entering our master bath. It's not big, but it is lovely, if I do say so myself. Dark cabinetry contrasts with white marble counters and modern his and hers rectangular vessel sinks. Oversize pale turquoise tiles fill one wall and are reflected in the large framed mirrors. There's no tub (our next remodel!), but the walk-in shower has multiple showerheads and a floor-to-ceiling surround of small glass tiles in shades of turquoise, sea-glass green, and pearl.

"Divine!" She runs a hand along the smooth ceramic wall tile. "What a fantastic color."

"The room's a bit small, but I made the most of the space we have." I could've designed the hell out of this room if it were bigger. I fantasize about having an en suite big enough to handle the scale of this chandelier I've had my eye on at Lime Light. Someday . . .

"I wish you lived closer. I'd hire you to redo my place."

Oh my God, I could use the work. Wonder if she'd be willing to pay my airfare up and back while the work's done? I could do it long-distance. Design via Skype? It could work! *Okay, stop. You're ridiculous. You are not going to long-distance design your husband's ex's place.* I shake my head, getting rid of my temporary insanity. Even with my money problems as bad as they are, and even if this woman were the last client on earth, I wouldn't want to work with this . . . what was it Wren called her? Oh yeah, this "lying nine-seventeen."

"You're too nice," I say, wanting to get this tour over with. "Let's go see the office." And let's make it snappy.

"This is lovely." Jade crosses the room, taking in the desk and book-cases. "Love the Paris theme."

I have a vintage travel trunk at the end of the bed, and a stack of old leather suitcases—my favorite thing in the room—forms a nightstand. A replica of the Eiffel Tower sits on the corner of the desk, and silver frames, filled with black-and-white photos of our tenth-anniversary Parisian getaway, stand out on the white shelving.

"It's one of my favorite cities," I say.

"Mine too." Well, there's something we have in common. Is she still in love with Barry? Do we have that in common too? She moves back toward the door and peeks out to make sure no one is coming down the hall. "Alex, I hoped to get you alone. I have a huge favor to ask."

Ah. So she didn't really want the tour.

I can't imagine what she's going to say, but I nod for her to continue.

"I'm sure you know Wren is still quite angry with me." She doesn't wait for me to confirm this. I mean, really, I'd have to be deaf and blind not to know. And even then, I'm pretty sure I could sense the annoyance radiating off Wren. "I did what I thought was best at the time, but she's determined to make me pay."

"Oh, I don't think she's trying to make you pay—" *Of course she's trying to make you pay, and she has every right to.*

"She simply refuses to listen to my apologies. I'm begging you to help me set things right with her." She looks around the room again. "Your home is so lovely, and I thank you so much for letting the girls move in. But wouldn't you and Barry like to have your lives back?"

Annoying as this woman is, she's got me there. I have to agree with her. *Yes, we want our lives back!* "Oh, the girls are no trouble at all." Why can't I say what I mean? I'm too used to being diplomatic in the extreme with my clients. *We need our lives back.* Can this woman help me get that?

"Still, it's best if they spend the rest of the summer back home with me. I'm going to be an empty nester soon enough when school starts. I need this time with my daughter. I had all these fun ideas planned for our last summer together. I even rented a cabin on Lake Tahoe for July and August. I'd pictured us spending weekends there." She looks down and blinks rapidly as if fighting back tears. "I'm just afraid if I don't mend things with Wren now, we'll grow further apart. And then who knows when I'll have a chance to make things right?"

I'm certain she's not the type to cry in front of a near-stranger. But even if those are fake tears, I've got to agree with her—it would be best if the girls went back home for the rest of the summer. This may be my out.

"I'm happy to help, but what can I do?" God help me, I can't help but feel like I'm about to sell my soul.

"Let me stay here." She brightens, blinking away potential tears. "I need a few days to turn things around. Right now, she barely takes my calls; I get one-word answers from her." She gives me a sad smile. "But if I was here, she couldn't shut me out. Not completely. And if nothing else, at least I'd have time with my Ruthie."

The devil and angel within me reappear. Should I do this, to help the mother-and-child reunion? That's a noble cause, right? I mean, Paul Simon even wrote a song about it. And wouldn't that speed up getting our lives back to normal? Or am I completely insane? Am I so anxious to restore calm to our home that I'd let the fox move into the henhouse? Well, I'll be here, the farmer keeping an eye on the fox. It'll be okay. It's risky, but it's my last, best chance at getting our house back for the rest of the summer.

I'm not sure I'm doing the right thing, I'm definitely not doing it for the right reason, but a girl needs her mom, doesn't she? And Wren still seems so angry with Jade that nothing's going to change unless we try something drastic. I swallow down my anxiety, my worries that I might live to regret this.

"Okay, well, we're . . . happy to do whatever we can to help you patch things up with Wren."

This definitely qualifies as drastic.

*

I shoo Wren out of the kitchen and tell her to go chat with her mom in the living room while Barry finishes dinner and I set the table. She tries to refuse, and almost wrestles the silverware out of my hands, but I insist. No time like the present to get them chatting again.

From the other room, I hear Jade's prodding voice, obviously peppering Wren with questions, and grunted or monosyllabic replies from her daughter. We're off to a slow start.

"I told Jade she could stay here," I whisper to Barry.

His head whips my way so fast I'm afraid he'll need to schedule a chiropractic appointment to get it back in line. He says nothing, but the furrows in his brow say this is not the way he'd have run with things.

"She begged. She says Wren'll barely talk to her. We need to help them mend their relationship."

"She can mend from her hotel room."

"This'll be better. It'll force Wren to interact with her mom." God, please let this be better. Have I just made the hugest mistake ever?

He returns to tossing the salad so aggressively that some of it flips up out of the bowl.

"It's only a few days. She flies out Wednesday. It'll all be fine," I say, trying to convince myself as well. "They need to make up, and this is the best way to help that happen."

Right?

CHAPTER 18

The next morning, a warm spot in the bed is the only reminder that Barry slept there. He gave me a quick kiss good-bye when he slipped out at the crack of dawn. As opposed to the last time he snuck out early, this time I'm pleased. I'm hoping it means he wants to avoid any more one-on-one time with Jade.

I'm still dying to know what went down in the kitchen between them last night. After a dinner filled with uncomfortable silences and a dessert course that would have been great with a side of Tums, Jade went back to her hotel to collect her things. Barry and Wren, early risers that they are, both claimed to be beat and went to bed early, leaving me to stay up watching TV until Jade got back. By the time I got her settled in the third bedroom and went to bed myself, Barry was asleep. And now he's gone already this morning. I'll call him later. He was pretty gruff last night. I'm not sure if he's pissed at me, at Jade, or at the whole situation. Hopefully he's in a better mood this morning.

At breakfast, Jade and I try to get a conversation going, but Wren focuses solely on feeding Ruthie. Ruthie fusses, as usual, rejecting the scrambled eggs Wren offers. Wren had been openmouthed annoyed last night after dinner when Jade announced she was going to "pop back to the hotel and grab her things," but hadn't said anything. She continues the mostly silent treatment this morning, making her seem even more like her dad.

"Try the airplane thing with the spoon," Jade suggests. "You loved that when you were little. Or let her feed herself."

Wren's jaw tightens, so I leap in. "Try telling her how much Marie loves eggs." I nod my head in Marie's direction, lying next to Ruthie's high chair. Marie's dark eyes follow the egg-filled spoon as if Wren were a hypnotist with a pocket watch. I can almost see the "Drop eggs, drop!" thought bubble over Marie's head.

"Marie *loves* eggs, Roo," Wren says.

Ruthie leans over her tray and checks with Marie to see if this is true. Marie's eyes widen with hope.

"All good puppies love to eat eggs," I say.

Ruthie looks at me, then back at Marie. She opens her mouth wide, while still contorted in her chair to watch the dog.

Wren quickly spoons in a mouthful.

Ruthie chews, woofs, and points at Marie.

"Is it okay?" Wren asks, moving to pinch a bit of eggs between her thumb and finger.

"Go ahead," I say. "It's for a good cause."

"Sit, Marie." Marie sits up and gently takes the eggs from Wren, gulping them greedily. Ruthie sits up higher in her chair. "Look," Wren says to me. "She's sitting up like Marie! I wonder how she learned that."

"Gosh, I wonder." I get myself some more coffee from the kitchen. Wren feeds Ruthie two more quick bites, and I pass and pat both dog and baby on their heads. "Good puppies."

Jade's sitting back in her chair, arms crossed, as I offer her more coffee. I guess I kind of usurped her helpful, all-knowing Grandma role. I fight the urge to break out in a self-satisfied grin.

"So do you three have plans for today?" I ask. "Because I was thinking the zoo would be fun. It's tiny, but nice. You can get close to the animals. Ruthie'll love it."

"That sounds delightful." Jade uncrosses her arms and leans into the table. "What do you say, Wren?"

"Will you come along?" Wren says to me.

"I can't. My client's waiting on me to finish her curtains, so I've got to go back to the studio and beat the sewing machine into submission."

"What kind of machine is it?"

"I forget the name. I've been calling it Voldemort. It's big. And angry. And it hates me."

Wren laughs. "I could probably figure it out. They all basically work the same." Before I can agree or disagree, Wren turns to her mom. "Take Ruthie to the zoo without me, maybe this afternoon after her nap. I've got to help Alex with her project." She splits the last of the egg between Ruthie and Marie, then gives them good-doggy pats.

"Wren, it's okay. I can figure it out. That's what YouTube's for, right? I'm sure there's some sort of how-to video on there."

"No. It's the least I can do to repay you guys for putting Ruthie and me up this summer."

So much for Wren spending time with Jade, but heaven knows I need the help. When Wren picks Ruthie up out of her high chair, I shrug and mouth "sorry" to Jade.

"Then tonight maybe we can get some takeout and play games or something," Jade says. "My treat!"

"My dad and I planned to watch some more *Next Generation* tonight."

"That sounds like fun too. Maybe you can fill me in on what I've missed?"

Wren doesn't answer. She simply hands Ruthie off to Jade and admonishes, "Don't let her eat any sugar at the zoo." Hmm. I think back to Cyn saying that her abs were the one thing she had control over. Maybe it's like that for Wren. In a world where she's controlled by her mom's purse strings, her vegetarian, organic, no-sugar rules give her some semblance of control. She gets to tell Jade what to do, not the other way around. I'm sure Wren would say it's for the environment, and for her and Ruthie's health, but maybe there's more to it than that. And maybe that's why she talks a better game at being green than she really is.

Wren points a finger at me and says, "*Don't* leave without me. I'll be ready in five."

Jade cranes her neck to see if Wren closed the bathroom door. "I'm sorry we're inflicting this drama on your life," she says softly while smoothing Ruthie's dress.

"It's okay. I remember inflicting some drama of my own when I was her age. I'll put in a good word for you while we're at the studio." *I have to. I'm not letting you stay here for no good reason.* This had better work.

"Thank you." Jade grabs for my hand and squeezes it, driving the prongs of my wedding ring into my pinky. "You're the best. Barry's a lucky man to have you."

Maybe I've been too hard on this woman all these years. I'm not saying I want to be best buddies with her, but I guess she seems like a decent enough person. I should have known Barry wouldn't have loved someone who wasn't.

"It's going to work out. You'll see." I gently extricate my hand. "I can ask Barry to plead your case with Wren too. I think his opinion pulls a lot of weight with her these days."

We hear the bathroom door open, so I grab my purse and a good-bye jerky treat for Marie. "Hi-ho, hi-ho, it's off to work we go," I sing-song for Ruthie's benefit. "Have fun at the zoo!"

*

"You run the thread around this thingy here, and then down here, back up here, and then down again and through the needle. See?" Wren's nose practically touches the hulking machine as she sets it up. "And there's this little doohickey here that helps you thread it."

"Don't go getting all technical on me." I try to watch, but her spiky hair obscures my view. "Don't just hand me a fillet here; I need to learn to fish." I push her to scoot over.

"Huh?" She looks at me.

"It's a saying." I bat at her shoulder again. "Let me. I need to figure out how to tame this beast." I lower my voice to an attempted baritone. "You are mine, Dark Lord."

Wren snorts, then applauds when I finally manage to thread it myself. "Can you show me how to figure out the tension too?" I ask. "Rache said you have to get it right or the stitches pucker up."

Wren shows me how to make adjustments while sewing some practice hems on scraps of extra fabric.

While she inspects the ironing job I've done in preparation for edging the curtains, I say, "So speaking of tension . . ."

She frowns at me. "You think I'm being too hard on my mom?"

"If you don't give her a chance and start talking to her, you're never going to work things out. Honestly, I thought your grandpa's funeral might bring you two together."

"Nope. We were busy getting stuff ready, and there were always a bunch of people around. It was pretty easy to avoid having a deep conversation. And then when she tried to, we got in that fight."

"You can't avoid her forever." Her intense glare says "watch me," so I add, "Well, you could. But she's your mom. I know what she did hurt you, but there's no going back and changing how it all happened. The important thing now is that you and your dad are getting to know each other."

"I guess," she reluctantly agrees while pinning the hems I've ironed.

"So you'll give your mom a chance? Talk to her? She loves you and Ruthie. She only wants what's best for you."

"Okay. I'll talk to her." She holds up one of the six panels I've prepped. She takes it to the window and turns it one way, then the other. "You ironed this one inside out."

"No!" I dash over and grab it from her. Yanking one of the other panels off the table, I hold them side by side in the daylight and notice the subtle difference in the fabric on one side compared to the other. "Ugh. I didn't notice under the fluorescent light, but you can totally tell by the window. Their place has tons of natural light. She would've noticed for sure. Please tell me I didn't totally eight-forty-three this? They didn't have any more of this color at the store."

"Nice use of the number system," she laughs. "We just have to iron it really flat again, then redo the hems. Good thing I noticed before we started sewing."

"You've totally saved my bacon." I give her a quick hug.

"No. You're the one who saved my . . . well, not my bacon, but you saved my tofu. Thanks for, you know, everything. With Ruthie and my mom and stuff." She half smiles at me, then grabs the iron. "Okay, let's fix this thing."

By midafternoon we've ironed, hemmed, hammered grommets in place, shared a huge vegetarian burrito lunch, and completed the project for Mrs. Marx.

"Thanks again. I appreciate your help with this," I say as we clean up the studio. I pick errant scraps of fabric off the table while Wren sweeps.

"It was fun. This was, like, one of the best days I've had in . . . months."

Poor thing. *This* day, hunched over the ironing board, nose to the sewing machine, has been her best day lately? The girl needs a treat.

"Let's celebrate. I know a great place where we can stop for sugar-free frozen yogurt on the way home. And it's right next to a second-hand clothes store."

*

The door into the house from the garage slams shut. Marie and I raise our heads to see what's up. I'm lying on the couch looking through *Architectural Digest*, and Marie was curled up asleep on the floor below me. The noise of the door is quickly followed by Barry flying in. Jade and Ruthie still aren't back from the zoo, and Wren's in her room with the door closed, listening to music.

"What's wrong?" I say, sitting up. I haven't talked to him all day. I tried to call him this morning when I first got to the office but got his voice mail. He'd texted me back: *Crazy-busy! Meetings all day.* Now he strides toward me, glaring. Marie normally runs to him when he comes in, but she carefully pulls her head into her shoulders and slinks forward. He ignores the sniff she gives his khakis, and she keeps going down the hall, glancing back at him, ears plastered to her head.

Oh my God. Today was the day. All those budget meetings, the cuts he's been mentioning. He got laid off. I glance at my watch; he's home at least an hour early. That has to be it. They always let people go on Fridays, right? My heart pounds.

"I just came from REI."

"REI? So you didn't get laid off?" Oh, massive *phew*. I sink into the sofa cushions again.

"What're you talking about? No, I left work early to go shopping."

Not laid off is good. Very good. Shopping shouldn't be a big deal. Barry buys almost nothing, not even presents for me. (I buy gifts for myself months in advance of my birthday and holidays and hide them in his sock drawer so that I'll forget.) He'll occasionally pick up some plants for the yard, and every six months or so he gets a new pair of running shoes, but I know there's enough room on our card for running shoes. He always buys the same pair, and they're always seventy-five dollars at REI. It's good to be married to a predictable man. Maybe someone cut him off in the parking lot? Their parking lot's always nutty, and people can be such jerks.

"Did you need new running shoes?"

"No. I did not." His nostrils flare as he sucks in air. "I went to get a baby jogger for Wren." Uh-oh. I know from Cynthia that they can easily be hundreds of dollars. Of course, Cynthia had to have the best one, and I remember she showed it to Barry once when he was giving her some advice on getting back into running after Bobby was born.

He stares at me, probably reading the thoughts racing through my mind. I can tell by the look on his face that I'm busted about the credit card. "And your card got rejected."

"Yes. It did. Do you know how embarrassing that is? I kept saying, 'There must be some mistake. Try it again.' But nope. *Denied.*" He emphasizes the last word, almost spitting it out.

"It's not as bad as it seems." I hold up a hand. I might still be okay here. "There *was* a decent amount of room on there until the other day when I had to buy a ton of this expensive fabric to redo Mrs. Marx's curtains. But we'll get that back as soon as she pays me for—"

"Why wouldn't that go on your business card?" he asks, but the snarky way he overenunciates tells me he already suspects that card is also at its limit.

"Okay, yeah, I know it should go on the business card, but I'm still paying that off from when Rache and I redid Salon Bellissima. But as soon as the work's done for Mrs. Marx, I'll have enough money to pay down part of our personal MasterCard with what she owes me for the fabric, and then I'll put the rest toward my business card."

"I can't believe you're sitting here acting like this is all going to be okay." He's still standing in the same spot he stormed to when he came in.

I sit up straight. "It will be," I say in a voice lacking conviction. There might as well be a question mark at the end.

"Don't even." He closes his eyes for a moment. "I thought at first there was a mix-up with the card. So I went to the ATM. I figured I'd get cash out of savings, then go back and get the jogger."

As soon as he says ATM, my heart hits the hardwood floor.

"The good news was, the ATM gave me the six hundred bucks I wanted," he says in a falsely cheerful voice. "But then, as I was putting the receipt in my pocket, I saw the balance." His voice steadily increases in volume. "You've almost drained our savings account. For your business. Haven't you?"

"Yes, but—" I stand up and move toward him.

"No. No buts." He turns away, looking out the front window. "I am so pissed at you right now, I can't . . ." At least he's not getting louder anymore, but he speaks slowly, choosing each word carefully. I don't think I've ever seen him this angry. No, I *know* I've never seen him this angry. We never fight. I'm completely unprepared for how he might act.

"I can still turn this around, Bear. I know I can make the money back—"

He raises a hand, cutting me off. "It's not about the money. It's about trust. You went behind my back." He finally looks at me. His eyes say it all—they look pinched and tired. Sad.

Now I'm the one who can't look straight ahead. A spot on the floor catches my eye, and for what might be the first time, I don't instantly bend down to spit shine it away. I study the spot. "I didn't want you to be disappointed in me. I know I should have talked to you, but I believed I could make this work." I take a deep breath. "I still believe it. I believe in *me*."

He grasps my shoulders, and I have no choice but to look into his sad eyes. "I believe in you too, Alex. But you didn't give me a chance to show you that." He walks away exasperated. "You took the money and then lied about how things were going."

"Well, things wouldn't be quite this bad if you'd come home the other day when I begged you to. But *no*. 'Take Ruthie with you,' you said. You've left way more of the burden with these girls on *my* plate." I try to deflect some of his anger. "I'd probably have the job with the Van Dierdons if you'd come home and watched Ruthie like I asked!"

"Don't try to turn this around on me. I told you I couldn't get out of that meeting. We're talking *serious* budget cuts at work. Like, I-could-lose-my-job cuts. And I've had a totally false picture of where we're at financially. I've been thinking we'd be okay if I got laid off. Not great, but we'd survive on your income and our savings. Now I find out we have no savings. What're we going to do if I get laid off? In this market, it might take forever to sell the house, and even if we did, we'd hardly make anything, thanks to our line of credit. We . . ." His voice starts to shake. "I can't even look at you right now."

"There're our retirement accounts. We could use those if we had to. Besides, you're not going to get laid off. You've been there your whole career."

"That doesn't matter. They could still cut me." He barks out a harsh laugh. "And as for our retirement savings, I guess I should thank you for not completely raiding our nest egg. That's fantastic. I applaud your good financial sense! Suze Orman would be proud!"

"I can still make this right. There's still time to save the business."

"I don't know if I can believe you. I thought all along the business was doing okay." He takes a deep breath. "I don't want to talk about this anymore. I need some time. To think."

"I'm really sorry. I know I should have told you, but . . . Look, uh, why don't you go for a run, and when you get back I'll go through everything with you. I'll be totally open."

"I'm not ready to process all of this, Alex. One run is not going to clear my head."

"Okay then, I could . . . go to my office for a while. I could suggest Jade take the girls out to dinner. Then we could have some quiet time here for ourselves. I could stop at Zen Noodle on my way home and—"

"No," he yells. "Bringing me my favorite Thai food is not going to smooth this over." His calm, methodical selection of words is gone. He's never yelled at me before. Sure, he's raised his voice in frustration here or there, but never flat-out yelled. "Do you have room on your credit card for takeout? Look, I want you to go."

"Go?" I ask quietly.

"Go! You can take the dog, but go. I don't know where. Your sister's. Rachel's. Wherever. But not a hotel room, because God knows we can't afford that. I'd go myself, but I'm sure you don't want to be here alone with the girls."

"No, you're right." At this point I'd pretty much agree to anything to make him stop looking at me with that hurt expression on his face. And to make the yelling stop. *God, has Wren heard all this? Please let her music be turned up too loud!* At least Jade's still out with Ruthie. "I'll go. I'll take Marie, and we'll go to my sister's. Please tell the girls I went to Cynthia's to, I don't know, help her redecorate Fuzzy's room or something. I don't want them to know we're—"

"Of course," he starts yelling again. "Because how things look is always what's most important, right?"

"I just—" But I'm talking to his back. And then he's out the front door. I don't know where he's headed. I didn't dare ask.

I retreat down the hall, Marie squirming behind me. She follows me to the bedroom, ears plastered to her head. I close the door so that Wren won't hear me crying.

I fall on the bed. How could I have screwed everything up so massively? God, if only Wren and Ruthie hadn't showed up this summer. Why couldn't they have showed up in the fall? Did she have to come down for school early? If they weren't here, I would have gotten the job with the Van Dierdons. I'd still have Rache working for me. I'd have money coming in to help me climb out of this hole. And I wouldn't be about to pack up and leave my own home. My home where my husband will be living with his ex.

Oh my God.

What the hell did I do, inviting Jade to stay with us?

Marie jumps up next to me. She frantically kisses my cheeks, lapping up tears. Her ears droop. She's not used to Daddy yelling and Mama crying.

I reach out and rub the silky spots behind her ears. After a few minutes of feeling sorry for myself, I start packing. I want to be gone before Barry gets back. I can't handle seeing the hurt in his eyes again. I shove enough clothes for a few days into my overnight bag. I don't know how long Barry wants me out of the house, but I'm hoping the weekend will be enough.

I splash cold water on my cheeks and swab at my wandering mascara with a tissue. A heavy hand with the face powder hides the worst of the redness.

Twenty minutes later, when I come out of the bedroom, followed by a rolling bag and Marie, Barry's still not back.

Wren is closed up in her room. Did she hear everything, or the gist of it? This place isn't that well insulated. Hopefully she just heard the raised voices, and not the stuff I said about Ruthie or what a "burden" they've been. I fight the urge to slink away and instead go tap on her door.

She opens it a crack. "Yeah?" she says, wide eyed.

"I'm going to visit my sister for the weekend. Kind of a last-minute thing." I tell myself I'm doing this not because I'm concerned about appearances, but because I'm saving Barry from having an awkward conversation with her. Yes, I'm doing this to be thoughtful. Right?

"Okay." She must've heard us fighting and doesn't know what to say. "Is everything cool?" She peers past me, presumably looking for her dad, and chews her lower lip. I'm going to work under the assumption she only heard our raised voices and not what we said.

"Yep," I say, blinking to keep from tearing up. "Everything's cool." More like ice cold. "I'm taking the dog with me."

"Ruthie'll miss her. We'll, uh, see you Monday, then?" She slumps against the doorjamb.

"Yeah, see you." I head for the garage, but stop and turn back. "Don't forget to give your mom a chance while I'm gone. Okay?"

She frowns, but nods.

I suppose it's not too surprising that she mentioned Ruthie will miss the dog, but not me.

CHAPTER 19

Saturday morning, I wake in Cynthia's guest bedroom/crafting room/ office. She's got a daybed in here so as to maximize space for her crafting supplies and work area. I try to stretch, but my feet smack against the white wooden bed frame. I yawn, loudly, since I didn't sleep much, trying to figure out how I can make things right with my business and with Barry. I must have yawned too loudly, because the bedroom door opens and A.J. pokes his spiky-haired head in.

"Are you awake, Aunt Alex?" he stage whispers. Marie thumps her tail on the carpet at the sight of him.

I pull the covers over my head and shout, "No!"

He jumps on the bed. "Are too!" Marie leaps on the bed as well.

Pretending to saw logs, I remain hidden under the quilt.

Marie paws at me, while A.J. lifts the blanket to peer underneath. I snap my eyes shut.

"You're awake. Come eat pancakes!" He bounces on his knees, shaking the whole bed. Marie woofs, excited at this fun game. "Mom says we can't eat until everyone comes down."

"What if I'm not hungry?" I emerge from the blankets and yank him down to snuggle next to me. Marie squeezes between me and the backrest of the daybed, wriggling onto her back, long legs kicking the air. While rubbing her belly with one hand, I pull the blanket over A.J.'s head with the other. "You look like you could use forty more winks yourself. Let's go back to sleep." If only I could sleep the next year or so away.

He comes out from under the blankets gasping for air. "No, it's time to eat."

"In a minute. You go ahead. Tell your mom I said you guys don't have to wait for me."

"It's okay. I'll wait." He snuggles back into me. Marie flumps onto her side, satisfied to wait with us. "I'm glad you're here. Is Uncle Barry going to come too?"

"Would you like that?"

"Yeah. He's cool."

It surprises me to hear that A.J. likes his uncle Barry, since Barry, to me anyway, always seems somewhat curt with the boys. "He's cool?"

"Yeah. He doesn't talk to me like I'm a kid, like Mom does. Or Grandma." That's true. No baby talk for Barry. He always attempts to give honest, scientific answers to the boys' nonstop "why is the sky blue?"–type questions. "He's smart about rocks and bugs and stuff."

"He sure is a fan of rocks and bugs and stuff." It's funny to see Barry through someone else's eyes, especially a child's. "You're right. I think he's cool too." I know it's only been one night, but I miss him. Hell, it's been more than one night since I saw him properly—as my partner, as my best friend. Why didn't I confide in him about everything that's going on?

"So is he coming?" A.J. asks, before I have time to think about the answer to my question.

"I wish he was, bud. But not this time."

"Bummer."

"I know. Total bummer." I tousle his hair. "Let's go stuff our faces with pancakes."

*

While I help Cynthia clean the kitchen after breakfast, she says, "I still can't believe Barry kicked you out. Jamie can't believe it either."

"You told Jamie?"

"He kind of guessed. You show up on our doorstep with a red face, an overnight bag, and the dog. The man's no Dr. Phil, but he knows a fight when he sees one."

"Do you guys ever fight?" Cynthia and I have never been the kind of sisters who call on each other for support. I only showed up here because I had nowhere else to go. Rache doesn't have room since her mom moved in with them, and I didn't want to drive all the way to my mom and dad's.

"Of course we fight. Everybody does."

"Barry and I never do."

"You guys are a practically perfect couple. That's why I can't believe your first big fight is *so* big he boots you out."

Her voice sounds borderline gleeful. I almost say, *I'm glad you're getting so much joy from my pain,* but instead go with, "We are *not* practically perfect." I've sometimes wondered if we never fight because our love isn't of the hot-blooded variety that brings great highs and lows. I know he used to fight with Jade, at least about having kids. "Maybe it's a bad sign we never fought. I mean, we've had disagreements now and then—over stupid things, like whether he'd wear his running shoes out to a nice restaurant. Or at first he was totally against that turquoise tile in our bathroom—but never a *fight*. Never yelling."

"I don't think it's a bad sign. I think it's amazing. I mean, it's not completely normal, but then you don't usually do things the way other people do them."

"What's that supposed to mean?"

"Don't get all defensive. I'm just saying, most folks who get married have kids, and kids bring stress. Yes, they bring joy too, but they also bring stress. And they eat up all your time. So between the kids' needs and the lack of time, it's fertile ground for arguments."

"Look, I know I'm not normal, you don't have to remind me."

"That's not what I'm saying. I'm saying you and Barry have a special relationship. You have *time* for each other. You *talk* to each other. You're together solely because you love each other. I wouldn't trade my boys for the world, but it'd be nice to have some alone time with my husband now and then. A lot of my friends are basically staying together for the kids' sake at this point. I . . . I'm saying I envy you that."

"You do?" I start crying. I try to wipe away my tears, but my hands are wet from rinsing the dishes. "We don't have anything to envy right now."

Cynthia hands me a paper towel. "You do too. This is just a bump in your relationship. You'll get through this." I told Cyn the whole story last night, but I'm still not sure if she gets how big a deal this is.

"I screwed up though. Big-time. I may not be able to get us out of this hole I dug. And if I can't, and if he gets laid off . . ." I practically start hyperventilating. I could soon be a divorced, homeless dog-mom, living in my BMW. The back room of my office is roomy, and there's a bathroom, but they'll evict me soon if I can't cover the rent.

"You'll get through this. You'll get through it together." She pats my shoulder and goes back to wiping down the counters. "If there's one thing I know, it's that Barry supports you. He's mad because you didn't tell him what was going on. He probably would've been the first one to suggest that you use your savings if you'd been straight with him all along."

"I don't know about that."

"I've seen how he is with you. Like the last time I was there—he was totally into your design ideas. He did that research on color for you. He helps you with your work." Her voice sounds caught in her throat. "He doesn't . . . tear you down." She sniffles.

"What's wrong?"

"Nothing. Same ol' poop. Different day."

"Is Jamie on you to go back to your dental work?"

"Yeah, but it's stupid. I didn't make that much money. And with what we'd have to pay for child care, it's just—it doesn't make sense. If I loved the work, sure, okay, I'd go back. But I don't even like it. And the boys are only going to be little for a few more years. I know you only see what a pain in the butt they can be, but they can be sweet too."

"I know they can be sweet."

"And let's face it, this is probably the sweetest they'll ever be. After this, it'll be homework stress and driving to baseball games, and then teenage hormones, and then they're off to college. It's going by so fast already, and I don't want to miss out. I want to stay home."

"Of course you do." I wouldn't want to rush back to poking my hands into strangers' mouths either. "Did you tell Jamie that?" I sit on the bar stool while Cyn rinses her hands.

"Sort of."

"What do you mean, 'sort of'?"

"He hates his job too, so he doesn't have a lot of sympathy for me not wanting to go back. I think he thinks I'm being lazy."

"You're the least lazy person I know. You're constantly running after the boys, not to mention literally running *with* them. You're like Mom, always on the go."

"Why doesn't he see that?" She grabs a fresh towel out of the drawer and drapes the damp one over the oven handle. While she fusses with the used towel, she says, "I . . . I wish my marriage were more like yours."

When she turns to look at me, I say, "You wish your husband had booted you out of the house, leaving him alone with his ex-girlfriend and their love child? Yes, it is an enviable position." I nod my head sagely, and we laugh until we're both crying again. I try to start laughing again and sputter, "Man, are we pathetic or what?"

Only half of Cyn's mouth manages a smile. She hands me another paper towel and grabs one for herself. We blow our noses in stereo. She comes around the bar, and we hug.

"Cyn, are you—when you say you have friends who are only together for the kids, do you mean . . . ?"

She looks as if she might start to weep too hard to speak, but after a moment, her lips stop trembling. "I don't know. It's not something we've said out loud to each other. But it's not like we talk about much of anything lately." Then she starts to cry again.

"I've been a crap big sister, all wrapped up in my own stuff. I want to do what I can to help. I don't want you and Jamie to go through the motions for the boys. I want you to be happy. Like Barry and I used to be."

"Like you *are*." Cyn sniffles and takes a jagged breath, starting to calm down.

"Anyway, I wanna help. Starting today. I know I don't look like a great businessperson at the moment, but let's assume it's the economy and not my lack of skills. If you want, we can sit down together and go over your business plan."

"Business plan?"

"Okay, we can put together a business plan. And let's do a spread-sheet showing how much you'd bring home if you went back to your old job, after taking out taxes and day care. And then we'll do some sales projections for your Baby Bath Time biz." Last night while helping me get settled, she'd showed me her latest idea—a set of natural soaps and butt balm (okay, she called it "diaper balm") for babies. The sample packages she'd put together smelled wonderfully of coconut, olive oil, and honey. I told her I knew a perfect test subject, and she said she'd actually already sold the first few small batches on Etsy. "We'll compare the two, and hopefully we can make a convincing case for Jamie to give you at least a year to get your business going."

"That'd be great. I definitely need help putting some numbers together. I've been feeling really alone in this."

"And"—I pause and look my sister in the eyes—"tonight, I'm going to babysit the boys, and you and Jamie are going on a date." Watching those three will at least keep my mind off my own problems. Why is it that other people's problems always seem easier to work out?

"Do you know what you're saying? All three of them?"

"A.J. and I are partners. He'll help me with the rug rats."

"Still . . . do you think you can handle it?"

"I managed to keep Ruthie alive for three days; I'm pretty sure I can keep the three of them alive for three hours."

"It's sweet of you to offer, but I don't know if Jamie'll want to. He recorded some car race the other day, and I know he wants to watch it tonight." Her mouth slants into the same pout I saw on Fuzzy's face this morning when he learned the pancakes were not of the chocolate chip variety. It makes me sad that she thinks her husband won't want to go on a date with her.

"I'll handle Jamie. You make the reservation at your favorite restaurant and figure out what you're going to wear."

"We don't have a favorite restaurant." Tears well up again in her eyes. "How pathetic is that? We've lived here almost six years and have never gone to a nice restaurant together. It's always Chuck E. Cheese–type places."

"We'll search online for someplace romantic. Your new favorite restaurant. No gigantic buck-toothed rats pimping pizza."

She sputters a laugh and dabs the corners of her eyes with the paper towel. "Okay. Will you help me pick out something to wear?"

Maybe because I pitch the idea instead of Cynthia, Jamie easily agrees to the idea of a date night with his wife. I make him promise to take the night off from talking about work. Then Cyn and I spend the rest of the day putting together the beginnings of a business plan. One of the great things about her idea is that the "all-natural" crowd doesn't go in for flashy wrappings; inexpensive brown butcher paper, a decent laser printer for labeling, and some twine is all she needs to package a cute gift set. The ingredients are top-notch and pricey, but buying them in bulk means the numbers look pretty good. Better, at least, than pumping everything she'd make at a dental office into day care costs.

We celebrate with a glass of wine while going through her closet. Having had few occasions to dress up lately, her choices are limited, but she tries each dress on, pairs them with this or that pair of heels, hair down, then up. She looks fantastic in all of them, which I tell her repeatedly while freely admitting to being jealous of her tight abs and tush. We settle on an emerald-green halter dress that makes her eyes sparkle. With her hair in a loose French twist, she looks ready not only for the hot weather but also for a hot date with her hubby.

When Jamie and Cyn say good-bye to the boys, they look a bit awkward-first-date-ish. Cyn reaches for the door to the garage as Jamie goes to open it for her, and they bump into one another. I hope that isn't the most contact they've had lately, but it may well be, judging by the way they both lurch back and mumble apologies. *Please let them have a good time,* I think as the door closes behind them.

"Okay!" I clap my hands as four sets of eyes—three human, one canine—stare at me. "Let's have some fun. Who wants root beer?" We crowd into the kitchen where everyone but Marie takes me up on the offer.

The boys drink their mercifully caffeine-free root beer, watching me over the tops of their glasses while they gurgle and slurp. "Slow down," I say. "We don't want this to turn into a burping contest." The boys bend over with laughter.

Belching humor. Gets them every time. Still, it's weird at first, because they're not used to alone time with me. While I get dinner ready, A.J. tries to take advantage of our buddy code. "Mom lets us eat at the coffee table in front of the TV *all* the time."

I assume it's not true but simply say, "We're doing it Auntie Alex's way tonight. And that means we set the table—which you're in charge of—and we all use napkins and not our sleeves."

We decide on a cowboy tablescape. We find red, white, and blue plates and napkins left over from the Fourth of July; A.J. donates his plastic horses for the centerpiece; and we make lasso napkin rings out of some brown raffia I find in Cyn's craft stash. I take a photo with my phone of them seated at the table saying, "Beans!" We feast on turkey hot dogs (Marie's a huge fan), canned baked beans, and baby carrots. I try to convince them that cowboys eat green beans, not pintos—and I almost have Fuzzy and Bobby buying it until A.J. sets them straight, like a good big brother should. I consider the meal a resounding success, especially since A.J. restrains himself to only one fart joke.

After dinner, we watch *Rustlers' Rhapsody*—the old Western parody starring Tom Berenger—which they've seen a million times. It cracks me up because they don't view it as parody. To them, it's a straight-up cowboy movie, and the three of them straddle various pieces of furniture, riding along on horseback and whooping. I have words with Fuzzy, though, when he tries to ride Marie.

"How many times do I have to tell you? No riding the dog! Ever." He settles for putting a cowboy hat on her, and I help tie a bandana around her neck.

When they're tucked in bed, after "just one more story" and drinks of water that they slurp from the sink, pretending it's a stream near camp, they finally crash.

I try to read a magazine, but instead sit and stare at the page while the type blurs. It's been good to forget my own troubles for a day.

The clock on the fireplace mantel chimes eleven thirty. Hmm. It's late. I know one dinner date is not going to turn back the clock to newly wedded bliss, but hopefully it's a start.

Maybe Barry and I need a new start. Cyn's words come back to me. "Barry supports you." I've been totally taking him for granted.

Marie sits up suddenly; her keen ears must hear Jamie's car. Sure enough, a moment later they come in through the garage door. They chatter as they enter.

"How was dinner?" I get up from the couch and follow Marie to welcome them.

"Great." "Terrible." They both speak at once, and I'm worried about the terrible comment, but then they look at each other and laugh.

"That restaurant was gross," Cyn explains.

"We left after the appetizers," Jamie adds. "Cynnie's salad looked like they'd pulled some of the lettuce out of the trash." I haven't heard him call her Cynnie in a while.

"Seriously, I don't know how that place stays in business. Those online reviews had to be from the owners' family."

"We ended up grabbing burritos at our favorite Mexican place and taking them down to the beach."

"Jamie still has this old blanket in the trunk of his car."

"I got it for like five bucks in Tijuana one time. Back in college."

They exchange a glance again.

"Memories," Cyn says.

"If that blanket could talk, eh, Cynnamon?" It's a very good sign that he's using her favorite nickname. I know this only because she heard Barry call me "Legs" once, and having always been a bit touchy about being shorter than me—maybe because I teased her about it relentlessly growing up—she made a point of letting me know Jamie liked to call her "his spicy Cynnamon." It's possible I made a gagging sound when she told me, which wasn't very nice, but right now I'm happy to see Cyn giggle like a prom queen as Jamie waggles his eyebrows at her.

Her eyes are glowing as she looks back at him. *Booze or bliss?* I wonder. Her messy hair looks speedily finger combed. *Hmm, bliss.*

"That's my cue to go to bed." I give them both a hug, and they smell like the ocean. Jamie has some sand on his shoulder, which I brush off with a raised eyebrow.

They giggle together as I close my bedroom door. I make a silent wish that this will be the start of happier times for them. They still clearly have a lot of stuff to work through, but hopefully tonight is a reminder of how good things used to be between them.

When I lay down, Marie hops up next to me. It's crowded on the daybed and a bit warm for cuddling, but I assume she's not sure what's going on and is wondering where Daddy is. I spoon her and stroke her fur.

"I'm confused too, babe." How did I let my marriage get to be such a mess?

I think back to the things A.J. said about Barry, and that Cyn said about our marriage. I've been blinded by the stress of all this business stuff. I lost sight of what matters most—my relationship with Barry.

Why didn't I tell him what was going on? Cynthia's right; he's always supported me. Why did I think he wouldn't?

Maybe I'm so used to my mom not supporting my reproductive decisions, I thought Barry wouldn't support my business ones. I've always been number two in my mom's affections and felt like that with Barry too. It felt good the other day to finally tell Mom the whole truth about not wanting to have kids. I have to tell Barry everything as well.

I can still turn my business around. I know I can. If I can keep the doors open until people are ready to open their checkbooks again, I can make it a success. But I have to own up to how I've messed up. I have to go over all the numbers with Barry. And I've got to come up with some ideas to stay afloat while the economy turns around.

I could sell my car.

I don't need a BMW. And luckily I own it outright, thanks to Barry's insistence that we save up to buy it instead of getting a loan. Oh, I whined at the time, but he was so right! Now I can sell it and get a used car: something big enough for the five of us, maybe a hatchback so that Marie can ride in the back. Sure, I've always justified having a fancy car because I sometimes drive clients to showrooms and antique stores, but I can make up excuses for why they need to meet me there. I can do this. The money will probably be enough to pay my office rent for at least two months. I could sell Voldemort too, if it comes down to that. I don't know how to use that thing properly anyway, and if things pick up enough someday for me to hire Rache back, I'll buy her a new machine.

I have to go tell Barry my ideas. I have to apologize and beg him to forgive me. I've been taking him for granted. He's the best thing that ever happened to me, and I need to make sure he knows that.

I reach for my phone. Almost midnight. Too late to call. I'll get up early and drive home. I want to catch him before he goes on his Sunday morning run. That means I'll have to get up really early, since it's an hour drive. He knows I'm not a morning person, so it'll be a surprise for him to see me there. If he tries to kick me out again, I won't take no for an answer. I'll make him listen, and he'll see that I know how badly I screwed up.

This has to work.

I try telling Marie her adoption bedtime story so that I can relax and get to sleep. It works for her, but I'm too excited. I can't stop practicing what I'll say to Barry.

I imagine him forgiving me and holding me tightly in his arms. For some reason, I imagine this scene playing out on the front lawn, and us kissing deeply, madly, in front of our neighbors, who stumble out for the morning paper in sleep-shaped hair and ratty slippers. Of course, every time I imagine this happy scene of us getting back together, it morphs into the hurt look in Barry's eyes when he told me to get out of the house.

Please let him listen to me. It can't be too late for me to make this right.

CHAPTER 20

I finally fall asleep around one, then wake at four. With this heat wave, Barry's been heading out for his weekend runs by six at the latest, so I had to set the alarm for oh-dark-thirty.

By the time I quietly dress, brush my hair, and put on some face powder, blush, and mascara (in no imagining of our happy reunion was I blotchy and uncoiffed), it's 4:20 a.m. I'll be home around 5:20. Perfect. I imagine slipping into bed with Barry; imagine the warmth of his skin, his musky smell, the coolness of the sheets—the good ones that I switched over while Wren was away. Everyone raves about "make-up sex." Fingers crossed this will be my chance to find out what all the fuss is about.

I grab a breakfast bar from the pantry, leave a note for my sis, and then Marie and I dash out to the car. I'd normally need at least one cup of coffee before even considering an hour-long drive this early, but nervous energy makes me feel like I've had a double espresso, even with only three hours of sleep.

The radio covers the top news and monotonously reports the "continued hot and dry" forecast. I try my favorite rock station, but the hyper beat frays my nerves; on the classical station a frenzied crescendo of violins matches my too-rapid heartbeat. I give up and shut it off. As I race north, I practice various ways of starting my plea to Barry.

I turn into our quiet cul-de-sac just before 5:15. I must've been speeding a bit more than usual. He should still be in bed. I park in the driveway, afraid that the noise of the garage door will wake everyone in the house. We need private time, not an audience of Jade and the girls.

Marie and I trot up the front walkway. The house is dark and silent in the predawn light.

Before we reach the door, an acrid, burning smell hits me. My breath catches in my chest. What the hell is happening? If my heart was beating fast before, it hammers double time now. Childhood memories of classroom fire safety lessons surface from hidden depths; I feel the door. It's not hot; neither is the handle. I turn my key in the lock and throw the door open. Marie balks at the fumes; smoke twirls and shape-shifts above our heads. There's an eerie light in the living room.

I remember another exercise we practiced in school, all of us dropping to the hard linoleum floor and scurrying down the rows between our desks. On hands and knees, I scramble across the foyer heading for the bedrooms. Marie stops and whines. Is she too afraid to follow? I look back and see Wren asleep on the sofa.

We rush to her. Marie licks her face. I shake her shoulders, kneeling beside her.

"Wake up! There's a fire."

"Uh . . ." She blinks a few times. Thank God she's not passed out. "Wha—?"

I squeeze her arm so hard I probably leave a mark. "Get Ruthie! There's a fire." I start toward the hall on hands and knees again. "Stay low!" I yell over my shoulder. "I'll wake Barry and your mom." Marie keeps licking Wren's face. She's not fully awake, but finally she pushes at the dog and swings her legs off the sofa. I call to Marie, "Come!" I can't lose track of her. Knowing Wren will run for the baby, I race toward the bedrooms with Marie behind me.

In the hallway, smoke billows from the guest bath on the left, accumulating against the ceiling. I don't see flames, only an eerie greenish-gray color. I squint; my eyes burn. I scuttle past, holding my breath.

The guest bedroom door, across the hall, stands shut, thank God, keeping Ruthie safe. Wren will have her out before I've even woken Barry and Jade.

I veer toward our room first. I don't consciously weigh the "Barry versus Jade" decision; all I know is I need my husband. I need him to help me get everyone out. I need to *see* him. I need to be sure he's okay. "Barry!" I scream as I near the door.

Before reaching our door handle, a loud pop sounds behind me. A fresh jolt of adrenaline shoots through me, reminding me to check the door before I open it—it's cool under my palms. I glance to my right, expecting to see Marie, but there's nothing but green-gray smoke. "Marie!" Oh God. Where'd she go? I try to swallow, but my tongue sticks to the roof of my mouth. Panic rises in me; I try to fight it. I want to cry. I need Barry. My hands shake as I thrust the door open. Thick ropes of smoke course into the room ahead of me. Barry's on the bed. He sprawls in his usual position—facedown, one leg kicked out from under the sheets, his right arm hanging over the edge of the bed. It's a surreally calm image in the midst of the madness swirling around me. Seeing him floods relief through my veins. Barry will know what to do. He'll help me find Marie.

"Barry! Fire!" I lunge for him.

He stirs. I sit back on my heels and shake his shoulder hard. He blinks. I let go of his arm as I hear rustling sounds behind him.

And then I see her.

Jade props herself up on one elbow, holding the sheet over her breasts with her other hand. Her hair falls, full and messy around her shoulders. She blinks several times, then her eyes widen at the sight of the smoke roiling along the ceiling.

Barry twists to see what I'm gaping at. "What the—" he yells.

"There's a fucking fire!" I pound his arm with the side of my fist. "Get up!" The acrid air rips at my vocal cords. Survival instinct wins out over any other thoughts. "The window!"

I don't want to see Jade climb, naked, from our bed. I just want to find Marie and get the hell out. I stand and try to run, stooped, back into the hallway, but it's too hot, and I can't see anything. Terrified, I drop back to my knees. "Marie!" I scream.

I fly past Ruthie's now-open door. Thank God: Wren must have gotten her out!

I'm still frantically trying to find Marie, when I crash into Wren in the foyer, passed out on the floor, alone.

"Wren . . ." If she doesn't have the baby—

I turn back to Ruthie's room. Crackling sounds come from the bathroom, but I only see smoke, thicker now, darker. The greenish tinge from before is gone.

Through the open guest bedroom door, I see Marie's cream-colored haunches in the dim light. I reach her just as she drags Ruthie by her pajamas to the edge of the bed. Ruthie, not fully awake, sputters and coughs. She starts to cry, and it's the best sound I've ever heard.

I scoop the baby into my arms. For a fraction of a second I consider dropping her and Marie out the window into the backyard, but I can't lose a moment in getting Wren out.

Cradling Ruthie with one arm, I hold my breath and press her to me, hoping to shield her from the worst of the heat. I scurry back to the foyer, crouching, staying as low as possible. "Marie, go!" I point out the open front door. She stays at my side. I clasp Wren's wrist to drag her out. Marie bites at the strap of Wren's overalls and helps tug her limp body over the front door's threshold.

As we collapse onto the stoop outside, we practically crash into Barry, who is leaping up the steps. He swings Wren into his arms and rushes her to a shady spot on the lawn at the farthest corner from the house.

Black clouds billow out the bathroom and garage windows.

Jade huddles in a short silk robe next to Wren. At least she's not still wrapped in my sheets. She trembles all over; her hand covers her mouth as she watches Barry with Wren. Incoherent words tumble out of Jade. She sees Ruthie in my arms and flails for her. "I've got her," I snap, moving toward Barry. I clutch Ruthie to me tighter than before. She cries against my chest, rubbing her eyes, and I stroke her hair, murmuring that she's okay.

Barry kneels next to Wren and holds two fingers to her neck.

"Is there . . ." I'm afraid to finish the question. Jade sobs behind me. Should he be doing CPR? They didn't go this in-depth in our grade school emergency training. We were taught the basics, not tips on how to handle someone unconscious from smoke inhalation. Not what to do after discovering your husband in bed with his ex while your house burns down. Anger, confusion, panic, and fear all fight to rule my head. Fear wins. I squeeze Ruthie, keeping her head turned into me so that she can't see her mom, seemingly lifeless on the ground.

"There's a pulse." Barry looks up at me, his face filled with relief. He turns back to Wren and pats her cheeks. "Wren? Can you hear me?"

At least he looked to me, not Jade.

Wren's eyelids flutter, and she rolls to her side, coughing. Barry rubs her back and tells her she's going to be okay. Jade flops down, hugging her and crying, "My baby. My baby."

Tilting my head back, I mouth "thank you" to the sky.

Now that I know Wren's okay, I look back at the house. Glass shatters as one of the windows blows out. Black fingers of smoke escape the narrow windows on the side of the garage, like a devil's hands, trying to rip the roof off.

"Did anyone call 911?" I ask no one and everyone.

Barry's wearing one of his ratty old racing T-shirts (one that I've told him he's no longer allowed out of the house in) and a pair of blue plaid boxers. He holds up his hands. "I didn't think to grab my phone."

"My purse." Did I leave it in the car? No. I took it inside with me. I must have dropped it in the foyer. "Mine's in the house." I point.

Barry jumps up. "You're not going back in there."

"No," I study his worried eyes. "Of course not."

"I thought you might want to try to save some of our things."

"I have everything I need here." I look down at Marie, Ruthie, back at him. The image of Jade sitting up, clothed only in my sheets, fills my vision. "Or I thought I did," I mumble. My throat burns.

"Alex," Barry starts. He's takes my hand, but I yank it away.

"Just go get Mr. Wilson or somebody to call 911."

Suddenly, I can barely hold Ruthie's weight. The adrenaline that propelled me drains away, along with what feels like all the blood in my limbs. I collapse onto the curb and let go of Ruthie. She crawls to her mother, who calls her name and reaches for her, crying.

Marie wriggles over to me, and I pull her into my arms. "You were a good, brave girl," I whisper in her ear, and she bathes my face with kisses. I rest my head against hers as my heartbeat struggles to return to normal.

A loud whoosh makes us all look back at the house. The guest bathroom shares a wall with the garage, and the fire must have reached the gas tank of Barry's truck. The shingles steam, then flames appear and lap at the eaves. Our house is small, a single story with only fifteen hundred square feet. The bedrooms are to the left of the garage, and the living room, dining room, and kitchen to the right. With the fire starting at the center of our home, and the huge old pine that's always provided lovely shade for our bedroom skimming the roofline, I fear it won't be long before our house is fully engulfed in flames. Another loud whoosh. Possibly the gas can Barry uses for the lawn mower.

"We need to get farther away," I say to Wren. "Can you walk?"

"Yeah. I'm okay." She sits up and raises her hand to her forehead, moaning as she delicately fingers a lump that's already turning mauve.

"What happened? I thought you might've stood up and inhaled too much smoke."

"No. I just wasn't totally awake yet when I tried to stand up. I took a sleeping pill last night. I got dizzy, and . . . I dunno. I must have tripped or something and whacked my head on the TV stand."

"Let me see." Jade pushes Wren's hand away and combs her bangs off her forehead.

Barry jogs over to us. "The fire department's on their way. They're sending an ambulance for Wren." He helps Wren up, and she drapes her arm around his shoulder.

"How embarrassing. I just tripped and fell. I'm fine." Wren pushes her mom's pawing hands away as we move to the other side of the cul-de-sac.

"The paramedics can take a look at you anyway," Barry says, as the Wilsons, an older couple, come out of their house offering blankets and hugs and kind words that disappear in the roar of our beloved house going up in flames.

We strain to hear sirens. In my peripheral vision I notice more neighbors gathering. Mr. Viera hollers, asking if he should call 911. Mr. Wilson yells that it's already done. Activity flashes around us, but it's all out of focus: muffled sounds, distant movements. I feel as if we're in a snow globe, just us and the house; I can't clearly see or hear anything outside that globe. Smoke puffs and whorls out the bathroom and garage windows. The myriad colors would be beautiful if they were paints or fabrics: pearl, dove-gray, tan, soft yellow, pale orange, greenish-gray again, pewter. My eyes won't look away; my ears fill with the hiss and crackle of the fire.

I sit on the curb on a crocheted blanket Mrs. Wilson set out for us, still holding Marie to me. I cough, cough again, and wipe my nose with the back of my hand. There's a dark streak of soot on my skin. Mr. Wilson pushes a bottle of water into my hands and sets down a bowl for Marie, who laps at it greedily, hacks, drinks again, and returns to my side. I drape my arm over her soft fur, noting its acrid smell. Barry sits on the other side of me, slack-jawed, watching the house. Wren leans against him, curled under his arm. Jade takes the far side of Wren, holding her hand and rocking Ruthie in her lap. Mrs. Wilson drapes a blanket across their shoulders. I look from my house to the family beside me on the curb. Is my marriage going up in flames as hot and hungry as those devouring my house?

CHAPTER 21

As neighbors circle and pray the embers won't drift to their tinder-dry yards, crews from three fire trucks beat the flames into submission, and our house hisses a final death rattle. The front side of the garage is almost completely black. The rest of the house's facade is black from the tops of the windows up. If I held my hand out horizontally to cover the upper half of the house, it wouldn't look too bad. But it *is* bad. Very bad. The roof is almost completely gone over the garage and our bedroom, and it sags precariously over the living room.

I'm too exhausted to think what happens next. But I've come back out from the Wilsons' house because the fire crew seems to be finishing up. They've stopped poking at and spraying down charred, steaming piles of rubble. They've strung yellow caution tape up around the property. They've begun to reel the hoses in. I want to hear what the crew chief is saying to Barry.

I walk out to join them on the curb, my limbs heavy. Water covers the street, and the smell of hot, wet asphalt mixes with the smell of burnt pine.

It's been the longest three hours of my life. Following the longest seven minutes and forty-five seconds (Mr. Wilson called out the time), while we waited for the firefighters to arrive. At one point there were the three trucks, an ambulance, and a police car in our cul-de-sac. A cop directed traffic and kept the looky-loos from turning down our street. Oh, yeah, and let's not forget, a helicopter from the local news station. With the dry weather and the drier hillside behind our houses, I imagine everyone in the neighborhood watched with dry-mouthed concern.

As for me, I stopped watching when the crew from the first truck climbed on top of the house with a chain saw, axes, and long poles, and began cutting, hacking, and punching through our roof. The rational side of my brain knew there was a logical, fire-fighting reason for the destruction, but the irrational side felt like they were abusing my already-ailing home. Wasn't it bad enough it was on fire? Now they had to beat the crap out of it too? When was the actual *saving* going to start?

I'd gone inside, head down, following Mrs. Wilson. I wanted to get away from Barry anyway. The ambulance had taken Wren and Ruthie to the hospital "for observation," even though Wren protested that she felt fine. Jade rode along. Before she left, I heard Jade tell Barry they'd get a cab back to her hotel after the girls got checked out.

"I want to get the dog inside, where it's cooler," I told Barry. But really I just couldn't look at him, or the house, anymore.

But then I did watch. I collapsed into an upholstered rocker in front of Mrs. Wilson's living room window and stared and rocked and stared and rocked. That pane of glass somehow separated me, shielded and numbed me from what was going on outside. Mrs. Wilson kept trying to get me to eat, but I felt like I couldn't keep anything down.

I watched from behind my "safety glass" as the firefighters aimed their powerful hoses at the roof, the pine tree, and the narrow strips of fencing and dry grass between our house and the neighbors.

I watched a kid I recognized from down the street point his phone at the chaos. No doubt our house would be a YouTube sensation for his friends within minutes.

I watched a perky, ponytailed reporter from the local morning news show interview Mr. Viera and Mr. Wilson. I watched Barry wave her off. I imagined the interview he might have given: *Well, I was sleeping soundly after a wild night in bed with my lover when . . .*

I watched, unblinking, the flashing red lights on the trucks until they blurred and I could still see flashes when I closed my eyes. I kept them closed until I heard one of the truck's engines roar as it started to leave.

In the street, I saw the chief pulling off his oversize, sooty gloves and tucking them, along with his white helmet, under his arm. He walked toward Barry, holding out his hand. I dragged myself up from the chair and went to join them. As I walked out, I looked at my watch for what must have been the hundredth time. I don't know why I kept looking. What did it matter? But that's how I knew three hours had crept by.

It's eight thirty, breakfast time. It feels so much later.

As I approach Barry and the fire chief, a firefighter emerges, walking out of our charred front door. His dirty yellow gear looks hot and heavy in the now-bright sunshine. He carries the small portable firebox we kept hidden in the office closet. He reaches Barry and the chief just as I do. He still wears his thick gloves. "Found it right where you said it'd be," he says to Barry, setting the shiny, wet box on the curb.

Half my brain rejoices: *At least we have a few things—insurance papers, passports, the external hard drive that Barry was good about backing up. Thank God all my business records are at the studio.* The other half screams: *That's a ridiculously tiny box! Why the hell didn't you buy the big, nonportable fire safe?*

I'm still staring at the stupid, minuscule box when the chief introduces himself. "You must be Mrs. Halstad." He holds out his meaty paw. "I'm Chief Paterka. Sorry we couldn't do more for you, folks." My bones might as well be linguini for all the force I'm able to put behind the handshake.

"Me too" is all I manage.

Barry turns to the gritty-faced firefighter still standing beside us. "What do you think started it?"

He shakes his head. "Your insurance company will send out an investigative team later. Maybe this afternoon or tomorrow. Have you called them yet?"

Barry looks at me, and I shake my head. "Not yet," I say.

"Sorry for your losses," the firefighter says. To the chief he says, "All clear inside, Chief," then walks away.

I don't need an investigative team. The smoke was pouring out of the guest bathroom. That overloaded plug was the cause. Since Jade and the girls are gone, there's no one for me to physically point fingers at, but in my head, blame is laid.

"So now what? We just leave?" Barry asks. The remains of the house, the tree, and our cars still drip. The *plick-plick-plick* of the water mixes with the idling truck engines. "What about anything that's salvageable?"

"I don't think you're going to find much," Chief Paterka says. "The things that might've survived the flames are likely to be too damaged to salvage. You don't need to worry about looters, if that's what you mean. Your insurance company will likely send someone out to board up the windows."

"It's very lucky no one was hurt," the chief continues. "Did your smoke alarms wake you?"

I put my hand to my mouth. It hasn't occurred to me until now. "Oh God. The one by the kitchen. We dismantled it the other day; something burned in the oven." I say "we," but think "Wren." *She* dismantled it.

And then I put the battery in the junk drawer. I was afraid she'd burn another batch of kale and scare the hell out of the dog again.

"We had one in the hallway too, though," Barry says. "It should've gone off. I changed the battery in the spring at the end of daylight savings."

"Do you know how old it was?"

Barry and I look at each other. I shake my head and shrug. "They're the same ones we had when we moved in. That was twelve years ago."

"Smoke alarms that old frequently fail. They should be replaced every ten years."

"I had no idea," Barry says.

"Unfortunately, not enough people do." He claps Barry on the shoulder. He's shorter than Barry, but probably outweighs him by forty or fifty pounds. After the morning we've had, I'm surprised Barry doesn't crumple under the weight of the man's hand.

Barry thanks him again. I don't say anything.

The chief walks away, and we stand back while the crew prepares to leave. They slam the doors shut on the backs of the trucks and, with a final nod in our direction, climb aboard and drive away.

Barry and I watch in silence until they turn the corner.

Beyond the contents of one small firebox, my overnight bag, and our wedding rings, we have nothing. No house. No credit cards. No phones. No cars—Barry's was a total loss, and mine is blackened and dripping from its proximity to the garage.

At least Wren's car and Jade's rental are okay. It was lucky they'd both parked on the street.

Jade. I picture her mincing across the hotel lobby in her bare feet and short silk robe.

I turn to Barry, "Maybe you can get one of the neighbors to drive you to Jade's hotel. I'm sure she'll take care of any . . . needs you have until we can get things sorted out with the insurance. I'm going to the

Wilsons' to get Marie and use their phone to call Cyn to come get me."
I turn to walk away.

"Alex, wait." He grabs my shoulder. "I'm not going to Jade's hotel."

I toss my hair out of my face and search his eyes. Why wouldn't he go there? What the hell else is he going to do?

She wins. The go-getter has gotten it all—the great career, the beautiful family, and the one that got away.

"I'm going with you to Cynthia's," he says.

"Why would you want to do that? I've got nothing, Barry. I've got less than nothing, considering the debt I've gotten us into." I feel completely beaten down, like I've got nothing inside me either. I've never been so wiped out in my life. My house is destroyed, and maybe my marriage too. All this on top of only about three hours of sleep last night. I close my eyes for a moment and feel myself sway a bit, so I jerk them open again. I need to sit down. I need coffee.

"I'm sure Jade can take you shopping. Get you some clothes and a car." I look down at his bare feet. "Some shoes." At least my overnight bag is in the back of my car. Since the front end took the brunt, I still have a couple of items of clothing, my toothbrush, my makeup bag. Even Marie, with her collar, leash, and favorite toys we'd taken along to Cyn's, is better off than Barry, who has nothing but a pair of boxers and a T-shirt that's not fit to use as a rag.

"I can borrow some things from Jamie," Barry says.

I shake my head again. "Don't be ridiculous. He's a head shorter than you. I'm going to the Wilsons' to borrow their phone; you do the same and try to call Jade at the hotel. And then I'll talk to you later, after I talk to the insurance company. Go; go call your precious Jade." I snort. "Oh no, wait—jade's *semi*-precious. So go and be with your semi-precious Jade. I'm exhausted, and I can't deal with you right now. Just go."

"I'm not going with Jade," he says. "Yes, I do need to call her later, to check on the girls, but that's it."

"You don't have to put on an act for me. I saw the two of you. In *our* bed." I stomp across the street in my sandals, while Barry picks his way across the wet asphalt on the balls of his bare feet.

He catches up as I hit the sidewalk in front of the Wilsons'. "Alex, I'm not interested in being with Jade."

"That's funny. It didn't look that way from my angle."

His eyebrows meet, and he pushes his hair off his forehead. "Wait, what were you doing here so early this morning?"

"Don't change the subject."

"I'm not. I'm just—my God, you saved us all, Alex. If you hadn't been here . . ." He pulls me to him. He hugs me hard, and I resist at first, but the emotion in his voice guts me. "The girls," he whispers into my hair. "We could've lost them." He leans back and looks into my face. Tears fill his eyes. "You saved them, Alex." He puts his hands on either side of my face and kisses me, his mouth covering mine with an urgency that hasn't been between us in months.

I melt into him. After the long, stressful morning, I want to collapse in his arms. But there's that flashback to Jade again. Sitting up in our bed, hair mussed, falling around her bare shoulders. My memory adds an extra heaping of bed-head sexy disheveledness to her tresses.

"No, Barry." I push against his chest so that he'll let go of me. "What's wrong with you? You probably still smell like her!" The old me would never have a fight like this on the street, where all the neighbors can view the airing of our charred laundry, but I don't care. I'll have my say, and I'll have it now. Right here in the middle of our street, across from the rubble that used to be our pride and joy. "Do you think I'm an idiot? You can't screw your lover one minute, and then stand here and kiss me the next. Even if it has been an emotionally exhausting morning." I smooth my filthy shirt and throw my shoulders back. Let the neighbors watch. I don't care. I've got nothing left, not even any pride.

He plucks at his shirt, then drops his hand to his side. "I don't smell like her. I smell like smoke. I didn't sleep with Jade."

I cross my arms, tilt my head and glare at him for a long moment. "I *saw* you."

"I guess technically we might've slept in the same bed, but I didn't *sleep* with her," he hisses. Apparently, he does still have some pride left, since he glances around, noting a few remaining looky-loos. He rests his right hand over his heart. "I swear on everything that's important to me, I was as shocked to see her in our bed as you were."

I think back to waking him up. I picture him rolling over, looking confused. "You said, 'What the' and I thought you meant the smoke."

"I looked up and saw the smoke, and then out of the corner of my eye, I saw Jade. I was so shocked—to see you, to wake up to the fire, but then to turn and see her in *our* bed. I was so angry. But there was no time to say anything. I just wanted to make sure we all got out of there."

I believe him.

I know Barry. I know how clueless he can be about women. Hell, it's the whole reason it was so easy for me to reel him in.

I slap my hand against my forehead and drag it down the side of my face, which must be a mess of soot, smeared makeup, and tear tracks. "Tell me everything that happened yesterday."

"After you left, I wanted to be alone. I suggested that Jade take the girls down to the wharf for a walk. I spent a long time in the yard, pulling weeds and thinking."

"Thinking what exactly?"

"I was mad. Mad at you, mad at Jade." He shakes his head. "You wouldn't believe what she said when I pulled her aside last night. That it was all *my* fault. She tried to turn it around on me—that I'd made such a big deal about never wanting to be a dad that *of course* she wasn't going to tell me." He looks up at the sky and scoffs. So that's what went down in the kitchen. "And I was mad about the money too. I was wishing you'd been straight with me. Weeding was good for my anger. Anyway, Jade called and said she and the girls would stop and pick up a pizza on the way back. We ate, and Jade said she wanted some wine, so I opened a bottle. She kept asking questions about you. About us. I didn't feel like talking, so I gave short answers."

He must notice my smirk. "I didn't tell her we were fighting. She's not someone I'd pour my heart out to. *You're* the one who invited her to stay. That wasn't my idea."

What an idiot I was to invite her. All I could think at the time was that I wanted her to make up with Wren so that they'd move out. I didn't realize how important Wren and Ruthie are to Barry. And to me.

God, what does it matter whose fault the fire is? All that matters is that we all got out okay. I contemplate launching into my "I was such an idiot—in so many ways" speech, but first I need to hear the rest of his story.

"Go on," I say.

"Anyway, I drank more than I realized." I picture Jade topping up his glass every time he turned his head. "And I hadn't eaten much, because I was still mad and my stomach was upset. When Jade suggested a movie, I said I was too tired. I went to bed to read, but I fell asleep. The next thing I know, you're beating on my arm and Jade's in the damn bed."

I take a deep breath.

"I swear."

I let out my breath. "I believe you. It's that bitch I can't believe. What a lot of nerve to pounce on you while you were vulnerable."

He shuts his eyes for a moment; he's done with the subject of Jade. When he opens them, he says, "Your turn. Why were you here so early? You're never up early. What time was it?" He looks at his bare wrist. A pale stripe stands out on his tan arm.

Poor Barry. His favorite sports watch didn't make it out of the fire. Thank God he's not a Rolex kind of guy. Replacing his watch will cost about twenty bucks at the nearest discount store.

I poke a finger into one of the many small holes in his T-shirt. This particular hole sits below the last *t* in "Santa Barbara Marathon," directly over his heart. I make tiny circles on his chest. "I came back to beg you to forgive me. Because I've been a total idiot." I look up into his eyes. "I'm so sorry, Bear. I majorly eight-forty-three'd everything."

He smiles and puts his hands on my shoulders. "Right now, all I care about is that you and the girls and Marie are safe. I don't care about the money. All that matters to me is *us*. We'll figure the rest out later."

I hug him and rest my head on his shoulder. He wraps his arms around me. It's true. He does only smell like smoke.

"Let's go call the girls," I say into his chest. I could stand here all day, but I suppose the Wilsons might start to wonder. "I want to hear Wren's voice. I want to make sure they're okay."

"I love you, Legs."

"I love you, Bear."

CHAPTER 22

Back at Cynthia's, after we've taken ridiculously long showers, eaten comfort food (macaroni and cheese with potato chips), and collapsed on the sofa with cold beers, Cyn says I have to call Mom.

"You do it for me. I'm completely and totally beat." I let my head, already resting against the back of the couch, slide down into my hand to demonstrate.

"She's going to want to hear the news from you." Cyn drops my cell phone in my lap. I'd found it, wet but still working, in the cup holder in my car. "Call her."

Barry, in a borrowed T-shirt and board shorts (which he looks surprisingly hot in), follows Jamie out back to help the boys bathe Marie in their kiddie pool, and Cyn goes off to check if our stinky clothes need another round in the wash. I'm alone in the living room. I pull my feet up under me and try to sit up straight.

My dad answers. "Hi, Daddy." I can't help it. I choke up when I hear his voice.

"Honey-bunny." His nickname for me brings tears. "What's wrong?"

"Nothing now. It's good to hear your voice. Look, everyone's fine, but there was a fire at our house early this morning."

"A fire? Oh my goodness. You're sure everyone's okay?"

"Yes, we're all fine." I tell him a shortened version of what happened—no need to go into the whole "I stupidly invited the viper into our den" story, so I gloss over the parts about Jade. He tells me he loves me, then hands the phone to my mom, who's been clamoring for it since she heard his gasps and oh-thank-Gods.

After retelling the abbreviated story again, I'm spent.

"Thank God you got that precious baby out of there."

Of course. The baby gets top billing on the "Things We're Thankful For" list. I suppose that's fair enough. Still, maybe I wanted my mom to make a fuss about *me*. "Yeah" is all I say. My muscles have turned to melted marshmallows, and I want to lie down somewhere dark. I rest my elbow on the arm of the sofa and prop my head up.

My mom lets out a peep of a cry.

"We're fine, Mom. The baby's fine. We're all fine."

Now she starts to sob. "Oh, Alex, the thought of losing you. It's more than I can stand."

"I'm fine. Please don't cry."

"You don't know what it's like. It's a mother's worst nightmare, worrying she might lose her children." Great. Time for another "it's a mother thing; you wouldn't understand" brush-off.

"I know, Mom. I mean, I know that I *don't* know."

She takes a gulping breath. "The first time I saw you . . . it was the most profound moment of my life. I didn't know it was possible to fall so instantly and so completely in love. You were the most beautiful thing I'd ever seen. You still are. I know you're a grown woman now, with a successful career and a family of your own, but to me, you're always going to be my baby. I love you very much, Alex."

"I love you too." Now I'm crying as well.

"I can't bear the thought you might have been killed in that fire, not knowing how precious you are to me. I know sometimes you seem to get, well, a little perturbed with me because of the extra time I spend with Cynthia, but she needs me so much more than you do. You . . . you're so together. So much more accomplished than I ever was at your age. But your sister, she's more like me. How I was when I was young with two small kids. She gets frazzled, and she needs my help. I hope you understand that."

"I do." Maybe I do *now*, anyway. I didn't really understand how stressed out Cyn could get until we talked . . . gosh, was that only yesterday morning? It seems forever ago. But maybe her projecting herself as Supermom all the time is like me putting on my career-woman facade. She has her mom-ness; I've got my career. If we're not both incredibly successful at those things, then where does that leave us?

"Ever since you two were little, she's always needed me more. Of course, the age difference between you didn't help. She's always been so in awe of you, and being six years younger, she could never keep up. She wanted to do everything you were doing—whether it was riding a bike or roller-skating or playing soccer. She took many a tumble trying to follow in your big footsteps, and I was always running a step behind, trying to catch her."

A laugh works its way through the tears. "Are you saying I have big feet?"

Mom doesn't laugh, but I can tell from the change in the timbre of her voice she's smiling more than crying now. "Oh, honey, I'm saying things seem to come easier for you than they have for Cynthia." I've always been so jealous of the attention Mom lavished on Cyn, I never stopped to think that Cyn might be jealous of me.

It occurs to me that because of our complicated love triangle, I've rarely shared my true feelings with my mom. "But . . . just so you know. I'm maybe not as together as you might think." One last tear rolls down my cheek, and I wipe it away with the back of my hand.

"When you're ready and things calm down a little, let's have a spa day. Just us two girls. My treat. We'll get massages and mani-pedis and then go get a decadent lunch somewhere. We'll have a long talk over some margaritas."

"I'd like that. It sounds nice. But let's invite Cynthia too."

"That'd be wonderful. I can't imagine a better day than one spent with both of my girls." She blows her nose. "Speaking of your sister, she called me this morning and told me about your successful babysitting services last night."

Was that just last night? "It was actually pretty fun. Maybe Barry and I can do that for them once in a while."

"I know she'd appreciate that."

"I'm glad we talked about this." I feel myself choking up again. "I love you, Mom." Through the sliding glass door, I see my sister trying to wrangle the boys into cleaning up the mess they've made in the yard. "But I better go; I think Cyn could use some help right now, in fact."

*

That night, with the daybed and trundle pushed together in my sister's guest room, Barry tries to bridge the gap.

As he lifts my sheet and tries to slip into bed with me, I hold my hand out. "Hang on." I know he loves me. I know he's pissed at Jade for crawling into our bed. But, there's a lot that's still unresolved between us. I've sorted things out with my mom, and now I need everything to be out in the open with him too. "I need to talk to you."

Marie harrumphs, annoyed with the movement, and gets up from where she's been curled in a ball at my feet. She flops down on the area rug and heaves a loud sigh.

"Sorry, Marie," Barry says. Turning to me, he creeps closer still and says, "You're right. We do need to talk. But I'm exhausted. You're exhausted. When's the last time you got up that early? Not to mention saved a house full of people, watched your house burn down, and had an emotionally draining phone call with your mom?"

At the mention of the house and my mom, fat, hot tears start to fall all over again. "You're right. I have never been this tired in my entire life."

"I promise we'll talk—about everything—later. Right now, I want to snuggle my wife and fall asleep next to her." He kisses away the tears on my cheeks, then burrows in next to me.

"Do I still smell bad?"

He sniffs and snuffles loudly against my ear, making me giggle. "No." He lets out a long sigh. "You smell amazing." At first his lips barely graze my skin, but then he kisses my neck, my temples, my eyelids and reaches for me with a quiet urgency.

*

Damn, people are right about make-up sex.

Barry collapses, falling almost instantly asleep, half on my bed, half on the trundle. He looks uncomfortable, but I hate to wake him. He's right; it's been an exhausting day. An exhausting couple of weeks.

I should be sleeping too, but my brain won't turn off. The last two weeks go by in View-Master slide-show fashion: Wren and Ruthie standing on our doorstep; Rache sitting at the mall, telling me Beverly wants her back; Ruthie sitting beside a pile of broken glass at the Van Dierdons'; Jade begging me to stay at our house; the fire. The flames. The firefighters. Over and over, I see that moment when flames first burst out of the garage window. I see the pine tree blazing. Squeezing my eyes shut, I try to make the images go away.

At least we all made it out alive. I try to replace the horrible images with calming thoughts. But the time has passed for being thankful that what I treasure most has survived. Now is apparently the time for dwelling on all that's lost, and my calm thoughts are replaced by a catalogue of all the lovely things from our house. My collection of beach sand from our trips. The Paris accents in my office. That perfect turquoise tile I picked out for our master bath. The huge collection of race T-shirts Barry built up over the years. His old college textbooks. Our wedding album; framed photos of us with Marie and our first dog, Louis; old black-and-white family pictures in a keepsake box in my closet. Albums dedicated to our favorite vacations; all the reminders of the special places Barry and I visited together.

The last image I see in my mind's eye is of the overloaded plug in the guest bathroom. And all the girls' stuff plugged in there. The fire . . . It had to have been started by the overloaded plug. One of Wren's chargers or something must have short-circuited. It's *their* fault. Hot tears slide down my temples as I stare at the ceiling. Why did she have to keep all that junk plugged in anyway?

My brain starts to replay how I stumbled over Wren as I tried to get out of the house. The image is hazy, as if I'm watching it through a veil. My God, what if I hadn't realized she was still in there? What if I'd thought she'd gotten Ruthie out through the window in her room? I might have thought they were safely in the backyard. Thank God Marie knew to go look for the baby.

"Marie," I whisper in the dark. "Come here." I pat the blankets next to me. It's a small bed for me, half of Barry, and a big dog, but I don't care. I need both her and Barry near me.

She springs onto the bed, and I scooch over so that she can squeeze in between Barry and me. As I rub her ears, I think, *Thank God you love that baby so much, girl.*

Dogs. They open their hearts so easily.

Maybe I could try to be more like Marie. I should've opened my heart to the girls more readily. Why did it take almost losing them in a fire to realize that I love them? I've been so self-absorbed. Worrying about myself, my business, and what other people think.

"I'm going to try to be a better person, Marie," I whisper. "More like you. Er, wait . . ." I get confused wondering if I need to be a better person or just a regular dog.

Of course, my path to self-improvement probably starts with not blaming others for things that've gone wrong in my life. Did Marie blame Wren and Ruthie when they moved in and stole her stuffed animals and encroached on her space and her mommy and daddy time? No, she embraced the girls.

But what did I do? I grasped at any opportunity to get rid of them. And I blamed Ruthie or Wren at every turn—for the Van Dierdon fiasco, for Rache quitting, for Jade moving in, and even for the fire.

Really, if I'm honest with myself, those things were all my fault.

I should've known better than to leave Ruthie alone in the living room at the Van Dierdons'. I should've trusted my gut and insisted we bring her into the dining room. The same with letting Jade move in: I totally let her bamboozle me with all her compliments about how tall and lovely I am and how beautiful my house is. *Was.* I let my stupid vanity cloud my judgment. Plus, I let her move in solely in the hopes it'd speed the girls along in moving *out.* Terrible.

But if I'd succeeded in getting rid of them, would my house still be standing?

Oh my God. I feel sick as I remember back to when I hired an electrician to change the switches and vanity lights when we redid the guest bath. He said that the wiring inside the wall between the garage and bathroom looked as if a monkey had done the electrical work. A *stoned* monkey. When we bought the house, we'd known that the previous owner had done some unpermitted work in the garage to add the laundry area. It passed inspection though. Of course, the inspector didn't look inside the walls. The electrician said we'd need to redo it someday. He figured an estimate for the work. But no, stupid aesthetics-obsessed me didn't want to "waste" precious budget dollars on something no one would see. I convinced Barry it would be fine to wait on the wiring—it's not like the guy said we were living in a death trap. He said it was something to be done "someday," and that's what I told him—"someday" we'd have it done. And then we forgot about it.

Maybe the fire didn't start in the bathroom after all. Maybe it was actually something in the garage.

Maybe this isn't the girls' fault. Maybe it's mine. Like everything else.

I curl into a fetal position facing the wall and listen to Barry and Marie sleep the sleep of the innocent.

CHAPTER 23

The next morning, my cell phone ring wakes me. I'm alone in the room, and the smell of bacon wafts under the bedroom door.

"Hello," I answer, groggy and wondering who's calling. It isn't a name or number I recognize.

"This is Deanna Humphrey, from KEYT NewsChannel Three." Her staccato greeting assaults my barely awake ear. "I got your number from your neighbor, Mrs. Wilson." Before I can acknowledge anything she's said, she presses on. "Mrs. Wilson told me that your dog saved your grandbaby in the fire at your house. That's a fantastic story, Mrs. Halstad. We'd like to have you and your granddaughter on our show tomorrow. Along with the dog, of course."

"I—uh."

She rattles off details about the human-interest segment KEYT runs every morning at 6:40 after the "serious" news, and tells me how everyone loves a story about a baby or a dog, so a story with a baby-saving dog—well, everyone's going to "eat it up with a fork." Thoughts stream through my head while she talks excitedly at me: that's damn early; I haven't had my hair colored in two months and don't have the time or the money to get it done; all my cutest clothes have been reduced to a pile of ash, and Cyn's so tiny I doubt I can borrow anything from her; when's the last time I whitened my teeth? Oh yeah, all my whitening strips went up in flames too.

"So can we count on you for the show tomorrow, Mrs. Halstad? Please say yes."

"I'm not sure I'll have a way to get there. We're staying with family in Thousand Oaks, and I haven't had a chance to arrange for a rental car yet." We talked to the insurance company at length yesterday after Cynthia brought us back here. When Cynthia showed up, she brought along a spare key for my car. I'd completely forgotten we'd traded house and car keys in case of emergencies. We couldn't get the car started, so we're having it hauled away to see if it's salvageable. Fingers crossed it's a write-off, and then I'll buy something cheaper.

"I know you must have a thousand things to deal with right now, but the station could send a car to pick you up. This is all still probably a huge shock, but we'd love to have you on as our guest. How about if I call back in an hour so you have time to think about it?"

I agree to think about it, and head to the kitchen where things are calm and quiet because Jamie already bundled the boys off to school on his way to work. The boys wanted to hear the story of the fire and my "daring rescue," as A J kept calling it over and over last night. Bobby tied his Superman cape around Marie's neck and kept calling her "Superdog." They were pretty cute. Maybe it is a good human-interest story.

Cynthia leans against the kitchen counter, and Barry sits at the bar sipping coffee, with Marie curled at his feet. She lifts her head, then gets up and comes to greet me as I stumble toward the coffeemaker.

"How'd you sleep?" Barry asks. "You were snoozing pretty soundly when I woke up."

"I only slept a few hours. I don't think I fell asleep until around four." I tell them about the phone call and Marie's possible impending stardom.

"You should totally do it!" Cyn says. "Everybody loves a rescued-baby story. Maybe it'll get picked up on the national news." Cyn pops a bagel into the toaster, which I assume is for me, judging by the crumb-filled plates in front of Barry and her.

"I doubt that." The rich smell of the coffee slaps my senses awake as I hold the hot mug to my lips. I can't believe I was considering making a decision before being fully caffeinated. "What do you think, Barry?"

"Sure, why not?"

"Well, for starters, I have nothing to wear except for the shorts and T-shirts I packed for the weekend. And, oh, how about the fact that we have a million things to do that are just a tad more urgent?"

"I'm sure I have something you can borrow," Cyn offers. "This'll be fun. And, yes, it's going to be a long, stressful haul dealing with the insurance and replacing all your stuff, but this can be a fun little bright spot in all that."

"Not to mention a potential PR boost for your business," Barry says.

Hmm. Barry does have a point. Lord knows I could use all the help I can get in that arena.

Marie sits on the kitchen rug, following my every move as I smear light cream cheese on my bagel. God, I love this dog. It'd be fun to share her amazing bravery on the news.

I bend down and kiss her on the soft spot between her eyes, then reward her with the cream cheese knife.

"All right. If Wren's okay with Ruthie being on TV, we'll do it."

What I really want to do this morning is talk to Barry. But there's no time now. There's too much to do. The dog, the girls, and I have to get camera ready.

*

"But what's she going to wear?" is the first question out of Wren's mouth when I call her at the hotel and ask if she wants to do the interview. "My mom took us shopping yesterday, but you should see the freak show of ruffles and sparkles she bought for Ruthie when I wasn't looking. I drew the line at anything pink, but it's all flowers and frogs and goofy stuff."

"At least she has new clothes. I'm going to be squeezing into one of Cynthia's hand-me-up skirts. What about you? Did you get some new things? I'll need you to hold Ruthie while we're all on camera."

"I've only got the overalls I was wearing when I ran out of the house. Mom had the hotel laundry run them through the wash like five hundred times 'cause they were so stinky. Thank God I fell asleep in front of the TV with my clothes on. I'd hate to only have my ratty sleep shirt, like my poor dad."

"How's your head, by the way?"

"It's fine. I've got a big honking bruise, but my bangs hide it pretty good."

"So tell me again what happened? Why were you on the couch?"

"I couldn't sleep. I guess I was stressed about my mom being there, you know? I was reading in our room, and then I got up around midnight and thought I'd watch some TV. I thought an old movie would knock me out. But I was still all wound up, so I took a sleeping pill at like one thirty. I swear, I almost never take them, in case Ruthie might"—her voice catches—"need me. Oh God, I shouldn't have taken it. I thought it'd be okay." The words tumble out, and I can barely follow. "I thought since my mom and dad were both there, if anything happened, she'd be fine. I could get away with taking one for *once*. And then, jeez, something *did* happen, and when you woke me up and I stood, I was *so* dizzy. I'd only been asleep for a few hours, so I fell and hit my head, and I was *useless*, and Ruthie could have—" She breaks off sobbing. It throws me, since I've never heard her cry before. She always seems so even keeled, so blasé about everything.

"Wren, it's okay. Everything's okay. You didn't know. And every-thing turned out fine in the end."

"Yeah, thanks to you and Marie, and no thanks to me." She sniffles loudly into the phone. "I should've been the one to rescue Ruthie, and instead I had to be rescued too."

"Oh, sweetie. It's okay. You didn't do anything wrong."

"I'm like the worst mother ever."

"Oh, come on, you are not. You're a great mom."

She blows her nose. "You think?"

"Yes, you're wonderful. And Ruthie's wonderful too, and that's because of *you*."

"You mean it?"

"Of course I do." And I actually *do* mean it. I might not have if this conversation had come up, oh, say, a week ago. "So what do you say? Want to show everyone in Santa Barbara that wonderful little cutie of yours on the news tomorrow morning?"

"She is pretty cute, isn't she? But seriously, what's she going to wear?" Okay, there's the Wren I know (and love). "I went to the Closet yesterday—have you been there? Killer secondhand stuff—and I got some jeans and a couple T-shirts. It's cool, right, if I wear jeans and a T-shirt? But what about Ruthie? When I was in the Closet, my mom took Ruthie to Macy's. There's no way I'm letting her wear that frog thing my mom bought her. No way."

"I tell you what. Cynthia's loaning me her minivan for the day, so I'll come get you, and we'll go to my office. There's a fabric store not far from there. I need to use the computer, and I can make phone calls while you whip up something cute for Ruthie. How's that sound?" I have to start compiling an inventory for the insurance company of what we lost. Luckily, I have a million photos of each room back at the office. I used a few of them as part of my portfolio. Oh! I kept all the receipts from our big home remodel project at the office too. Bonus.

"Is my dad coming? He doesn't have to go back to work today, does he?"

"No, he has a few days' leave. I'm dropping him off so he can pick up a rental car. He's going to deal with getting my car towed, and I'll figure out a rental for myself later."

"Cool. I'll get my mom to watch Ruthie."

"Uh, so your mom's there? In the room with you now?"

"She's in the bedroom in our suite. Do you want to talk to her? I know she probably wants to thank you for everything."

"Yes. Yes, I *would* like to talk to her. Can you put her on?"

There are a few moments of silence while I wait for Jade. I hadn't planned this out, so I'm not sure what I'll say. I feel my face getting hot, the anger building in me.

"Alex, I'm so glad you called." Jade puts on such an oh-so-gracious voice that I know Wren must be within earshot. "I was going to call you today. I owe you a huge debt of gratitude for everything you did yesterday."

"Sure you were going to call. I'm sure you *really* wanted to have a conversation with me after what you pulled at our house."

"I . . . uh," Jade stammers. I'm sure that with her business experience, she's good at talking herself out of tough corners, so I charge ahead before she can gather her thoughts.

"You just keep your mouth shut. Wren doesn't need to know about any of this. Plaster that fake smile of yours on your face and listen to me. You are *never* going to try to slither your way between my husband and me again. You may be in our lives now because of Wren, but you are Wren's mom and nothing more to us. We are done with you. Now, thank me again. Make it sound good, and put Wren back on the phone."

"I . . . I just don't seem to be able to find the words," Jade says. "Thank you. So much. Again. I don't know . . . what I . . . Uh, here's Wren."

I hear the phone pass between them, while my heart rate slowly returns to normal. Then Wren's voice comes across the line. "You should see my mom's face," she whispers. "She's still really upset about everything. She didn't know what to say to you just now. And she's *never* at a loss for words. Anyway," she continues, louder. I'm relieved Wren clearly didn't pick up on any of what Jade and I were really discussing. "See you in an hour? Oh, hey, guess what? My cell was in the pocket of my overalls. I didn't lose everything."

So we did have a phone when we got out of the house. We could've called 911, what, a few minutes earlier? Would that have made a difference? Probably not.

How could we lose *everything*? The magnitude of all that lies ahead of us—the rebuilding, the paperwork, everything we have to replace—crushes me. I want to crawl back in bed with the dog. And maybe a glass of whiskey. But there's too much to do, and plenty of time to stress about all that later. Now, I need to get ready to be on TV!

Cynthia was right. It is a good thing we're doing this news spot, because otherwise, I'd crawl right back under the covers and possibly never come out. The new me should march out there and thank Cyn and tell her she was right (how often have I said those words to her in my life?) and give her a big hug.

So I do.

*

At my office, Wren sees the curtains for Mrs. Marx laid out on the sewing table, ironed, and ready to deliver.

She runs a hand over the fabric. "Do you need me to come along and help hang these?"

"That'd be great, but we don't have to do it right away. I called Mrs. Marx and explained about the fire. She said she saw it on the news last night, but didn't realize it was our house. Anyway, she said to come when I get a chance." I better squeeze her in soon though. I need her check so that I can pay down our credit cards. "Maybe we could go tomorrow."

"Cool."

Wren spreads out the fabric she picked up on our way to the office—black, naturally, with some black, white, and gray camouflage print for the trim. She quickly cuts out a simple jumper shape, then gets to work pinning and prepping. I head out to the front office so that I can use the phone and my laptop at my desk.

Later, Wren takes a break from sewing, and I push aside my long to-do list, which only has a few meager items scratched off. She checks the containers of pad thai we had delivered. "Chicken for you." She passes me the takeout box.

"So my mom said that when she climbed out her bedroom window"—I note Jade's lie, forcing my face to remain impassive by focusing on my lunch—"she thought she'd find me and Ruthie in the front yard. When we weren't there, she started freaking out. She said it was like everything went in slo-mo, and she realized what was happening and started running for the front door when she saw you and Marie dragging me out on the porch." She opens her own pad thai—tofu for her—and digs in.

"She must have been terrified. When I didn't know for even a minute where Marie was, I panicked. I can't imagine how horrible those moments must have been for your mom."

"We really owe you. A lot."

"No, you don't owe me anything. I did what anyone else would've done. Besides, Marie was the real hero, going back for Ruthie. Like I said before, it's over, and we all got out, and that's the important thing." I hope she won't start to cry again, but who could blame her? We've been through a lot. But no, happily, she just scrunches half her face into that funny little crooked smile I've grown so fond of.

"Hey, my mom said she has a spare key for my car at her house. She'll overnight it to me when she gets home. Good thing I wasn't parked in the driveway like you were."

"Is she still going home on Wednesday?"

"Yeah. She wanted to stay longer, but I told her it was fine, she should go. I'm sure she's freaking out about missing so much work anyway."

"So did you guys get a chance to talk? You must realize now how important you and Ruthie are to her."

She pokes at her meal with her chopsticks, tumbling a block of tofu end over end. "Yeah, we talked. It was kind of hard to avoid her, being in the same hotel suite and stuff. Plus, she was still kinda freaked. She kept hugging me and Ruthie and crying. And then she apologized for how everything went down." She finally raises the hunk of tofu to her mouth. "She *never* apologizes."

"So you guys are good?"

"Mostly."

"What's that mean?"

"I still don't want to start school in September. She was begging me last night to come back to San Francisco with her. She started in again on the whole Berkeley thing. Said I could look into transferring."

"Did you tell her you don't want to go to school?"

"No. If I do, she'll just say she won't fund that 'lifestyle.' And then I'll have no choice but to go home. I'd rather stay down here and go to school than *not* go and have to move back." She drops the chopsticks into the container and pushes the remains of her lunch aside. "Speaking of home, my mom said that once she sends me my car key, Ruthie and I should drive back up for the rest of the summer. She said we need to get out of your way while you guys, you know, put your lives back together."

I know she's referring to our house, but she's right; it's our lives—and our marriage—we need to focus on. I'm still working on the last bite of my lunch, so I don't say anything.

"She said we can come back with Sarah when our apartment's ready right before school starts," Wren continues. "Plus, she said she can help me replace the stuff we lost in the fire."

"Do you want to go home for the rest of the summer?"

"No, but, like, we don't have anywhere to live now, so I don't have a choice."

"You can still live with us." Wow, how things have changed! Nothing like a major emergency to make you realize that your perspective is totally eight-forty-three'd. Before the fire, I'd have been overjoyed to hear Wren and Jade had finally made up, and I would have pushed her to move home. But now, I'm just relieved that everyone's okay, and I'm excited about finding our new normal. "When Barry and I talked to the insurance company, we told them we'll need to rent at least a two-bedroom place while the house is rebuilt." Nodding my head toward my computer behind me, I add, "And I'm including the stuff you and Ruthie lost on my list. I was going to ask you to help me finish it after lunch."

She smiles a full smile, nothing halfway or uncertain about it. "You don't mind if we keep living with you? Even though everything's gonna be all crazy for a while?"

"Of course not. We want you guys to stay. It'll definitely be a summer we'll never forget." I toss my empty container in the trash. "And as for school in the fall, well, that's six weeks away. There's still time to figure everything out, so let's not worry about it right now." I stand and pull my purse out of my desk drawer. "What we need to focus on is how we're all going to look on camera tomorrow! If I go grab some hair dye at the drugstore around the corner, will you help me color my hair in the sink?"

"Ooh, sure! But I'm coming along. Let's get some fun nail colors too."

We close up the office and head to the drugstore, just two girls discussing the latest trendy colors.

CHAPTER 24

"So you headed down the hall, thinking your stepdaughter was following behind to get the baby?" the TV reporter asks, a look of studied concern on her face. I wonder if she really needs those glasses or just wears them to look more serious.

We're on set and the studio lights bake my head. I'm hoping the makeup lady knew what she was doing so that I don't look like a melting cupcake. I sit up very straight on the stiff-backed sofa, because if I slump, my belly will pop the buttons on the blouse I borrowed from Cynthia.

"Yes, that's right." I reach over and rest my hand on Wren's shoulder, catching a glimpse of the fantastic job she did on my nails. This "mimosa" color may be *so* in today, gone tomorrow, but the bright orangey yellow is perfect for summer. Wren's own nails, visible around Ruthie's middle as she bounces the baby on her knee, are so eggplant purple as to look almost black, but they shine like raven's feathers under the bright lights. Meanwhile, Ruthie looks adorable in her new black jumper with the black-and-white camo trim. With Wren's white T-shirt and black jeans, they look perfect together. Marie, wedged between our legs, leans up against the sofa, panting from the heat of the lights.

Every once in a while, Ruthie says, "Og!" and reaches for Marie's ears. In response, Marie leans her head back and stretches her nose toward Ruthie's face. Now she flicks a long tongue at Ruthie's chin, making her squeal. A honey scent floats up to me every time Marie moves; she smells wonderful from Cynthia's Baby Bath Time bar that the boys used on her yesterday. I can't help but think again: Cyn was right. This is a moment to savor before the onslaught of dealing with the house.

"I thought Wren was awake, and at first, she was. But I didn't know she passed out before we got to the hall. She got dizzy from standing up so suddenly." I'd promised her that I wouldn't mention the sleeping pill, since she felt it was a blemish on her Permanent Mothering Record. "And she fell and hit her head."

"And when did you realize Marie was no longer at your side?"

"It was right before I warned my husband and Ruthie's grandmother they should climb out their bedroom windows." I add an extra window to the story. "I thought I'd boost Marie out the window to my husband, then climb out myself, but when I turned, she was gone. I was terrified. I had no idea where she was. Luckily, she's very bonded to Ruthie." I glance at Marie who is again stretching her neck to get a good look at the baby, and add, "As you can see."

"You said everyone except your stepdaughter was behind closed doors. So how did Marie get into the baby's room?"

"It's funny. You never realize how a design decision you make might impact your family's life someday. As you mentioned before, I'm an interior designer, so over the years I've changed everything about our house, literally from floor to ceiling. I wanted high-end bedroom doors, but we couldn't afford them with our budget at the time, so instead I updated the look of the existing doors with new handles. Thank God I replaced the old knobs with stainless-steel levers. I had no idea the dog could work them, but I guess she instinctively jumped at the door to get to Ruthie and managed to open it."

"Talk about form meeting function!"

"Exactly!" I reach out and stroke Marie's head. Although we're here to focus on her heroic story, Barry was right—it can't hurt to put in a wee plug for my business, right? *Be marketing all the time!* "As I always tell my clients, don't choose form *over* function. It doesn't matter how beautiful something is if it doesn't work for you. Luckily, this ended up being a choice that both looked beautiful and also *worked* beautifully at a crucial moment. Anyway, when I saw the bedroom door open, I thought Wren had already been in and out with Ruthie. It wasn't until I practically fell over Wren that I realized what was going on."

The reporter takes us through the rest of our story, with Ruthie being a perfect angel the whole time, thanks to Marie keeping her entertained. Wren barely makes a peep until the reporter comments on Ruthie's "unusual" dress. Wren takes it as a compliment and mutters, "Thanks. I made it."

The reporter, forgetting that Wren is my stepdaughter, says, "Design talent runs in your family." She adds, again, how lucky we are to have a "terrific" dog like Marie.

"Can I say one more thing? I want to give a shout-out to the local Humane Society, where we got Marie. Even before all this, she's been such an amazing addition to our family. I hope anyone out there thinking of getting a pet will consider all the gorgeous, sweet dogs at the shelter waiting for a home."

"What a great reminder," the reporter says with a smile. "Now, back to Lisa at the news desk."

Lisa, the anchor with gleaming hair and heavy makeup, thanks us for sharing our "amazing" story and adds, "Maybe I'd better check out those rescue pups." She straightens the papers on her shiny desktop. "And consider changing all the doorknobs in our house." Maybe I should leave her my card. She beams her thousand-watt smile in our direction, then transitions to her serious-newscaster face as she turns back to the camera. "Now, to recap today's top story, Councilman Burman is recovering after falling from a horse during practice for the upcoming Old Spanish Days Fiesta parade." Leave it to Santa Barbara to have *that* as our top news item.

We're quietly hustled off to the greenroom, where we meet up with Barry. (He refused to go on camera with us, which was just as well since he's in a pair of Jamie's shorts and flip-flops, his heels almost hanging off the ends.) The producer tells us what a great job we did. She bends to pat Marie's head, and Marie sits and holds out a paw.

On the way out, all the production and office staff want to meet Marie and Ruthie. We run a gauntlet of pats, waves, and an "Oh, how cute!" and then head to our favorite dog-friendly breakfast place, Esau's Cafe, to celebrate.

Our fifteen minutes of fame are over.

*

"Your mom didn't want to join us for breakfast and celebrate your big TV debut?" I ask Wren while we wait for our meals. I knew there was no way Jade would join us, but I'm curious what excuse she gave Wren. I gulp my coffee. I don't know how newspeople get up at this ungodly hour every morning.

"She had some work call she needed to make, but said she'd watch from her hotel room." She pulls a few folded twenties out of the bib pocket of her overalls. "Anyway, she gave me some cash and said breakfast is on her." I'd *love* for my breakfast to be on Jade. Egg literally on her face would make me happy. Maybe mashed into her shiny hair as well. Wait. The new me is supposed to be nicer. But then, she did try to sleep with my husband, so screw it.

"Did it seem obnoxious that I talked about my design biz?" I ask Barry.

"No, you were great."

My phone rings. I pull it from my purse—or rather, from the purse I'm borrowing from Cyn. Mrs. Van Dierdon. Ugh. Though she said the vase was one of a kind and there was nothing I could do, I should've at least called to apologize again. But I was too embarrassed. She's probably calling to ream me out for that, on top of everything else. Normally, I'd let the call go to voice mail, but the new me is trying to consider the other person first. No time like the present to get started. If she needs to yell at me to feel better, let the yelling begin.

"Hello, Mrs. Van Dierdon." I scoot my chair to the left, away from the table, to hear better. We're seated on the patio, and since it's a weekday morning, it's fairly quiet.

"Hello, Alex."

I know I'm supposed to let this be about her and let her say her piece, but I can't help it. I dive in with my apology. I need her to know that I'm not completely insensitive to the fact I've handled this whole thing badly. *Then* she can ream me out. "I'm sorry I haven't called you. I should have—"

"Oh, don't be silly. With what you've been through this weekend, why, I can't imagine—losing your house. It's so dreadful."

"Thank you, Mrs. Van Dierdon."

"Please, call me June."

"Okay, June." That's weird.

"We saw in the paper someone's home had burned down, but I confess I only glanced at the picture, so I had no idea it was *you*. And then to see you on the news this morning. With your beautiful grand-baby! Oh my, it was such a shock. I said to Vincent, 'Why, Vincent, can you imagine if anything had happened to that precious baby?' and he just couldn't. We were both so upset by it all—we haven't even gotten out of our pajamas yet! But I had to call you right away and tell you how wonderful it is that you and your dog—what's his name? Marty?—how wonderful it is that you were able to save that precious baby."

"Thank you so much, Mrs.—er, June."

"I know you're going to be supremely busy with the work to restore your own home, but, my dear, we simply loved that romantic beach getaway you designed for our master bedroom. And we're willing to wait however long we must until you have time to squeeze us in."

My heart does a backflip of joy, and I silently scream while shimmying in my chair. I turn and give Barry a big thumbs-up while he mouths "What?" at me.

I turn away again and take a breath to regain a modicum of composure. "I'm so glad to hear that, Mrs.—sorry, June! It's true, things are a bit hectic right now, but I'd love to get you on the schedule as soon as possible. But first, I want to apologize again about the vase—"

"It's fine, dear. In fact, I'll let you in on a little secret—and if you ever tell anyone in my family, I'll deny it to my dying day—but Grandpa wasn't, well, let's just say he wasn't at the top of his craft. Certainly the vase had sentimental value, but my dear, sweet Vincent went out and bought me a Piero Magro to replace it. Are you familiar with his work? To die for! Wait until you see it. It's the absolute focal piece of the living room."

I am familiar with Magro's work, and it's breathtaking—both in its artistry and price tag—so when I do see it, I'll be sure to suggest having doors installed on the shelves.

"I'm sure the piece is divine, and I'm so glad that worked out. I felt so terrible—"

She cuts me off again. "Don't give it another thought." I wonder if she's going to keep interrupting me when we work together. Who cares? I'm too excited about getting the job. I've got to call Rache after this.

"Thank you. You're very generous. I'll call you later this week when things have calmed down a bit, and we can set up a time to go over the design and the contract, scheduling, et cetera."

"I do hope you'll bring that precious Ruthie with you again! We'd love to see her."

I almost laugh out loud at the thought of taking Ruthie back to their house, but what the heck. Gotta give clients what they want. But Ruthie's not getting anywhere near that new vase. After we hang up, I do laugh, a long hoot of joy.

"I have fantastic news! I got the job with the Van Dierdons after all!"

Barry holds his juice glass aloft. "Here's to you!"

"Here's to good news." I raise my glass as Wren helps Ruthie join in with her sippy cup.

My phone rings again. I intend to ignore it and concentrate on eating with my family—my egg-white omelet arrived while I was on the phone—but when I see it's Rache, I hold up a finger. "I'll be one sec. I've got to tell Rachel the good news."

"Holy cow, I saw you on TV," she screams. "You looked amazing. Have you lost weight? I'm sorry! Damn, that sounds shallow. I mean, I'm so glad you guys are all okay!"

"Ha. It's fine; it's nice to hear."

"I was getting ready for work when I saw you. I couldn't believe it! My God, you didn't tell me your house burned down!"

"I was going to, but it's been a crazy few days. Anyway, I was going to call you later. The Van Dierdons want us after all!"

"No way. Beverly thinks she's getting the job. They called her last week with some follow-up questions. She was all pissed because they wanted to make some changes to her design. She wouldn't say, but I guessed that they were trying to get her to do something more like your design."

"As of this morning, she's definitely not getting the job. Apparently, they've forgiven me for the, uh, fiasco at their house." I don't mention Ruthie's name since I never did tell Wren about the vase.

"That's fantastic. But I better get to work. I want to see Beverly's face after they cancel on her." She pauses. "Look, I know you said they want 'us,' but I understand if you're not ready to hire me back. I've gotten better at standing up to Beverly and her BS. I can wait it out until you're sure you're ready for an employee."

"I really want us to work together again. But you're right, I do need to look at the numbers. If you have time, maybe you could at least work for me part-time, on the weekends or whatever. I mean, I don't want to take away your time with Kaitlin, but if you'd like to make some extra money . . . We'll figure it out."

"Some extra money would be great. Especially since Mason was late with child support *again*. Anyway, I better run so I don't miss the fireworks at the office. I can't wait to talk to you more about all this!"

I turn back to the table again. "I'm so sorry. I know it's rude to take calls at the table." It rings before I can set it aside.

"The rigors of fame," Barry says with a smile.

"I don't recognize that number." I drop the phone into my purse. "They can leave a message."

"Even strangers want a piece of you now," Barry says.

I take a bite of my eggs, which have gone cold, and push the plate away.

"Do you want some of my blueberry wheat germ pancakes?" Wren asks. They look better than they sound, covered in plump indigo berries. "They're still warm. And I'm stuffed."

"It's okay. I'm too excited to eat." I pinch a bite of omelet off my plate and slip it to Marie, who's sitting quietly next to me. "What started off as a pretty crappy week is suddenly looking very good. And I owe it all to my two favorite little girls." I reach across the table and tickle Ruthie with one hand as I ruffle Marie's curls with the other.

"Tee Lexsch!" Ruthie says, and I laugh.

CHAPTER 25

"Those look fantastic," Mrs. Marx says, setting foot in the living room. Wren, still up on the step stool, finishing with the last panel, smiles. I can tell she's proud of her work, and I'm so thankful she was around to help.

"I'm happy that you're happy," I say.

"Could I talk to you for one second in the other room?" Mrs. Marx asks.

"Sure."

Mrs. Marx leads me into her boring beige dining room. "I have a small project, and I'm hoping you can help. Your assistant, Wren . . ." I'd introduced her as such, rather than as my stepdaughter, since I thought that sounded more professional. "It strikes me that her, uh, style is very similar to the look my Jenny's been leaning toward lately. It's very . . . what's the word?"

"Edgy?"

"Yes! Edgy. Anyway, Jenny's away at horse camp for the summer. She's been texting and calling me every day, complaining about how much she hates it. Cost us a fortune, so no way I'm letting her come home early." She smiles at me conspiratorially, as if I can relate to how much summer horse camps cost. Possibly more than our kitchen remodel. "But I thought it would be a nice welcome-home treat to update her room while she's away. She's fourteen going on a very jaded forty, and the purple pony haven is not cutting it for her anymore."

Other than for my nephews, designing kids' rooms has never been my thing, but designing for a teen might be fun. With Wren as my "edginess" consultant, plus my own cred as a fairly jaded forty-year-old, we might be able to pull off a look a cynical fourteen-year-old girl will love. It's not a big enough project to get us completely out of the hole, but still, together with the Van Dierdons' master suite project, this simple bedroom makeover might be the start of turning my business around. If I can do great work for both of them, hopefully they'll spread the word to their friends.

"Let's have a look," I say in my most professional tone. I step back into the living room and signal for Wren to come along.

Mrs. Marx shows us the room. Wren peruses Jenny's bookshelves while Mrs. Marx and I talk about the changes she wants: bedding, curtains, lighting, new furniture if I think the room needs it. (I do.)

On the way back to the office, Wren says, "I can't wait to be your assistant again."

"Great. And this time I'll pay you."

"I'd totally work for you for free. Especially since you guys are putting us up and all."

"It's nice you'd work for free—they say that's the trick to finding work you'll love, think about what you'd do even for free—but we'll figure out something that's fair."

"I already have a ton of ideas for Jenny's room." She turns to me and presses her hands flat against the car's center console. "We should totally do a steampunk theme."

"I don't know what that means."

"It's sort of like this cool mix of old-fashioned, like Victorian-era stuff, but with a weird futuristic look mixed in. There's usually, like, clocks and mechanical moving parts, and . . ."

We come to a red light, so I raise an eyebrow at her.

"It's hard to explain, but I'll show you some pictures online when we get back to the office. It's totally killer. I looked at some of her books, and she'd be really into it."

"Hmm. That does sound kind of cool. But Mrs. Marx is pretty straight and narrow in her design choices, so we might have to push her a little. Oh, hey, I never listened to the voice mail from the last call I got during breakfast." I hand her my phone and ask her to play the message over the speaker.

"Hi, Alex. This is Leann Perkins, the TV producer from this morning?" Her voice rises at the end as though she's not sure she's the producer from this morning. "I wanted to get in touch because we had a few people call and e-mail the station after you were on. They want to know if your stepdaughter sells those baby clothes she makes? Call me back when you get a chance."

I glance at Wren, who bugs her eyes out at me.

"Oh my God, that's so cool." She bounces in her seat and pulls her skinny legs up to sit on her feet. "This has been the best day ever."

She stares out the front window, and I can practically hear the gears turning under that spiky hair of hers.

"Did you ever think of making your own line of baby clothes?"

"Well, yeah, like, I've fantasized about it. But I didn't know where to start."

"You start by making a business plan."

"You know how to do that?" I nod. "Would you show me?" I nod again, and she pounds her fists on her knees. "This!" She shouts. "This is what I want to do."

"Have a baby clothes business?"

"I don't know if it's that *exactly*, but, yeah, something creative. Something where I can use my hands and see my ideas become a real thing. It's something I would totally love. I'm not going to school. I'm going to start this baby-clothes business."

"Whoa, let's slow down one sec." We stop at another light, but she's still bouncing, which shakes the tiny rental car. "Let's talk this over with your dad tonight. You know, school can be a big help, even if you want to do something creative. I mean, look at me—I have a very creative job, but I had to go to school and study to learn how to do this. And I took a lot of business classes too."

She stops bouncing and slumps back in the seat.

"But I don't think I'll like school. Business classes sound *so* boring." She throws her head back against the seat and lets her mouth fall open.

"Just keep an open mind. Like I said, we'll talk to your dad. Maybe you can try going to school for a quarter or two, and then if you really don't like it—and you can honestly say you aren't getting anything out of it—maybe you could talk your mom into letting you take the next quarter off and see how that goes."

"My mom will never go for it, and she won't support me if I'm not in school."

"I'm not making any promises, but *maybe* by then, I'd have enough work to hire you."

Her bouncing resumes.

"I said *maybe*. Seriously, I'm emphasizing the *maybe* here."

"Let's not go back to the office. Let's go find my dad and talk to him right now. If he agrees, my mom will too."

"Okay. But remember—*your* part of the deal is to commit to giving school a try."

"Can I work for you part-time while I'm in school? Or will you help me get my baby line going?"

"If it works out with your classes. Studying comes above all else! But we'll see."

"Okay, deal."

"Whoa, again, *whoa*. I'm only outlining a possible deal here. You have to work out the details and sign and seal it with your parents. And we're not doing any of this if it interferes with your schoolwork."

"Right. Right." She keeps bouncing and snaps her gum, obviously deep in thought about her possible future.

I haven't seen the girl this animated about anything since we first met. Hopefully, she'll get this excited about school once she's there. But if not, I've got a good feeling about her future as a baby-clothes designer. She could be pretty fabulous.

*

Barry ends up telling his boss that he needs the entire week off. We spend the rest of Tuesday finding a cute two-bedroom house to rent while our place is being rebuilt.

When I speak to our insurance agent that afternoon, she says the remains of the house will be demolished on Wednesday and Thursday. They want to do it as soon as possible for safety reasons. Lord knows there's probably nothing to loot, but potential looters won't know that until they've picked through the place. She also says their inspector determined the cause of the fire.

"It started in the garage."

So my second guess was right—it wasn't the overloaded outlet in the bathroom. The agent goes on to explain that the inspector found melted copper, proving the garage wiring where our spare freezer was plugged in was the cause. I don't totally understand how they figured it out—something about how the heat of an arc (the only arks I know about are the kind you put pairs of animals in . . .) in the wiring is greater than the heat of a house fire, and copper only melts at the higher temperature.

I hear her still talking, but I can't process any of it. I won't be able to explain any of what she's saying to Barry. "I'm going to let you talk to my husband, okay?" I hand the phone over. I can't think of anything other than the fact I should've listened to that electrician. God, I was so stupid. And shortsighted. But he'd said we could fix it "someday." I was waiting for someday when we had some extra money.

I'd finally gotten up my nerve last night and told Barry that I wondered if the fire might have started in the garage, not the bathroom as I'd originally thought. "The wiring," he said, remembering the decision we'd made. In my memory of that remodeling project—what was it, five years ago? Six?—I pushed him into the "let's wait; let's not spend our limited budget on that boring stuff" decision, but he insists it was mutual. At least he doesn't seem to blame me, or at least not as much as I'm blaming myself.

When Barry hangs up, I'm still lost in my memories.

"They're knocking the house down tomorrow."

"Yeah, she told me."

"We should try to go by there—in case we might find something—before they get started."

So at seven on Wednesday morning, Barry and I pull into our driveway, armed (well, *footed*, I guess) with heavy boots that we picked up cheap at the Closet. Slowly, carefully, we comb through the rubble wearing great fumble-fingered gloves and face masks so that we won't breathe in the ash we stir. I don't want Barry to go in our bedroom.

"Not worth it," I say, pointing at the precariously sagging remains of our roof. He goes in anyway, but comes out empty-handed a few minutes later.

"Nothin'," he says.

We turn to the office. The blades from the ceiling fan hang like a rotten banana peel. We find the tower from the desktop computer under what was once my beautiful desk next to a hunk of misshapen metal that used to be my replica Eiffel Tower.

"The hard drive might've survived," Barry says pointing at the computer. "We can take it somewhere and see. At least I'd backed it up recently." With luck, we might have most of our photos from the digital era on.

Back in the living room, I try to find my glass bottle collection, hoping for a miracle, but all my trip mementos are gone.

Optimistically, we'd come in with two cardboard boxes, which I manage to load with items from the kitchen, the room farthest from the worst of the fire. I pack up some dishes, a few stainless-steel pots and pans, silverware, a teakettle. Barry finds the cheese grater, then stumbles upon his UCSB beer bottle opener and gets excited.

But none of the things we truly cared about—our framed wedding pictures, our photo albums, the cut-crystal cake plate from my grandparents' wedding—can be found.

At least I'd never been much of a fine jewelry wearer, always preferring fun and funky costume pieces. I have no diamond earrings to search for, no gold bracelets whose loss I'll mourn. I was wearing my wedding band and engagement ring, Barry his plain gold band, and that was all the jewelry we cared about.

We leave the house with our meager findings as a tractor-trailer lumbers down our street toward us with a backhoe. I've already watched my house be destroyed once. I'm not up for watching it again.

CHAPTER 26

Thursday evening, Barry and I decide to drive by and look at our empty lot.

We park in the driveway and sit together in our rental car, shocked. The dusky light illuminates the few bare reminders that someone lived here: the poured-concrete driveway, the plants around the perimeter of our yard, the flagstones out back.

"Wow," I say as Barry turns off the engine.

"Yeah."

"Do you think we're going to get screwed on the insurance?"

"Depends how good our records are."

"I still have all the receipts and before-and-after remodel pictures up the wazoo back at the office."

Barry reaches for my hand and squeezes it. "That'll be a big help. You're amazing."

"No, you are." I turn in my seat and look at him. This isn't exactly the setting I'd pictured for our big talk, but it's been a crazy week, and between staying at Cynthia's, shopping for or borrowing basics, getting started on Mrs. Marx's project, and moving to the rental house with the girls, we haven't had a moment to ourselves. "Really. You're the best. But . . ."

"But?" Barry pouts with feigned concern.

"Not so much a *but*. It's . . . I want to say some stuff to you. I want us to have that talk we've been needing to have."

"Now? Here?"

"No time like the present."

"Okay, but I want to start by saying—"

I hold up my right hand. "No. Me first. I've been thinking about this for a long time." He's still holding my left hand in his right. With the index finger of my other hand, I outline the bumps of his knuckles as I speak.

"Look, I appreciate what a stand-up guy you are, and that's exactly what I'd expect from you, Bear. But it's been an emotional week. Hell, it's been a draining *couple* of weeks, and now with the fire on top of everything else . . . What I'm trying to say is, I know you said you don't want to be with Jade, and you chose me. And I should probably keep my mouth shut and be happy, but I need to say this. I . . . I know she's always been the One. And I know I'm . . . the runner-up."

"What? Runner-up? God, Alex, that kills me." His eyes go soft and sad. He tugs on my hand, squeezing it. "No, you are *not* runner-up."

I pull my hand away and forge ahead, staring at the patch of raw dirt that used to be our home.

"It's okay. I know I am. Let me finish. Do you remember when we went to see *Jerry Maguire*?"

"Is this relevant?"

"Listen!" My fingers curl into my palms. "Do you remember how you snorted when Tom Cruise told what's-her-name . . ." Barry's raised eyebrows indicate he has no idea where I'm going with this, and no idea who I'm talking about. "You know—that blond actress. Crooked smile. Whatever. I can't think of her name right now." I shake my head. "Anyway, when he told her she 'completed' him, you scoffed. And I thought, yeah, Barry's right; that's so corny. But then I thought about us. Thought about when I fell in love with you. And I knew what that Tom Cruise character meant. I'd had this . . . empty space in me—I didn't know it at the time, because I was used to it. I got used to that feeling, like I was always searching for something or trying to remember a great dream."

I turn to face him and continue, "But then one day, that feeling was gone. It was the first time we went away together. Remember when we went to Mammoth Mountain for that long weekend?"

"Of course."

I stare out at our yard again. "When you dropped me off afterward, I was alone in my apartment. I expected that longing to come back, but it didn't. It was like I was . . . filled up inside. That probably sounds dumb." I shake my head. "Anyway, I knew it was because I was in love with you. And I didn't ever want to be without you."

"You called my answering machine before I got home and said you loved me." He reaches for my hand again, and I turn to look at him. "I kept it until the power went out and it got erased."

"You did?"

"Yes. I loved you too. I *still* love you."

"I know you love me, Barry. The problem is you loved Jade more. She was the love of your life. *She* was the one who completed you."

"Alex—"

"Let me finish. I've been thinking about this for a long time, and I have to get it all out. I've known all along she was your *one*. I mean, on our very first date, you told me how gorgeous she was, how smart. How she lights up a room. Yada, yada. I knew you guys only broke up because of the whole baby issue. It took me a long time to let myself be convinced you were over her. But I always knew, deep down, you never stopped loving her. I remember we'd gotten engaged shortly before we went to see that movie, and when you scoffed at that stupid line, I knew what you were thinking. That I'd never be the woman who completed you."

"Wow. All that from me laughing at a stupid movie line? Honest to God, I just didn't think Tom Cruise and . . . and that blond actress had any chemistry."

"It wasn't just the stupid movie. Whenever Jade's name would come up, you would say what an amazing person she is. Like you'd never be able to forget your time with her."

"Yes, I was nuts about her because I thought she was an amazing person. Yes, she's smart, and 'yada, yada,' but it's not like she's perfect. She'll get her way no matter what. She can be very manipulative; you think she's being nice, but she's really just working you. She comes across as friendly, interested, but she's the least genuine person I know. There's always an ulterior motive with her. After we broke up, I realized there was nothing that special between us."

My lips purse, transmitting my disbelief.

"I swear," he continues. "I remember the exact moment I realized it. I'd gone to the deli where we always used to go."

"Renée Zellweger!" I throw my hands in the air. Then I notice Barry's hurt-puppy-dog expression. "Sorry. That was bugging me. Go on. I'll shut up."

"Anyway . . ." he overexaggerates a pause to make sure I'm done. "She used to rave to the owner how it was the best pastrami anywhere, even better than on the East Coast. She used to have these rapt conversations with him about his bread, telling him it was better than stuff from her dad's bakery. I went in there one day not long after—well, the *Wren* incident. After running into her at the bar, I thought maybe I'd run into her someplace else too. So I went to the deli, and the owner asked me where Jade was. I told him we broke up, and he's trying to console me, telling me how great she was. Saying how I must be devastated at losing the 'perfect' woman. And at first I was like, Okay, buddy, this is not helping. And then it hit me—she'd had the same effect on him she'd had on me. On everyone. She makes everybody feel better about themselves. She's got this way of paying attention and complimenting you. You feel like you can do anything."

I interrupt. "Yeah, so I've heard you say many times." I want to borrow his own line: *Okay, buddy, this is not helping.* But I have to admit that when I first met her, she made me feel . . . special. What a sucker I was.

"She's always had this knack for making people feel good about themselves. Which would be great if she were doing it because she was interested in you—I thought she was for a long time. But she was really just working people over. Like the deli guy. He used to give her free stuff all the time—add some cookies to our takeout bag, give her free drinks, ask her to try the batch of potato salad he'd made and then send her home with a tubful after she raved about it. She was working him. She was always working people. Trying to get what she wanted from them. It didn't matter how small or how big a thing. I think it was like a game to her."

Hmm. Like she worked me, telling me what a great designer I was and getting on my good side to finagle an invite into our home.

"I used to cut her slack for it," Barry continues. "I knew she was manipulative, but I also thought she was a good person, that she wouldn't intentionally hurt anyone, so I made excuses for her in my head. But what she did—manipulating me so that she could get pregnant and then not telling me, lying to Wren about me and my family, hell, climbing into our bed the other night—that's the *real* Jade. I know she'll always be in our lives to some degree through Wren, but I hope we'll have as little to do with her as possible. In fact, while you were calling Cyn the other day, I called Jade's hotel to check on the girls, and I told her as much."

"You did?" Oh my God, I wish I could have seen her face! "Well, I'm glad we're a united front, because I told her the same thing. Did she have anything to say for her sorry self?"

"She said that when she saw me, she supposedly realized she'd never stopped loving me. And that when she saw me with Wren, she realized what a fool she'd been to try to keep Wren and me apart. She said she could see that I loved Wren, and she should have known that I'd change my mind about kids once I met my *own* kid. She said she regretted all that time that we could have been together as a family."

"And you said?"

"That she damn well should regret keeping Wren and me apart, but she shouldn't be delusional enough to think that the three of us ever would have been a family. I told her nothing would ever come between me and my wife, certainly not her and her games."

I suck in my upper lip to avoid busting out in a grin. When I'm sure I've got the corners of my mouth under control, I say, "So I guess this means you don't think she's Saint Jade?"

"When did I ever call her Saint Jade?"

"Well, never, I guess. That might've been me."

"When did *you* call her Saint Jade?"

"I might've muttered it under my breath a time or two."

"Believe me, she's no saint. I guess I always knew that. But that day at the deli, I finally realized that the feelings I had for her, *about* her—they were the same feelings the deli guy had. What I'd felt . . . it wasn't love. And she wasn't in love with me either. She wanted something from me—security, validation, *kids*, hell, I don't know, but whatever it was, it wasn't *love*. I looked at the deli owner, and I wanted to hug him. I didn't need to search for her anymore or mourn what I thought we'd had." He reaches over and tucks a strand of hair behind my ear. He knows I fall for that move every time.

"Anyway, then you and I started dating, and when I heard you say on my answering machine you loved me . . . I knew I was in love with you too. I realized what it *really* feels like to be in love. I'm so grateful Jade and I broke up, or I might never have met you. It's you, Alex. *You* are the love of my life. And I don't ever want to be without you."

"Oh, Bear. I wish you'd been wordy about all this before." I reach for my purse and find a tissue.

"It makes me sad to know you've been thinking all this time that you were 'runner-up.'"

"Yeah, well, there's a whole lotta neurosis between these ears." I tap my temple. I think about my mom and how I've spent most of my life feeling like I was runner-up with her too. With all the honest conversations I've had in the past few days, I guess it's a shame our house didn't burn down sooner. Nothing like a brush with death to make you take a good hard look at your life. "Of course, you're not exactly Mr. Open and Expressive when it comes to feelings, are you?"

"We're quite a pair." He gently tugs at the strand of my hair he's been twirling around his finger. "I'm sorry if I ever did anything to make you feel less than. You're the most important person in the world to me. And I'm going to make sure you never forget it." He slips his hand behind my neck and kisses me.

It's a wonderful, tender kiss, but I pull away. "I'm not done."

"I'm not done either." Barry kisses me again. "But we probably need to go home for what I have in mind in the way of finishing."

It's nice to know my husband can still make me blush. "Soon," I whisper, then lean back in my seat. "I'm not done having my say. I have to apologize for not being straight with you about my business."

He's still turned in his seat toward me, and he tilts his head and lets it fall against the headrest. "That's yesterday's news."

"No, it's not. I'm so sorry. I know we've had other fish to fry since you found out about the money—and now all our fish are fried to a crisp." I survey the empty lot where our home used to be. "But I never should've kept all that a secret, and I never should've taken the money from our savings without asking you."

"If you had, I would've told you to take it. I believe in you. And I'm sorry too. I shouldn't have gotten so angry with you. I just . . . I guess it was bad memories from how Jade used to manipulate me, and all the stress at work, and finding out about Wren. I was overwhelmed with everything, and I took it out on you. I should have just come home and talked to you like a rational human being."

"Wow. When you think about it . . . If we hadn't had that fight, I'd have been home with you."

"And Jade never would have had a chance to . . ." He shakes his head in disgust.

"No, I mean I would have been asleep along with everyone else. I wouldn't have come home. With Marie. We might not have . . ." Tears slip down my cheeks.

He realizes what I'm saying and hugs me tightly. "Oh my God, I never thought of it that way. I've been feeling really bad about how mad I got."

I laugh through my tears. "No. Turns out it was a good thing." I dab under my eyes with the tissue and hope my mascara isn't a total mess. "Anyway, you were right to be mad. I shouldn't have touched that money without talking to you. I just—it started out slowly, and then just snowballed."

"It's okay. Look at you—you've already got two new jobs lined up. You're going to make this work. I know you are."

"That's very sweet, Bear, but it's only two jobs. I don't know what's going to happen next. But I want you to know I'm going to work hard to build our savings back up. I'm going to try my darnedest to make this work. I know I can make a go of this if we can get through the next year or so."

"I know you can do it too. And if we need to borrow against our 401(k)s to tide the business over, that's what we'll do."

"Hopefully we won't need to do anything that drastic. But I promise if they total my car, I'm buying something way cheaper. A used car. The extra money will cover the office rent for a couple of months."

He takes my hand and squeezes it again. "I know how much you loved that car."

I shake my head. "No. It was just a thing. I get that now. What I really love is you and our family."

We kiss again, then sit back in our seats, taking one last look at the remains of our home.

"I have every faith in you, and I'm sure our new house is going to be even more beautiful than the old one."

"Oh, yeah," I say. "I've already got lots of ideas."

He grimaces, and I know he's wondering if I'm already backtracking down the path to big-budget ideas. "For instance?"

"For instance, getting rid of the office."

"Yeah?"

"We don't need it. On the rare occasions when you bring work home, you sprawl on the sofa with your laptop, and I've got my office downtown, or I can use the dining table if I bring stuff home."

"So we're only planning for a two-bedroom?"

"No, silly. It'll still be three bedrooms. But the third room will be Ruthie's." He smiles at me, and I continue. "I know it's going to be hard. I know sometimes I might think, 'What the hell have I done?' And I know Wren will still probably want to move in with Sarah, which she totally should, but the girls can come and stay with us whenever they want."

His smile spreads wider, revealing first one, then both, of his sexy Halstad fangs.

I lean over and kiss him, stroking the back of his neck. Then I press my forehead against his. "That make-up sex thing. I think that's good for more than just the first time postfight, right?"

Starting up the car, he says, "Copernicus and I are ready and willing to test that theory."

ACKNOWLEDGMENTS

What I'd *really* like to do to thank the folks who helped me finish this book is get together with them for a beer/margarita/cupcake/cup of coffee or whatever their treat of choice is. The funny thing is that I've never met the majority of the people on this list. Hopefully, someday we can meet, and when we do, I'll owe you that beer/margarita/cupcake/cup of coffee.

To my local(ish) readers and friends: Leslie, Louisa, and fellow authors Dee DeTarsio and Liz Fenton, you gals are the best. Let's get together soon!

To my long-distance writer pals who helped with early critiques or support along the way: Tracie Banister, Kathleen Irene Paterka, Samantha Stroh Bailey, and Jami Deise, this journey would not be as fun without all of you! A special shout-out goes to Kathleen's volunteer firefighter hubby, Steve, for his expert help.

To my sister, Terry: thank you for being retired so that you can spend countless hours proofreading early drafts and newsletter copy! I really appreciate all your help!

To my agent, Kevan Lyon, and also to Patricia Nelson and the whole team at Marsal Lyon Literary Agency: thanks so much for your efforts with the manuscript, and for helping me make my publishing dream a reality. I'm also very grateful for my editor, Amara Holstein, who is such a pleasure to work with, as are Jodi Warshaw and everyone at Lake Union Publishing.

I have a whole other slew of long-distance friends out there in the dog/pet-blogging community (yes, that's really a thing!), and I've hardly met any of them. I wish I could name you all individually (and list all your blogs that I love to read), but it would go on for pages. Thank you for your support for me and my writing, and thanks so much for reviewing my books or mentioning them on your blogs. You are great pet parents and inspire me to try to be a better dog-mom—and a better person as well! Just like Alex.

READERS' GUIDE

1. Alex finds puppies irresistible, while she finds babies a bit frightening. How about you? Do your own maternal/paternal instincts run more toward babies or pets? Is that simply the way you've always felt, or do you think something in particular influenced you either way?

2. Alex quickly agrees to go along with it when Barry wants to let the girls move in. How do you think you might react if your spouse or partner suddenly had a child or grandchild show up on your doorstep?

3. Alex does things she never would have thought she'd do (i.e., agreeing to care for a sick baby and letting Jade move in to her home) in the hopes that Wren will reconcile with her mother and move out again. How did you feel about that? Could you understand her wanting to get the girls out of the house? Can you imagine any circumstance under which you'd invite your spouse's ex to move in to your home?

4. Alex and Barry are childless by choice. Do you feel people judge those who choose not to become parents? What would your response be if someone criticized a friend of yours for not wanting to have children?

5. Barry's method of dealing with stress is to literally run away from it, even if only temporarily. Given that Barry is overwhelmed by finding out he's a father and grandfather, on top of the stress of the severe budget cuts at his work, how did you feel when he left Alex alone that first morning with the girls? Could you understand his need for stress relief, or were you angry with him for Alex's sake? Did you feel he let Alex do all the "heavy lifting" with the girls?

6. Alex thinks she has always been the runner-up to Jade in Barry's eyes. What did you think of Barry and Alex's relationship?

7. Many couples fight about money, and it's not unheard of for a spouse to perhaps hide a purchase or two from their other half, but what about the financial mess Alex gets herself into? Could you understand how the problem snowballed and got away from her even while she kept thinking she'd be able to pull herself out of the hole? Or did you see it as a huge betrayal that she would keep something like that from Barry?

8. Alex mentions ways in which people judge others, including stay-at-home moms versus working moms, "breast-milk wars," and arguments with people at the dog park over dog food and training methods. Have you experienced these types of social pressures, where people try to press their choices on you, either as a parent or a pet-parent?

9. Marie is definitely the hero of the story. Do you know any stories of heroic pets? What happened?

10. If you knew a fire was imminent and you only had fifteen minutes to grab a few items from your home (and assuming all your loved ones and pets were already safe), what would you want to save?

ABOUT THE AUTHOR

Photo © 2012 Theresa Hunten

Jackie Bouchard, a *USA Today* bestselling author, writes what she calls Fido-friendly fiction: humorous and heartwarming stories about women and the dogs that profoundly impact their lives.

Bouchard has lived in Southern California, Canada, and Bermuda and now lives in San Diego with her husband and dog. Her novels include *What the Dog Ate* and *Rescue Me, Maybe*.

For more information, visit www.jackiebouchard.com.

Her blog: www.poochsmooches.com

Facebook: www.facebook.com/JackieBouchardWriter

Twitter: http://twitter.com/@JackieBouchard